MW01242887

Cowboy Brides

By

Leann Harris
Renee Riva
Cindy M. Amos
Christina Rich
Rose Verde
Martha Rogers

Copyright © 2018 Forget Me Not Romances, an imprint of Winged Publications

All rights reserved. No part of this publication may be resold, reproduced, stored in a retrieval system, or transmitted in any form or by any means, electronic, mechanical, recording, or otherwise, without the prior written permission of the author. Piracy is illegal. Thank you for respecting the hard work of this author.

This is a work of fiction. All characters, names, dialogue, incidents, and places either are the product of the author's imagination or are used fictitiously. Any resemblance to actual events, locales, or people, living or dead, is entirely coincidental.

ISBN-13: 9781730923500

i

Going Home

Leann Harris

Chapter One

January, Denver

Melissa Danner hurried around the outer hall of the Denver Coliseum looking for seating Section XX where her family's seats where located.

"Next up is barrel racing, and we have some sharp and eager ladies wanting to show their talent." The announcement vibrated in the hall.

"Hurry up, Tony." Missy glared at footwear her co-worker had chosen for his first time at the rodeo--loafers without socks. Her break-up with her long-time fiancé had left her vulnerable to Tony's quest for a date. He'd been asking for months.

"I'm trying, but I've got something in my shoe." He limped toward her.

"We're almost to the right section. According to the signs, we're one more entrance over."

"I want you to give a good Colorado welcome for our first contestant, Julie Long, from Mesa, Arizona," the announcer continued.

"We don't have time. Let's go inside and I'll locate my family." She helped Tony climb the stairs. They emerged into the bright lights of the arena just as the first rider finished.

"Miss Julie's score is 17 seconds. Next up is Carol Jones out of Oklahoma City."

Missy spotted her family in the next section. They took up the entire row. First in line was her father. Behind him sat Nathan Winters, her oldest brother's best friend.

Once at their seats, Tony tapped Nate on the shoulder.

He glanced up. Missy quickly made the introductions.

"Your brothers were taking bets if you'd make it on time," Nate murmured.

She leaned over her oldest brother's shoulder. "I'm sure you started this entire thing."

Noah didn't deny it but grinned.

She turned her head and kissed her father's cheek, tucking a strand of chin-length brown hair behind her ear. "How are you, Dad?"

He grunted, but flashed a smile.

Nate cleared his throat. She jerked upright realizing she had her backside in his face. He didn't appear upset but had a twinkle in his green eyes. Missy's cheeks went hot. Tony frowned. She moved to his right and sat.

After the next two contests, Tony asked if that was all that barrel racing was--racing around barrels.

Missy's gaze met Nate's. "These women clock some of the fastest in all of rodeo."

"And our last contestant is Kylee Danner out of Silverdale, out on the Eastern slope. Let's welcome a hometown girl."

Her sister raced into the arena on a bay horse Kylee had named Morning Lightning. She and the horse rounded the first barrel, heading to the barrel on the other side.

"Go, Sis," her brothers shouted, but Kylee cut the corner on the second barrel and rocked it as she raced to the finish line. The announcer said, "What a ride...16.8 seconds, which is our best time today, but there will be penalty points added for the brush with that barrel."

Missy and her brothers all sat down.

"I thought she had it," Wyatt shook his head.

"It was good ride," Noah added.

The entire Danner clan stood and made their way to the exit where the contestants were housed.

"Are you going, too?" Tony asked her, sounding like a five-year-old.

"Yes. My sister just lost her event and I want to be with her. If you want, you can stay here and watch the bareback bullriding."

He opened his mouth to reply, but she hurried away before he could say anything. Backstage, Missy made her way to where Kylee stood forehead to forehead with her horse. Brandi Jo had her hand on Missy's shoulder.

"It wasn't your fault. I just cut that corner," Kylee reassured the horse.

"But it was a great ride, Sis. You'll learn from this experience," Missy called out.

Kylee looked up and threw herself into her older sister's arms. No tears followed. The Danner girls learned early not to cry in front of their brothers. It always turned out badly. Showing emotion was not a wise move in their household.

The girls separated and each sibling gave Kylee an awkward smile.

"Where's your date?" Nate asked, searching for the man Missy hauled to his seat.

"He had a burning desire to see bareback bull-riding."

Every brother gave her a look of disbelief. Brandi Jo held back a grin.

Late in November Noah had driven to Denver to pick up a special order of bridles and dropped by Missy's office, surprising her. He filled her in on how their father was dealing with the sudden death of their mother. Tony, Missy, and Noah shared an early dinner. Tony wanted oysters. Noah, who loved most other fish, hated raw oysters since getting sick after trying one. He couldn't stomach watching Tony slobber over his dinner. It'd been a quick meal, and Noah drove back to the ranch that night. Over the holidays, no one mentioned the incident. Nor did they mention her recent break-up with her fiancé months before.

"Ah, Sis, you're too smart to date someone like Mr. Big Shot. I haven't liked him since I had dinner with you two in November. All the man cares about is himself. I'm surprised he could walk through a door and not turn sideways, his head is so big."

The brutally honest truth tumbled out of Noah's mouth, sparking a smile or a laugh from everyone. No doubt Noah' had told everyone about that dreadful dinner in great detail.

Missy kissed Kylee. "Let's talk later."

Rushing back to her seat, she pushed away her embarrassment. All her family knew her miserable track record with men. A fiancé who ran off with another woman, taking the money they had saved for a house, then she showed up with fancy pants Tony. Denials were useless.

The outside hallway was crowded with fans leaving the show. Nate stepped to her side. "I hope you find your date among all these folks."

"I'm wondering myself. I didn't realize we spent that much time with Kylee." Missy ducked into the TT section. Most of the people were gone. Medics were further down the aisle near where Tony sat. She broke into a run.

"Do you have a way to get to your car? Anyone with you?" Nate called after her.

"I rode with him," Missy replied, coming to a stop by Tony's side.

A medic finished taping the bandage on Tony's foot. "Those blisters will be painful tonight. I'd recommend he not drive home."

She nodded and waited until the medics were gone.

"Where have you been? I had to call the coliseum and say I needed medical help." He held up his wrapped foot.

Tony's behavior shouldn't have shocked her. She thought he had manners.

"Why doesn't Missy get your car," Nate suggested, stopping behind her, "drive it to the main door of the coliseum, and I can help you get in."

She'd never driven Tony's BMW and wondered if the man would surrender his keys. With a sigh, he pulled them out of his pocket, handing them to her.

Twenty minutes later Tony was on his couch in his upscale condo in downtown Denver. As Missy and Nate turned to leave, he said, "Aren't you going to stay with me?"

She locked eyes with Nate. He shook his head.

"I think you'll be okay without my help. Call downstairs if you need anything." She placed his keys on the coffee table within reach. "Take tomorrow off."

Never did Tony ask how she would get home.

"Don't worry about Missy," Nate added. "I'll drive her home."

Once back in his truck, Nate glanced at the girl he'd known all his life. She was Noah's little sister, who always tagged along with them. Tonight, however, having her backside in his face for several minutes changed things. This was not the skinny tomboy he remembered. When she turned, bringing them face to face, he didn't remember her eyes so blue or her lips so kissable. Whoa——what was going on? The electricity scrambled his brain.

When the boyfriend cleared his throat breaking into Nate's out-of-body experience, he turned his attention to the barrel racing, wanting to put the incident out of his mind. Unfortunately, his body remembered. And all too well.

He wanted to grill her when she had lost her common sense by dating such a jerk, but the last time they talked was at her mother's funeral.

"Thanks for helping with Tony."

He glanced at her. "No problem."

"If you met him in a different setting, you'd like him." She sighed.

He couldn't imagine that. He had Tony nailed as a self-absorbed jerk. A good looking one, he supposed, but a first-class jerk. "Really?"

"No." She snorted and laughed.

"You've always been a terrible liar."

Another round of laughter echoed through the cab. When it died down, she asked, "How are things at the ranch?"

"My folks are fine."

"You know what I mean."

"Why ask me? You need to talk to your family."

"Because they'll sugar-coat everything. Who's cooking? Cleaning? Doing the laundry? And no one wants to say, if mom hadn't wanted to see me after my jerk of a fiancé ran off, she'd be alive today."

He debated how much to tell her. Things had gone from bad to worse. Each sibling claimed a job at the ranch, but there was no coordination. "Everyone is working, but it's hit or miss."

"So it's chaos right now?"

"It's not that bad," he hedged.

"Says my older brother's best friend. You aren't exactly a neutral observer."

"Hey, you know me, and I'm not going to rat out my friend." He clamped his teeth together, not wanting anything else to slip out. There were some things Noah had told him in confidence.

"So it's a mess." She fell silent.

She didn't question him further, which worried him. From experience, when Missy went quite, that meant trouble was brewing.

He pulled up to her apartment. "Everything is okay."

"Thanks for the ride and the help with Tony."

From the angle of her chin, he knew something was up. "What's going on in that brain of yours?"

"Solutions." She grinned at him and walked to her front door.

He waited until she entered the apartment and saw the lights come on. What had he just done?

Stirred up trouble.

Chapter 2

Missy pulled her truck behind her brother Noah's beat-up green F-150. Hopefully he was out working with cattle and not home. She wasn't ready to spar with him over her plans. He knew cows, but nothing about accounting. Dad and Mom had kept the books for the ranch, but after seeing Noah in Denver, she worried things weren't running smoothly.

Before she could get out, the back door swung open and her mom's best friend, Betty Vance, emerged. "Hello, Missy. What are you doing here?"

Good question. Nothing had gone right since the rodeo. Tony had made her life at work miserable, spreading all sorts of lies. He'd also made sure that she wouldn't get a promotion any time soon.

And there was that urgent call from Kylee last week, telling her that all her brothers were jerks. They wouldn't agree to let her drop out of college and rodeo full time. When Missy sided with them, the conversation ended abruptly.

She slipped out of the truck and hugged the older woman.

Betty pulled back and studied Missy's face. The woman could read her as accurately as her mom. She glanced at the bed of the truck. "What's going on?"

Betty's question undid Missy and her eyes watered. "I quit my job and decided to come home." The words tumbled out, shocking her. She hadn't planned to tell anyone until she told her family.

"You quit? Why? You were first in your class in high school and college." Betty wiped away the moisture from Missy's cheeks.

The words pricked Missy's heart. "I didn't want to play the political games at work with one of my male co-workers."

Betty shook her head.

"I made the mistake of going out with him. Things didn't work out, so he set me up with reports that were wrong. I knew he wouldn't stop until I was fired."

"I'm sorry, dear. Couldn't you get a job at another accounting firm in Denver or Colorado Springs?"

"I could've tried, but this man wanted to ruin my chances of getting another job in the city or in the state. I watched him slice up other colleagues and knew what he did."

"Sounds like that boy needs his mother to grab him by the ear and give him a good talking to."

Missy choked on a laugh.

"You don't think that would've worked? Well, it did with my son, Fred!"

Everyone in the county heard how Betty grabbed Fred's ear at the 4th of July picnic, even if he was 39 years old, and gave him a talking-to.

"Well, not everyone has your talent." Missy grinned.

"Your momma had that talent."

"She did, and she ran a tight ship."

"And she wouldn't put up with your brothers' behaviors. They need a good referee, and a full-time housekeeper, and your sister doesn't want the job. Sometimes that laundry room smells worse than our barn when it needs a good mucking out."

"That bad?"

"Yup. This is the last meal I can bring. I'm going to Florida to be there for my first great-grandbaby's birth."

"So who's caring for your hubby?" Hard to believe Betty would leave Harold to fend for himself.

"He's coming with me. Church friends are helping at the ranch, each taking a day to do morning and evening chores. The pastor's teen-age son will stay at the ranch overnight. This is our first vacation in thirty years. You know ranchers and farmers don't take vacations."

"Well, if you need someone to take a day, let me know. My brothers owe you and can take up the slack."

"Deal."

"Is Dad inside?"

"No. The house's empty. I left the stew on the stove, biscuits and brownies on the countertop."

The roar of an engine filled the air.

"Looks like someone got here in time to help you unload. Lucky it's such a nice day." She brushed Missy's cheek with her fingers. "I'll pray for you. There are problems here that need to be sorted out. Maybe you'll find some good in this mess."

Betty waited until the truck parked before she backed up, turned around, and left.

Missy recognized the truck as Nate's. The doors opened like wings and Nate and Noah hopped out in unison.

"Sis, what are you doing here? It's the middle of the week." He glanced at the items in the bed of the truck. His brow shot up. "What's this?"

She clamped down on her teeth and took a breath. "My things."

"Why are they in your truck and here at the house?"

Most of the small furnishings from her apartment were stuffed into the back of the truck. Missy's next-door neighbor and good friend would bring her bedroom furniture this weekend along with the other boxes she couldn't fit into the truck.

Noah stared. She turned toward Nate. Questions filled his eyes, too.

"I've decided to move back home."

Stunned, they gaped at her. A feather could've blown them over. But it was the knowing glow in Nate's eyes that spurred her into action.

"Really?" Noah stepped closer. "I thought you couldn't wait to go to the big city to get to a fancy job and make a name for yourself."

Resting her hands on her hips, she replied, "You going to help me move these things into my old room or just stand there, watching?"

She didn't wait for his response but pulled the truck gate down and climbed up. Yanking her suitcase from the side of the pile, Missy gave it to Noah, followed by a smaller bag. Snatching several baskets and artificial plants, she shoved them in Nate's direction. It took less than thirty minutes to unload her truck.

"All your things are inside. Now you want to tell me what's going on?" Noah folded his arms and pinned her with a big-brother-knows-all look.

Her first thought was her room needed a good cleaning, postponing the moment of reckoning, but she had a brother--no, brothers--sisters, and a dad who'd want an explanation. Taking a deep breath, she nodded. "But before we do that, I need a cup of coffee and one of those brownies Betty just dropped off."

Noah nodded his agreement. They made their way to the large kitchen and grabbed mugs and treats.

~

Nate should leave, since this was family, Danner family, business, but wanted to hear her explanation, guessing it had something to do with the loser she brought to the stock show.

Once they'd settled at the table, Noah waited for her to speak. After several moments, he said, "Now that you've gotten your chocolate and coffee, Sis, I need an explanation."

"I quit." The words landed like lead balloons.

Dead quiet reigned except the ticking of the clock over the stove.

"Why?"

The simple question vibrated in the air.

She didn't answer.

Noah glanced at Nate. He nodded toward his sister, as if Nate knew what she would say. He shrugged wanting to stay on the safe side of this argument between brother and sister.

She cleared her throat. "You remember Tony from the rodeo?"

Noah nodded, gripping his coffee cup so hard his fingers turned white. The muscles in Nate's shoulders tightened, waiting for what he knew was coming.

"Yeah, how could anyone forget someone so dumb?" Noah's upper lip curled.

"Well, not only did he not know how to dress for the rodeo, the following Monday, he acted like we'd never gone out, and made it clear there would be no further discussion of what happened Saturday night. I was happy to ignore the whole thing."

"Well, the situation went downhill from there. He claimed the work on my accounts unacceptable, whereas before it was excellent. The third time he made a big deal out of a mistake, the boss called me into his office to question me. The smug look on Tony's face told the story. He sandbagged me."

"Did you defend yourself?" Noah demanded, pounding his fist on the table.

"Of course I did, and the errors Tony found weren't mine. The numbers had been altered, and the only person who reviewed those accounts was him. The last report which was about to be sent out, and the largest account I was in charge of, Tony claimed he wanted to double check my work. The error he pointed out wasn't in the file I gave him."

Noah jerked to his feet. "I'll show that little weasel—"

She grabbed her brother's arm and pulled. "Sit."

"Did your boss believe you?" Noah demanded.

Nate felt outrage bubbling up in him. She'd been set up by the little whiny man who probably didn't know the north end of a mule from the south.

"I didn't have the seniority and, to boot, was the new hire, so before I got fired, I quit. I didn't want to tell anyone I'd been fired from my job. I could just say the job wasn't a good fit for me."

"Did you at least kick the jerk in the shins or let the air out of his tires?" Noah wasn't going to let this go.

Nate agreed. The snake needed to be taught a lesson.

"No, but I did warn the boss if he ever wondered why he couldn't keep a person in my position, he should ask all the other women who came before me. His eyes widened, then narrowed. He caught my meaning. When I left the room, I heard Tony make up excuses about my lack of qualifications."

"That weasel shouldn't skate," Noah shot back. One look at his sister's face, he clamped his mouth shut.

"So what do you plan to do now?" Nate asked.

The back screen slammed and her other brothers walked in.

"What's Missy's truck doing in the driveway?" Wyatt asked.

She turned and greeted him. "Hello to you, too, bro. Good to see you."

Wyatt stopped and swallowed. "Hey, sis. You're home. Why?"

"Get yourself a brownie and join us."

Rait and Wyatt grabbed brownies and found a chair around the table.

"Is Dad with you?" Missy asked.

Wyatt frowned. "Last time I saw him is when we rode out around noon. I thought he was following, but we never saw him after we crested the hill. So what's up?" Wyatt asked.

Well into her explanation, their father, Bill Danner, and Brandi Jo walked into the kitchen. "What's going on? Y'all having a family meeting without us?" His gaze touched each person but when he got to Missy he stopped.

She rushed to her dad's side. "I was explaining to everyone why I decided to move home."

Her father blinked. "So why are you home? You think I can't run this ranch without your mother?"

The harsh words were so unlike the man they knew growing up that everyone in the room squirmed.

"That's not it, Dad," Missy hastily replied. "I had a little problem. Why don't I heat up stew Betty brought and I'll explain."

Nate stood and stepped toward the back door. "I'll be on my way. We can talk about those bulls we saw today later."

"No, don't you go." Bill put his hand on Nate's shoulder. "I think all of us would like to hear your opinion on a new bull."

From the look on everyone's face, Nate knew the brothers and sisters wanted him to stay. His stomach growled.

"I'm not quite sure Missy will enjoy the discussion."

She waved away his concerns. "As if this isn't my first discussion on the subject of bulls."

Missy didn't hesitate with her answer. That's what Nate always admired about her. No matter what her brothers threw at her, she didn't back down. "Thanks for the invite, Bill."

"We'll have to thank Betty for the wonderful meal." Wyatt placed his spoon in his bowl and stood.

"Where are you going?" Missy asked.

"I'm going to turn on the TV to see what the weather will be like tomorrow. This nice weather shouldn't last long."

"You going to leave that on the table?" Missy nodded to his bowel.

His brow wrinkled as he looked from his dish to his sister. Several coughs dotted the air.

"I'd planned to-"

"To what?" she asked.

He met each sibling's gaze. "Well, since you're home, I thought you'd be taking over the cooking and cleaning. Brandi Jo keeps complaining about it."

"Mom didn't let you get away with walking away from the table without gathering up your dishes."

He shuffled his feet. No one said a thing.

"No matter what you think, brother, I didn't come to be the maid." Missy's voice rang with steel. "There are going to be chores, and each of you will help on a different day until we can hire a housekeeper. And we can start with you, Wyatt, tomorrow morning. You'll get drafted for breakfast."

His eyes widened as he sat back down.

Missy knew this would be a battle, and she had to stand her ground now. The sooner she established how things were going to work, the better off everyone would be.

Glancing around the table, she noted there were no objections. "I'll make up a schedule tonight and post it on the fridge until we can hire a housekeeper and a cook.

"But you're a gi—" Wyatt swallowed the rest of the word.

"You're right. I am a CPA and worked hard to get that degree."

"I think your sister has a good idea," Bill added. "I know your mother wouldn't want your sisters stuck in the kitchen. Besides, if I remember correctly, Missy isn't that gifted in the cooking department."

She heard several snickers. Her lips twitched. "You're right, Dad, we need to hire a cook, someone who enjoys cooking."

Later that evening, she made the call to line up a cook her top priority."Thanks, Carrie. I know my brothers will appreciate a good cook and your mom is the best."

"It's just until her new job opens up."

"I understand." Missy hung up the phone just as a knock sounded on the door. "Come in."

The portal slowly opened, and Wyatt's face appeared. "Can I talk to you, Sis?"

"Sure."

"I want to apologize for that crack earlier about you being a girl." He looked like he stood in a patch of prickly pear and didn't know where to move. "Mom wouldn't have approved."

He shook his head. "We all feel lost without her. And Dad, we're all worried about him. He says one thing then does another. Like this morning, he said he'd ride out after us, but never showed. Who knows where he went. He isn't dealing well with Mom's death."

She slipped off her single bed and walked to Wyatt's side and gave him a squeeze. "We all miss her. What you're feeling is okay. I think if you talked to your brothers, you'd find they miss her, too." She knew he'd never talk to Brandi Jo about his feelings. She was a girl.

He nodded. "Thanks for understanding."

"No problem, but I expect to see you in the kitchen at 5:30."

"I'll be there."

That's what she liked about her younger brother. He kept his word.

Five minutes later someone knocked and opened the door. Brandi Jo stood there. "Thanks for handling the schedule of chores. The first time they expected me to do everything Mom did, and I told them no. We all needed to share the load. They didn't listen to me. Noah stepped in and said it wasn't fair to dump on me." She leaned down and gave her sister a kiss. "You're a God-send. You're better at corralling the boys."

"No, just determined I wasn't going to try to take Mom's place, and they needed to know."

Chapter 3

Missy stared at the owner of the feed store, who gave her a tight smile. She couldn't believe her ears. She'd volunteered to run errands in town this morning.

"Are you aware that your account for grain is 60 days overdue? I wish I could carry your family's bill longer, but things are tight right now."

"No, Ted, you shouldn't have to go that long without being paid."

He shrugged. "With your mom's passing, I figured things were in an uproar at the ranch and would settle down."

"There's no reason to apologize. I'm glad you brought this to my attention."

He rubbed his chin. "I can fill this order today, but..."

"I understand, Ted. Let me know what we owe, and I'll cut a check and get it to you tomorrow."

He blushed, but pulled up the account on his computer screen and told her the balance.

"I'll take care of things."

"Kinda like your mom."

"I'm not that good."

"Don't sell yourself short."

"Thanks."

He printed off a copy of the bill. "So, what are you doing here, Missy? I thought you took a fancy job in Denver?"

It was the question everyone in Silverdale would ask and the one she dreaded.

"Sometimes, Ted, living in the big city isn't what it's cracked up to be. You ever feel smothered when you go into Denver, the Springs, or Pueblo?"

He nodded.

"I just needed time on the plains where I could see the horizon, clear my head, and breathe clean air."

"I understand. Let me load your order."

She needed a strong cup of coffee to steady her frazzled nerves. "I'll be next door at the Branding Iron."

He nodded and disappeared into the back.

On wobbly legs, she made her way to the café and ordered coffee.

"Would you like one of our new Danishes?" the waitress asked.

"They're mighty good," Nate interjected, startling both women. He took a seat at the table before asking permission. "I'll have coffee, too. And one of those Danishes."

He turned back to her. "What's wrong?"

Of all the people in the world, Nathan Winter had to sit across from her. When they were growing up, she could never bluff her way past him. She could Noah, but not Nate.

Before she could answer, Ted stuck his head in the doorway. "You're good to go, Missy. Everything's loaded."

"Thanks."

The waitress appeared with coffee and Danishes. It took several minutes for her heart to settle down. Nate didn't take his eyes off her which didn't help.

She stared at her food. He reached across the table and rested his hand on hers. Her head jerked up and their gazes clashed.

"Missy?"

She needed a friend, a non-relative to talk with. "Apparently, Dad hasn't paid Ted in months. We have a large outstanding bill." She took a deep breath. "Why hasn't someone done something about the situation? Didn't anyone wonder about the money situation?"

Nate squeezed her hand, then motioned with his fork to the Danish. He took a bite and chewed, enjoying the sweetness of the treat.

She wanted answers, but apparently Nate was in no hurry to answer. Again he nodded to the food. She cut a bite and popped it into her mouth. The man wasn't lying. The wonderful blend of cinnamon, walnuts, and butter rolled over her tongue. It took the edge off her crashing emotions. She followed up with a swallow of coffee.

The corner of Nate's mouth kicked up. "Feeling better?"

"You were right, it is good, but do you have an answer to my question?"

15

A grin crossed his lips. "Maybe your brothers and sisters were too busy wrestling with their own grief to realize your dad hadn't paid the bills. Men aren't as good in the emotion department as women. As for your sisters, can't say."

At Christmas she tried to talk about their mother and how things were running at the ranch, but only received single-word grunts and stares in response. Even Brandi Jo seemed reluctant to say anything.

Nate took another bite. "I know Noah asked your dad if he needed any help with the books. He nearly bit Noah's head off. Everything was fine. Bill didn't need any help. Noah needed to take care of his chores and not worry about the finances."

She put her fork down, shocked. "So what you're telling me is things are not good at the Danner ranch."

"Confused and unsettled would be more like it."

Missy didn't know how to respond.

"Your family needs a push in the right direction. That's all. Someone to organize things, and you're the best of the bunch." He finished his Danish and took the last swallow of coffee. Leaning in, he added, "The guys might not be the only ones who've lost their direction."

She flinched.

He got up and tossed enough money to cover both their orders on the table.

"I can pay," she called out.

He paused at the door and grinned. "You can get the next round." He didn't wait for an answer.

The waitress appeared beside her and picked up the generous tip. "He's a hunk. I've tried to get his attention, but there aren't any sparks." She sighed.

Missy shook her head. That was Nate. Sure he was a good guy, but he was the guy who threw mud at her one summer when she was fourteen and trailing behind him and Noah. The man who walked out of the diner had certainly matured. His arms filled out his shirt and he'd have no trouble picking up a calf, and turning it on its side for branding.

She blew out a breath, picked up her purse and headed home, and worried how she would confront her dad. Apparently, there was another reason for her to come home.

Once at the ranch, she parked by Nate's truck. Noah, Nate and Wyatt walked out of the barn. "Guys, I need help unloading all this feed."

"Can't, Sis. Nate and I have to be at that auction in Pueblo by 12:30."

She glared at Nate. "You could've said something."

"Nope. It had nothing to do with Danishes."

"What are you two talking about?" Noah looked from her to Nate.

"Money, bro," She explained about the overdue bill at the feed store.

Wyatt stopped and stared at her. "That can't be. No one has mentioned anything about overdue bills."

She rested her forearms on the bed of her truck. "Has any one of you checked the ranch's bank accounts? And if you buy a new bull, how are you going to pay for the animal?"

Wyatt threw Noah a glance. "Is she right?"

"I haven't had any problems with the bills. Dad's taking care of it. He and I had a discussion about it after Mom died. He told me he could do the job and not to underestimate him and threw me out of his office." But Noah stared down at his boots.

"Well, you and Nate go to the auction. If you want to bid, give me a call first. I'll talk to Dad."

Noah hopped into his truck and didn't waste any time zipping out of the driveway.

Wyatt paused by her. "I can't believe that Dad hasn't been paying the bills."

"Let's pray he's paid gas and electric or we'll have a cold weekend." She walked into the house, praying she'd find her dad.

~

They were half-way to Pueblo before Noah said anything. "I didn't know." His hands gripped the steering wheel. "I tried helping Dad, but you know what happened. I knew Mom and Dad did the books together, but...

"Mom never asked about my time in the Army, but when I would sit out on the porch, looking out at the familiar horizon, she'd bring out a glass of sweet tea and sit with me. Didn't ask questions, didn't pry, but would grab my hand and say she was proud of her eldest son."

Struggling with the truth wasn't easy, no matter who you were. Nate's sudden and unexpected attraction to Missy flashed in his mind. "You offered to help but your dad would have nothing to do with it. He assured you everything was okay. Normally, we don't question our dads since they've had a truckload of experience beyond us. Maybe Missy can do things that none of the rest of you can do. As I recall, your dad has a soft spot for his girls."

"Yeah, he does. When it came to the girls, Mom had to dish out the discipline. Dad didn't have any problem whipping us boys."

"As you said, maybe Missy can do a better job at coaxing your dad into letting her do the books. I wonder how many other creditors he hasn't paid. Since it's early in the year, did he pay the County and State taxes?"

Noah went pale. "That's a frightening thought."

It was.

Chapter 4

Missy sat at the kitchen table, nursing a cup of coffee, her mind racing over all the things she needed to do. First was to get signed onto the ranch accounts, so she could write checks for the bills. Talk to the bank and creditors. Know what the balance was.

"Hey, what are you doing sitting here a-lolly-gagging?" Her dad smiled. I thought you ran errands in town this morning. You finished already?"

She'd been praying on how to start this conversation. "Dad, why don't you pour yourself some coffee and join me at the table?"

"You sound so serious." He grabbed a cup, filled it, and sat beside her. "So what's up?" He studied her. Taking a deep breath, she stood and pulled her purse from the cubbyhole at the end of the kitchen that had been hers. She laid the bill on the table.

He put his coffee down and ran his fingers through his hair. "I didn't realize..."

She scooted her chair closer to his.

"How'd it get so big, Dad? Why didn't you pay it?"

He stared at the table. "Every time I went into the office, I was overwhelmed with your mother's presence, hearing her voice, reliving a funny time together. The feelings became too much, and I couldn't stand to be in there." He picked up the bill again. "I didn't realize it had been that long."

Her heart went out to this strong man. She understood how grief could devastate a person. "Why didn't you have one of us do it?"

"And have my children think their dad couldn't handle things." He blew out breath.

She could understand him not wanting to show weakness in front of his kids.

"You should've called me. I could've come home on a weekend or done something over Christmas holiday."

"And have your brothers ask why? I'd look like an old coot who couldn't control his emotions."

She laid her hand on his arm. "Dad, grieving for your wife of thirty-five years doesn't make you look like an old coot. It only shows that you loved Mom. Each of us kids has our own way of grieving. None of us are immune." She rubbed his arm. "Maybe that's why I accepted a date from Tony. That's got to be it. So I guess we all had our way to cope." Hers stunk.

"My guess is this isn't the only outstanding bill. Have you paid the taxes on the ranch?"

He studied her, his mind reviewing what he'd done. "I don't know."

"Why don't we go to the office and check what you've done in the last few months."

"I like your idea."

Over the next hour, Melissa and her father went over the bills.

They worked on the accounts and wrote checks to the county for taxes and to the power company for electricity. She informed her dad of this new and fancy system called e-check that would make writing checks easier.

"And we'll need to go to the bank, and put me on the signature card, so I can take over the books. It might make it easier on you."

He grabbed her hand and squeezed. "Thanks for your help. It won't take long for your boss to discover his mistake."

She wouldn't hold her breath.

~

The drive into town was a peaceful affair. They stopped at the bank and had her name put on the accounts. As they visited each retailer, Bill handed the owner a check. If Missy thought girls gossiped, she'd forgotten the information swamped among the guys, but each owner sympathized with Bill and had a story of his own. Their last stop was the feed store. At the sound of the chime, Ted emerged from the back.

"Bill, Missy, what are you doing here? Was there something wrong with the feed?"

Bill held out a check. "After talking with my daughter this morning, and realizing what had been going on, we wanted to come in and pay you. This isn't the full amount, but the bulk of what the ranch owes." The men continued to talk, but Missy could see the animation in her father's body language.

As it turned out, the best thing that could've happened was to lose her job in Denver. She was needed here.

As Ted and her dad ended their conversion, she handed Ted an envelope. He frowned. "What's --"

She shook her head. He peeked inside the unsealed envelope.

"That's my contribution. Credit it to the ranch's account."

Ted eyed her dad. "You got it."

~

Saturday morning, Missy's friend from Denver arrived with her mother and the balance of Missy's belongings.

"Anna," Missy yelled as she exited the backdoor of the ranch house with open arms. Squeals ensued. Her family followed her out of the house and others out of the barn.

Rait had a spatula in his hand, dripping grease. "What's going on?"

A woman in her mid-fifties opened the passenger door of the U-haul van, climbed out, and walked toward him. She nodded to the utensil he held. "Furniture and the cook have arrived, and I'd say you left the bacon on the stove, frying."

"Oh." He turned and hurried into the house. The skillet had begun to smoke.

"Use a hot pad," the woman yelled.

The family followed them into the kitchen.

It didn't take long for Rait to follow the woman's directions. Before he could move the skillet, she leaned in, turning off the fire beneath it.

With the situation under control, the woman introduced herself. "I'm Mary Jardin, your temporary cook and housekeeper."

Sighs of relief sounded. "But, I'm going to lay down some ground rules. I'm sure your mother required you to do things. After we eat breakfast, I'm going to tell you what I expect. We'll all be happier after that."

No one complained. Mary nodded and smiled. Turning, she observed the partially fried bacon. Rait tried to hand her the spatula. "I don't want to interfere with your cooking. Continue. While you finish there, I'll start on the biscuits."

Mary's daughter, Trisha, whispered, "It's amazing to see her take on this rowdy group of guys and bring order within minutes." She glanced at her mom. "It never fails to awe me."

"Good job," Noah whispered.

Missy introduced her brother.

"How full is the rental?"

"Let's go out and see."

Missy, Noah, Wyatt, and Trish went to the van and Trish unlocked it. Noah stepped up on the tailgate and looked inside. "Where do you plan on putting all this stuff?"

"I'll need to see where it will fit, but until it's all unloaded, I won't know where I'll put it."

"Well, that flowery couch isn't going in the den," Wyatt declared. "We'll be the laughing stock of the neighborhood." He'd thrown down the first marker. "Come to the Danner place to sit among the flowers."

"Don't worry, bro, no one will question your manhood or make you sit on that loveseat."

His eyes widened. "That's even worse, me sitting on that flowery little bench. If any of my friends saw that, they'd run me out of the Professional Rodeo Riders Association."

Missy shook her head. "Quit complaining."

By the time they made their way back into the house, the family had gathered in the kitchen, waiting for the biscuits to finish baking. The last thing she heard was Noah calling Nate to come and help.

Finally, there was some hope. Missy could only thank Heaven Above for Mary.

~

Sunday, after the morning chores were done and the family fed, they made it to the community church for the 11:00 service. The first person who greeted Missy was Nate's mom, Sandra, pulling her into a big hug. "I heard you'd come home." She pulled back and studied Missy. "How are you doing?"

A prickling chill ran up Missy's spine. Nate's mom had always been friendly, but not this friendly. It could be chalked up to the circumstances of not seeing her since her mother's funeral, but there was more to Sandra's enthusiasm. Missy was sure of it.

"Things are starting to look up. I miss Mom, but that seems to be a theme at the ranch. No one realized we had that big hole in our hearts since we're running so hard."

"I hear you."

Over Sandra's shoulder, Missy spotted Nate and his dad. His Dad stepped forward and shook her hand. He was studying her, but why?

"Welcome home, Missy. Nate's been telling us how much difference you've made at the ranch." He glanced over her shoulder to Bill.

"Sometimes, home is the best place to be." Currents swirled around her.

"I can second that." Darrell nodded, stepping to his wife's side.

Nate moved closer to Missy. "I'm sorry if my folks embarrassed you. They're glad Bill is looking so good. And your trip back into town set everyone talking, about how you took over and paid bills." His eyes roamed over her face, settling on her lips.

Fireworks exploded in her stomach. This was church, for Pete's sake, and of all places to have those feelings, Sunday morning service was the last place she wanted to experience those feelings.

The church started filling up with neighbors greeting her and the family. Organ music floated through the sanctuary and most of the polite chatter ceased and services began.

Missy felt like a bug under glass with all the stares directed her way. She didn't think it was a big deal she'd come home. Some of the other ranchers' children had done the exact same thing. The Souters, the ranch north of them, had both of their sons return with families in tow. She wasn't the first, nor would she be the last wandering child to return home, so why was it such a big deal?

The answer occurred to her on Tuesday when she went to town with their new cook. Every store owner where they went congratulated her on how she'd put the Rockin' D on solid footing and handled the crisis. A couple of ranchers asked if they could hire her to help with their books. An entire new opportunity opened before her. Had there been more than one reason she needed to come home?

"What's got you so puzzled over there, Missy?" Mary asked, as they drove home.

"The realization I might be on right track and needed to come home."

"Good for you. Something about how your job in Denver ended didn't feel right to me. Maybe you weren't on the correct path in the first place and needed a little nudge."

"Well, I would've liked a different ending." Missy tried to concentrate on driving, turning onto the gravel road leading to the ranch. The temperature had dropped and the skies to the west had darkened. But each time she tried to focus on her driving, lots of little facts that didn't add up popped into her head, and for her, the accountant, things needed to add up.

"I'll say your need for a cook/housekeeper came at the right time," Mary added. "I'd run out of unemployment insurance, then bam, there was your job offer. You couldn't have planned it better."

"There was no planning. It just happened."

"Well, it certainly worked out well for me. I didn't know what I'd do, but you were an answer to my prayer."

"We answered each other's prayers."

"And if I don't miss my guess, I know a certain cowboy who thinks you were an answer to his prayers."

"What?" She glanced at Mary. "My brothers don't count."

Mary waved off the statement. "I wasn't talking about your brothers, and you know it."

"No, I don't." She wasn't going down without a fight.

"Please, it's obvious as the nose on your face, unless you're purposely ignoring it."

She was.

Nate?

"You hit the nail on the head."

Missy jerked. She didn't realize she'd spoken his name out loud.

"That cowboy is so lovesick he doesn't know what to do with himself." Mary reached into her purse and pulled out a package of gum. "Want one?"

Missy shook her head. How could the woman offer her gum when she'd just thrown that grenade into the front seat? Now, Missy had heard Nate described several different ways. "The most stubborn hard-headed cowboy that ever mounted a horse," or "Never back-down cowboy 'cause he thinks he's right," but never a love-sick cowboy.

"Cat got your tongue?" Mary pressed.

"No, that cat stole my tongue." She glanced out at the road. "I've known Nate most of my life, and he's always considered me a pest. A tag-a-long little sister of his best friend, who had to be endured." She swallowed, remembering the electricity that arched between her and Nate when brushed by him when taking her seat at the rodeo.

"So, I'm not so far off the mark."

When Missy looked at the other woman, her satisfied smile landed right between her eyes.

"No."

"You don't sound excited or delighted at the news."

"It's like you're telling me I've got the flu."

"What, you don't want to fall in love with Nate? He seems like a nice young man. And he's the same every time you meet him. My ex—" She shook her head. "When he was on, he could charm the world, and make me feel like a million bucks. When he wasn't, the man was impossible to live with. He thought of no one but himself, and when he got his paycheck, he spent most of it on himself, before thinking about his wife and babies at home. Give me a steady, unexciting man any day of the week, a man I can depend on."

Mary's words cast Nate in new light. He was as steady as one of the pillars in the capital building in Denver. He could be counted on, no matter the situation. She understood Mary's viewpoint having to deal with a mercurial man.

"It's such a shock to even think of Nate in that light." Her mouth grew dry; Missy swallowed.

"Well, Sugar, you better come to grips with it, 'cause it looks like you have a case of love-sickness, too."

"No, don't tell me that."

Mary smiled.

Chapter Five

Nate looked across the kitchen table at Missy who sat sandwiched between Rait and Wyatt. She didn't look up from her food, but concentrated on the pork chops as if they held the answer to world peace. She also didn't glance at Noah.

Nate knew they'd have a hard time convincing her that buying that bull was a good idea, but the owner had called him this morning, asking if he and Noah were still interested. They were, and went by the bank, had the check cut, and drove to pick up the animal.

He caught the glance Missy threw at him and couldn't identify her expression. His heart skipped a beat. The brothers stood, carrying their dishes to the sink.

"Come on, Nate, let's show everyone the new bull we bought." Noah grabbed him by the arm and headed out the door.

Still no objection from Missy.

Out in the barn the brothers talked about the latest purchase.

Nate stepped closer to Noah. "Did your sister say anything to you?"

"No, and I was prepared to defend our purchase with several different arguments using cost and profit analysis on our investment. She didn't say anything, which took me by surprise. I had all the logical reasons why it was a good investment. She asked you about it?"

"No, and that's what's got me worried."

Noah rubbed his chin. "You think I need to talk to her?"

"No." Nate held up his hand. "I'll do that, leaving you out of the line of fire."

The pat on the back Noah gave him wasn't much comfort. Leaving the guys in the barn, Nate made his way inside. The kitchen stood empty. Next he went to the living room. Bill sat in his chair snoring. Nate turned

26

to go, but Bill woke.

"I'm sorry to disturb you."

Bill re-adjusted the paper. "Not a problem."

"I was looking for Missy."

"Ah, to explain the new purchase?"

Nate cleared his throat, shifting his weight from one foot to the other. "I thought I'd take the hit, since it was my idea."

"She's either in the ranch office or in her mother's office."

Nate found her in her mother's very feminine room.

"May I come in and explain what happened today?"

She shrugged.

He'd found where they put Missy's flowered couch, and she sat at one end, hugging a flowery pillow with ruffles. This wouldn't be easy. He sat gingerly on the other end.

"What happened this morning with your brother and me buying that bull is my fault. When the rancher called, offering the bull at a better price, well, I couldn't pass it up."

"You got the animal for less?"

"Yes."

She nodded and stared down into her lap. "Good."

He waited. That was all?

"You're not upset?"

"If you and Noah had the money, there's nothing to be upset about."

He stared at her. Something was wrong, but what?

She set aside the pillow, stood, and plopped down next to him. Cupping both his cheeks, she planted a kiss on his lips.

His brain shut down and instinct took over. His mouth responded to hers, and his arms wrapped around her waist, pressing her to his chest.

Finally, after what seemed like an eternity, he pulled back. Her eyes fluttered open, the pupils large and dark. He brushed her hair from her face.

"What was all that about, not that I objected?"

"I told Mary that you weren't attracted to me, and I returned the feeling. You and I can't be. We just can't."

"Why?"

Jumping up, she backed up. "Because Noah and you are best friends."

"That's true. So?"

"And you and I can't have feelings for each other for that very reason. It would complicate things."

"So why'd you kiss me?"

"Why'd you kiss me back?" she demanded, gesturing wildly. "You just should've kept your lips to yourself."

He sat there, stunned. Words failed him.

The door to the room flew open and Noah stood there looking guilty. "I'm sorry, Sis. I thought Nate could explain things better than I could about the bull."

"Bull? What are you talking about?"

Noah explained about the purchase.

"Well, he has a funny way of explaining things."

Noah frowned, looking from Missy to him. "What's going on?"

Missy pointed at him. "He kissed me."

"Only after you sat beside me and kissed me. I only reacted."

"What?" Noah's eyes narrowed. "Why are you kissing my sister?"

"Because she kissed me first." Nate couldn't believe his ears. How'd the situation go from him trying to explain about the bull to ease the way for their purchase to him defending himself, who innocently sat there on the couch.

"That true, Melissa?"

Her cheeks reddened, and her gaze bounced off Nate's, then she stared at the floor. She didn't defend herself but left the room, pushing past the crowd gathered at the door.

Noah collapsed onto the sofa. "What happened?"

Bill walked into the room. "Is there a problem with your sister?" He closed the door behind him, waving off the others.

Nate leaned forward resting his arms on his thighs and shook his head. "I wish I knew." He combed his fingers through his hair. "She didn't ask any question about the arrangement we worked out for the new bull. Nothing about the benefits, profit or loss, or where the money came from.

"I was sitting here trying to explain. Missy was at the other end clutching a pillow." He jabbed his hand at the far end. "Before I knew it, she threw the pillow over her shoulder, launched herself at me, grabbing my face, and planted a kiss on my lips."

Noah's jaw went slack.

Bill grinned. "Good for her."

"How can you say that, Dad?"

"'Cause your sister needs to be interested in a good, solid man compared to that poor excuse she showed up with at the rodeo. I think Nate qualifies. He's got his head on straight and is one of the hardest working cowboys around. I've always liked him, and your mother did, too. Apparently, love's come and bit your sister."

The older man's gaze narrowed. "You got feelings for my girl, don't you, Nate? I don't want her to be hurt."

Nate stared at the older man. Sure he had feelings for Melissa, but they were all over the map. "Well, it's like I've been struck by lightning and my heart races when she's near. I nearly passed out when she kissed me. But I kissed her back with an eagerness I haven't felt before."

Bill slapped his thigh. "That's all I need to know."

"That's all you have to say, Dad?" Noah asked.

"The first time I saw your mom, I got her alone at the church picnic and stole a kiss. Her older brother saw it and cleaned my clock, but the important thing was how your mother responded. She kissed back."

"But Missy wasn't happy." Nate rubbed his neck.

"Did she kiss you?"

"Yes." And with vigor. He couldn't help but smile.

"Then let her deal with the fallout. My girl's smart enough to know what she wants."

"But Dad," Noah objected. "He's my best friend."

"Can you think of anyone better to deal with your sister?"

Silence greeted the question.

"All right. Let's leave Missy and Nate to deal with the fallout." He pointed to his son. "I expect you have enough common sense not to interfere. Do you want to lose both a sister and good friend?"

"No."

Bill nodded. "You always were a smart boy."

Once they were alone, Nate didn't know how his friend would react. He didn't know how to react.

Nate stood. "I need to get back to the ranch. We've run across some issues that we had thought about. I'll call you later this week." He left without any objections from his best friend and drove home in fog.

~

Sleep eluded her. Every time she closed her eyes, she relived Nate's kiss. She could feel his surprise when she put her lips on his, but it didn't take him long to get with the program. And when he did, there was no doubt that he was totally committed. He raised no objections. If she didn't miss her guess, he liked the kiss, and she was in deeper with this "attraction to" Nate than she imagined.

Her brain kept going over Mary's words, so when Nate showed up in the sitting room, Missy gave into the idea of kissing him. It would answer the question if she was attracted to him and vice-versa.

She had her answer and it only added to her confusion. Nate was supposed to kiss like her brother's friend, cold lips and mashing of teeth. It'd been nothing like that. If she touched a live wire, her senses couldn't have been that overloaded. His warmth surrounded her and his lips went from slack to welcoming to demanding in a matter of moments.

29

She felt surrounded, loved, comforted.

Sitting up in bed, she ran her fingers though her hair. What had started with a brilliant plan had exploded in her face. Now that she tasted the man, felt his strength, how could she look him in the eye?

Of all the spur-of-the-moment rash things she'd done, kissing Nate ranked as number one. Sometimes she'd outsmarted herself. The man deserved an apology.

She stretched out again. That would fix things and their relationship could go back to normal.

She had a plan.

Chapter Six

The next morning, Missy went down to breakfast as if what happened between Nate and her had been a fluke, and things were back to normal.

The first person she encountered was Wyatt. He nodded as he put his hat on his hook. "Well, our mild temperatures didn't last long. Snow's predicted for later today."

The others slowly drifted in and grabbed a plate and silverware. Each person stopped by the coffeemaker. When Missy reached for a cup, her hand met Noah's. He stepped back and motioned her to proceed. He didn't say anything, but questions lingered in his eyes.

Fortunately, the conversion drifted to today's chores. Just as she began to relax and all seemed normal, the phone rang. Wyatt answered.

"Sure, Mrs. Winter, Missy's here." Wyatt held the phone out to her.

Missy felt the blood drain from her face. She hurried to the phone. Nate's mother. "Hello, Mrs. Winter."

"Missy, your mom was the head of the committee for organizing the Valentine's banquet for church. She had all the notes, and several of the other ladies asked what we wanted to do this year. I thought your mother would want us to continue with the banquet. The only problem is she was the only one with copies of our plans. Do you think you could locate her notes and then we'll figure a way to get them to the committee? Not everyone has a computer they're comfortable using. If their kids are still at home, everything's fine."

For a moment her mind went blank.

"Missy, are you there?"

"I'm sorry, Mrs. Winter."

"Please call me Sandra. You make me sound like my mother."

"Of course, Sandra. Let me check Mom's files, and I'll get back with you." When Missy hung up, she straightened her spine and turned to her brothers. She explained about the Valentine's Day Banquet. "So any of you know where I might find the information for Nate's mom?" She couldn't bring herself to call Mrs. Winter by her first name.

"It's in your mom's desk," her father replied. "I remember her telling me she had the only copy of the plans, and she needed to be careful with the file."

"Good. I'll check after breakfast." She slowly walked back to her seat. The only response was the sound of slurping and utensils clanging on plates.

After the kitchen cleared out, Missy went to her mom's library. She stood in the doorway, overcome with memories and feelings from last night that she didn't know what to do with. If she let herself, she'd collapse on the floor and have a good cry. "Get a hold of yourself, girlfriend. Things will only change if you let it."

In the center drawer of the desk, she found the file labeled 'Valentine's Banquet.' Just as Nate's mother described, inside were detailed notes, including a long description documenting her conversation with the pastor.

As much as she didn't want to be involved with Valentine's Day, she knew how much her mother loved the holiday. She said there was no better group of men than ranchers, but they needed a lot of help in showing their emotions. This was the wives' opportunity to help.

Missy called Nate's mom. "I found the folder just where Dad told me I'd find it. All her notes are inside." Usually, the committee had six to eight weeks to plan and do things. Because of her mom's death, they were down to four and a half weeks, which meant Sandra needed this info ASAP.

"I could wait and bring this file to you Sunday but, because of how close the holiday is, would it help if I drive the file out to you this afternoon?" She glanced out the window and the snow hadn't begun, and the temperature had risen eight degrees.

Sandra didn't respond right away. "You know they predicated a storm today."

"True, but the temp's up, and you and I know it takes less than a half-hour if I use the county roads to drive to your place. The committee could start work today."

"Okay, but you're going to need to drop off the information and turn around and go home."

Missy smiled. "Deal."

She hurried downstairs to the kitchen where Mary worked on dinner.

"I'm going to take this file to the Winters' place. I should be back in less than an hour." She pulled her cell phone from inside her purse, making sure she had a way to communicate if something happened.

"Be careful." Mary pointed her rolling pen at Missy. "Remember the forecast."

Slipping the file in her purse, she brushed a kiss across Mary's cheek. "I will. Since the snow hasn't started yet, I'll have plenty of time. I'll be back in in less than an hour."

That was the last time weather crossed her mind.

~

The sound of a back door slamming broke into Missy and Sandra's concentration. "Mom, what's Missy's truck doing here?"

The women looked at the clock above Sandra's sewing machine. It read 4:30.

"Where'd the time go?" Missy asked. "It was just 10:30." She gathered her papers and notes and followed Sandra down the hall. Nate, his father, and another man stood in there, dripping snow.

"Time got away from us. The rumbling of our stomachs should've warned us, but things fell so easily into place. Lucky I have spaghetti sauce in the freezer and it won't take long to fix." Sandra hugged Missy. "You were a huge help. I think we can pull this off. And be careful driving home."

Nate pointed at Missy. "She's not going anywhere."

"Son, that's no way to greet a guest."

"Sandra, have you looked outside?" Darrell pointed to the window. "It's a blizzard. We've already put up the guide rope from the side door to the barn."

Both women looked out the kitchen window. The snow storm howled, the wind whipping the snow sideways.

Missy's phone rang. She opened her purse and answered. "Where are you, Sis?" Noah roared.

Before she could answer, her father took the phone, "We've been panicked for hours, searching for you."

Her purse had been buried beneath several pillows on the sofa and she hadn't heard a thing. "I'm safe in Sandra's kitchen. Time got away from us. Before we knew it, we spent the day organizing Mom's banquet. Everything's in place. I'm sorry for worrying you."

"Let me talk to Darrell," her dad demanded. Missy handed the phone to Nate's dad.

"Right, there's no way she can get out of our drive." He paused, listening to her father's loud words. "Of course, we'll keep her here until traffic's moving on the county roads. No problem, Bill." He handed back the phone.

"Sorry I worried you, Dad."

"I've lost one of my girls. I didn't think I could lose another one and survive."

Tears clouded her vision. "I'll see you tomorrow or when it's safe." She hung up her phone. "I guess I'm your unexpected guest. How can I help, Sandra?"

She glanced at Nate. The frown that gathered between his brows didn't bode well.

~

Nate's heart nearly stopped when he spotted Missy's truck parked in their drive. He knew his mom had called her this morning, but expected she'd have gone home hours ago. The storm predicted this morning quickly turned into a blizzard. While riding in from the south pasture and final check, his phone rang, with a frantic call from Noah. The reception had been so bad; understanding any words through the howling wind was impossible. Nate and his dad had managed to make it in to the barn. They found their hired man had finished the evening chores, but no one was leaving and going anywhere in this storm.

That's just what he needed. A hostile woman he'd suddenly found himself attracted to confined to the house. What he wanted was time to himself to sort out this crazy attraction he felt for Missy. When had things changed from childhood friendship to adult attraction?

At the rodeo when she passed by you, making her way to her seat. Logistics had been awkward.

No matter how much he denied his feelings, they were there, stubborn and giving him no quarter. He could've handled it, but then the woman kissed him and knocked his socks off, followed by her going crazy blaming him for the situation. He hadn't been the aggressor, but the victim. Well, he couldn't complain too much about it. He grinned.

But with awareness came a whole new set of problems. She was stuck here at the house until the weather changed. Could he gut it out, endure, survive several days? He had no idea, but didn't have a choice.

~

Dinner was the spaghetti Sandra promised. Both Nate's parents seemed unaware of the tenseness between Nate and her. After his dad stole another strand of spaghetti, Sandra banished the men from the kitchen.

"Show me where the dishes are, and I'll set the table." Missy wanted to stay as busy as possible.

Pointing to the end cabinet, Sandra told her where she could find everything. Missy went on automatic. If she thought too hard about the

34

situation of being snowed in with Nate after she made an idiot of herself last night, she'd run out into the raging storm, screaming at the top of her lungs.

Nothing had been settled between Nate and her and it sat like a huge boulder between them. "Why are you frowning, Missy? I'm sorry you got caught here, but we got things resolved. We're lucky the guys came in, making us aware of the weather outside. I wouldn't want you to start home and be caught in this storm," Sandra put back the top of the skillet.

Ranchers knew the hazards of a blizzard, and paid attention to the weather, which is something she hadn't.

"I guess I'm going to have to start thinking like a ranch kid again instead of a city-slicker." She rubbed her arms.

"Those are hard lessons to learn." Sandra pulled out the colander, placed it in the sink, then drained the spaghetti. "Last winter we had a couple of twenty-somethings from the Springs who bought a ranch, thinking they were going to breed llamas. Let's just say Darrell had to pull them out of a ditch during a storm and brought them home. They had a mild case frostbite. They moved back to the city the next week. We ended up with the llamas spread among the different ranchers."

"You telling Missy our experience with the spitting wonders?" Nate asked, walking into the kitchen.

"She is. I told her I need to brush up on my rancher's kid do's and don'ts. Dad sounded panicked when I talked to him earlier."

"Well, you're safe here, and we'll have one more person for our survive-the-blizzard games. Stoney can join in the games." The ranch hand grinned.

Just what she needed. One more person to hide her feelings from.

The evening passed quickly, with several games of Gin Rummy. Who knew that Nate was such a card shark? He took no prisoners and showed no mercy. The man was out to win.

"We should've warned you about Nate." Sandra laughed. "He's the 'Blizzard Gin Rummy champ'. His sister won't play with him."

"I guess I'll discover those hidden skills." She didn't need any further surprises. She didn't have her life under control.

~

Sandra pulled out sweats that belonged to Nate's younger sister. "These should do." Opening a drawer in the chest of drawers, she grabbed a couple of pairs of wool socks. "You'll need these, too. There's a heavy flannel robe in the closet. Feel free to use it." With her hand on the doorknob, Sandra added. "You're welcome to anything in the kitchen, in case you have an attack of the midnight munchies."

"Thanks."

Sandra nodded and left Missy alone.

Now what?

There was nothing she could do to change the situation of being stranded but to deal with it. Changing, she put on the warmer clothes, and loved the wool socks. She might be able to feel her toes again. The flannel robe made her feel she could meet any challenge.

The tension between her and Nate nearly killed her. They needed to clear the air between them. Hopefully, she could talk to him privately, saying she'd made a mistake and was sorry.

Tightening the belt of the robe, she opened the bedroom door to find Nate with his fist raised to knock.

"Good, I want to talk to you."

"I had the same idea. Let's go make hot chocolate in case my folks stumble into the kitchen and wonder what we're doing."

"Works for me."

She trailed him down the hall and into the large kitchen.

They worked together to make the hot chocolate, including marshmallows. For a moment, it was the way it used to be between them, friends, but when they sat down across from each other, the truce disappeared.

She put a finger on a marshmallow and stirred it. "I guess I need to explain why I kissed you."

"That would be nice. I went to the library to explain about what happened with the purchase of the bull, and Noah thought I could do a better job than he could."

"So why did you buy that animal?"

He explained the entire situation with the sale that didn't go through and the reduced price they paid. "It was like Heaven looked down and okayed the deal."

"Oh, please. I've heard some lame excuses, but that one tops it."

"You asked why I was there. That's why. Why'd you kiss me?"

She opened her mouth to tell him exactly what she thought, but the man deserved a reasonable explanation. "You're right. I kissed you, but only to prove Mary wrong in her observations about you and me. She said the electricity generated between us could short-circuit the kitchen clock."

"I told her she was mistaken. We've known each other for years, and she was wrong."

He didn't respond, but took a sip of his hot chocolate.

"Don't you have anything to say?"

"Mary is an observant woman."

"That's the reason I kissed you. To prove her wrong."

"Was she wrong?" he quietly asked.

She couldn't look at him. The spark generated by that kiss turned her world upside down. "No."

His hand covered her. She jerked away. He took another sip of his drink.

"You seem awfully calm over this situation."

"If you want to know, I liked that kiss and wouldn't mind repeating it."

She choked on her drink.

"What about your friendship with my brother?"

"I don't think he'll object."

"How can you be so sure of yourself?"

"Because he saw how upset you were at the rodeo. Noah knows me and said he appreciated how I drove you home that night."

"Is that what he said last night?"

"No. We just listened to your father." He swirled the last of his chocolate in his mug.

"What did he say?"

"You need to ask him. I'm not going to tell stories out of school."

"This involves me," she protested.

"And me." He stood and set his mug in the sink.

She stood and glared at him. "So you're not going to tell me."

He smiled down at her. "I think you already know."

She had the sinking feeling she did. "But what if I want to go back to the way it was?"

He ran the tips of his fingers across her jaw line then brushed a kiss across her mouth.

"That train has already left the station, and we're in a brand new world, which I like." He walked out of the kitchen, leaving Missy with her jaw hanging open.

Recognizing the truth of his words, Missy knew she'd have no help from him in turning back the clock. Now what was she going to do?

When his mouth brushed across hers, she wanted him to stop and put a little effort into the kiss. She wanted more.

Oh, she was in trouble.

She didn't see a solution to her attraction to Nate except maybe give in.

No, that wasn't in an option.

Nate knew that his attraction to Missy could turn into something more durable if the stubborn woman would give in. He certainly didn't expect his body's reaction to her, but since it happened, he wasn't to give up without a fight.

He knew what a fierce warrior she could be. If she thought something was wrong, or someone was being abused, she wouldn't tolerate it. He didn't doubt her experiences in Denver colored her outlook on men and no one would roll over her again.

That was what was needed in a ranch wife. Someone with grit.

He sat up in the bed. Ranch wife? He was getting ahead of himself. Easing back down, he rolled the concept around his brain.

He could see her in that role. She knew what it took to live out on the prairie, and what was required of a rancher's wife. And she certainly knew how to kiss, that's for sure. From their conversation tonight, she wasn't willing to move forward. That's what her words said, but her lips said something entirely different.

They probably had a couple more days of being stuck in the house. He was willing to let their attraction play out and see where things stood when she left.

He closed his eyes, satisfied.

Chapter Seven

The next morning, Missy felt like she'd wrestled a calf the balance of the night. When she appeared in the kitchen Nate and his father were in the barn feeding the animals.

"Morn'," Sandra cheerful voice greeted. "I've got coffee if you need some."

Missy welcomed the news of coffee. Cheerful wasn't in her vocabulary today.

As she poured herself a cup, the back door opened, and a bitter wind raced around the mud room and into the kitchen. After a moment, Nate and his father appeared. Her stomach did a little dance. She thought she could ignore her attraction, but one look at Nate's face destroyed that fantasy. Suddenly, she was out of control.

He smiled, and his eyes sparkled with mischief. "Morning."

Before she could respond, his father called out, "Why don't you pour a couple more mugs, Missy? Black for me but put cream in the other one for the sissy, here." He clapped Nate on the back.

She poured the extra mugs.

"Ignore Dad," Nate said reaching around her for the small pitcher that held real cream. "If he keeps drinking his coffee straight, he going to develop a bad ulcer just as the doctor warned." He raised his voice.

Darrell claimed his mug. "The man doesn't know what he's talking about. That incident was just a round of bad potatoes."

Mother and son traded looks.

Nate took a sip of his coffee. "Sleep well?" He softly asked.

To the others in the room, it sounded like a normal greeting, but the look in his eyes told her something else.

She could play this game. "Yes, I did." Too bad the bags under her eyes didn't agree.

"Good. It looks like traffic might be moving tomorrow. The county will be out clearing the roads as soon as they can."

"We'll have to listen to the county broadcasts tonight on road status," his dad commented.

They sat down for breakfast of pancakes and sausages, but sitting next to Nate the food didn't have any taste for her. The rest of the morning followed the pattern of breakfast with coffee and togetherness. After lunch the women retreated to the craft room to finalize plans for the Valentine's Day Banquet.

The telephone thankfully worked and as much as could be done by phone, Sandra did it. Everyone was in the same position as they were, stuck inside until the temperatures rose allowing movement on the roads. When they rejoined the guys late in the afternoon, they played a game of Rummy, which Missy won.

Darrell headed toward the back room where the short wave radio was located. As he signed on, Nate put on his boots and bundled up for his trip to the barn.

"I'll help," she volunteered, wanting to break the spell the day held. Cold could do that.

Nate glanced at her stocking feet.

"Give me a moment, and I'll be ready to go." Dashing to the bedroom assigned to her, she put on her socks and shoes. By the time she arrived back on the porch, Nate was ready to go. Before they stepped outside, he put a leash around her waist.

"We'll hook up outside."

Glancing down she said, "But it's calm outside."

"True, but if the wall of snow collapses, I'll be able to rescue you quickly."

Once seeing the path through the wall of snow, she appreciated his caution.

Inside the barn they quickly saw to the animals, feeding and putting out fresh water.

Nate patted his horse on the back. He re-adjusted the blanket on her back.

"Hello, Lady," Missy said, peeking over the side of the stall.

The horse turned her head and butted Missy's hand.

"You remember her?" surprised rumbled in Nate's voice.

"Do I remember your sister's name? Of course I remember your mount's name. She was a star in our county rodeo. She kept tension on the rope while you tied up the calf. You worked well as a team.

He smiled. "She still is the most reliable of all our horses."

Missy moved into the stable. "Of course she's the most reliable of all your horses, aren't you, girl."

The horse nodded and leaned into Missy. The smell of horse and the warmth of her breath wrapped around her heart.

"Did you miss riding when you were away?" She felt his presence behind her. "I did in college. The last couple of years, I didn't have time to ride, but..."

She promised herself she'd find a stable once she established her career and started riding again.

"Did you?"

She glanced over her shoulder. "No. Maybe that's why I started dating Tony."

"You were really desperate."

She snorted, startling Lady. "Sorry, girl. I just couldn't help myself."

He turned her in his arms, took off his gloves, stuffing them in his pockets and cupped her face. Slowly he leaned down. Her heart pounded, and she didn't try to avoid his lips. It was a curl-your-toes, take-no-prisoners kind of kiss that every woman longs for. But it was more than a kiss. The tenderness in his lips broke through the barrier she'd built around her heart.

When he drew back, the soft welcoming smile he flashed nearly crippled her.

"We can't be doing this."

"Why? Didn't you enjoy that as much as I did?"

She touched her lips. "I did."

"And you don't have a fiancé hidden away somewhere?"

"You know I don't."

"You liked it. I liked it. So what's the problem?"

"The problem is—" She started to explain, but nothing came out. She turned toward the side door and jerked it open, raced to the house. She ran through the kitchen and didn't stop until she reached his sister's room. The door slammed behind her. Leaning back against the wood, she asked herself why they couldn't fall in love.

She didn't have an answer.

~

Nate followed Missy into the house.

"What happened out in the barn? Did she fall and hurt herself?" Sandra demanded. "She raced through here like trying to outrun a fire."

Nate took off his coat, gloves and hat, hung them up on the hook beside the outside door and sat at the table.

"I kissed her."

Sandra stared at him. "Why'd you do that?"

His dad chuckled. "That's the silliest question you ever asked, dear."

"Because she kissed me."

His parents stared at him. "Two nights ago out of the blue, she kissed me. I haven't seen straight since."

"I knew something was off," his dad commented.

"What happened, son?"

He explained why he'd been in the upstairs study with her. "And out of nowhere, she kisses me." He finished the story, ending with her father's approval of the situation between Missy and him.

"But you've always considered Missy a pest to what you and Noah were doing. When did that attitude change?"

"There are some things a guy doesn't talk to his mom about. Know our relationship has changed. Missy's not ready for it to change. Inside, I can't undo the kiss, nor do I want to."

"Oh," his mom replied. She stared at her hands. "Had she given you a reason, yet?"

"No, and I don't think she has one."

"Well, give the girl some time to organize her feelings." Sandra squeezed his hand. "When she realizes what a marvelous man you are, she'll come to her senses."

"So says my mother." He rolled his eyes at his dad.

"Ignore her." Darrell smiled. "Missy is one of the most practical women I've met. I don't think her plans were to come back to Silverdale and stay here. But maybe the good Lord had a different idea for her. God sees everything."

He'd hang onto to his father's words, because at this point he was thoroughly confused.

~

Her attraction to Nate made no sense. Their kiss the other night hadn't been a fluke. The man knew how to kiss, turning her insides to a big quivering mess.

If she was honest with herself, this entire situation was her fault. She started it. No, it was Mary's fault, implying she and Nate showed signs of attraction. Well, to prove her wrong, Missy tested out the theory and kissed Nate. Of all the men who made her heart beat like a drum, it was her brother's best friend. Why couldn't it have been one of the sophisticated men she dated in Denver or her former fiancé? No, the only male who shook her to her core was a man she'd known most of her life.

What was the matter with her? Where had her common sense gone? Of course if you kiss a man, he's going to kiss back.

But what happened in the barn wasn't a spur of the moment event. It was a deliberate, focused action on his part. If the man hadn't held her up, she would've been a puddle on the floor.

So what was she going to do about it? She drew her legs up to her chest and laid her head on her knees. She changed back into the sweats and wool socks.

Did she want to ignore this "thing" between her and Nate? Or see where it would lead? Did she want to gamble she might lose her heart and her freedom from Silverdale?

Her very nature said 'don't take the chance.' Her CPA side wanted to stay with the sure thing. But what was the sure thing in this instance?

She tried managing her love life in Denver, only to have her fiancé run off and marry another woman, that's why she asked Tony he'd like to go to the rodeo. She told him about her sister's competing in the barrel racing at the livestock show and wondered if he'd like to go with her. He agreed.

A knock sounded at her door.

"Come in."

Sandra appeared with a tray of chili and crackers. "I thought you might be hungry." She set the tray on the desk. "If you want something to drink, I've got coffee."

Missy shook her head. "That's okay."

"I'm sorry for that little drama earlier." Sandra ran her hand up and down Missy's arm. "Don't worry about it. Nate told us what happened."

Missy's cheeks heated. She would love to have heard his explanation. "I didn't handle things well. I'll admit I enjoyed the kiss. But I shouldn't have."

"Why?" Sandra sounded as confused as she was.

Missy shrugged, feeling like an idiot. "I can't say. That's what makes me crazy. Maybe I just need time to deal with reality."

"If I say so, there's no better man I know than Nate, except his dad." The older woman smiled.

"True."

Sandra nodded and left the room.

The smell of the chili tickled her nose and she moved to the desk, sat and ate. Ready for a cup of coffee, she opened the door and found Nate standing there.

"The county extension service issued another warning the temperature would drop below zero tonight and for some reason, the heater isn't working properly. Mom's got the living room set up for these emergency conditions with air mattresses, sleeping bags, and a roaring fire. It will be too cold to spend the night in the bedrooms."

She'd noticed it seemed a litter cooler, but chalked it up to her faulty instincts. She followed him into the kitchen, setting the bowl in the sink. She looked up into eyes.

"I'm not sorry about earlier. Your kiss was better the second time. If you'd let yourself go, who knows. The unexpected could be exactly what you need." He grinned and walked away.

His words let her know where she stood. The man wanted to pursue a relationship with her. A smile curved her mouth.

Although she was still unsure of what she wanted, the prospect of Nate not quitting appealed to her.

~

This wasn't the first time the family had spent the night in front of the fireplace on an extremely cold night. The last time this happened to the old ranch house was when he was a senior in high school and his sister a freshman. Teresa and he treated it as a big party. This time, his feelings wandered in a different direction.

His mom ran interference for him, but the pull between him and Missy spoke for itself. If the woman was within three feet of him, his heart started beating faster, and his brain disconnected.

The coffee table had been moved to the side of the room and the chairs opposite the couch were pushed against the wall. Air mattresses lined the floor, topped with sleeping bags. A bowl of popped corn sat on the coffee table along with a pitcher of water, and plastic cups.

"What does your family do on these super cold nights?" Sandra asked.

"Kylee and I shared a bed. What the boys did, I don't know. They were in a separate wing of the house, but I think Dad had to sort them out when they were in the same room. I remember one time Noah complained Wyatt kicked him in the face. I don't know how that happened."

"Boys can be creative when pressed." Nate smiled, picturing how Wyatt managed to kick Noah.

They all faced the fireplace the sound of the crackling wood and heat lulled them to sleep.

When Nate woke, his backside was cold, but a little toasty bundle snuggled in his arms. He glanced down. He hadn't moved, but she managed to find him.

Contentment filled him. She burrowed deeper into his arms, sighing. Her lids fluttered, and it took a moment for her to realize where she was. "I'm sorry," she whispered.

"I need to feed the fire." He stood, allowing her to scoot back to where she started, and added a couple of logs to the fire. He resumed his position in his own sleeping bag.

He wagged his brows at her. She rolled over, curling deeper into her own sleeping bag. Even in her sleep, she came to him. The prospects looked good for her deciding to go with her heart.

~

The next morning, the shortwave announced the county roads were passable.

Missy helped Sandra prepare breakfast while the men did chores. When they came back inside, Darrell announced the driveway had been cleared and Missy could drive home.

She could go home. Mixed emotions raced through her. Her gaze met Nate's.

"Well, before you leave, Missy," Sandra interrupted. "I'd like to go over the banquet schedule one more time.

"We can do that."

During breakfast Nate recounted several stories of Noah and him finding Missy trailing them. "I remember the time we went fishing our freshman year. Noah told Missy to stay home, but we discovered she'd followed and, as I was casting, my hook caught onto something. When I gave the line a good tug, I heard 'ouch' and found a piece of T-shirt on the end of my hook.

"Missy came out of the trees where she hid. I caught the sleeve of her shirt. The first thing she said to me was 'look what you've done to my new shirt.'" He grinned.

She shrugged. "I didn't want to help Mom with cooking dinner. Fishing sounded better."

"And you boys always complained about her," Sandra added.

Several more embarrassing stories surfaced, tying Missy to him. Their history was a comfort. She knew him and what to expect.

After breakfast, they huddled in the office. When they emerged from the office, Sandra gave Missy a hug. "I know your mom would be proud of you."

"I'd like to think so."

She kept that thought in her mind as she drove home. "Would her mom be proud of her? And what would she think of her and Nate dating? Missy always talked about being a professional woman and having a job as an accountant. Her mother's response was, didn't she run a business? Manage the ranch and all the men?

That stopped her. Missy hadn't really appreciated the job her mother had done. And she did it without any acknowledgement.

Missy couldn't believe she was considering doing the very thing her mother did and which she tried to escape.

But her mother was well loved and very happy.

Could Missy count on Nate to be the partner her father had been to her mother?

Was love the key?

Chapter 8

It wasn't until after dinner that Noah cornered her. He found her in the ranch office.

"We were worried when we didn't hear from you."

"I'm sorry, but Sandra and I are continuing Mom's favorite event during the year." She pointed at him. "I'm warning you to pass the word on to your brothers that pastor will announce the banquet on Sunday at church. If you have a girl you're interested in or is interested in you, you better ask her or have a good excuse why you're not taking her to the banquet."

He frowned. "Thanks for the heads up." He ran his hands over his jeans. "How'd it go these last few days?"

Leaning back, she studied him. She had her suspicion he knew about her kissing Nate. "It went well."

He picked up a glass paper weight and shifted it from one hand to another. The muscles in his jaw flexed.

"What do you want to ask me, Noah?"

His head jerked up. "I talked to Nate earlier."

This ought to be interesting. "What did he say?"

"He warned me of his intention to court you."

She coughed.

"That was my reaction, too. I nearly swallowed my tongue, but with what happened the other night, I wasn't surprised."

"So how do you feel about our dating?"

He couldn't meet her gaze. "Shocked. When Nate explained you kissed him, I couldn't believe it. I mean, Nate and I spent time thinking of ways to ditch you."

Missy felt the heat run up her neck. "I know."

Shaking his head, he asked, "How'd that happen?"

"I'm as puzzled at the change as you. It was like a bolt of lightning struck me. I don't know what to do about it. Nate was the last man on my list of prospective dates, let alone boyfriends."

He rubbed his neck. "I don't think he's thinking causally about this 'thing' between you two."

She swallowed.

"He's a good man, Sis. I can count on him for anything."

"So you don't have any objection to him dating me?"

"The idea takes some getting used to, but he's much better than those clowns in Denver."

She smiled. "I agree."

"So how do you feel about it?"

A bark of laughter escaped her mouth. Noah asked the question she'd been wrestling with. "I'm as confused as you. The only person sure about this thing between Nate and me is Nate. He doesn't have any doubts."

Noah nodded. "Well, I'd trust him. Just look at his persistence at acquiring that bull for the ranch. He doesn't quit."

She supposed the comparison should be encouraging, but being compared to a bull...

~

At church on Sunday, the pastor announced the Valentine's Day Banquet. "Bring your sweetheart or your wife." Chuckles rumbled through the congregation.

The pastor's wife, who played the organ, glared at him.

He cleared his throat. "I think Sandra and Missy will welcome all the help they can get to pull this event together in short order."

The head of the Woman's Ladies Auxiliary committee stood. "Pastor, my team will meet in the foyer after service, and we'll take care of things."

Applause greeted her announcement.

Sunday started the race to the Valentine's Day Banquet. They had less than two weeks.

In addition to volunteers taking on all the different chores, Nate kept showing up at the ranch and always found an excuse to stay for dinner. Not only stay, but found a way to sit next to her at dinner. He was in full-frontal attack. That first night, after dinner, he asked her to the banquet. He followed the question with a kiss.

She didn't know whether or not to laugh at his persistence or stomp her foot and tell him to knock it off.

Things came to a head the following Friday. The church had borrowed folding chairs from the city. Neither the city nor the church owned enough folding chairs to use at the banquet, or use at city council meetings, so they shared. Nate brought over the chairs stored at the city council meeting room.

"Where do you want these?" He stood at the doorway to the church hall. She pointed to the wall. "Bring them in, and we'll set up the tables and arrange them."

She stood at the glass door and held it open for him. He took off his short coat and they went to work setting up the tables. In less than thirty minutes they were ready for the ladies to come and decorate.

He caught her hand and drew her to his chest. That overpowering thrill raced through her.

"I look forward to seeing you each day. When are you going to accept the fact we're meant for each other?"

He'd slowly put all her doubts to rest.

She stared at the buttons on his shirt. "You're a persistent man."

"I'm a man in love." He grinned.

She still couldn't believe she'd found love in the very place where she grew up. "Well, you've convinced me what's between us is real."

His fingers ran over her chin. "I never thought I'd hear you say that."

She laughed and looked up. "It's nice to admit it."

"It's about time. I haven't worked so hard since I learned to rope when I was eight." He grinned and brushed a kiss across her lips.

"That's not very romantic." She poked him in the chest.

"Hey, I'm just a simple cowboy and can only go with what I know."

"Oh, please." She rolled her eyes.

Nate had a couple of years in college, and was active in the Rancher's Association, setting up classes and continuing education of the latest techniques. No way was he a simple man.

After her heart had been so battered while in Denver, his love soaked into her soul, healing wounds she didn't know she had. She understood Nate, knew where he was coming from. The ease between them was welcomed. She didn't have to put on a show for him. He understood her.

"Do you need anything else done for the banquet? I need to be working out in the fields, making sure the cattle survived that last storm."

"So I'm behind your cows?" Her eyes danced with merriment.

"Those bovines pay the bills and will support any children we have."

She knew the routine. "Children?"

"That's my goal. Dad and I work together, but I'd planned on building a home a couple of miles from my parents. Probably my wife might prefer privacy. She could yell at me without an audience."

Since she hadn't planned on spending her adult life on a ranch, she never thought about it.

He kissed her again, then he was off.

She stumbled to the closest chair and sat, overwhelmed with the implications of their conversation. He had proposed, hadn't he? In her mind she'd agreed to date him, but marry him? Is that where her future lay?

If his kisses were any indication, they were perfect physical match. So the only question, would she be happy out here on the ranch?

Which dream did she want? Being an admired CPA with maybe her own firm in the city or a ranch wife, jack-of-all-trades woman, whose efforts went unnoticed and her children would think she was behind the times? Which dream was stronger?

~

True to his word, Missy didn't see or hear from Nate for the next several days. She had no time to stew about things as she stamped out little fires that flared up as the banquet came together. Each couple had the choice of brisket or a steak. The numbers were evenly divided.

Most of the women baked their prize desserts. Baked potatoes and beans would be furnished by the mayor, who was running for re-election.

Since the holiday fell on a Tuesday, the banquet would be held the Saturday before.

Friday morning, the phone started ringing at seven. By nine she'd put out three fires and talked to Peggy McSally, who'd dropped her prized three-layered chocolate cake on the floor. Peggy managed to keep the dogs from eating it, but not her husband, who picked up the pieces.

"You make the county's best cherry pie, Peggy. Make that." Problem solved.

"Missy," her dad yelled. "You've got a stranger here to see you."

Now what? She rushed into the kitchen and came to a dead stop. Sitting at the table drinking coffee with her dad was Vince Paudet, the head honcho of the accounting firm she'd worked for in Denver.

He stood. "Hello, Melissa."

"Mr. Paudet."

He sat down and motioned for her to join them. "Your dad and I've been discussing your merits as a CPA. He's told me I was an idiot to let you go. And Tony, the poor excuse for a man, should've been the one I fired."

She glanced at her dad. He nodded.

"I told your father that I'd already taken care of the problem. Tony is no longer with us."

If little green Martians appeared in the kitchen, she couldn't have been more surprised. "You did?"

"I got to thinking about what you said. Had the other women been abused by Tony like you were? I checked it out and discovered you were right.

"I'd like to offer you a job. It wouldn't be your old one, but it would be Tony's job."

Satisfaction swelled in her chest. V. Paudet had just offered her a better position than she had before.

"I told Mr. Paudet you've been doing the books here at the ranch and you had thought of opening your own business here in Silverdale. Ranchers need accountants, too."

"You did?" Her father had come up with idea out of nowhere.

"I told your father the job offer comes with a hefty raise. He didn't seem too impressed."

"Money can't buy everything," Bill mumbled.

Missy hid her smile. "Dad is right. Money isn't everything."

"True," Vince shot back, "but it solves lots of problems, as you know keeping different company's books."

Her old boss offered everything she went to Denver to accomplish, but that dream didn't hold the appeal it once did. It'd been replaced with another one. . . one centered here on a ranch with the man she's fallen in love with.

The admission came easily, now. What she'd found here in Silverdale was what she really wanted.

"It's a tempting offer, Mr. Paudet, and I thank you, but I found the dream I'd been chasing here, right under my nose."

Bill grinned and nodded at the other man as if to say, I told you so.

"Are you sure? I'd love to have you back."

"I'm sure. As Dorothy learned in the Wizard of Oz, there's no place like home."

He held out his hand and shook hers. "Any time you want to come back, or need a recommendation, let me know."

"That's generous of you."

Bill stood. "I'll walk you out."

Vince laughed. "You were right. She's not going anywhere."

So, her dad had warned Mr. Paudet she wouldn't return. How'd he been so sure?

She'd been tempted. Oh, she'd been tempted for a moment with her old dream reappearing.

Mary entered the kitchen. "Who was that?"

"That was the owner of the firm I worked for in Denver."

Mary settled her fists on her hips. "What did he want?"

A smile curved Missy's mouth. "He offered me my job back."

"You're kidding."

"Nope. It seems he took my word for what Tony did to the other woman who had that job before me. He wanted to offer me Tony's job."

She laughed. "What sweet revenge is that? Are you going to take it?"

"No. I'm happy here."

Mary pointed at her. "It's that cowboy. I wish I had one of my own."

Bill came back into the kitchen. "I knew you wouldn't go back and told him you wouldn't. Love bit you and Nate hard, and numbers won't warm you in bed at night."

Her dad was right.

"Ain't that the truth," Mary mumbled.

~

Four that afternoon, Nate showed up at the church hall. Noah had called, warning him that her old boss visited the ranch, this morning, offering Missy her job back.

Panic shot through him. She hadn't said she'd marry him, but he hadn't "officially" asked but knew he had to lasso his bride before she talked herself out of marrying him. That was always Missy's problem. She thought too much.

He parked by her truck and went inside. The ladies had done a bang-up job of decorating the room where, during the winter, the church held basketball camps and other activities for the youth.

"Hello," he called out.

Missy walked out of the kitchen. "Hey, Nate, what are you doing here? I thought you left this part of the banquet planning to the ladies."

He looked around. Red and white crepe paper streamers hung from side to side of the room. Cupid made more than one appearance in the room. "Well, I'll say, this room is decorated in the right theme." He walked to her side, pulled her into his arms and kissed her. He couldn't resist. They had a physical connection and he would use it to convince her she belonged here with him.

She searched his face. "Noah must've called you and told you about my old boss showing up this morning."

He wasn't going to lie to her. "He did, but he also said that you turned him down."

"Men are worse gossips than women."

"Were you tempted?" He had to know. He loved her so much, that if she wanted to go back to Denver, he wouldn't stand in her way. He'd wrestled with that fear the days he was on the range tracking down the scattered cows. And would she be dissatisfied with him and ranch life and, later on, up and leave?

"For about 30 seconds, then I realized I love you, and being with you is more important than anything Denver has to offer. I am home, Nate."

His heart nearly stopped at her words. This was the first time she admitted she loved him. He cupped her face. "Well, lady, the feelings are returned." His mouth covered hers. When he came up for air, he rested his forehead against hers.

"We could walk over to city hall and apply for a marriage license, just in case. There's no waiting period in the state and it's good for ninety days. What do you say?" His heart pounded as his suggestion put her claim to the test.

"Yes. Let's go."

~

Saturday morning dawned clear and cold. The forecast called for the temperature to be in the mid-sixties.

None of her brothers were happy.

"So what time is that shindig tonight," Wyatt asked for the fourth time since breakfast.

"Six," Missy replied, "As you well know. If you'd asked Linda when you had the chance, she'd be going with you."

Wyatt's brows gathered in a frown. "She knew I was going to ask. Why didn't she wait?"

"Because, Bro, you couldn't wait until Friday and expect an answer," Noah answered.

"Do you want to know the real reason she's going with Gary Ford?" Missy smiled into her coffee cup.

"Tell me, Miss-Know-it-all."

"Because girls hate to be taken for granted. You just assumed she'd go with you."

"And did Nate ask you?"

"Yes. We've spent a lot of time together this week helping to pull this thing off." A smile curved her mouth. "Not only did he ask me to the banquet, we applied for a wedding license yesterday."

"What?" came the shouts.

"You're pulling a fast one on us," Wyatt pointed to her.

"No. I'm not."

"What about all that talk in high school about going to Denver and make a big splash?"

"We all have dreams, Wyatt, but sometimes when those dreams become reality, it's not what you think you wanted. Living in the city isn't what it's cracked up to be. At least it wasn't for me."

"So you're going to marry Nate, and give up those dreams you had and talked about in high school?" The sincerity in Wyatt's voice took the sting out of his question. "Ouch," he complained, glaring at Rait. "Why'd you kick me?"

"Because, even I know that's not the kind of question you ask a girl."

Missy knew her younger brother was sincere. He didn't understand.

"Dreams can change. Mine did." Admitting the change out loud made her smile.

"Oh." Wyatt nodded his head, a frown crinkling his brow.

"I'm going to check things at the church hall. You better finish any chores you have, so you can enjoy dinner."

She waved good-bye, snatched up her purse, garment bag holding her dress and shoes for tonight, and raced to her pick-up. She wasn't in the mood to face twenty questions. Reviewing her decision wasn't on the breakfast menu. She sped to the church, thankful none of the local law enforcement was out.

As she pulled into the church parking lot, the knot in her stomach tightened.

Shoving aside her nerves, she opened the church hall and went inside. At the head table sat a beautiful arrangement done by one of the ladies on the committee. Missy wondered if the woman had ever thought of becoming a florist.

As she walked around the gym, her stomach calmed.

The door opened, and Tony walked in. His hair wasn't combed and his shirt was out of his pants. He held a bottle in his right hand.

"It's your fault." He pointed the bottle at her.

He didn't need to explain.

"What are you doing here?" she asked.

"I'm going to ruin your life like you ruined mine."

"You're drunk, Tony, and not thinking too clearly."

He shook his head. "I see all too clearly now. You and that stupid rodeo."

"I'm sorry you lost your job." But you deserved it, she silently added.

He slammed the bottle onto the table. "No! You're not, but I can fix that." He pulled a handgun from his overcoat.

Her eyes widened, and she took a step back.

"Not so smart now, are you?" He fired into the ceiling, bringing ceiling tiles raining down. She hid on the far side of the tables.

"Think about what you're doing. Now, all you have to do is find a job. If you hurt me, you're looking at jail."

"You should've thought about that before you opened your big fat mouth." Another shot whizzed by her head, hitting the stove's hood.

She wished she had her phone, but her purse was hanging on the coat tree beside Tony.

Nate hummed as he drove to Danner Ranch. He'd told his parents he planned to propose tonight at the banquet and would try to convince Missy to get married after church on Sunday. When he pulled into the Danner driveway, his truck came grill to grill with Noah's.

Noah leaned out of the driver's window. "She not here, but at the church, making sure everything is right."

Nate backed up his truck, turned around and followed Noah.

As Nate drove, the back of his neck itched and a sense of urgency hit him in the stomach.

He sped to town, down the main street, and pulled into the parking lot. There was that miserable little sports car Tony drove parked cock-eyed in front of the side door. Panic shot through Nate. He lunged out of the truck, not bothering to shut the door.

The clear sound of a gunshot echoed in the air. He yanked open the door and heard the sound of pots bouncing off the floor.

Tony turned to Nate. "So it's you." He shot in Nate's direction, taking out the glass door. He missed, and Nate dove under the table.

The next thing he heard was another pot banging against something. The sound of a body hitting the floor, then Missy yelled, "Nate, are you okay?"

She emerged from the kitchen and ran into his embrace. She had the gun in her right hand and placed it on the table. "Are you hurt?" She patted him down. He flinched when she got to his upper arm.

"I'm okay. Got cut by flying glass. Where's Tony?" He glanced over her shoulder.

"Laid out flat on the floor thanks to the church's iron skillet."

After a moment he grinned.

Her dad appeared at the shattered door. "What's going on here?"

"Had a bit of trouble, Dad." They walked into the kitchen. Tony lay sprawled on the floor, the skillet a few feet from his head.

"What's the dude doing here?"

"He didn't take losing his job well."

She explained the events of the last few minutes to her father. Others arrived and found a piece of plywood to cover the door, while some ladies cleaned off the tables. The wonderful arrangement for the main table lay shattered on the floor.

Missy pulled Nate into the kitchen to look at his wound.

"I've gotten worse on our barbed wire fences at home."

Tears filled her eyes. "But the wire wasn't shooting at you." She buried her face in his chest.

Having her against him felt so good. It was worth the small wound.

"Take your shirt off, and I'll clean you up."

He readily obeyed.

Her hands shook as she wiped the wound. Sandra appeared at her side. "Would you like for me to take over?"

Missy nodded. "I don't know what's wrong with me." She folded her hands under her arms to stop them from shaking.

It took moments for Sandra to finish cleaning the wound and wrapping it. "Lucky you had a tetanus shot, son."

After the sheriff hauled Tony to jail, Nate announced the banquet would go on as planned.

The food arrived, and the ladies of the auxiliary took over, setting up the serving lines.

Nate still shook inside. His blood ran cold when he stepped inside the church hall to find Tony waving around a gun. He didn't want to spend another night without her. He didn't have a ring, but that could be taken care of.

He pulled Missy to the side of the room.

"Would you marry me?"

"Yes."

"Tonight. Here. We have the license and pastor right here with us. And a room full of witnesses."

She searched his eyes.

"No, no," Sandra said. "You can't do that to your families. Your sister isn't here, Nate, my sister isn't here. Family members want to see the only Winters son married. Give us until May to get things organized."

Nate wasn't happy with the delay. He looked into Missy's eyes wanting to hold her tonight.

"She's your mom, and that wedding license will still be good in May.

"Okay, Mom. We got the license yesterday, so in early May, we have to have the wedding."

Sandra smiled and hugged both Nate and Missy.

"You've won over my mother and can count on her to take your side if we have an argument." He kissed her.

"Good to know, but I don't foresee any problems as of this moment."

"I don't either."

Epilogue

May 10 – 89 days later

The church gym rang with laughter and talk. Family members Nate hadn't seen since he graduated from high school shook his hand and teasingly warned Missy about Nate's exploits as a youth.

"As if I wasn't there and saw most of what you did," Missy whispered in his ear.

"And you still found me charming." He brushed a kiss across her cheek.

Eighty-nine days had passed in a blink of an eye, with all her siblings finding loves of their own. The ranch had been teasingly renamed the Sweetheart Ranch. If you needed a sweetheart, the Rockin' D was the place to work.

In the midst of all this happiness, her dad took comfort in his children finding love. He wished his own bride could've witnessed it. Instead, a picture of her sat at the head table as a tribute to her. No one forgot.

Missy picked up the frame and smiled. She knew her mom was rejoicing in heaven.

"You miss her." Nate's arm slipped around her waist and drew her close.

"I do. I once remember her telling me the girl who married Nathan Winter would be one lucky woman. She said that when I was in high school and thought you were a toad. Mom was right."

Her heart overflowing with love, she whispered, "Thanks, Mom."

Leann Harris was born at Fitzsimmons Army Hospital there in Denver and grew up in the city until her family moved to Houston. Rural Colorado & ranches are two of her favorite topics.

More books by Leann Harris

STAR-SPANGLED HOMECOMING

LAST TRUTH

LAST LIE

STOLEN SECRETS

To Love A Cowboy

By Renee Riva

Prologue

Cross Creek Elementary School
Silverdale, Colorado

Mrs. Brink clapped her hands to get the children's attention. "Okay, class, time for reading circle." Brandy Jo Danner popped up from her desk, dodged a chair in the aisle, and skidded to a halt before the big circular red carpet. Reading circle was her favorite activity—next to recess. There was nothing better than reading aloud to speed up the time 'til she was turned loose on the playground.

She glanced across the circle at Dane Bronson, who joined the circle last. Brandy Jo liked the way he looked. He had a kind face with cute dimples when he smiled. He wasn't smiling now. He was quiet and thoughtful, unlike big loud Hank Halverson, who was neither quiet nor kind.

"Hey, Dane, you gonna read today?" Hank asked, nudging the smaller boy in the back.

Dane shrugged. "If I have to."

Hank whispered something to cute Victoria Langley, who looked at Dane and giggled.

"Settle down class, settle down. We're going to finish the story *Dusty the Cattle Dog*. Who would like to read?"

Brandy Jo's hand shot up before anyone else had time to think about it.

"Alright, Brandy Jo, go ahead. Top of page fourteen."

Brandy Jo jumped right in. " 'Timmy and Mary Walker skipped

home from school in the rain, splashing through mud puddles along the way. When they came through the back door, they smelled something good. Mrs. Walker had baked a big chocolate cake with white frosting that she'd left on the counter. But Dusty, their cattle dog, snuck into the kitchen and found it before Mary and Timmy did. Dusty had frosting all over his face.' "

"Thank you, Brandy Jo." Mrs Brink glanced around the circle. "Dane, how about you read the next page?"

All eyes turned to Dane. He glanced down at his book and cleared his throat. " 'Mom! Mary yelled. D-D-D-usty is eating our c-c-cake...' "

Hank burst out laughing and Victoria started to giggle at Dane's nervous stutter. Dane stopped reading and looked down, his face flushed.

A sharp pain pierced Brandy Jo's heart. She balled her fists, wanting to silence both Hank and Victoria.

Mrs. Brink moved on to another reader.

By the time the recess bell rang, Brandy Jo was burning mad. When everyone else ran out to the playground, she held back and walked out next to Dane. "Want to play four-square with me?" she asked.

Dane looked up with big blue eyes. "Sure," he replied. A set of dimples quickly appeared.

As soon as their game was under way, Hank and Victoria showed up. When Dane hit the ball to Brandy Jo, Victoria yelled, "Hey, D-D-Dane, can you say d-d-dog?" She and Hank roared with laughter.

Brandy Jo grabbed the ball and tucked it under her arm. She marched over to Victoria ready to smack her a good one but remembered what the Good Book said about turning the other cheek. Instead she stared her down. "Victoria Langley, you apologize to Dane right now."

Victoria looked over at Hank who quickly came to her aid. "Oh, you must be in love with D-D-Dane," he taunted. He started singing, "D-D-Dane and B-B-Brandy Jo sitting in a tree, K-I-S-S-I-N-G ...."

At the moment that Brandy Jo was ready to start swinging, Dane stepped in and stood between her and Hank. He looked Hank right in the eye. "Leave her alone."

Hank glared back at Dane.

Brandy Jo never knew what Hank saw in Dane's eyes, but at that moment, Hank shut his mouth and walked away.

"Come on, Brandy Jo," Dane said, and the two went back to their game.

Before the recess bell rang that day, Brandy Jo had made up her mind. She was going to marry Dane Bronson.

Chapter One

Fourteen Years Later....

"Order's up, Brandy Jo!"

Brandy Jo's chestnut ponytail swung around as she turned toward the kitchen. She narrowed her gaze on the cook who'd yelled her name. "That's Brandy to you, Hank," she replied, and grabbed her eggs Benedict special.

Hank smirked.

The door chime drew Brandy Jo's attention.

A tall, handsome cowboy walked through the door of The Branding Iron Grill and tipped his hat. "Hey, Brandy Jo."

"Good morning, Dane," she answered sweetly. "I'll bring you some coffee if you want to grab a seat."

Dane slid onto a stool at the counter and removed his Stetson.

Brandy Jo grabbed the coffee pot on her way back from delivering Mr. Sander's breakfast. She smiled while filling Dane's mug. "Cheese and bacon omelet today?"

Dane met her gaze with a bashful smile. "Yes, please."

Brandy Jo jotted "Omelet cheese bacon" on her order pad, and shot Hank a warning glare as she clipped her ticket to the order carousel.

Hank leaned in close as he snatched the ticket. "I just don't get why Dane Bronson can call you Brandy Jo but I can't."

She looked Hank square on. "Because Dane was grandfathered in from grade-school when everyone was allowed to call me Brandy Jo. Only family and close friends are allowed the privilege anymore."

"Well, well, maybe we should rename the café The *Brandy* Iron Grill." Hank chuckled. "So, why don't you just tell your cowboy that you want to go by Brandy?"

She raised a defiant brow. "Because maybe I like the way he says Brandy Jo."

"I think she got you on that one, Hank," Marv, the sous chef, interjected. He slid a hot plate onto the heating shelf. "Bacon cheese omelet up!"

"Thanks, Marv." Brandy Jo grabbed her order, flung her ponytail back, and swung around to deliver the omelet to Dane.

Hank shook his head. "That girl has more sass than anyone has a right to."

"She's a Danner," Marv replied. "No doubt about it."

~

After ringing up Dane, Brandy Jo headed to the wait-station to refill the ketchup bottles.

"Excuse me, Brandy Jo?"

She loved the sound of his voice—calm and low—like a gentle breeze across the prairie. She turned and gazed into his deep blue eyes. "Yes, Dane?"

"I was…uh, wondering if maybe you'd like to join me for an evening ride along the river." Dane nodded toward the Silverdale Slough flowing past the back deck of The Branding Iron Grill.

Brandy Jo's heart nearly stopped beating. She'd waited fourteen years to hear those words from Dane Bronson, and just wanted to be sure she'd heard him correctly. "You mean, like a date?"

Dane peered around. Another set of eyes watched intensely from behind the grill. He shifted back to Brandy Jo. "Yeah, like a date."

Brandy Jo's instinctive reaction was to toss her dish towel up in the air with a victory shout, but she restrained her excitement. "I'd like that," she replied, calm as a girl in love could reply, without giving herself away.

Dane's shoulders relaxed at her affirming words. "I'll pick you up at your place about five then?"

"I'll be waiting with my boots on," Brandy Jo blurted out, acting more herself now that the date was secured.

Dane tipped his hat goodbye, then strode out the front door.

~

"What on earth does a girl like Brandy Jo Danner see in a wimp like Dane Bronson?" Hank mumbled to Marv. "Especially, when she could have a rodeo stud like me?" A loud chuckle escaped his lips.

Brandy Jo's gaze darted toward the grill. "Well, Hank, not every girl wants a cocky, bull-bustin' cowboy for a boyfriend."

"I think she got you again," Marv remarked.

"That girl's too sassy for her own good," Hank mumbled, out of earshot from Brandy Jo this time. "What's Dane got that I don't have?"

"Brandy Jo."

~

Shortly after Dane left, Brandy Jo returned to the grill with another order.

"Hey, Brandy?"

"Yeah?"

"What do you say you come watch me ride the meanest bull in town at the rodeo next weekend? My fans dubbed me *Hang-on-Hank* for holding the best record in town. Next Saturday's the county championship. I got a front row ticket if you want to see what a real cowboy can do."

Brandy Jo took a large sip of coffee, then looked Hank in the eye. "Hank Halverson, the last place I would want to spend my Saturday night—or any night for that matter—is at a rodeo."

"Why on earth not? Everybody has a good time at the rodeo."

"Everybody but the bulls. I am not into watching those poor animals suffer for the sake of entertainment."

Hank scoffed. "Don't worry your pretty little head over it, darlin'. There are plenty more ladies who will jump at the chance to watch me ride."

Brandy Jo rolled her eyes then glared back at Hank. "Then I suggest you go find yourself one of those ladies—although, from the way I hear you talk about women around here, I don't know that your type of gal would qualify as a lady."

The front door chimed, and Brandy Jo grabbed a coffee pot. She turned back toward the grill. "Oh, Hank?"

"Yes, darlin'?"

"Don't ever call me darlin' again."

Hank chuckled under his breath, but his gaze slowly turned to a glare.

~

Dane stopped his Dodge Ram pickup under the imposing wrought iron arch that read Rockin' D Ranch. The gate opened automatically, so he pulled through and rolled up in front of the sprawling ranch home, known as Danner Manor. He checked his hair in the mirror to make sure he'd remembered to comb it before going to fetch his date, then stepped out of the truck cab and glanced around. *Whoa.* He'd driven past the ranch for years, eyeing it from the road, hoping to work up the nerve to ask Brandy Jo out someday. But standing on the property of this magnificent home with its rich woodwork and massive beam architecture was another story. He tried not to compare it with his own family's turn-of-the-century farmhouse passed down from his great grandfather. He reminded himself that it's not the house that makes a man, but the man that makes the house.

"Hey, Bronson, what are you doing on my property?"

Dane turned toward the barn where Brandy Jo's older brother, Rait, stood in the doorway. To his relief, Rait sported a big grin. "Hasn't anyone tried to warn you yet about Brandy Jo?"

"Warn me about what?" Dane asked, hoping he was joking.

"There's not a sassier woman this side of the Rockies." Rait covered the distance between them in a few long strides. The two men shook hands. "You sure you're ready to take her on? I don't think there's a man alive who's ever won an argument with my little sis."

"Well, sir, I don't plan on arguin' with her," Dane replied. "Thought I'd just take her for a nice ride along the river."

Brandy Jo was leaning over the railing on the front porch trying to catch what the two were discussing when she realized she was the main topic. "Rait Danner, what in the name of Pete are you telling Dane about me?"

Rait pulled a look of innocence. "Why, Brandy Jo, I am just lookin' out for my little sis."

"Looking out for me?" Brandy Jo shifted her gaze quickly to Dane and smiled. "Hi, Dane. Don't you believe a word he tells you. Ever since Mamma passed, Rait thinks it's his job to protect me from everyone who comes calling for me."

"Protect *you*?" Rait threw his head back, laughing. "I'm trying to protect Dane here! You've never needed anyone to protect you, little sis. I think you've chased off more men yourself than I can shake a stick at."

"Maybe if you're referring to Hank Halverson, then yes, because some men are just too thick-headed to take a polite 'no thank you.'" Brandy Jo smiled again at Dane to reassure him, then glanced back to Rait. "Don't worry, big brother. I'll go easy on him."

Brandy Jo hopped down the front stairs and headed toward Dane's truck. "Come on, Dane. We'd better get a move on before he talks you out of taking me with you."

Rait gave his sister an endearing smile. "You two have fun." He turned his gaze to Dane. "Don't worry too much, Bronson, when it comes to amiable young ladies, they don't come any better than Brandy Jo."

"I don't doubt that," Dane replied.

The two men parted with a hardy handshake.

Dane opened the passenger door for Brandy Jo and helped her inside.

"Don't take my brother too seriously. For an April Fool's joke, Rait and
Daddy chased Melissa's boyfriend off the ranch with a shotgun full of blanks."

Dane's eyes grew wide. "Really? Did he come back?"

"Yeah. They're getting married."

Chapter Two

Dane pulled away from the Danner home relieved that he hadn't been the one chased off the property by a shotgun. He turned onto the main highway and got his truck up to speed before stealing his first glance at Brandy Jo seated beside him. Fourteen years was a long time to wait to finally ask her out. It wasn't as tough as he thought it would be— probably because she'd said yes. He was finally alone with her for the first time. He loved the way she sang to the country music playing on the radio, all dolled up in her jean jacket with a pink bandana tied around her neck. She caught him stealing side-glances and smiled. One look into those brilliant blue-green eyes of hers told him the wait was worth every minute just to sit beside her and have her smile back at him.

"Seems you've come to the grill most every morning since I've been working there, haven't you?"

"Best bacon in town." He grinned, knowing he'd never told another living soul he thought the coffee was awful and the eggs were too well done, but the service was worth the suffering—so long as Brandy Jo was the one serving him.

"So, do you have an extra horse for me to ride or are we going double?"

"I've got a horse for you," he replied. "My sister doesn't ride much now that she's away at college, so it'll be good for her mare to get out. She's a real beauty."

When Dane turned off the county road onto his long dirt drive, he feared his homestead may be a letdown for someone used to living at Danner Manor.

Before he had a chance to guess what Brandy Jo was thinking, he saw her eyes light up.

"What a great farmhouse! I've always loved traditional white farmhouses with red barns!"

"Really?"

"I've dreamt about places like this since I was a kid. My grandma lived in a farmhouse just like this."

"Huh. That's funny. I've dreamt of building a place like yours ever since I was a kid."

Brandy Jo laughed. "I guess it's true what they say about the grass bein' greener on the other side of the fence." She peered around. "Where are the horses?"

"They're generally out to pasture, but I brought them up to the barn while you finished your shift at the grill. They're all saddled and ready to go."

"I can't wait to see your sister's mare."

Dane swung his pick-up to the side of the barn. "C'mon, I'll introduce you."

~

As Brandy Jo jumped down from the cab her boot caught on the door rim and she fell headlong out of the truck. Preparing herself for a full-on faceplant, she was pleasantly surprised to find herself suddenly in the arms of Dane Bronson, staring into his blue eyes. The moment lingered long enough to bring a blush to both faces before a loud whinny distracted them.

Dane set Brandy Jo back on her feet and led her toward the corral where the horses were hitched to the railing. The palomino mare whinnied again from the corral and shook her proud head. Her long shaggy mane rippled in the sunlight.

"Brandy Jo, meet Sunny, short for Sunshine's Glory." Dane held out a gentle hand and the mare snorted as she sniffed his palm.

"Wow. She is a beauty."

A muscular buckskin, quarter horse gelding stood beside Sunny like a protective guardian. Dane felt the same protective way about Sunny's rider. "This big boy here is Danny Boy. He's mine." Danny Boy nuzzled Dane's pockets in search of treats.

Up at the house, a squeaky screen door opened, and a woman stepped out carrying a wicker basket.

Brandy Jo turned and waved.

"I'll bridle the horses if you'd like to grab the food hamper from Mamma. I'll transfer it into a saddle bag."

"Oh, sure." Brandy Jo started toward the house. She was already acquainted with Dane's mamma from the years she worked as a Sunday school teacher at church. Having called her Mrs. Bronson from childhood, she couldn't help but refer to her as Mrs. Bronson still.

"Hello, darlin," Elma Bronson called out. "Looks like the two of you have a lovely evening for a sunset ride."

Brandy Jo greeted Dane's mamma with a warm hug, just as she had since she was small. "Dane says I'm to gather up the picnic basket. I hope you haven't gone to much trouble."

Elma laughed. "No trouble at all. As a matter of fact, Dane prepared and packed the entire basket. I have no idea what he has in store for the two of you but it sure smells good."

That little tidbit of news surprised Brandy Jo. She'd never pictured Dane possessing culinary skills, seeing as how he bought his breakfast every morning. She figured his habit was partly due to a lack of cooking skills—as was the case with many of the morning regulars. That didn't include the old farmers who hovered around booth #8 every morning for coffee, donuts, and a good grumble with fellow farmers. Or the gossip-monger ladies group whose soul existence seemed to revolve around being the first to hear the latest tidbits and the first to spread them around town. Establishments like The Branding Iron Grill counted on their loyal busy-bodies for their ongoing prosperity.

~

After adjusting Brandy Jo's stirrups, Dane packed the hot meal into the saddle bag behind his saddle, then mounted Danny Boy. The two headed down the dusty road toward the Cross Creek trailhead. Riding along the creek through shadowed woods, Dane allowed Brandy Jo to ride in front. He enjoyed watching her thick chestnut ponytail sway side to side and loved the way she whistled as she rode along—like a child without a care in the world. Beneath her rough and tough exterior, Dane knew that Brandy Jo was a sweet, gentle soul. He'd watched her grow up. He'd seen her soft side many times over the years—especially in dealing with the elderly folks at the grill—some he was certain came in just for the attention and care she showed them.

The only time Dane saw Brandy Jo's assertive side was when she was confronted by antagonistic or aggressive people—like Hank Halverson. Dane saw what happened to women who dated Hank, and he kept a protective watch from his side of the breakfast counter in case Hank should decide to try and add Brandy Jo to his list of conquests. Not that she couldn't stand up against a guy like Hank, but he'd seen how cold and calculating *Hang-On-Hank* could be. He 'd be hanged if he was going to let Hank do the same to Brandy Jo.

"Hungry?" Dane asked, and pulled Danny Boy to a halt beneath a shady grove of trees.

Brandy Jo circled back around with Sunny and joined him.

"Whatcha got in that saddle bag that smells so good?"

Dane reached in and pulled out a foil pouch. "I brought finger food so we don't have to get off the horses to eat." He lifted a deep fried corndog on a stick from the pouch and handed it to Brandy Jo.

Her eyes lit up when she took hold of the stick."Oh, man, I love these things!"

"Mustard?"

"You bet!"

Dane handed her another small foil pouch filled with mustard to dip her corn dog in.

Brandy Jo crossed herself, then bit in. She closed her eyes and chewed slowly. "Oh, Yuuum."

"Glad you like it." It was fun to see the joy on her face over something so simple as a corn dog. "I made brownies for dessert."

Her eyes popped open. "Dane Bronson, marry me right now and cook for me for life!" she joked. Her melodious laughter followed, carried to his ears by the wind.

Dane prayed it wasn't really a joke.

~

The following Saturday, Brandy Jo looked forward to going to work, hoping Dane might ask her out on another date. She watched the clock, knowing he usually arrived around eight each morning. Unfortunately, she'd have to put up with Hank until Dane arrived.

"Your hash 'n eggs are up, Brandy!" Hank intentionally flexed his muscles when he handed her the plate.

Brandy Jo glanced at the bulging biceps beneath his rolled up T-shirt sleeves as she grabbed the plate. "Don't strain yourself there, Hank—those eggs must weigh a ton by the looks of what it takes for you to lift them." She had an uncanny way of deflating both his ego and muscles in one simple blow.

Truth be told, as far as chefs were concerned, she was glad that Hank came to fill the position left by Consuela when she went to work for the Danner family. He was efficient as far as his cooking, and agreed to work part time until he went on the rodeo circuit.

On the flipside, he spent the majority of his time behind the grill scanning the joint for his next female conquest. His crass comments were often overheard by Brandy Jo. She was fully aware of Hank's appeal to the fairer sex. He was, by far, the epitome of the ruggedly handsome rodeo cowboy. Every girl in town gawked whenever he'd stride through town in his bull-ridin' chaps and cowboy boots. Included in his machismo image was a five o'clock beard that contrasted against his sun-bronzed face and added a hint of mysterious to tall, dark, and handsome.

All that, and a Stetson cowboy hat to boot, made him the real deal when it came to big, brawny cowboys. But for those who knew better, he came with a big warning tag attached.

Brandy Jo clipped a new order onto the carousel and swung it around to face Hank. "Bacon cheese omelet."

Hank glanced out to see who the order was for. When his leering gaze landed on Dane Bronson, his eyes narrowed in a way that sent a chill down Brandy Jo's spine. She turned away and tried to shake the feeling, hoping it was her imagination.

When the front door chimed, Brandy Jo glanced up. "Hey, Sarah, I thought you only worked nights. What brings you in on a Saturday morning?"

"I switched my shift so I could get tonight off."

Brandy Jo smiled at the attractive young waitress she'd worked with over the past year. She was a sweet girl and the two had become fast friends. "Oh? Do you have something special planned tonight?" she teased.

"As a matter of fact, I do," Sarah replied, sporting a coy smile. "Hank got me a front row ticket to watch him ride in the rodeo. The winner goes to the state championship."

Brandy Jo's stomach suddenly knotted up. *Oh, not sweet Sarah.* "Oh. Well, that should be … quite an event." She said a silent prayer that Sarah would be wise to what she was getting herself into.

Brandy Jo swung by the grill with a new order. "Ham with two eggs, over easy."

Hank peered up, then looked right past Brandy Jo. "Hey, there, Sarah. You sure are lookin' nice today."

Brandy Jo stared back at Hank. "Looks like you got yourself someone to watch you ride after all."

Hank flashed a sly grin and cracked two eggs in one hand onto the hot grill. "I told you it wouldn't be hard to find another girl."

"Sarah isn't just 'another girl,' Hank. She's my good friend." The comment was delivered with a warning tone.

Hank responded with a challenging grin. "Sure you don't want to take a chance on me? Between your sass and my brawn, we could have ourselves a good time ."

Brandy Jo's eyebrows shot up as she looked at Hank square on. "You and me? Together? You have *got* to be joking. We'd kill each other before we even got out of the gate."

Hank threw his head back, laughing, then slid a plate of hash browns across the serving shelf.

"Mr. Ridley's hash browns," Brandy Jo announced, aloud.

"Strikes me funny that a potato farmer comes in here every morning for freezer potatoes when he's got a whole field of fresh potatoes outside his back door," Hank commented.

"Maybe he just likes the company here," Brandy Jo replied.

Hank grinned. "You seem to have that effect on everyone ."

"Save your butter for the biscuits," Brandy Jo quipped, and headed off to Mr. Ridley's table.

Chapter Three

Church on Sunday was the only reason Brandy Jo would don a dress rather than blue jeans. Her little sister, Kylee tromped down the grand staircase in a denim skirt and cowgirl boots. It was hard to take the tomboy out of her, even for church. As the Danner family gathered in the front hall foyer, Brandy Jo detected a hint of sadness in her father's eyes. It usually had to do with missing his late wife and mother of his six children, but this sadness seemed different.

"You okay, Daddy?" she asked softly.

Bill Danner shifted his eyes to his daughter with a winsome smile. "I was just trying to take in my family all together for the last time. Come Missy's wedding, we won't be the Danner seven any longer."

Missy grabbed her sweater from the front closet and turned back to the clan. "Hey, now, don't look at it as losing me. You'll be gaining another son." she tried to sound cheerful, but Brandy Jo could see it had little effect.

"It's not the same," Kylee countered. "Daddy means there won't be seven of us all driving to church together anymore." She swooped in to give her daddy a hug. That at least brought a smile to his face.

Noah grabbed the keys from the hook by the door. "I say we all make the best of it while we can, so let's all crowd into the Silver Bullet and get on the road before we're late."

As the Danner family piled into the silver Expedition, Brandy Jo realized Kylee was right. It never would be quite the same once her sister walked down that aisle. She sympathized with her father who had lost his wife, and now a daughter. His sadness reminded her how fleeting life could be, and she didn't want to take for granted all the blessings she'd been given by being a Danner.

~

When the service let out, Brandy Jo spotted Dane working his way over to her from across the sanctuary. She quickly tucked her long bangs behind one ear and smoothed the front of her dress.

"Morning, Brandy Jo, you look real nice in that yellow dress."

She couldn't help but notice how nice Dane looked, too, and blushed at the thought.

"I was wondering—if you're not already busy, if you'd like to go on a date with me this afternoon?" Dane asked.

She tried to look surprised instead of relieved that he'd finally asked. "Uh, sure. Where are we going?"

"You'll have to wait and see—it's kind of a surprise."

Brandy Jo wasn't big on surprises, but she'd tolerate it coming from Dane. "Okay. Can I put my jeans back on? Or is it somewhere fancy?"

"Nope, not too fancy. But it may be too warm for jeans. Maybe just stay in what you've got on. Okay to pick you up about noon?"

Brandy Jo nodded. "Okay. See you then." She hustled out the door to join the rest of the family for the trip home.

~

Brandy Jo glanced in the mirror one last time trying to decide what to do with her hair. *A dress is one thing, but I will not curl my hair for anyone.* She quickly twisted and flipped her hair back into its familiar ponytail, then decided she'd put in a little more effort and went with a French braid instead.

A knock at the door made her jump, even though she'd been expecting Dane. She grabbed a light sweater and opened the door.

"Wow, you look…"

Brandy Jo tilted her head to the side, and raised her eyebrows waiting for Dane to decide on the right word.

"*Really* nice."

"Well, I don't know about that but thank you for saying so."

"All set to go?"

Brandy Jo flung her cardigan over her shoulder. "All set." As soon as she stepped outside her eyes doubled in size. "You've got a boat back there!" she announced, referring to an old wooden rowboat tied down in the bed of the truck.

"I thought we could go for a row and have a picnic."

"Where are we going?" she asked, eagerly.

"My secret place."

When the truck pulled off the county road onto a dirt road that led to a grove of trees, Brandy Jo's heart began to pound. "We're going to Little Lake!" Little Lake was Brandy Jo's favorite childhood haunt; her

74

secret hidden lake in the middle of a grove. "How did you know about Little Lake?"

"I used to come here as a kid all the time."

"So did I!"

"I know."

Brandy Jo turned to Dane. "How did you know that? I don't remember seeing you there."

He pointed to a giant lodgepole pine. "See that big crook in the tree up there? I used to sit up there and watch y'all but was too chicken to come down."

"Oh, my gosh. I was being stalked at age eight and never knew." Brandy Jo laughed.

Dane swung the truck around in a small clearing, then backed down to the edge of the lake. After lowering the tailgate, he slid the rowboat out, straight into the water.

Brandy Jo grabbed the wicker basket from the cab of the truck. After kicking off her flip-flops, she hiked the hem of her dress up above her knees and waded toward the boat's stern. Dane grabbed the basket, then helped Brandy Jo into the boat.

"Ready to cast off, mate?" Dane asked.

"Aye, aye, captain," she replied, and took her seat in the bow.

Dane locked the oars into place and began to row.

Brandy Jo filled her lungs with a long, deep inhale. The air was warm and sweet, and smelled like the summer days of her childhood. A smile appeared as she closed her eyes and turned her face to the sun. "I'm so happy to be here again."

Dane smiled back. "I'm glad."

They rowed along in silence, taking in the familiar sights and sounds. Brandy Jo loved the swirling water caused by the oars and rhythmic sway of the boat.

Half-way across the small lake, Dane pulled in the oars and just allowed the boat to drift, carried by the rustling breeze. He turned around on the seat to face Brandy Jo.

"How long has it been since you were last here?" Dane asked.

Brandy Jo thought about it. "Gosh, it must be longer than I thought. I had to have been pretty young. I always came with my mamma. I don't think I've been back since she passed."

Dane nodded. "I'm glad you have those memories with her."

"Me, too." After a thoughtful moment she added. "I'm so glad you brought me here. It reminds me that I need to bring my own children here someday, so they can have memories like mine to grow up with."

Dane grinned. "Planning on having a lot of them?"

"What? Memories or kids?" Brandy Jo smirked.

"Both, but I was talking about kids."

"Planning on as many as the Lord wants to give me. I guess when you come from a big family, you just imagine having a big family yourself—at least I do. I know some girls just want to get out there and have a career, but family and ranching are all I've ever known, and they're all I've ever wanted."

"Yeah. I know what you mean. I don't come from as large a family as yours, but our family is pretty tight, and ranching is all I've ever learned to do. I can't imagine doing anything different. I love being outdoors at dawn with nothing but the herd, the sunrise, and The One who created it all."

Brandy Jo glanced back at Dane and felt as though she'd known him her whole life. Sure, she'd known him since grade school, but at that moment, she felt as though she really *knew* him. She found comfort and peace just being with him.

Chapter Four

Brandy Jo used the front of her catering cart to bump open the double doors of the town hall meeting room. "The Branding Iron Grill is now serving lunch to the High Plains Restoration committee." The savory aroma of warm fried chicken swept through the doors along with her announcement. "Boxed chicken lunches—all packed full!" She wheeled her cart through the room, delivering the greasy goodness to one and all. Her eyes scanned the room for the woman Rait had chosen as his top pick to direct the restoration project of Old Town. She zeroed in on an attractive blonde—the only unfamiliar face in the room. "You must be Serena." As Brandy Jo slid a boxed lunch in front of her, she couldn't miss the reaction on Rait's face. She knew in a glance; her brother was smitten. *Well, I'll be.*

Rait shot his sister a warning glare. Brandy Jo hadn't seen that look in her brother's eyes since she'd told Rait's sixth grade crush that her brother was in love with her. Brandy Jo had no intention of interfering this time. But no harm in encouraging Serena to get to know the Danner family a little better. Besides, it would take the pressure off her brother having to ask her out. No need to let this one slip away without a fair chance.

Serena thanked Brandy Jo for the boxed lunch.

Brandy Jo shot her brother a smug look that struck terror in his eyes, then turned back to Serena. "Hey, in case I don't run into you again before the weekend, we're having a cookout Friday night at the Rockin' D Ranch." She invited Serena to come as her guest.

Brandy Jo shot Rait a victory smile when Serena accepted, which triggered a choking fit on Rait's end. Brandy Jo came to his rescue with a hardy blow across the back with the palm of her hand.

"Okay, enough," he growled, red faced.

"Thank me later for Friday night," she whispered. It was the least she could do for her favorite brother.

~

The Danner clan was in full swing Friday afternoon pulling together the bride-to-be-feast for the oldest daughter. Melissa would be the first Danner to head down the matrimonial aisle. No one was more excited than the sister of the bride. In her attempt to decorate, Brandy Jo managed to tangle herself right into a strand of twinkle lights meant to adorn the railing on the back deck that overlooked the ranch. "Get me untangled, Wyatt," she called to her youngest brother. Having only a year between them, they were often mistaken for twins growing up.

"I think we should include you as part of the light show," Wyatt teased.

"Get me free before Dane comes and sees me like this!"

"I'm sure Dane would enjoy seeing you all lit up as part of the party decorations."

Her biggest brother Noah stepped in and lifted his sister off the ground while Wyatt untangled the strand from around her body.

"Only you, Brandy Jo." Noah chuckled, and set her back down.

Finally free, Brandy Jo moved on to carrying huge bowls of salads and side dishes to the banquet tables. Thank goodness for their new cook, Consuela, or Brandy Jo would have had to prepare a good deal of the food herself. Her eyes teared up at the thought of her mother missing out on the first Danner wedding festivities. How she would have loved to plan her daughter's special celebration. No one could cook like Mamma. Thankfully, they hired Consuela in the nick of time. No one could fill her mother's shoes, but Consuela was pretty amazing at keeping the Danner clan fed day in and day out. The Danner men, all grill-masters, had the beef BBQ handled down at the grilling pit.

As the steady flow of guests slowed, Brandy Jo wondered if Dane was going to show up after all. He'd told her he'd be a little late due to moving the herd that day. It's impossible to know what will come up when wrangling cattle. One stray cow or runaway calf could change the whole game plan.

While Brandy Jo waited for Dane to arrive, she made a point of making sure Serena was introduced to the whole Danner family. Rather than make the introductions herself, she grabbed Rait by the arm. "Hey, big brother, I need to check on the banquet table. Do me a favor and introduce Serena to the rest of the family, will you?"

Rait took a quick glance at Serena, then shifted his gaze back to Brandy Jo, who was openly smirking at him.

"Sure, I'd be happy to," Rait replied. Passing by the banquet table with Serena at his side, Rait gave Brandy Jo a discreet warning pinch in the back, letting her know he was onto her matchmaking efforts and to lay off. Brandy Jo responded with a sly grin as she carried an empty potato salad bowl to the kitchen for a refill.

Just as the sun was setting over the fields, Dane's truck pulled up. Brandy Jo's heart skipped a beat at the sight of him stepping down from the cab. He was all clean shaven with a nice, crisp plaid shirt tucked into his jeans. Cowboys didn't get much better than the one Brandy Jo had her gaze glued to. She untied her apron, tossed it on the table, and hustled out to greet him. As far as she was concerned, her shift was over and the night was just beginning.

"Get up here fast as you can!" she yelled from the deck railing. "The food is going quick!"

Dane laughed, then took the back steps to the deck two at a time. When he reached the top, he pulled Brandy Jo into a warm embrace, taking her by surprise, and planted a kiss on her cheek.

"That fast enough for you?" he asked.

She nodded, visiably flushed. She took his hand and led him through the banquet line, making sure he got the best cuts of beef. The two of them grabbed an isolated table off to one corner and watched the sun go down while Dane inhaled a huge plate of some of the finest home-cooked barbecue he'd ever tasted.

Somewhere between the barbecued beef and dessert, Brandy Jo sprang her long-awaited question. "So, any chance you'd be agreeable to accompany me to my sister's wedding and reception next weekend?"

Dane looked up with a mouth full of food. He didn't answer until he'd swallowed, then wiped his chin with a napkin. "I guess that would depend on one thing."

Brandy Jo's eyebrows pressed together. "What's that?"

"Do I have to dance?"

"Are you trying to tell me you don't dance?"

"I'm not sayin' I don't dance. I'm sayin' I'm particular about which kind of dancing I'm willing to attempt."

Brandy Jo cocked her head to the side. "So, what kind of dancing are you willing to agree to?"

"Only the slow ones."

A smile spread across Brandy Jo's face. "Deal."

~

When Sarah came to clock in for her shift the following Friday afternoon, Brandy Jo was just clocking out. "Hey, cowgirl. You got plans this weekend?" Sarah asked.

"Just my sister's wedding."

"Oh, that's right!"

"Since I'm in it, it looks as though I'll have to attend," she joked.

Sarah laughed. "You got your cowboy all lined up to go with you?"

"Dane has agreed to be my date, but he's not much for kicking up his heels. I had to agree to only dance the slow ones with him." The comment came with a blush.

Sarah zeroed in with a clever smile. "Oh, I do believe Brandy Jo has finally gone gaga. Never thought I'd see the day." Sarah hummed as she gathered her apron and order pad. She went from humming, to singing along with Patsy Cline. *"He Called Me Baby…"*

Brandy Jo was determined to find out what or *who* was making Sarah so deliriously happy. She grabbed Sarah by the shoulders. "Okay, out with it. Who are you crooning over?"

Sarah gave her a coy smile. "What makes you think I'm crooning over someone?"

"Okay, fine. Tell me then, what are you doing this weekend?"

This time Sarah blushed. "Goin' to the rodeo."

"Oh, my *gosh!* Please don't tell me it's Hank Halverson."

"Why not? He's the best catch in town—not to mention, he happens to feel the same about me."

Brandy Jo's heart sank. She couldn't hide her disappointment from Sarah.

Sarah squeezed her friend's arm. "It's not what you're thinking. I know all about Hank's bad boy reputation, but he says I'm different from the others. Besides, if he wins tomorrow night, he's taking me with him on the road for the circuit." Sarah looked at Brandy Jo and giggled. "Hank says I might just be the next Rodeo Queen."

The next Rodeo King's victim. Lord have mercy.

Chapter Five

Saturday was one big blur from sun-up until Melissa Danner walked down the aisle of holy matrimony and changed her name forever. Brandy Jo wasn't one for weeping, but a single tear did escape the moment they announced her sister as Mrs. Winters. She cheered up only when Dane pulled her onto the dance floor whispering, "Let's get this over with." He drew Brandy Jo into a close embrace, swaying slowly to a Garth Brooks song, *If Tomorrow Never Comes.* "Boy, this one's a tear-jerker," he said. "Isn't this more a funeral song than a wedding song?" At the thought of losing Brandy Jo, he tightened his arms around her.

Brandy Jo felt Dane's heart beat against hers and was sure their hearts started keeping time with one another. She was so exhausted from the long day, she let herself completely relax in his arms, hoping she wouldn't fall asleep and drool on his shoulder.

"This isn't so bad," Dane whispered in her ear, and refused to stop dancing when the next song *I Hope You'll Dance* started up. "I have a confession," he said half-way through the song.

"What's that?"

"The only reason I was hesitant to dance was because you're the first girl I've ever danced with."

Brandy Jo smiled against his warm neck. "You're the first man I've ever *slow danced* with," she admitted back. She was well-experienced in line-dancing, but nothing as intimate as this.

"I actually really like this," he replied. "It's kind of like a nice, long hug to music."

For the duration of the evening every time a slow song came on, Dane pulled Brandy Jo back out on the dance floor.

The reception came to a crescendo with Brandy Jo catching the bridal bouquet. Dane looked both pleased and nervous.

Brandy Jo fell into bed that night exhausted. She drifted off dreaming of Cinderella, but she lost a cowgirl boot instead of a glass slipper, and the prince had dimples.

~

An hour later, the shrill ring of Brandy Jo's cell phone jolted her from a deep sleep. She glanced, blurry-eyed at the screen as Sarah's name lit up the room. *Sarah? Why is Sarah calling so late?* "Hello?"

"Brandy Jo...." Her name was followed by a sob.

"Sarah, what's wrong?"

"It's Hank."

"What did he do to you?"

"Nothing. He's hurt bad. C-can you meet me at the hospital—they took him by ambulance from the rodeo." Another sob followed.

"Oh, my gosh!" She wiped her eyes and shot up in bed. "Yeah, I can head right over." She jumped out of bed so fast it made her head spin. Stumbling from her room, she called for Rait.

"Down here," he yelled, from the family room. He was still up watching a movie. Dad Danner was fast asleep, snoring away in the Lazy Boy. The other Danner kids had headed for the rodeo after the wedding.

"Hank's been injured at the rodeo! Can you drive with me to the hospital?"

"Halverson's hurt?"

"Yeah, Sarah just called. Sounds pretty bad." Brandy Jo returned to her room and pulled on a pair of jeans draped over the back of a chair, then threw a jean jacket over her thermal night shirt. By the time she was dressed, Rait had the Expedition fired up and was waiting for her out front.

"What all did Sarah tell you?" Rait asked, putting his foot to the gas.

"Not much—she was crying and just said he was hurt—then cried some more. Oh, she said he went by ambulance."

"That doesn't sound good." Rait stroked his beard. "I've never been a close friend of Hank's, but I helped with their round up when they were short a few wranglers a while back. I recall his dad being pretty hard on Hank. He expects a lot from his sons."

Brandy Jo's thoughts shifted from Hank to her little sister. She'd always been so bent on barrel racing in the rodeo. "I sure hope Kylee thinks twice after watching what happened to Hank tonight."

It didn't take long to reach the hospital given the speed Rait was driving. He pulled the SUV into the emergency room parking lot. They both jumped out and headed for the entrance. Not surprising, between

Hank's big family, concerned friends, and rodeo-goers, it seemed half the town was gathered in the small waiting room awaiting news on Hank's condition. Rait spotted Wyatt and went to get the story while Brandy Jo scanned the room for Sarah.

"Brandy Jo!" Sarah called from behind her.

Brandy Jo spun around. "Sarah, tell me what happened."

Sarah calmed down enough to relay the story. "Hank had just finished his ride on Big Red with top scores and was walking away. The rodeo clown was distracting the bull, but suddenly Big Red turned and charged at Hank. He hit him full-force in the lower back. Hank never even saw him coming, he just flew up in the air then landed flat on his back." Tears started up again. "He just laid there groaning, unable to get up." A small sob escaped. "The medics rushed in and put him on a stretcher, then loaded him into the ambulance. Nobody knows yet how bad it is."

What was left of Sarah's black eyeliner ran in streams down her face. Brandy Jo wrapped her arms around her friend and tried to comfort her. Over Sarah's shoulder she saw a doctor come through the ER door to the waiting room. Hank's parents immediately stood and went to speak with him. They talked quietly, huddled together for several minutes before Mrs. Halverson let out a cry and collapsed into her husband's arms. At that point, everyone thought the worst. Mr. Halverson kept a stone-face expression and just nodded.

Quiet whispers rippled out through the group like after a stone has been tossed into a pond. By the time they reached Sarah and Brandy Jo, the story was that Hank was alive but they didn't know if he'd walk again—he had no feeling in his legs as of yet. The doctors were not sure if it was a temporary paralysis or permanent.

A group of folks who attended the community church gathered in prayer in a corner of the waiting room. The only ones admitted through the double doors into the ICU were Hank's parents. At that point, Hank's uncle announced that it might be best if everyone went on home and continued to keep the Halverson family in their prayers.

"There's not much they can tell us at this point but we will get the word out when we know more." He thanked everyone for their concern and support.

The crowd slowly started to disperse. "You want to ride home with us?" Brandy Jo asked Sarah.

"No, I'm just going to stay for now. I want him to know I'm here for him." She slumped into an empty seat.

"You'll let me know if you hear anything?"

"Sure. Thanks, Brandy Jo."

Brandy Jo considered whether or not she should call Dane but decided against it until she had something more concrete to tell him about Hank's injuries. Besides, Dane would likely show up at the grill for breakfast. She'd tell him then if he hadn't already heard. Dane and Hank never had resolved their childhood differences. Most kids it seemed outgrew childhood grudges, but Hank and Dane still kept an obvious distance from one another.

~

The following morning the whole community was abuzz about Hank Halverson, especially down at the grill. A few rumors had spread that he was now a quadriplegic who would never recover, but no one had a solid source for where the information came from. It was hard on the Branding Iron staff to be at work without Hank behind the grill.

Marv was devastated without his head chef and friend working beside him. Brandy Jo thought of Sarah and wondered if she'd spent the whole night in the hospital waiting room. Shortly after opening, Dane came through the front door and headed for his seat at the counter. When Brandy Jo showed up with her coffee carafe, she realized he'd already heard the news.

Before long, Sarah came through the front door looking for Brandy Jo. "Oh, thank goodness you're here," she exclaimed.

"What's the news on Hank?"

Sarah's tangled hair stood out from her head and wrinkles criss-crossed the front of her blouse. Dark circles marred the skin beneath her eyes, but considering she'd spent the night in a chair, that wasn't surprising. "Hank was awake and talking this morning, but when I sent a message to him that I was there, he told the nurse he didn't want to see me." She looked down at her feet.

"Oh, Sarah, don't take it too hard—he's probably in pain and not in his right mind."

"Yeah."

"So, what did the doctors say?"

"It's still uncertain which way things are going. He has feeling to his waist but he's numb from his waist down. They say it's all a matter of time and nerves working together." She looked so sad, more from the rejection than the news, Brandy Jo figured.

"Why don't you go home and get some rest? Maybe Hank will feel more sociable when the shock wears off."

Sarah nodded and wandered back out toward her car parked at the curb.

Brandy Jo only hoped she was right about Hank being nicer to Sarah—he had never been known for his kind ways toward women.

~

As the week went on, it was clear that Hank would not be returning to the Branding Iron anytime soon, so they had to hire on an extra hand at the grill. It didn't take Brandy Jo long to realize she'd never appreciated how efficient Hank was at getting his orders right, cooked well, and on time. Never before had orders been returned by customers for not being cooked through, being overdone, or taking so long to arrive. It was mayhem during the lunch rush every noon hour. After the third order in one hour was sent back to the kitchen, Brandy Jo pulled Marv aside. "If I get one more burnt grilled cheese sandwich, I'm going to go to the Silverdale hospital and tell Hank to hurry up and get back to work!"

~

Two weeks out, Hank started receiving a few visitors, mostly good rodeo buddies who could give him the latest scoop on upcoming competitions. If anything could motivate him to get back on his feet, it was riding bulls again. Unfortunately, the short list of visitors Hank allowed did not include Sarah. Brandy Jo agonized for her friend as she knew Sarah spent every waking moment that she wasn't at work down in the Silverdale Hospital's waiting room hoping to hear her name called in for a visit. After three weeks of waiting and sending requests in with the nurses, her name was finally called.

Sarah all but ran toward Hank's room to see him for the first time since the accident. It happened the same afternoon that the doctors agreed to give Hank's friends and fans an update on his prognosis. So many calls and visitors flooded the hospital daily, they were jamming up both the phone lines and the small waiting room. Hank agreed to let the doctors release a brief statement to the public regarding his condition in order to decrease the chaos his well-wishers were causing.

Brandy Jo fully intended to attend the briefing once her shift ended. She swung by the counter to give Dane a coffee warm-up. "Hey, how would you like to go with me to hear how things are looking for Hank this afternoon? Hopefully we'll hear some good news."

Dane hesitated and set a ten-dollar bill by his plate, then he grabbed his jean jacket from the back of the bar stool. "I don't think I'll join you this time."

"Are you in a hurry to get to work?"

"Not particularly. I just don't feel compelled to catch up on Hank right now." He pulled on his jacket.

Brandy Jo's gaze narrowed. "Do you realize Hank could be paralyzed?"

"That would be unfortunate. I hope that's not the case." He took a last gulp of water, fixing to leave.

Brandy Jo glared at Dane. "Are you telling me you would let a third grade spat keep you from attending a briefing on an injured man who may never walk again?" Her gaze held him in place.

Dane stared back. "That's not really the point, Brandy Jo. I have my reasons and I'm not comfortable accompanying you right now. Maybe another time." He turned and walked out the front door. Starting the truck, he shot Brandy Jo a questioning glance, and drove off.

Brandy Jo was dumbstruck. When she finally snapped back, she threw her dish rag into the wash tub with a dramatic splash. *What kind of man have I got myself involved with? When the chips are down, he's not even able to rise to the concern for a fallen soldier? And all over a stupid third-grade squabble.* Brandy Jo stewed over the thought of it for the rest of the morning. She stewed over it while she took lunch orders, and she stewed over it when she returned a burnt grilled-cheese sandwich to Hank's replacement chef.

In an attempt to pinpoint what she was so upset about, she decided she did not care for the way Dane responded to her when she merely asked a simple request. Nor did she get a chance to give him her two bits about what she thought of his answer. *If this is the way he's going to act whenever there's a conflict between us—just turn and walk away from me—I may as well call it quits right now.* Brandy Jo started home as the anger continued to build. Halfway home, she decided she was going to go to the hospital on her own, because she *did* care what happened to Hank.

Brandy Jo pulled into the visitor parking lot and followed a group of folks into the conference room to hear the update on Hank. The seats around the large table were all taken so Brandy Jo joined the others standing along the back wall. Dr. Stoddard entered the room shortly after and the room went quiet.

"I'm sure Hank appreciates all of you who are following his progress in this unfortunate situation. He apologizes for not being able to receive all of you who have requested a visit, but I can tell you from a medical standpoint, it takes a lot of energy to recover from what he's been through. It takes rest for the body to heal. It also drains energy to speak with visitors who understandably have a lot of questions. For now, please respect that Hank needs every ounce of strength it will take to recover." The doctor paused and looked around the room, as if to make sure everyone listened to his words. "At this point, we're encouraged that the reduction in swelling has begun to allow for more nerve connection in his lower extremities. We're hoping this will continue to improve. The next step will be physical therapy. He will be moved from the hospital to rehab when the team feels he's ready. I can't give you any timelines on any of this right now. I can't disclose more details, but just know we're hopeful he'll have use of his legs again. That's all I have for now. Again, on behalf of Hank, thank you all for coming."

"Will he ever ride again?" Buddy Thomas from his rodeo team yelled out.

"I can't answer that at this point," Dr. Stoddard replied.

It was true that Brandy Jo did not like the rodeo one bit, but she knew how much it meant to Hank, and she couldn't imagine what it would be like to have the one thing you love most in your life taken away from you, possibly forever.

As Brandy Jo prepared to leave, she saw Sarah standing just outside the door. Her eyes were red as though she'd been crying again. Brandy Jo dodged her way through the crowd to Sarah's side. "What's going on?" she asked.

Sarah pulled Brandy Jo out into the hall and into a private corner. "Hank finally let me in to visit. He broke up with me." Tears started flowing the instant she said it.

"What? After all this time you've been here and waited to see him?"

"He says it's hard enough for him to deal with all that's going on, but he doesn't feel he has anything left to give to a relationship right now."

Brandy Jo just had enough with insensitive men for one day. She wasn't sure who she was more upset with right now, Hank or Dane.

"Come on, Sarah. I think we both need an afternoon off without cowboys. We're going for a nice, long walk along the slough to chill out." She grabbed her friend by the arm and led her out of the hospital.

~

When Dane's name appeared on Brandy Jo's cell phone that evening, she ignored it. Let him think twice over the way he'd behaved that morning. She would talk to him about it when she was good and ready.

The following morning at work, for the first time for as long as Brandy Jo could remember, Dane did not come into The Grill for breakfast.

Fine. Two can play this game. Maybe Dane and Hank both need a little time alone to grow up and learn to appreciate the women who care about them.

When Dane didn't call or show up for the rest of the week, Brandy Jo just got angrier. She refused to give in to his childish way of dealing with conflict. As more time passed, the memories of the good times she'd had with Dane came to mind, and she realized how much she missed him. She missed his kind, gentle ways, and his soft, sweet kisses. But how could she be the one to break the ice now? It would give the message that it was okay to treat her the way he had over something as stupid as not wanting to visit Hank Halverson. The longer the silence between them lasted, the worse Brandy Jo felt.

When Sunday came, Brandy Jo looked for Dane at church. He wasn't where he normally sat, but near the end of the service, she finally spotted him. Maybe he would come talk to her after the closing hymn. She knew he had seen her sitting with her family. No one could miss the Danner clan, they took up an entire pew.

She waited right where she was sitting to make it easy for him to find her, but when the service ended, she watched Dane walk out of the sanctuary without so much as a backward glance.

While the rest of the Danners dispersed to join church friends at coffee hour, Brandy Jo sat and stewed. Rait was the only one still remaining in the Danner pew. Her brother glanced over with what she considered close to a glare.

"What are you looking at me like that for, Rait?"

"I just don't get you, Brandy Jo. I don't get why you're doing what you're doing to Dane. He doesn't deserve this kind of treatment from you."

"From *me*?" Brandy Jo scoffed. "How can you say that about a man who wouldn't even accompany me to an update on a man who may be paralyzed for the rest of his life just because of a little squabble in the third grade?"

Rait's eyes narrowed to a definite glare and he spoke to her in a tone he'd never used with her before. "Do you really believe that's the reason Dane didn't want to go with you?"

"What other reason is there? He hasn't liked Hank ever since third grade and that's why."

Rait shook his head. "Brandy Jo, sometimes I can't believe you're a Danner—not giving a man like Dane the benefit of the doubt. You should know by his character that he's not that petty. If you weren't so stubborn and prideful, maybe you could have afforded him a chance to explain himself—but then Dane's probably too much of a gentleman to say anything that might hurt another and that's probably why he just kept his mouth shut."

"Rait Danner, what on earth are you talking about? If you've got something to say about Dane, you tell me right now."

Rait glanced around the empty sanctuary. "I don't know if I should be the one to tell you why he reacted that way toward Hank, but, I can tell you that Dane deserves another chance. I happen to like him enough to set you straight before you lose a good man over this."

Brandy Jo pleaded with her eyes. "Rait, tell me."

Rait considered her plea with a heavy sigh. "Alright. I will, but know this doesn't go any further than this sanctuary—you got that?"

"I got it," Brandy Jo replied, looking somber.

"Dane Bronson's little sister happens to be one of Hank Halverson's most innocent victims."

Brandy Jo felt as though she'd been punched in the stomach.

"He hurt that girl so bad, I don't know if she'll ever recover from that kind of humiliation."

"Dane's sister, Charlotte?"

Rait nodded. "I don't know if Hank did it more for sport or to spite Dane, whom he's always been jealous of, but it hurt their whole family. I don't feel it's my place to relay the details, but I'll say enough for you to get a clear picture." Rait drew a deep breath, exhaled, then began. "Back when Charlotte won the title of Silverdale Rodeo Queen, she was given the honor of riding on the float in the Old Settlers' Day Parade with the Rodeo King of her choosing. Hank and his rodeo buddies made bets with each other that whoever got chosen as her Rodeo King would win the pot between them. For the next month they all went after Charlotte, trying to woo her and get her to fall for them. Well, Hank finally won her over with his charm. He had Charlotte believing that she was the stars and the moon to him. Lord only knows how swept up she was by him.

"Come the end of the parade, Hank's rodeo buddies, all drunk as skunks, gathered around Hank on the float, and brought him the pot of money he'd won, exposing the whole mean prank publicly."

Brandy Jo gasped.

"The worst of it was, Hank just had a good laugh right along with his buddies and left Charlotte standing there, brokenhearted, to face the humiliation alone."

"Where was I when all of this happened?"

"Well, B-Jo, considering you dislike parades as much as you do, I gather you didn't attend."

Brandy Jo nodded. The memory of getting pummeled in the head by a handful of candy from a creepy clown didn't help her affections for parades. "All I remember is seeing a pair of huge red lips and a mass of orange hair when I looked up at the float, then, wham! Right in the noggin." She shook off the feeling with a wave of her hand. "But why didn't Dane tell me?"

"That's not the kind of thing a guy goes around telling people about.

Besides protecting his sister's honor, Dane's too much a gentleman to be bad-mouthing someone—even someone as mean as Hank Halverson. Sounds to me like you accused Dane without giving him much of a chance to explain anything."

Brandy Jo covered her face with her hands. "Oh, my gosh. What have I done?"

"Well, that's a good question to ask yourself. You should have known that a man like Dane is not going to hold a grudge over some grade school spat."

Tears spilled from Brandy Jo's eyes. "What am I going to do?"

"If I were Dane, I'd probably like an apology to begin with. From there it will be his call to decide if you're worth taking another chance. And while you're sitting here, you might want to start by asking for God's help with the matter."

Brandy Jo felt Rait's arm gently wrap around her. She released a heavy sigh and leaned on his shoulder.

"I'm not saying this to put you down, Sis. Lord knows I'm the last guy to claim to know the ways of the fairer sex. I'm just giving it to you from a man's viewpoint. I really hope you two can work through this—because I like Dane. I know I don't say this often, but I love my little sister too."

"I love you, too Rait," she whispered.

Chapter Six

On Brandy Jo's way over to the Bronson's farm, she felt an urge to stop one other place first. She pulled her Jeep into the parking lot of the Silverdale Hospital and hopped out. Passing through the lobby, she stopped by the main desk. "Hank Halverson's room number please."

The receptionist scrolled down her computer screen. "Room 403 west. But, there's a note here he's not receiving visitors."

"Okay, thank you." Brandy Jo went to the elevator and rode up to the fourth floor. She bypassed the nurse's station, made her way down the hall to room 403, and knocked.

A gruff voice answered back. "Yeah?"

Brandy Jo opened the door and stepped inside.

Hank was lying in bed and looked surprised to see her. "How'd you get past the nurses?" He didn't sound too pleased that she had.

"I walked," she replied matter of fact.

"Sounds like a Danner." Hank smirked and shook his head. "Well, have a seat then." He sat up, pulling the covers up with him.

Seeing Hank's 6ft 4in. frame in a skimpy hospital gown made him look more vulnerable than Brandy Jo had ever seen him. She scooted a chair up near the bed. "I know you're not up for visitors, and I'm real sorry about your accident, but Hank, I've got a bone to pick with you."

Hank raised an eyebrow in surprise. "That's refreshing. Most folks come in here with nothing but pity."

"I'm not going to pity you."

"Well, okay then. Let's hear it."

Brandy Jo released a loud sigh. "I think sometimes we're given an unexpected chance to re-evaluate our lives and decide if we want to stay on the same destructive course, or, if we're willing to, change our ways and become something better. Now I'm not just saying this to you—it applies to me as well, and I hope for everyone's sake we both change for the better."

"Brandy Danner, what are you talkin' about?"

She squared her shoulders. "Hank, you have a bad reputation around town for the way you treat women. And, I'm not known for the tactful way I say things to people. I think we both have a problem with pride— among other things. But you need to know that the way *we* act hurts other people."

Hanks brows pressed together. "And your point is?"

"My point is, that there is a kind, sweet, wonderful friend of mine who happens to care deeply for you."

"Are you talkin' about Sarah?"

"I am. Whether you realize it or not, Sarah has been sleeping out there in the waiting room day in and day out on your behalf just hoping to hear how you were doing or that maybe you'd want to see her. Instead, you broke her heart. You sent her away without giving her the time of day."

Hank released a heavy sigh. "Well, there's a reason for that." He took a moment to consider his words. "Whether or not you believe me, I am not proud of the way I have treated women in the past—as a matter of fact, I'm ashamed of it. Now, I happen to really care for Sarah, more than I've cared for any other girl. But, I am not used to people seeing me this way." Hank glanced down toward his still legs. "I can't expect a beautiful, young woman like Sarah to be stuck with some broken-down guy who may or may not ever walk again. I just want to be left alone and have everyone else just get on with their lives. I'm no longer Hang-on-Hank the Rodeo King. I'm just this disabled nobody—just like my Pa always said—a good for nothin' that won't amount to much of anything."

Brandy Jo's mouth fell open. "Your Pa told you that?"

"First words out of his mouth every time he drank."

"But Hank, that's just the alcohol talking. Your Pa…"

Hank cut in. "Why do you think I always had to prove I was better than everyone else; better at bull riding, better at getting the women I wanted? I have had plenty of time in here to think, and all I can come up with is, my Pa was right."

"Oh, Hank, your Pa has been worried sick over you. I even saw him in church for the first time in ages—he's been coming ever since you got hurt—probably praying his heart out for you."

"My Pa, in church?" That brought a smile to Hank's face. "Now that's something I never thought I'd hear."

"Your misfortune has the potential to change a lot of lives." Brandy Jo placed her hand gently on Hank's arm. "A lot of people are pulling for you out there. You've got to let God turn this for the good—mostly for yourself."

Hank looked at Brandy Jo with a vulnerability she wasn't used to seeing. "So, Sarah really slept out there for me?"

"She did. And she's been here constantly. Whenever she's not at work, she's here asking nurses how you're doing—even after you sent her away. She's probably out there now."

"Really?" He looked visibly touched. "C-could you go check—and if she is, would you ask her to come in?"

Brandy Jo smiled. "I sure will. If she's not out there, I'll call her and tell her to come." Brandy Jo got up. "I have a mess of my own to go fix now, but you just fight to get well, you hear me?"

Hank smiled. "Yes, Ma'am!" He chuckled. "And Brandy?"

"Yeah?"

"Thank you."

Brandy Jo gave Hank a sincere nod. "You're welcome. And Hank?"

"Yeah?"

"You can call me Brandy Jo."

~

Brandy Jo headed her Jeep down the highway toward the Bronson Ranch. As soon as she had the ranch in sight, she spotted Dane's hay baler in the middle of the field. She could barely make out Dane hoisting the bales into the back of the farm truck. As she got closer she realized she'd have to drive her Jeep into the middle of the field to get close enough to talk to him. The afternoon sun was beating down and she knew Dane would be hot and tired, but she couldn't stand the thought of waiting any longer. As her Jeep plowed over rugged hay fields, she felt like she was on a bucking bronco.

As she pulled up beside Dane's truck, he was heaving a huge bale of hay with gloved hands. Sweat dripped from his muscular arms as he flung the bale into the hay truck. By the number of bales already loaded, Brandy Jo knew how exhausted he must be. He looked up and dropped the bale he was lifting. Sweat beaded up on his tanned, shirtless chest and dripped from his brow. He reached for his shirt hanging on the side of his truck and wiped his face. He shot Brandy Jo a curious look as she stepped down from her Jeep. Before she could even say hello, tears began rolling down her cheeks. Dane tossed his shirt into the back of the truck and walked toward her. His puzzled expression turned to a look of concern.

"Are you okay?"

Brandy Jo shook her head and continued to cry.

Dane hurried to her side. "What's wrong? What happened?"

She barely lifted her eyes. "I'm so sorry, Dane."

He placed his hands on her shoulders and tried to catch her gaze. "Sorry for what?"

"F-for everything." The tears came faster.

He reached for a loose strand of hair and tucked it gently behind Brandy Jo's ear. "Hey, it's okay."

"No, it's not. I accused you unfairly for something I knew nothing about, then blamed you for walking away. I completely misread the whole situation, but never gave you a chance to explain anything." She wiped her face on her sleeve, knowing she must look like a blotchy mess. "I just wanted to come tell you how sorry I am and hope that you can forgive me."

Dane took a step closer and cupped her face in his hands. "Of course I forgive you." His dimples reappeared, and he added. "I'd kiss you right now but I'm a sweaty mess."

Hearing that he wanted to kiss her, Brandy Jo threw her arms around Dane and kissed him anyway. "I missed you," she whispered in his ear.

Dane kissed her back with an intensity that told her he missed her, too. Stepping back, he gently wiped her tears away. "What do you say I get cleaned up and we can pick it back up over dinner?"

Brandy Jo smiled through glistening eyes. "I'd like that."

"Pick you up at five?"

She nodded.

He placed a soft kiss on her forehead before returning to the bales waiting to be loaded.

She climbed back into her Jeep and glanced over at Dane one last time. "That's *my* cowboy," she whispered, and drove home.

~

Dane pulled up to the Rockin' D Ranch at three minutes to five. Brandy Jo was sitting on the log rail fence out front, waiting for him. She wasn't sure what had gotten into her, but she'd nixed her blue jeans for a long western skirt with a white cotton peasant top and her best cowgirl boots—in case they went somewhere fancy. The minute Dane stepped down from the truck cab, Brandy Jo ran into his arms and hugged him like she wasn't planning to let go anytime soon.

Dane chuckled softly. "Did you want to eat before sundown?"

"Just making up for lost time," she replied. "That was the longest three weeks without you." She slowly released him and hopped into the truck beside him. "So, where're we going?"

"How about the Cliff House?" he asked.

"The *Cliff House?* Woohoo! I've never been to anything that fancy."

"Well, then, it's time you go." He looked over with a grin. "The sunset should be beautiful from there tonight."

The drive to The Cliff House was a steep, winding road into the Rockies, ending at the top of a mountain, overlooking the Flat Irons. The restaurant was considered the best in three counties for view, cuisine and ambiance. The cedar lodge sat perched at the top of a sheer peak and had a panoramic view for miles around.

Brandy Jo slipped from the truck cab, awestruck at the view surrounding her. "Whoa." She took Dane's hand and moved as though she were walking on clouds toward the lodge. Entering the lobby, Brandy Jo continued to gawk at the magnificent windows and big beam construction that drew their attention right back outdoors to the sun setting over the horizon.

"Bronson, party of two."

The hostess led them to the best window seat in the house. The dining room extended out over the cliff so looking down gave one the sense of being suspended over a massive chasm below. After her first glance downward, Brandy Jo shifted her eyes back on Dane to relieve the slight queasiness she experienced from such a drop.

Dane chuckled over the expression on her face. "You gonna be okay sitting here?"

"Oh, yeah. Must just be the altitude up here making me a little dizzy. I'll be fine—as long as we don't have an earthquake."

Dane laughed and reached for her hand across the table. "It's so good to be with you again. That was the worst few weeks of my life."

"Me, too."

After placing their orders, Dane glanced across the candlelit table at Brandy Jo. "I did try to call you to explain my reaction to visiting Hank, but when you didn't answer or call me back, I felt I should give you some space until you were ready to approach me again. When I didn't hear from you for a few weeks, I was hoping it wasn't due to you taking a shine to Hank."

A spurt of ice water escaped from Brandy Jo's lips as she was taking a sip. "Opps, sorry." She quickly moped up the water with her napkin. "Me taking a shine to Hank Halverson is about as likely as a dozen pigs flying through this dining room right now."

Dane glanced up at the ceiling, then back at Brandy Jo with a smile. "I hoped that was the case, but seeing your Jeep at the hospital a few times had me wondering."

"Just a friendly visit," she replied.

"Dane nodded. "I want you to know, I wasn't intentionally ignoring you—just trying to pick up on your cues. As a guy I may not be very good at this, so I'm sorry if my reactions hurt you."

Brandy Jo tightened her hand around Dane's. "No, you got it right, and being as stubborn as I am, it just took me a while to work through it." She didn't feel the need to bring up the information she'd learned from Rait. That would only add more pain at this point. She was just thankful for another chance.

Following a fabulous meal of plank salmon and Black Angus steak, Dane and Brandy Jo wandered out to the observation deck to watch the last fleeting moments of the sunset. They reclined in two lounge chairs holding hands between them and watched in silence as brilliant lavender and orange streaks spread across the sky. Watching the sun slowly sink behind the Rocky Mountains felt like a wonderful gift of God's grace settling over their budding young love. Brandy Jo sent a silent prayer out over the canyon. *Thank you, Lord.*

~

Monday afternoon, Sarah came into work all smiles. Brandy Jo's heart felt lighter just seeing her that way. After Brandy Jo clocked out, Sarah pulled her into the girl's room and locked the door.

"What are we doing in here?" Brandy Jo gasped.

"It's the only safe place for privacy around here." She turned Brandy Jo around to face her. "After you told me to go to Hank's room the other day, he apologized to me for the way he'd treated me. Then he said, if I don't mind hanging around with a cripple while he recovers, he would really like to give us another chance." Sarah's face beamed with the news.

Brandy Jo hugged her friend. "I am so happy for you, Sarah. I think this is the first time I've seen Hank take a girl seriously." She didn't mention anything to Sarah that she and Hank had talked about that day, but had a good feeling about Hank's attempt to change his ways—especially toward her friend.

"So, how are things with you and Dane?" Sarah asked.

Brandy Jo grinned. "Much better, thanks."

"I'm so glad. I'd better get back to work."

"Oh, right." The two left just as Marv walked out from the men's bathroom.

"What's going on in there—am I missing a good party?"

"Girl talk," Brandy Jo replied, and winked at Sarah, before heading home.

~

The following week, news spread quickly that Hank had some feeling back in both legs and was beginning physical therapy. Knowing Sarah, Brandy Jo figured she'd be there to encourage Hank every step of the way. The other big news in town was that the neighboring county of Cross Creek was putting on a small spring fair to coincide with their Lavender Festival. If anyone loved the fair, it was Brandy Jo. It didn't take much for her to talk Dane into going with her opening night. "We have to go after dark, though—that's when all the dazzling lights are flashing, and the rides are way scarier."

"For someone who's afraid of clowns and parades, I'm surprised you like scary rides," Dane replied.

"Hey, there's a big difference between scary fun and just plain creepy."

"So how many rides did you want to go on?" he asked as they neared the ticket booth.

"All of them! Just buy the bracelets so we can go on them all, as many times as we want."

"I'm glad I haven't eaten yet," Dane replied. "Doing the Zipper on a full stomach could pose a real risk."

"Okay, we'll ride first, then eat." Brandy Jo slid her ride bracelet on and pulled Dane over to the Ferris wheel. "We can start easy and work our way up to The Slammer."

Dane didn't look as excited as Brandy Jo.

She couldn't help the kid in her from coming out on the fairgrounds. She hadn't missed a single fair since she was tall enough to climb on the rides. As the two of them dodged their way through the crowd to the Ferris wheel, Brandy Jo nearly ran right into a man with a cane. "Oh, excuse.... Hank!"

Hank and Sarah were equally surprised to see Brandy Jo and Dane.

"I can't believe you're already getting out and about," Brandy Jo exclaimed. "That's great."

Hank smiled in return, then glanced at Dane. "Hey, Dane," he nodded in a friendly manner. Hank actually held his hand out to Dane. "It's good to see you."

Dane nodded in return and gripped Hank's hand. "I'm glad to see you're on your feet again."

Something passed between the two men that Brandy Jo could only interpret as a truce. As the couples parted ways, a palpable heaviness parted as well, replaced by a lightness of heart. It was a moment Brandy Jo would not easily forget.

Climbing aboard the Ferris wheel, Brandy Jo slid to the far side of the seat. Dane hopped in after her and slipped his arm around her shoulder. As the big wheel arched upward into the night air, Brandy Jo closed her eyes and snuggled into Dane's side. "This is the first time I've ever been on a Ferris wheel with a guy I have a crush on," she announced.

"Is that right?" Dane laughed. "Well, I'm glad to know that." He pulled her closer. "This is the first time I've been on a Ferris wheel with a girl I'm in love with," he whispered softly.

Brandy Jo's eyes shot open. She pulled back slightly, just enough to look Dane in the eye. "What did you just say?"

Dimples appeared as Dane reacted to the look on Brandy Jo's face. "I said, I'm in love with you."

Brandy Jo's eyes teared up. "Wow. I always wondered what it would be like to hear that for the first time."

"So, how was it?"

"It was just like I hoped, because I always imagined you when I tried to imagine hearing those words."

"Really?" Dane tucked a wisp of hair behind Brandy Jo's ear.

"Yeah. And just so you know, I'm in love with you, too."

Dane's smile broadened. "I'm really glad to know that." Then he leaned in and kissed her the way he'd always imagined he would after hearing that she loved him back.

After hitting all the rides in the fairground, Dane finally convinced Brandy Jo that it was time to eat. That's when he realized she had a fair food agenda too. First, the deep-fried corn dogs, with sweet onion rings, followed by the strawberry shortcake scones. The cotton candy and elephant ears were only for backups if the scones had sold out. Fortunately, the strawberry shortcake was still available.

A trip through the bunny barn and livestock barns were last on the list—to help walk off the fullness from dinner. By the time they left the fairgrounds, the only inch of ground they hadn't set foot on was the rodeo arena. Brandy Jo thought of Hank as they passed it by on their way back to the parking lot. She said a silent prayer—that it wouldn't cause him too much pain to be a bystander for the first time in his life.

Chapter Seven

"I'm not interested in just dating you," Dane told Brandy Jo one night sitting on her front porch swing at sundown. "I'd like to court you—as long as you feel the same about me."

"You mean exclusive dating—just me and you?"

Holding her hand, he gave her a more extensive definition of courting. "Well, that's where it would start, but if all goes well, it could lead to something more permanent."

Brandy Jo's eyes widened. "Ohhh, *that* kind of courting." A grin spread across her face. "Does that mean you might want to marry me one day?" she asked, playfully.

"I sure hope that's where it goes," he replied. "But, I was thinking, I should probably ask your fathers's permission to court you before we get too far down the road, don't you think?"

A deep crease suddenly formed between Brandy Jo's eyebrows.

"What is it—am I going too fast with this for you?" Dane drew his hand back slightly.

"Not for me," Brandy Jo reassured him, "but I am a little concerned for my dad. He's been acting funny lately, having just married off Melissa, and after losing Mamma. I'm worried he might not be ready for any more losses just yet." Brandy Jo's brows knitted even closer together, as she thought harder about the matter. "If we were to get married, would we still be able to live here in Silverdale?"

"I've never considered living anywhere else. My family's homestead has been here for three generations. It's the only place I've ever ranched or called home." Dane glanced at his watch, then at the light in the sky. "We still have a little daylight left—let's go for a drive. I have something I want to show you."

Ten minutes later, Dane was pulling off the main road by his family's ranch. Instead of taking the driveway up toward the house, he veered off on a more primitive road that cut through the field along the fence line. With the farmhouse fading in the background behind them, another roofline appeared in the distance. The structure sat in a green oasis at the foot of a small valley.

"Are you building a new barn?" Brandy Jo asked.

Dane smiled and kept driving. They wound down the tree-lined road until they pulled to a stop in from of an unfinished two-story building with a protruding roofline.

"It's...it's a farmhouse." Brandy Jo stared out the window, wide-eyed. "Is...it...yours?"

"My folks sectioned off a portion of land for me to build a house on. I've been working on it for months—it still has a ways to go." He smiled over at Brandy Jo. "I was saving the final details for input."

"Really?" Brandy Jo's excitement was over-the-moon. "You mean like the colors of the rooms and the flooring and all that kind of stuff?"

"And the inside layout of the kitchen and family room—I figured that should be geared toward what the woman has in mind."

Brandy Jo's hands covered her mouth as she blinked over and over. "This is so amazing. It's even got a creek—and look at all the trees growing along its path."

"I was hoping you'd like it here."

"Like it? I *love it*!"

"Come on, let's go take a closer look."

Brandy Jo stepped down from the cab. She took hold of Dane's hand and walked slowly toward the house, taking in every detail. "Since I'd only be down the road from Rockin' D, I'm sure my dad wouldn't feel too lonely. I could always pop over and see him and he could drop by here for a visit whenever he wanted to see me." She turned to Dane and gave him a quick hug. "Oh, Dane, he would just love it here. We could have a porch swing to sit on and watch the creek go by, and a tire swing up in that big pine tree, and...."

Dane breathed an audible sigh of relief. "Alright then, I'll try to work up the nerve to talk to him soon."

Brandy Jo's head was already off in La-la Land. "My own ranch kitchen... I've always wanted one of those shiny silver Universal cook stoves and a cozy little kitchen nook with wood benches, and ...." Her ideas rambled on as Dane gave her a guided tour of their future farmhouse.

~

Brandy Jo had everyone trying to guess what in the world she was whistling and sing about—more so than usual.

"You got something to tell us?" Rait asked, over the rim of his morning coffee.

"Not unless you've got something to tell me about Serena."

"What makes you think I have anything to say about Serena? I'm not the one whistling *Dixie* around here."

Brandy Jo laughed. Of her three brothers, Rait was the most fun to tease—especially about girls. He still got nervous when Brandy Jo figured out who he had his eye on, knowing her potential for embarrassing the daylights out of him.

"Don't think I don't know that look in your eye whenever Serena arrives on the scene. Seems to me you hired her so you wouldn't have to work so much, but every time I drive past her car in Old Town, there's your truck parked right behind hers."

Rait did not look amused. "I'm warning you stay out of it, you hear me?"

Brandy Jo smirked. "Fine. Then neither will I tell you why I happen to be whistling and singing more lately." Thank goodness her father had agreed to keep the courtship between her and Dane a secret until, Lord willing, something more official was announced. She left Rait stewing over his coffee as she strode away belting out, "Oh, I wish I was in the land of cotton…"

~

As spring rolled into summer, Dane and Brandy Jo spent almost all their free time on the building site of the farmhouse. The construction was only a few months away from completion, and Brandy Jo was itching to get into her ranch kitchen and start calling the shots. But she wasn't making a peep until she had something official on her finger to prove her status as the Cowgirl of the Cottage. It was going on three months of courtship—the minimum amount of time Dad Danner had requested they wait before making final plans.

When opening night for the Silverdale County Fair rolled around, it was Dane who suggested they attend this time. Brandy Jo was surprised, remembering how queasy Dane had looked by the time they left the Cross Creek county fair.

"You sure you're up for another fair with me?" she asked.

"Yeah, it's taken me this long to recover, but I think I can at least handle the Ferris wheel."

Brandy Jo was all for it and threw on her fancy western skirt and cowgirl boots for the occasion. She even curled her hair for the first time in ages and donned her cowgirl hat just before answering the door.

Dane nearly tripped back down the stairs when he got his first glimpse at Brandy Jo. "Whoa…. you look…. amazing."

Brandy Jo shrugged. "Just something I tossed together."

Dane continued to steal side glances of her all the way to the fairgrounds. And Brandy Jo pretended not to notice.

When they reached the ticket booth, Dane suggested they just buy a few tickets at a time rather than the all-inclusive bracelet—after all, Cross Creek had been a fraction of the size of the Silverdale fair with half the number of rides. There was no way Dane was going to get himself talked into every ride this time.

"Okay, which ride first?"

"Let's start out easy. How about the Ferris wheel?"Dane suggested.

Even the Silverdale Ferris wheel was bigger than the one at Cross Creek. "Let's get number three—it was our lucky number last time," Brandy Jo suggested.

The ride attendant acted slightly put out by her request.

"That's the seat we had when this cowboy told me he loved me for the first time," Brandy Jo informed the man.

A smile broke out over the man's face and he was happy to accommodate her.

Once they were safely buckled into seat number three, the big wheel began to turn. Brandy Jo took in all of the flashing, dazzling fair lights, but they were no competition for the stars appearing overhead. "Look how brilliant the Milky Way is tonight."

Dane nodded. "Yeah, pretty amazing."

Just as seat number three crested the top, the big wheel slowed to a stop.

"Hey, what's going on?" Brandy Jo asked, startled.

"I don't know, but if we're stuck, at least I'm stuck with you."

"Stuck!" Brandy Jo glanced down over the side to the attendant far below. She quickly pulled back. "Do you really think we're stuck?"

Dane calmly poured a handful of Sugar Babies into his palm. "I don't know, but we may as well have a snack while we're waiting." He held his palm out in front of Brandy Jo, who, distractedly grabbed a few off the top and looked down at her hand.

"Ohmygosh!" she shrieked. "It's…. it's…. a *ring*! A *diamond* ring! Is this….?" She looked at Dane, her eyes glistening with tears.

Dane smiled. "Marry me?"

Brandy Jo threw her arms around Dane with a full-force kiss of acceptance that rocked their Ferris wheel car.

"Shall I take that as a yes?" Dane asked.

"Yes! Yes, I will marry you!" She screamed so loud the entire Ferris wheel of riders burst into applause and cheers. The big wheel roared back to life and continued its descent downward. To make up for stalling, which Dane had secretly requested before they climbed on, the attendant gave everyone aboard an extra-long ride. Meanwhile, Brandy Jo spent the remainder of the ride staring at her new ring, kissing her fiancé, and discussing wall and floor colors for her new ranch kitchen.

As soon as the ride was over, Brandy Jo leapt down from the Ferris wheel. "C'mon!"

Dane could barely keep up with his bride-to-be, who sprinted across the fairground in a pair of cowgirl boots.

By the time they reached the truck, both were breathing hard. "Is there a reason we need to get back in such a hurry?" Dane asked, between breaths.

Brandy Jo shot Dane a curious look as she belted herself into the passenger seat. "Only that it's the most exciting day of my life! I have to tell someone, and who better than my family? Besides, my siblings have teased me all my life saying that I'm so sassy, any man would be crazy to take me as a wife. They're all convinced I'll die a sassy old spinster!"

Dane shot back a look of concern. "Should I be worried about this— being the one crazy enough to take you as a wife?"

"Not a bit. I just have to show them all how wrong they are. Nothing to fear."

Dane just shook his head and drove.

Brandy Jo led the way through the front door of Danner Manor. The Danner family was sitting down to a steak dinner when Brandy Jo burst into the room with Dane in tow. "Hey everyone, guess who's gettin' hitched?" She held out her hand and flashed her shiny stone for all to admire.

"Oh, my goodness!" Kylee exclaimed. "Would you look at the size of that rock?"

"Woohoo!" The boys all howled.

"Our sassy little sis finally landed herself a man to take on the Danner challenge," Noah announced.

Everyone was in good cheer, apart from Dad Danner, who was giving his best smile of support, but still looked a far cry from cheerful. He did give Dane his heartfelt sentiments. "I couldn't be more pleased that it's you, Dane."

"Thank you, Sir." Dane nodded, respectfully. "It's going to be an honor to be a part of the Danner family."

The brothers, one by one, shook the hand of their new brother-in-law-to-be. "Welcome to the family," Rait greeted with a firm handshake.

"In all honesty, you are getting yourself the cream of the crop with this little gal here," he added.

"Thank you, Rait. I kind of see it that way myself."

Dad Danner lifted his glass of wine. "To Dane and Brandy Jo, may you be as blessed as Brandy Jo's mother and I were in our years together."

The rest of the family raised their glasses and chimed in. "Hear, hear! And many years!"

Brandy Jo could barely sleep that night—having to hold her engagement ring up in the moonlight every few minutes to watch it twinkle.

I finally got my cowboy.

Chapter Eight

On her way to work the following morning, Brandy Jo caught sight of Serena hard at work staining the walls of the old Mercantile building. She pulled her Jeep to a halt and ran down the sidewalk, flashing her new ring at Serena.

"Oh, Brandy Jo, it's gorgeous! Congratulations!"

By the time the two finished chatting, Serena had already agreed to do the makeup at Brandy Jo's wedding for all the bridesmaids and made plans to meet her after work to go dress shopping.

"Come by at two when my shift ends!" Brandy Jo yelled and headed off to work, honking her horn all the way through Old Town while waving her ring out the window.

It didn't take more than two minutes before everyone at The Branding Iron heard the big news. Brandy Jo's customers were shown the sparkling token of Dane's affection before they even had a chance to order their coffee. The entire café was instantly set in a festive mood. Brandy Jo kept it going all the way through breakfast and lunch, until it was time to go shopping for her dress.

When Sarah arrived for work, Brandy Jo pulled her aside. "Don't scream, but I'm engaged."

"Oh, my gosh!" she yelled. "When? Let me see that ring." Sarah grabbed Brandy Jo's hand and gawked. "That is the best news I've heard in ages. I am so happy for you!"

"So....?" Brandy Jo cracked a sly smile.

"So, what?" Sarah replied.

"So, how are things going with Hank?"

Sarah blushed. "They're actually going really well. I mean, his progress is slow. But, as far as he and I, it's going really well. He's asked me to be his personal bodyguard while he recovers." She laughed.

"Well, that's a cute thing to say coming from big Hank."

Sarah looked thoughtful. "Yeah. It is, isn't it? He's really a different guy than when we first met. I like him much more this way—I don't mean crippled, but as a kinder version of Hank. I think in time he's going to recover physically, but God's doing some work on him in the meantime."

"That's awesome," Brandy Jo replied. "Hey, by the way, I wanted to ask if you would do me the honor of being one of my bridesmaids."

"Are you kidding? I would love to!" She narrowed her gaze at Brandy Jo. "What color am I wearing—I just hope it's not orange. Copper hair and orange do not go well together."

Brandy Jo laughed. "You're in luck. It's turquoise."

"My best color," Sarah replied, visibly relieved.

"Okay, it's settled then." She gave Sarah a hug. "Gotta scoot! Have a good shift." She was out the door and on her way to shop for her wedding gown with Serena. She hadn't known Serena long enough to include her in the wedding party, but if Rait played his cards well, they could end up as something more endearing than friends—like, maybe, sisters-in-law.

~

"I have no desire to wear a brand-new wedding dress," Brandy Jo announced, as the two gals entered Second Go Round Shop. "I want something that has a timelessness about it—kind of a vintage feel, you know?"

"What are your bridesmaid colors?" Serena asked.

"My signature color. Turquoise blue, with gold accents."

"Oh, nice. I'll have to look for something to wear to your wedding with at least a hint of turquoise." As her eyes scanned the racks, they fell upon something she thought might interest Brandy Jo. "Did you say something about a timeless look?"

"Yeah, why?"

"Check that out."

Brandy Jo twisted around to the gown that Serena was pointing out. Her eyes froze in place."Oh, my gosh." She strutted straight to the window display, then ran her fingers over the bejeweled bodice and embroidered trim on the antique, cream-colored satin gown. Long woven vines cascaded down the back, into a long train that wound around the mannequin modeling the dress.

"That's the one," she whispered. "*That's* the dress I have always dreamt of."

The shopkeeper rushed over, trying to assist Brandy Jo, who was already wrestling the gown off of the mannequin.

"Let's unzip it first, shall we?" the shopkeeper suggested.

"Oh, it's got one of those hidden zippers. No wonder I couldn't get it off." She stepped back and let the sales lady take over.

While Brandy Jo swept the gown off to the dressing room, she noticed Serena had found something turquoise that she was holding up in front of the mirror. "Oh, that color against your blonde hair is faboo—go try it on!" Brandy Jo insisted, while pulling the curtain closed behind her. She wasn't thinking about how great she thought Serena looked in that dazzling blue dress as much as how great her brother Rait would think Serena looked in it. It would definitely get his attention.

In a matter of moments, both Brandy Jo and Serena were parading around the shop together in their two gorgeous dresses. After being handed a pair of too-small sandals, Brandy Jo twirled from the platform she was posing on. "Can someone please grab me those cream colored cowgirl boots over in that window display? I'm marrying myself a cowboy, not a beach bum!"

The boots were the perfect finish to the look Brandy Jo was going for. "I love it! I absolutely love it all! This is dress I want to wear when I say 'I do' to Dane." Brandy Jo sighed with relief. "This has been so Providential in the biggest way. Given how much I hate to shop, and that we both found the exact dress we both needed at the same place, it's nothing short of a miracle."

Serena, on the other hand, was having second thoughts. "Are you sure this dress isn't too…revealing on me?"

Brandy Jo just stared at her. She wasn't about to say that her oblivious brother could use all the help he could get to notice a woman in a beautiful dress. If that one didn't get his attention, she didn't know what would. "It's perfect, Serena. Go with it."

Brandy Jo and Serena walked out of the Second Go Round Shop carrying dress bags larger than themselves. "Well," Serena sighed. "We found our dresses. Now all we need to worry about is our hair, our nails, and our makeup."

"Mercy me, the things we women go through to make ourselves presentable. Men just pull on a pair of blue jeans, jump into cowboy boots, don a flannel shirt, and give no thought to the matter. So unfair."

~

While Brandy Jo sat on a newly installed countertop in her soon-to-be ranch kitchen, she and Dane decided on a wedding date. The week prior to Old Settler's Day in July seemed to be the only weekend that wasn't already scheduled for some kind of celebration. Neither Dane nor

Brandy Jo had any reason for prolonging the engagement any longer than they had to. Neither had big grandiose wedding plans –they just plain wanted to get married. The fact that they only had six weeks to plan didn't seem to bother either one of them.

"All I need is my dress, a bouquet of flowers, a church, and my cowboy," Brandy Jo remarked to anyone who told her she was crazy to try to plan a wedding in that short amount of time.

The completion date of the farmhouse fell close to their wedding date. "As long as the walls are up and the roof is on, I'm planning to move in on our honeymoon, even if it means sleeping bags and air mattresses."

On the Fourth of July when the rest of the town was out blowing up fireworks, Dane and Brandy Jo spent a peaceful evening around the firepit that Dane had built down by the creek behind the new farmhouse. They sat in Adirondack chairs and roasted hotdogs. Brandy Jo brought all the fixin's for S'mores in case they got hungry later.

Somewhere between the hotdogs and S'mores, Dane decided it was a good time to make certain that Brandy Jo was really ready to take on the life of a rancher's wife. "Are you absolutely sure you don't want to pursue anything more as far as college?"

Brandy Jo dropped her stick in the fire and turned to face her fiancé. "Dane Bronson, if you want to see me wither up and die, then you just put me in a school room to study books and take exams that will qualify me for a future job at a desk plucking away at a computer keyboard."

"Shall I take that as, you are happy to live on a ranch and raise kids and livestock?"

"You shall indeed. And speaking of livestock, apart from the cattle, we are getting a few of our own farm animals, right?"

Dane stirred the fire with his roasting stick. "What do you mean by a few?"

"Oh, I don't know. There's the obvious, like horses and dogs. And, it might be nice to have our own laying chickens. And, maybe a few ducks—being as how we have this big creek and all. Then there's goats that can keep all the grass down for us –but I'm not real fond of goat milk."

Dane stood up and held out his hand. "Hey, before your list gets any longer, I have something to show you."

"To show *me?*"

"Yeah, c'mon." He pulled her up from her chair. "I was going to wait to show you this, but maybe it will help to postpone having to commit to turning our place into Mrs. Pigglewiggle's Farm."

Brandy Jo got to her feet and strolled beside Dane out to the new barn. Sliding back the double doors, he flipped on a dim light hanging from a rafter. "Over here." He guided her to the last stall and slowly opened the stall door. A shiny black mare with a white blaze and three white socks lowered its head and sniffed Dane's outstretched hand full of grain. "Hey, girl, meet your new mistress, Brandy Jo."

Brandy Jo's heart swelled as she stared at the gorgeous young mare. "She's...she's mine?"

"All yours," Dane replied. "Her name is Ebony's Pride. Ebony for short. I was going to give her to you for a wedding gift but tonight seemed like a good night."

Brandy Jo held out her hand and took a step closer. "Hey, sweet girl." The mare nuzzled her hand with its soft muzzle.

"Oh, Dane, I can't believe she's mine." She ran her hand gently over the horse's back and stepped beside her, wrapping her arms around her warm neck.

"She's only green broke, but I thought you might enjoy working with her."

"I will. I've always wanted to train my own horse. Besides, I'd never be able to take my own horse away from the herd at our ranch. It's all she's ever known."

"Well, you can work as much or little as you like once we're married, so if you want to spend more time with the animals, it's fine with me."

Brandy Jo turned back to Dane, her arms held out to him. "I know I just hugged a horse, and I probably smell like one, but I just want to say thank you."

Dane grinned. "I happen to love the smell of horses, so c'mere." Then he pulled her into his arms and kissed his eau de horse-scented cowgirl, as Ebony's Pride nuzzled their pockets in search of treats.

Epilogue

The Big Red Barn Wedding Reception

Following a quiet, poignant exchange of wedding vows before God and family, the double doors of the chapel burst open as Brandy Jo and Dane stepped out and were bombarded with birdseed and rose petals. He took time out for a passionate kiss on the church porch, then Dane Bronson scooped up his cowgirl bride and carried her down the front steps to the getaway car—which by the looks of it, had been tampered with by someone fond of Cheerios. They covered the floors, seats, and cup holders.

One maiden of honor, and three bridesmaids in turquoise gowns, sporting cowgirl boots beneath, tromped down the church steps behind them.

Out of respect for her shy cowboy, Brandy Jo had honored Dane's wishes for a small, intimate, family ceremony—so long as she got her full-blown, foot-stompin' reception down at the newly restored, Barton's Big Red Barn. The huge historical structure survived for over one-hundred years and was recently opened as an event center for celebrations and gatherings.

Banquet tables were piled high with fine country cuisine inside the big red barn. Festive tables were set up along the perimeter of the newly laid dance floor. A freshly mowed, green meadow surrounded the barn, and a flower-strewn walking path led to Barton's Bird Pond out back. The pond boasted a magnificent fountain in the middle that rained down peals of water and light mist that fell near the surrounding picnic tables. It was the perfect spot for avid nature lovers and guests who wanted to cool off. Knowing that many of the guests would venture out and stay past dark, Brandy Jo had spent all week hanging twinkle lights from trees to light up at dusk like little stars among the pine branches.

Dane and Brandy Jo were the first to arrive to Barton's Big Red Barn. They kicked off the celebration with Dane carrying his bride through the double red barn doors, stealing as many kisses as he could before the wedding entourage arrived behind them.

Garrets Barber shop quartet sang a few oldie goldies before the country-western band arrived. The song *As Time Goes By* was included in the playlist for the Father-daughter dance. Brandy Jo knew it was the song her parents had danced to at their own wedding and she hoped it might comfort her father to have her in his arms while hearing it again.

Dane wasn't so sure it was the right choice, as Bill Danner looked far from happy. The groom waited until the song was nearly over before cutting in, hoping his father-in-law would cheer up a little first. Fortunately, Brandy Jo reminded him that she was moving only a few miles away—which finally brought a smile to his face.

Amid all of the festivities, the bride made sure that Serena was not left alone as a wall-flower without a dance partner. Brandy Jo made a point of insisting that everyone join in the dancing—including her reluctant brother. There was no way Brandy Jo was going to allow Serena, or her new dress, to go unnoticed by her oblivious big brother. By all appearances, her plan appeared to have worked. She spotted Rait and Serena all cozied up at a corner table together.

The biggest surprise of all was the barn-shaped wedding cake with dozens of plastic farm animals surrounding it. "I couldn't resist," Brandy Jo confessed to Dane when he first laid eyes on it.

"Why am I not surprised?" he replied.

~

When it came time to cut the cake, the newlyweds were given the cupola piece that sat at the top of the barn and housed the weather vane. As a special touch, guests were handed little plastic pitchforks in lieu of regular forks to eat their cake with. While everyone was enjoying their cake, someone clanged a champagne glass with a fork to get everyone's attention. All eyes fell upon Rait Danner standing at the head of the wedding party table with a microphone in hand.

Oh no. Brandy Jo's heart quickened. She knew Rait could completely roast her with all of the childhood antics they'd been through together. She suddenly recalled the last wedding they'd attended for Rait's best friend. Rait wrote "Help Me!" on the souls of the groom's shoes. When he kneeled at the altar beside his bride to take their vows, the entire congregation burst out laughing.

"I'd like to raise a toast to my sister, Brandy Jo, and to my new brother-in-law, Dane." Rait waited until folks were paired with a glass of champagne, then continued. "There are so many things I could share with you about my little sister, but I'm going to try and let her off easy today. I will share the two things that stand out more than anything else in my mind."

Brandy Jo squeezed Dane's hand under the table for support, and shot Rait a silent plea for mercy.

Rait sent her a reassuring wink in return.

"First off, I'm not sure how many of you are aware that Brandy Jo has been in love with Dane Bronson for fourteen years. That's right folks, since third grade. I know this because I used to have full access to my little sister's diary and knew she hid the key rolled up in her red ball of socks."

Brandy Jo's blush now matched the shade of the said red socks.

"Now, to sum up those diary secrets in a nutshell, there were a few things she wrote over and over, year after year: "I love Dane Bronson, I'm going to marry Dane Bronson, BJD + DB = True love, and my favorite, where she signed her signature as: *Brandy Jo Bronson.* How prophetic is that?"

A ripple of laughter swept through the crowd. Brandy Jo squirmed slightly, hoping he was done.

"As far as Dane goes, my brothers and I often wonder how long our sister will give him before she shows her full colors. Now, I don't mean that in a negative sense. My sister is just a very colorful person as far as vigor and attitude. One might be so bold as to call her a little bit sassy. But somehow, Dane Bronson seems to bring out the best in Brandy Jo. It's a joy to see my sister so happy. We are all curious what it is about Dane that seems to have calmed and tamed Brandy Jo, but whatever it is, God bless you, brother. I wish you both a lifetime of happiness together. If I were to guess what each of your headstones might say at the end of your lives together, my guess would be this:

"Brandy Jo Bronson: Still in Love

Dane Matthew Bronson: I Was Never Bored.

"May God bless you both and grant you many wonderful years together. Cheers!"

Glasses went up and the clink of fine crystal rang clear throughout the rafters. Dane turned to toast his bride. "To you, my sassy bride," he joked.

"I am *not* sassy! For the love of Pete, I don't know where he gets that idea."

Dane smiled. "I'm looking forward to spending a lifetime together to find out. Cheers to you, Mrs. Bronson."

Brandy Jo placed a sweet kiss on Dane's cheek. "Cheers to you, my BCF."

"What's a BCF?"

"Best Cowboy Forever." She intertwined arms with Dane as they shared their first sip of wedded bliss.

Renee Riva is an ACFW award winning author who writes for WaterBrook/Random House, David C. Cook, and Winged Publications. Renee has been writing inspirational, humorous stories ever since she won her first writing contest in the second grade. She began her writing career as a greeting-card verse writer and Young Author's Instructor; teaching writing workshops in schools throughout the Northwest and as far South as Alabama. She loves working with children of all ages, hoping to inspire and spark young imaginations. An animal lover and kid at heart, Renee has published two children's books: Izzy the Lizzy, and Guido's Gondola, as well as a humorous, family, YA-Adult trilogy: Saving Sailor (which took 3rd place in the ACFW Book of the Year 2008), it's sequels are; Taking Tuscany, and Heading Home. She now enjoys writing sweet, clean romances for **Forget Me Not Romances**, and coming-of-age stories with **Take Me Away Books**; both a division of **Winged Publications**.

For more books by Renee Riva Visit
Visit Renee's Book page at Amazon Author Central

Or visit her website at www.reneeriva.com

Renegade Restoration

By Cindy M. Amos

Rebuild
what you believe
about love & life -

Cindy M. Amos

"The day will come when I restore the derelict buildings.
My hand will repair the broken places, restore what is ruined,
and build it back to its grandeur, so the homeland will bear
my name."
Amos 9:11-12

Chapter 1

Rait Danner eased past the welcome sign outside of Silverdale, confident he would arrive fifteen minutes early for his lunch meeting. A long-awaited juncture, his favorite nonprofit endeavor received leadership power today, a move intended to propel it forward. That promised to take the burden off his shoulders as interim director—praise the Lord and pass the salsa.

His community work meant the world to him, and helped balance the rigors of ranch work, which, as of late, seemed to be never-ending. All brawn with no brain input held only slight merit, in his consideration. Add a little heart to a well thought out activity in Silverdale, Colorado, and it probably had Rait Danner's signature written all over it.

He turned on Windrow Lane to take the back way to downtown. His favorite approach, it gave him direct access to the rear entrance of town hall. As his truck rolled down the block, he recalled his father had once attributed his civic-mindedness to his mother's strong society connections. Though his brothers ribbed him about it later, he cherished the cloaked compliment. He would do his best to make her proud of him, should she be looking down from heaven.

With the clock tower in sight, he eased the truck to the curb. Several parking spaces remained open, so he pulled into the front spot, shifted the truck out of gear, and turned off the ignition. Since the first week of May had ended on a friendly note weather-wise, he decided to leave the windows cracked open. Almost an afterthought, he reached across the cab for his hat and popped it onto his head.

Not hearing any approaching traffic, he started to cross the street. A mourning dove flew up from its dust bath at the road's edge. Scenic, the historic part of town stood like a picture postcard of tranquility on the high plains, even if it needed some restoration work.

"Hey—stop that car," a woman shouted.

Rait looked up to find a miniature European-styled sedan rolling his way. A glance through the windshield quickened his pulse. The moving vehicle lacked a driver.

"Please, Cowboy—hit the brakes on that runaway." She ran toward him, frantically waving her arms. At her dainty pace, she had no chance of catching it.

Possessing a split second to get ready, he toed the center line and tried to time his leap for the driver-side window. More like a rodeo move without a horse, he dashed over and lunged fully outstretched. His hat flew off, but he made a successful landing against the upholstery.

Now with something to grip, he climbed down the seat, ducked the steering wheel, and shoved his palm against the brake pedal. Operating blind while buried in the floorboard, he soon gauged a lack of momentum to mean success. That allowed him to borrow a long breath. Not the most comfortable he'd ever been, the head rush began to make his temples throb.

"Lord, help me," a woman lamented. "How near to catastrophe can you get?"

"Uh, pretty close, I reckon," he replied, faintly amused. "From where I sit, distance is a bit tough to estimate."

Two hands clamped on his calves and began to tug him back out. His belt buckle hitched on the door rim, posing his next problem. Unwilling to have his jeans shucked in such a public spectacle, he decided some intervention might be in order. "Whoa up a second. Let me drop into the driver's seat and get turned around here a minute. I'd rather not have my bare assets dangling out the door panel."

"Oh, right. So sorry." She began to push him back inside.

At this rate, he'd have to eat lunch with a crick in his neck. He hand-walked across the console until his legs dropped inside, then he righted his back pockets into the driver's seat. A set of keys hung in the window's opening when he had the wherewithal to look up.

"Can you park it along the curb for me?" The owner knelt down to eye level as if to extract a cooperative answer.

Rait stared into a pair of feminine blue eyes framed by bouncy blonde hair that curved under the stranger's delicate chin. When she followed the question with a hesitant smile, her charm nearly struck him blind. With her perched on the far end of pretty, he'd not been prepared for such sensory onslaught. A sensation that he still remained in motion caused him to stomp the brake pedal involuntarily.

"Please—I forgot to say please. Can you hurry? We're going to block traffic out here." Her quizzical stare perpetuated.

Without a single good reason to deny the request, Rait snatched the keys to get the perfunctory deed underway. He started the toy car and maneuvered hard right, parking several lengths in front of his Silverado. As a safety measure, he manhandled the emergency brake into service before glancing up again.

The woman walked toward the vehicle, her gait unsteady. She tugged at the overly long sleeves of her sheer shirt, balling the cuffs in her fists. "That's so much better. Thank you."

Sighting her approach in the side view mirror, Rait noticed her exterior in a state of complete tatters. His heart skipped a beat. *Had she been dragged by the renegade rambler?* Reactive, he shot out of the door to see to her well being. Almost at arm's length he froze—unsure what to do next. "Are you hurt? Did it drag you?" A trio of slits in her fitted jeans testified to minor damage, but where were the telltale scrapes and blood smears?

Her hands traced the potential injury zone from her hips down her legs. "No, I'm not hurt. I'm fine." She smoothed her hair next as if to prove it.

Stupefied, he gestured to her knees. "But your jeans are shredded. I'd better have a look."

A hand covered her lips, but failed to muffle her laugh. "No, Cowboy. I'm not an accident victim. I simply had a runaway car because I parked on a slight rise. The torn jeans are...a fashion statement." She flexed one of her high-heeled sandals as if to show off the finer points of distressed clothing.

The wind blew something down the road—his hat. Ready to break the tension, he darted for it, dusted it against his thigh, and set it on the crown of his head. A might off-kilter, Rait spread his stance right across the center-lane stripe. Certain he'd won the opening round against the Euro-car, a feeling of incompletion left him two steps short of the victory stand. The bell tower rang in the noon hour, reminding him of his original mission.

"Well, if your sideshow is over now, I've got a meeting to attend. Your keys are in the car. Try not to park on any more slopes—or at least stay downhill of my rig." He tipped his hat toward his truck and left her standing in the middle of Windrow Lane, her mouth agape—just like her fashionable jeans.

~

Serena Thornton ducked through the heavy oak door to enter the designated room at town hall. At first glance, several members of her restoration committee had huddled along one side of the table. An animated tale of lassoing a stray echoed around the room. When the storyteller mentioned a "European horse cart," she caught on that he described the rescue scene which had just transpired. Shame pinned her as the brunt of the joking tale.

Determined not to let gravity and a sticky parking brake cast needless dispersions on her ability to make a professional first impression, she walked to the head of the table and set her master plan binder on the conference room table with a bang. Once all eyes focused on her, she unbuttoned her navy suit jacket and smiled. "Welcome to the High Plains Restoration kick-off meeting. I'm Director Serena Thornton, reporting for duty."

An elderly woman squared around and stumbled down two spaces to regain her seat. "Welcome to you, Miss Thornton. We've been highly expecting your arrival. I'm Marvella Lutes, at your service." She nodded and folded her bent fingers together, which seemed to stop her hands from shaking.

She fixed her attention on the old woman, sensing an opportunity for camaraderie. "Please, call me Serena, Miss Marvella. I'm grateful for your participation on the committee."

"Well, I've been a family friend of the Danner clan for years. When I heard Rait wanted to get this restoration going, I signed right up."

Recognizing the Danner name from her hiring paperwork, Serena acknowledged the confession with a nod. She glanced down the table's length to find a familiar face, the car-rescuing cowboy with a smart-mouthed attitude. Too bad those entrancing blue eyes had to go to waste on such a cocky cowpoke. As introductions went, he deserved the silent treatment. Skipping down to a middle-aged man, she locked gazes to continue her inquiries. "Are you Interim Director Danner?"

The man turned a deep shade of red. "Oh, no, Miss Thornton. I'm Cal Prang, head of municipal services. You know, street sweeping and such. I'm here to coordinate your dumpster needs for the restoration."

"Well, thank you for being here, nonetheless. I wouldn't want to turn downtown into a trash heap, now would I?" To remedy her growing discomfort, she slid an arm out of her jacket and inadvertently shifted part of her flowing over-blouse with it. She took a personal moment to correct the situation, but that jacket had to go.

The cowboy snickered. "Let me save you the trouble, though process of elimination might soon have me pegged. I'm Rait Danner, interim director only out of necessity, as per city statutes. Otherwise, they wouldn't recognize us as an official committee. At your appearance today, I hereby relinquish my temporary status, but I will remain on the general committee, hopefully for the good of all involved." He crossed his arms, emulating a blockade.

Serena picked up copies of her agenda and began to circle the table to hand them out. "In proper acknowledgment, I couldn't have arrived today without Mr. Danner's assistance. First, he's the individual who hired me straight out of Colorado State, so thank you for allowing me to graduate last week before reporting for duty here."

Rait sat forward in his seat and tipped his hat in wordless response. A smug look sharpened his expression. "I may have robbed the cradle a little on that one."

"Considering historical restoration represents my second Bachelor's degree, I don't think my age will be an issue." She placed an agenda in front of him accompanied by an icy stare, meant to direct him away from additional negative comments.

"You're as young as you feel," Marvella quipped. "I look at seventy in my bathroom mirror, but don't let it slow me down one bit."

"Good wisdom," she replied. After slipping one more agenda onto the table for Mr. Prang, she strolled back to the head of the table. "You've heard one version of the second reason I wouldn't be here today without Mr. Danner, but let me add that Edgar's Ridge probably should be translated as 'don't park here' for newcomers to town."

Marvella fanned her face with the agenda. "Oh, dear. Set yourself up for trouble from the outset, did you?"

"The car's previous owner wore out the emergency brake, likely up in the Rockies," she replied. "Anyway, once I'd arrived all the way from Fort Collins this morning, what's a few more hundred feet in the grand scheme of things?"

"A fender bender waiting to happen, that's what." Rait feigned a glance at his agenda.

"So that's my last thank you, because the 'renegade horse' Mr. Danner lassoed was my mini-sedan. I think we can dispense with introductions and get to our business agenda now." She took her seat, eager to conduct the meeting.

The double doors on the side wall flew open. Within seconds, a serving cart appeared stacked with boxed meals. A peppy young woman with a sleek ponytail entered the room and gave a cordial wave. "The Branding Iron Grill is now serving lunch to the High Plains Restoration committee." Stopping short of the table, the pretty young woman singled out Mr. Danner and soon planted a brazen kiss on his clean-shaven cheek.

The sting of losing control shot through Serena's midsection. She counted to ten in hopes of corralling her knee-jerk reaction and tried to keep her eyebrows from arching. No matter that he represented the only person approximately her age in the room, of course he had a girlfriend. Maybe two or three, for all she knew. Working past the nettling sensation, she recalled with some reluctance that it had been intended for a lunch meeting in celebration of her arrival. She crossed her legs under the table. Her tattered jeans scraped her kneecap like burlap.

"That is Rait's second sister Brandy Jo," Marvella whispered. "You can see the Danner resemblance if you compare them side by side. Their mother was a real beauty, rest her soul."

"Boxed fried chicken lunches—all packed full," Brandy Jo announced. She offered a box with a smile, her gaze fixated on Serena. "We're so excited you're finally here. Nobody is more over-the-moon about it than Rait. He had his pick of candidates, but claimed you were a real standout. Maybe he was boasting about the picture on your resume." She chewed her cheek to amplify her conniving wink.

Serena needed to get that clarified in a heartbeat. "No, I didn't post a picture. I hope my credentials and project experience got me the job. Thank you for the down-home welcome—and for delivering our celebration lunch."

Brandy Jo slid a box in front of Marvella. "Hope you'll like Silverdale. It's a sweet little town. In case I don't run into you again before the weekend, we're having a cookout Friday night at the Rockin' D Ranch. Please come out as my guest. Six o'clock or there about." She tucked her thumbs into her silver-studded belt and actually stood still a split second.

"Thanks, Brandy Jo. That might be fun. I'd enjoy meeting the rest of the Danner family. It sounds like your clan enjoys quite the reputation around here. I accept your invitation."

While Marvella opened her lunch box, a choking noise reverberated from down the table. Rait Danner had begun an onslaught on a drumstick, which now sounded like an obstruction in his windpipe. Without looking up, his face turned red.

Brandy Jo wandered over and gave him a hardy slap between the shoulder blades. "He acts starved for attention, but don't let him fool you. Deep down, he's really worth knowing, even if he does give me a hard time about my tomboy ways. See you Friday, Serena." She hooked the cart with one hand and headed for the door.

Rait twisted off the lid on his water bottle and downed a long drink. It took a french fry or two for his color to return to normal. Between bites, he finally looked up at her. "Family members don't know how to keep any secrets." The inference seemed to play with his demeanor as his eyes sparkled with a moment of lightheartedness.

"Thank you for the indirect compliment via you sister, Rait." She found her fork and let the coleslaw tempt her.

"And thank you, God, for this great food," Cal added.

Marvella wiped the fried chicken off her lips. "Amen."

"Please glance over your agendas while we eat," Serena said. "I don't want to miss this delectable chicken trying to talk about interpretive plaques and stain selections for building facades." She swirled her fork in the air and plunged into the fries.

Rait held up a nearly stripped drumstick. "Best in the west," he quipped.

Cal nodded and tore into a chicken wing with enthusiasm.

Not to be left out, Serie stuck her fork into the split breast next and drew out a chunk of moist white meat. Once in her mouth, it didn't disappoint. She caught Rait staring at her in fixed assessment, so she focused on her boxed lunch and celebrated a meal for which she didn't have to pay. Steady income meant no more worries in that department. Still, a frugal lifestyle made one appreciate the finer things in life, like someone else picking up the tab.

Chapter 2

Not opposed to doing his share of the prep, Rait hauled over two empty trash cans a reasonable walking distance from the banquet table. Brandy Jo had been working double time to get the tabletop decorated just right. A string of party lights draped the deck rail, making things look festive. Having his oldest sister Melissa tie the knot so soon after being done with college made him shake his head. Count that a major gain for the Winters' ranch, but at least she would live right down the road.

Brandy Jo had been bubbly with excitement all day. This romance thing triggered something in the womenfolk he didn't understand. Shouldn't Brandy Jo be sad about losing a sister? Her merriment didn't add up. A door slammed by the deck, and he saw his older brother Noah appear, balancing a tray of thick-cut steaks. *Must be time to get the barbeque grill going.*

He beat Noah to the custom-built brick grill and began to clean off the grate with a wire brush. "Hey, those look great. Do you think the coals are ready?"

"We're about to find out. Brandy Jo has me on a tight schedule. She told Melissa and Nathan to get here at six-fifteen, which means the grillmaster has to get cranking. Are you done with the cleanup?"

"Just finishing. Say, you'll get to meet our new restoration director this evening. Brandy Jo couldn't help but invite Serena, thinking she was new in town and therefore lonely." He leaned a bit closer. "In truth, she isn't hard to look at, so maybe you two will hit it off."

"Don't run your cheap fix-up game by me, little brother." Noah picked up the first steak with a long set of tongs and maneuvered it onto the grill. The meat sizzled on contact. "Since she came to town at your specific request, that makes her all yours."

Rait wiped across his lip with the back of his hand, worried there might be an ounce of truth in that rendering. Maybe if he stayed busy with hosting duties, he wouldn't be burdened with keeping up small talk with his new director. Outside of restoration work, they probably had little in common anyway. In a pinch, he could hook his younger brother Wyatt up with her and duck out of sight. That guy had turned into a first-class flirt, to hear Brandy Jo tell it.

The door slammed again. Brandy Jo led Wyatt down the table's length, each carrying a big bowl of tossed salad covered with plastic wrap. Both dear to him, he couldn't imagine not having them around the ranch. Losing Melissa was more than enough to contend with—which would happen in short order.

The grill sizzled with the addition of several more steaks. Rait patted Noah's shoulder and headed onto the deck to check out the seating arrangements. The placemats of their guests of honor were crowned by swags of meadow flowers, sure to turn his oldest sister sentimental. How many times had the girls wiled away the afternoon roaming the pastures for a collection just like this? Maybe they'd been dreaming their teenage angst away, and now they stood at the cusp of sending Melissa down the aisle of holy matrimony. He shook his head to think more logically. "Hey, B-Jo, can I do anything up here?"

Wyatt shouldered the screen door. "Let me go get dad to come out. He's missing all the set-up fun, but he claims he can't find his new hat."

Brandy Jo straightened like she was straining to hear. "Rait, you greet the guests as they arrive, will you? I have to get the condiments and salad dressing in place next."

"I reckon you're sure missing Kylee's assistance tonight, since Melissa is the guest of honor. Another set of female helping hands would be handy right now."

Footsteps sounded on the deck steps. "Count me in as family then," a sweet-toned female voice offered.

Rait glanced up to see Serena standing there, the sun playing off her blonde hair. The breeze tickled the uneven hemline of her sundress, making it sway in a rippling rhythm. Lace-up sandals drew his attention to her shapely legs. A coral-colored feast, he forced his gaze away to check on Noah's progress at the grill.

Brandy Jo shifted to their guest and gave her a hug. "Serena, thank you for coming out tonight. This is a special celebration, because our oldest sister Melissa is getting married later this month. We're surprising her with this cookout tonight."

She raised a hand to her throat. "Oh, should I have brought a gift?"

"No, certainly not," Rait replied. "The gathering is the gift. We value time spent together over material clutter. Tonight, we'll all be here except for the youngest, Kylee, who felt compelled to hit the rodeo circuit right after her final exams, much to dad's consternation. Come down to the grill and let me introduce you to our senior member." He hooked a smile into his cheek, having gaffed Noah before he could even meet Serena. Not that he had to sabotage anything, but he certainly held no obligation to make it easy.

"Hey, Noah, here's Serena Thornton, the new restoration director I mentioned earlier." Rait gestured to the flowing figure at his side and waited for his brother's reaction.

The grill-master scanned her for a moment, but when a spatter drew him back to the open pit, he had to divide his attention. "Welcome to the Rockin' D, Serena. Thanks for being a part of this special occasion. Our family is expanding by a married-in member, who happens to be my best friend since grade school." He gestured with the tongs between adjustments.

She leaned in to take a whiff of grilling beefsteak. "Mmm, it smells wonderful next to the grill. I think the party-goers might congregate down here, if given the chance."

Rait didn't want to give Noah any advantage. "I think Brandy Jo prefers us up on the deck where she hung the lantern lights and all. You know how I like my steak, brother, so don't overdo it on my account."

"Why would I start now, Rait? Everything you touch turns out undercooked." He snickered and shook his head. "Serena, how do you prefer your steak cooked?"

Her gaze shifted between them, a scanning evaluation. "I like my beef the far side of medium, but not by much. Too much pink makes my stomach flip."

Noah chuckled and moved a thinner steak to the perimeter of the fire. "Sure, not everyone has to play caveman with their food allotment." He shot Rait a corrective glance and went about his business.

"Yoo-hoo," a woman called from the gate. "Parents of the groom are now arriving."

Rait took Serena's elbow and guided her back toward the deck. "This is Nathan's parents. The Winters operate the next spread over, so we've known them all our lives. Nate and Noah are buddies, which is why he's taking this hitch-up a whole lot better than me." At that disclosure, he pasted on a smile for the moment and made the requisite introductions.

When Wyatt signaled him by the kitchen door, he pulled away and let the newcomer hold her own. "What's up, kid brother. Can't get your lasso around the steak sauce?"

Wyatt winced. "Dad's being a pain. He won't come out of his room. The party starts in five minutes. Can you use some leverage on him?"

"Yeah, let me work on him." He headed down the familiar hall, original to the sprawling ranch house. Two-bedroom wings had been added as the family grew, giving the sons a separate wing from the daughters. He chuckled, figuring that had held the peace under one roof on many occasions. Turning into the master suite, he found his father planted in a chair, staring at a photograph of his mother. "Hey, Dad. You're not in here raining on Brandy Jo's party for Melissa, are you? We don't want to risk getting B-Jo foot-stomping mad."

He returned the photo to its spot on the nightstand. "No, we'd better not go down that trail. I just needed a moment. Feels like I'm starting to lose control of my herd, that's all."

"You and me both. I've always looked up to Nate Winters, so I don't mind gaining a brother-in-law in this case."

"Melissa won't be around much anymore, I reckon. That hits a tender spot for me." He stood and took a few steps toward the door, looking like a kicked puppy.

"What did Mamma always say? 'We're raising them to be independent.' Funny that Melissa's first step toward freedom is matrimony. I don't get that at all, but I respect her right to choose it."

His father faced him, man to man. A calloused hand clamped his shoulder. "When the time is right, you'll recognize marriage for the blessing God intended it to be. Until that day, it might behoove you to not play devil's advocate so convincingly." Mirth showed in his eyes as the shoulder grip turned into a pat on the back. "Let's get out there and whoop it up, Colorado-style. That'll keep two of your sisters happy at the same time."

"Noah's pretty happy, dominating the barbeque pit. And when Wyatt sees you exit with me, he'll be happy, too. Well, as content as B-Jo will let him be." Rait nodded to the hallway, returning to the party action with his father's approving hand riding his shoulder. They arrived at the deck door to find several more guests had come in, Marvella the loudest and liveliest of all.

"Who's the pretty blonde?" Dad asked.

"My new restoration director," he replied with a trace of lament in his tone.

His father raised one eyebrow at him and banged out of the door to join the festivities.

Rait spied the old man's hat right on the peg where it should be. He grabbed it and followed his father out into the celebration, just like he'd trailed him all his life on the ranch. Tonight seemed to hold a higher risk, one that a dab of saddle soap or twist of baling wire couldn't fix. No, he had to put on his affable mingling airs, the ones he used in town to get the outcome he wanted.

The trouble was, he didn't know what he wanted—besides the steak. Good beef covered a multitude of sins, and tonight he'd likely need the main course to live up to its reputation. When Serena threw her head back to laugh at some wisecrack Wyatt had made, Rait mentally added a heaping spoonful of potato salad to the penance offering.

"Smile, Rait," Brandy Jo said under her breath as she walked by. "Remember, this is a happy occasion. Melissa and Nate are due in five minutes."

He flashed a smile he didn't mean and bypassed his incorrigible younger brother. Once he'd tamped the white hat in place on the crown of his father's head, he redirected to converse with the Winters. When Marvella glanced up from chit-chatting with Noah, he tossed her a wave.

Wrought with both the familiar and unfamiliar, the evening began to play tug-of-war with his contentment. Not fond of such unlevel terrain, it left him flatfooted and lightheaded all at the same time. Altitude sickness would have been a relief, as this imbalance had no change in elevation attached. Set against the light of late afternoon, the mountain ridge on the western horizon appeared to give a hazy smoke signal of warning. He would heed that cautious landscape omen, if he had any sense at all.

~

No wonder everyone in town thinks so highly of the Danner family. Serena glanced up the table at the soon-to-be-newlyweds, their affection obvious. The father of the bride had swapped stories with the father of the groom until hunger overrode the need to entertain. By the taste of things, the engagement dinner was a huge success. She leaned in to better transfer her message. "Noah, this steak is simply the best. Great job at getting my custom order accomplished to perfection." She hoisted a triangular chunk on her fork to demonstrate her appreciation.

"Thank you kindly," he replied. "I do most of the grilling, but we're set to lose our main cook with Melissa headed out."

She looked directly across the table at Rait, who seemed subdued. "Maybe you can get your middle brother on chef duty." She raised a brow and ate the succulent steak.

Noah chortled. "Rait isn't half bad on the ranch, but he sure doesn't know his way around the kitchen. He can't cook anything that has more than two ingredients."

"Peanut butter and jelly," Rait replied with a clap of his hands.

"There's never been a more classic combination. Plus, it has kept many a neglected soul alive."

Imagining the slapped-together concoction, Serena had no desire to venture into his "neglected soul" comment, so she opted for higher ground. "Melissa looks euphoric over her pending wedding."

Brandy Jo slid back into her seat. "There's plenty of that kind of happiness to go around," she whispered in a tone laced with intrigue.

Serena wanted to fish for more information on that leading comment, so she leaned close enough to touch shoulders with her bubbly hostess. "Do you have an iron heating up in that fire, Brandy Jo? You know—the romance department?"

She picked up a piece of Texas toast and hid her lips behind it. "I have an old school chum by the name of Dane Bronson who holds my heart. He traded in his boyish stutter for an entrancing baritone voice, especially when he calls my name. He makes me melt like butter."

"Are the wedding bells going to ring a second time for the Danner clan?" The thought of it made her stomach flutter for some unexplainable reason.

Brandy Jo bit the tip off the toast, shook her head no, and then gave her a wink. After taking a drink of lemonade, she shifted closer again. "Time will tell. Now that Melissa has broken the ice, the damage to the family unit is done. I think Dad feels it, that sense of no turning back. We all have lives to lead as adults. He knows that."

"Surely his sons might stay on the ranch to help keep things running."

Brandy Jo shrugged her bony shoulders. "Probably Noah will. I can't say about Rait and Wyatt. Rait's devoted to his involvements in town, and Wyatt has some wanderlust to rid from his spirit twixt now and settling down. Dad will have to hire help, if they should leave."

Serena sorted through the inference. One area of the disclosure deserved a bit more probing. She raised her napkin and drew out wiping her mouth. "Is part of Rait's devotion to town a special lady friend living there? You'd think with those soulful blue eyes, he'd be targeted for that kind of attention. Some women aren't that...discrete."

"Right you are about that one. Several gals at church bat their eyelashes at Rait, but he seems oblivious. Dad often says that love takes its time. For Dane and me, it's roaring like a freight train rolling down the tracks."

Satisfied that she'd cleared the air regarding Rait's availability, she focused on his enigmatic middle sister. "Remember what the Apostle Paul said. 'It is better to marry than to burn.' If that train rolling down the tracks catches on fire, you might heed the warning."

Brandy Jo caught the snickers at that point. To her credit, she tried to bury them in her napkin. She glanced over at her with a knowing look.

Rait cleared his throat, a hand on his glass. "Just what are you two whispering about over there? Maybe the rest of us would like to know." His eyes widened for emphasis.

Brandy Jo's expression grew anxious, perhaps in fear of immediate betrayal.

"Oh, just being impetuous about not waiting our turn," Serena replied.

Rait cocked his head to the side. "Your turn for what?"

When all three of the Danner brothers focused on her, Serena had a rare moment to compare and contrast the options. Wyatt held a youthful dash of good looks, while Noah was more staid in his rugged handsomeness. But Rait's dark hair framed his flashing blue eyes in a breath-stealing combination that arrested her attention. Were those the eyes of a brother-in-law she might regard platonically across the Danner family dinner table years from now? The doubt-filled answer leaked down her veins like ice water.

"Listen, everyone," Melissa called from her seat of honor. "I've just requested our post-dinner activity at Dad's timely suggestion. I'd like to ride horses over to the south gate where we share a fence with the Winters' ranch, symbolic of my passage to the other side. All are welcome to ride along. Let's leave out in ten minutes to conserve daylight."

Serena pulled the hem of her high-low dress past her knees, wondering how she'd manage the intricacies of mounting a horse. Her Bohemian bent would be the shame of her yet. She caught the smirk on Rait's face and froze under his intense inspection.

Brandy Jo leaned closer. "You can borrow my old boots, no worries."

"But my dress—I'll look like a bawdy saloon gal up in the saddle."

"You've got great legs," Brandy Jo replied. "So let the cowboys stare. You don't go fishing without a worm on your hook, do you?" With that, she shoved away from the table and disappeared inside.

Unsettled by that particular analogy, she toyed with the last bite of potato salad. Riding a horse struck her akin to saddling a smoothie shaker after such a heavy meal. No one else seemed to be having any qualms about it.

Rait stood and lifted his cleared plate. "Are you thinking to go, Serena?" His stare landed more direct than his question.

"Yes, it sounds like an adventure I wouldn't want to miss. Brandy Jo is lending me a pair of her old boots. That should keep the pasture grasses from scratching my legs, don't you think?"

He exchanged looks with his older brother as a crooked smile slid onto his face. "I don't know about that, but you're welcome to ride along. I'll saddle a gentle mare for you, if you trust my judgment."

Marvella laughed from midway down the table. "Of course Serena trusts your judgment, Rait, or she wouldn't be sitting here eating steak with the finest men in the county. Now, get on with the saddling job, pray tell, so the gate posse can ride out."

Noah stood beside Rait. "I'll get your horse saddled, Melissa."

"No, let Nate do it for me instead," she replied. "That should symbolize something between a bride and groom."

"Sounds like servitude," Rait teased under his breath.

Serena gasped at his irreverent treatment of the selfless bond represented by marriage. Whether blue-eyed or black, the man's attitude had a long way to go to reach worthy marrying material. She shoved away from the table, needing some distance from the Danner men and needing it quick. Trailing into the kitchen, she called for Brandy Jo and soon heard footsteps on the landing above.

"Come on up," Brandy Jo replied. "You can take off your sandals up here and try the boots. My brothers are forbidden to enter this hallowed hall."

"Good, as I could use a refuge." She ran up the stairs, mindful of the ten-minute warning. Trying not to dwell on the potential for further embarrassment, she soaked in the beauty of the solid oak planking and blew out a laden breath.

~

Rait glanced at his trek-mate and sensed her tenseness. "Hey, relax up there. You'll be fine. I'm going to tie a knot in this excess hem, as the fabric is tickling Lady's withers. See how she's flinching?" He gestured to the horse's trembling hind quarter to authenticate the claim.

Once Serena nodded, he took a handful of soft cotton fabric and wound it into a half-hitch. Working past the tactile pleasure, he took in an eyeful of toned calf muscle before stepping back toward his mount. "Those beat-up boots actually look good on you. Maybe you should dress western more often."

"I wouldn't want to appear predictable." She adjusted her CSU baseball cap and took the reins in her hands. Two dimples appeared above her smug smile.

"You won't need to steer much, if you ride beside me. Lady will fall in step with Fleet, and let him set the pace. Would that suit you?" He looked up to gauge her receptivity, but only got a clouded reaction to sort through. Deciding to mount, he'd let it work out one way or the other.

She didn't have to stay strapped to him, if another rider seemed more promising.

Ten minutes into the ride, she broke the truce of silence. "It's so beautiful here."

Her admission stirred a heartstring in his chest. Unsure what kind of validation the remark needed, he tipped his hat and reined Fleet a step closer. The endless meadow offered its peace, a territory he now inhabited alongside an eye-catching woman. Despite its odd unfamiliarity, he drew nearer to his riding companion, unable to counter the attraction.

Chapter 3

It had taken Serena two weeks to get the stain samples sent over from Colorado Springs. She'd spent the time getting more familiar with the street front of historic buildings flanking both sides of Main Street, fourteen structures in all. With keys to all the buildings, she had worked like a housemaid sweeping and scrubbing the dust and dirt off the authentic wood surfaces. Though she'd made a cursory list of improvements to be made to interior décor, the building facades would lead the restoration efforts.

Given that the town's Old Settlers' Day celebration lurked only two months away in mid-July, the committee had agreed to focus on the street appeal of the buildings in last week's meeting. Rait had remained in town to begin some of the carpentry repair work, aided by Cole Davis, a sheriff's deputy who volunteered when he could. At least the wheels of progress had begun to roll during her first month on the job.

She stuck the foam brush into the first small container and stroked stain across the end of her sample board. The color turned out dark, almost walnut brown. Maybe it would dry lighter. Since the high-end line of recommended stains only contained eight hues, they would have to repeat the use of several—which she'd let the committee decide. After completing the square, she tried to paint the brush dry and then stuck it into a cup of mineral spirits.

Rait Danner popped to mind as she drew a new brush from the multi-pack and selected the next stain. As her most devoted committee member, he seemed enigmatic to her. Maybe that stemmed from his deep-set engagement in the restoration work, contrasting with his skim-the-surface non-interest in her. The more she considered getting to know him better, the less she thought of the idea. The second stain turned out to be an ochre color, like mustard that had withered on a forgotten board, faded by the sun. The old jail might look good in that color.

She ditched the brush into the cup to let it soak and opened the next stain option. The first brush stroke unleashed a magical hue resembling olive green, but with gray-tones to it. The apothecary might look best in that hue, a point she would surely suggest. She might need Marvella to weigh in on her sample board this afternoon when she closed her shop. Meaning to check out her Junktique Shop, this would be her chance. She spread the olive stain into its sample block and soaked the brush.

With the wipe of her hands, she reached for her phone and sent Marvella the text requesting a meet-up at closing time. After sending it, she noticed the lateness of the morning. If only the delivery had come earlier, she'd have the sample board finished by now. She could catch up by working through lunch, her only apparent option. Two more stains, an off-black and a flat gray, soon finished out the left half of the board.

The door to her workspace rattled open. When she turned to look at her visitor, there stood Rait with a bag in his hand. In a final sweep, she finished off the gray sample and dunked the brush.

He stepped into the cluttered room. "Hey, I thought you might be in the workshop today."

She wiped a smear of stain off her fingers. "Yeah, the set of exterior stains came in. I'm creating a sample board for the committee's consideration. I sent a text message to Marvella, requesting a meeting at her place around five o'clock." She shrugged her shoulders and threw the paint rag across the sawhorse holding up her sample board.

Rait stepped past her and fixed his gaze on the half-painted plank. "Man, that yellow is some ugly stuff. Who'd paint anything to make it look like a shellacking of cod liver oil?"

"Repulsion has its place. I was thinking maybe it would be best suited for the jailhouse. You know, a subliminal avoidance hue for its façade."

He glanced up at her like she'd spoken Greek. A furrow between his eyebrows deepened. "I planned to be back at the ranch by four, so we might need to hurry up on the approval meeting."

Her stomach betrayed her with a rumble. "Do I smell onions?"

His expression eased. "Brandy Jo found me on Main Street and delivered three hamburgers, thinking I'd have a crew. Cole got called out for a stranding on the highway, so I walked over to share this windfall with you."

"If we could get the rest of this display finished, we could head over to Marvella's for lunch. Are you up for a bit of painting?" She held up the next miniature can of stain.

Rait placed the bag on the shop counter, took the stain, and shook it.

"Let me get you a clean brush." She picked one and scraped the mineral spirits out, and then wiped in across the rag to clear away any residue.

"This is a good way to compare all the options. Thank you for thinking of it. Stain is definitely the way to go, but I had no idea they made so many color choices." After knocking back the brim of his hat, he keyed the can open and motioned for the brush.

She handed it to him with a fleeting smile. "If you don't mind, I'll work beside you to hasten the process. Stop at the pencil line, and I'll work from the other side." Her phone pinged, so she dried her hands to examine the message. "Marvella says earlier is better for her. What should I tell her?"

"How about 'see you in twenty minutes?' We'll be done by then. I'll drive us over in my truck. If the stain isn't set, it won't matter since it's riding back in the bed."

"Oh, good. I didn't think about that. Not that my upholstery doesn't have a blemish or two already." She opened a can and readied her paint brush. By the time she settled opposite Rait, she could hear him chuckling over her last remark. "You don't like my car?"

"I'm not fond of Euro-anything. There's plenty of good American stock to choose from."

"My mother gave me that car when I returned to college. One day, I'll get to pick my own style...maybe a small SUV so I can haul stuff in back."

He took a stroke and laid out a tobacco brown color in his square.

"Umm, that's a good hue to put the brown back into the age-bleached wood. What's the tallest façade we have in the historic block?"

"Guess it would be the old post office. Being a federal building, they wanted it to stand out. There's no second story, though. The tall façade is false."

She dabbed a bit of her stain, which turned out to be mule brown. "I noticed you're the tallest one in your family, so I guess that makes you stand out like the post office." She swept the stain over toward his brush, looking up when he did.

His tight lips finally hooked up at the corners. "Don't mention that in front of Noah. He's a might sensitive to that particular subject. I tease him that he stunted his own growth drinking all those sodas in high school. Wyatt, on the other hand, thinks he's still growing and dreams of passing me. I keep quiet and let him think he can best six foot-two."

"I'm only five foot-nine, which is tall for a Thornton. I have two younger sisters, but they're short like my mother."

Rait nodded and scraped the excess stain from his brush.

"Soak it in the cup there, and switch out for another one. Here's the rag to wipe it dry." She tossed the torn cotton rag, and it landed in his vicinity.

Rait took the cloth and wiped the sample board with it, changing out the contact surface with each square. "This really helps me see the project as a whole, since the buildings adjoin one another. I think this will give the historic district the exact type of distinction we intended." A genuine look of appreciation followed the comment.

"Good. I'll take that as validation that you're glad you hired me," she teased.

He looked away, fetching the next can of stain. After cleaning a brush on the rag, he opened it and painted a swath across the next square. His brush tip pointed skyward as he paused to examine the hue. "Lord above. Brandy Jo would love this one."

She glanced over to see an enjoyable tint of turquoise with brown undertones. "That might do justice for the mercantile. Let's leave ourselves open to the possibilities. There's a right stain for every building." This time, when their gazes met, he seemed less apprehensive, maybe even downright cordial. She flipped him a smile and worked as fast as her fingers could go to get the last stain onto the sample board. A dampened russet red, it resembled a rusted nail.

"Let's leave these brushes in soak and get over to Marvella's place. She can reheat those burgers, and we'll get the match-up assessment underway. Got your list of buildings?" He looked at her, his gaze holding a question.

She finished out the red square, perplexed as to what building might wear such a bawdy color. If it bordered on outlandish, maybe Marvella would have some insight. She dunked the brush into the cup and wiped her sticky fingers on the cloth. "Yes, I have the building list in my pocket." She tapped her shoulder near the pocket.

Rait glanced at the inside-out seams anchoring her sleeves and shook his head. "Most folks would wear that shirt the other way around."

"Well, I'm not most folks." She attempted to hoist the sample board, but he wrestled it from her in short order.

"Grab the bag of burgers, will you? And then you can get the shop door open for me."

Serena saw the grease-soaked paper bag and thought to carry it with both hands. She flicked off the shop light and shouldered into the door. "After you, Mr. Danner."

He turned the plank lengthwise and passed through the threshold, easing past her with a sideways glance.

"I hope you like the clutter of old junk," she teased.

"Not in the least," he replied, dipping his hat brim to counter the midday sun.

Serena pulled the outside door closed with a snicker. Marvella seemed to manage the favor of the Danner clan, despite being a purveyor of junk. That hinted of redeeming qualities that lurked beneath the surface. She had a few character qualities that might count in that department. If the opportunity availed itself, she wouldn't hesitate to demonstrate them. As Rait loaded the sample board, she slipped into the cab, determined to be more than an inside-out complication.

~

Rait backhanded a fallen stack of empty egg cartons, repulsed by the tick-tacky mess. Marvella, bless her heart, would let the whole thing cave in on her, she piled junk so high. "Let's get it up here where everyone can see. Thanks for dropping by, Cal. You can vote if you want. Now, think about the storefronts downtown, and how these stains might spruce up the historic block. Maybe we can start with what we like."

"Oh, my," Marvella replied. She scanned the board and seemed perplexed.

"Man, I hate that mustard color," Cal said. "That would be the first to drop out of contention for me."

He offered an agreeable nod, but held his peace. The committee needed to speak.

Serena stepped closer. "Still, look at it in light of another color being adjacent to it. The turquoise, for instance. It steps down the hue change, but still uses the width of the color wheel."

"I think the turquoise is my favorite," Marvella replied. "Let's consider having two buildings in that color. Can we do that?"

"We'll have to double up, if this is all our choices." Rait looked at his new director for a confirmation.

"Yes, this is the complete restoration line for aging wood structures. The stain contains conditioning oils to treat weather-damaged wood. It comes highly recommended, but only has eight shades. We have fourteen buildings to cover, so we'll repeat stains on separate sides of the street. That should keep the overall effect alternating from building to building."

"Preservation with enhancement," Rait said. "I like this approach, as opposed to making everything the same. Still, I don't want it to come off like some avant-garde interpretation of the Old West. Flashy is phony."

Serena put a hand on her hip. "Fresh doesn't have to be phony. We can avoid tones that clash by placing a more neutral tint between them, like the gray here."

Marvella laid her broad palm across the ochre stain. "I'm afraid I'm siding with the men against the mustard yellow. I don't think storefronts used to be painted yellow. If we have to double up, I vote we use the black fewer times, as opposed to gray or brown."

"But avoid the brown next to another brown," Cal added. "Keep the color mix alternating from bright to neutral. And drop the mustard. That's all the opinion I have." He shrugged his shoulders and left the shop.

Marvella looked up, her eyes twinkling. "Good, now we can eat. I have a bag of chips and some lemonade. Let me reheat the burgers, and we're all set. Be back in a flash."

Serena began to wander down the nearest aisle, past a display of lacy note cards. "Wow, this place is interesting."

Rait followed a step or two back, his hands crammed into his jeans pockets. "Yeah, if you thrive on sensory overload. Guess that makes me a simple man, because I can hardly take it."

She turned back toward him. "No, you're not that simple, Rait. In fact, I find you incredibly complex. Now, I know yet one more thing about you—that you disdain the color of mustard—but likely not the taste of it." She sniffed at the bar of wrapped soap in her hands and put it back on the shelf.

Her evaluation struck a pleasant note. At least she had a list going of his attributes. Maybe lack of cooperation shouldn't lead the list. "My mother loved it here in Marvella's shop. She would pretend to come in looking for a gift, and spend half the morning helping her restock and dust the place. Mom considered Marvella the great aunt she never had."

Serena brushed some dust off the price labels along the edge of the shelf. "I bet the sentiment worked both ways. It's thoughtful of you to keep the ties alive, Rait. I'm sure Marvella sees traces of your mother when she looks at you."

That recognition touched a tender spot, though he tried to squint and shuck it off. A rustle up the adjoining aisle alleviated the need to respond. He caught a whiff of onions and stepped back toward the front counter. More than the shelves held a jumble, as his insides fell into imbalance. Maybe he just needed to eat, and Brandy Jo's burgers were the tonic he craved. He had to stave off the effect of Serena's comments. Or maybe it was her presence here, mixing old and new in an amalgamation of unsettling proportion.

A bag of barbeque potato chips appeared on the counter. "Thank you God, for this sustaining food," Marvella said, "and bless our town restoration, amen."

Rait opened the bag and handed their hostess the first burger. "Branding Iron Grill's known for keeping cowboys happy across the generations."

"I've not stepped a foot inside yet," Serena replied, holding out her hand for a burger.

Marvella sucked in a gasp. "Rait, tell me that isn't so. We have only one restaurant in town, and you haven't treated Serena to a meal there yet? Where are your good manners hiding?"

Caught short, he had to play the oblivious card. "Shoot, Marvella. By dinnertime, I'm usually back at the ranch. Serena lives in town and could drop by the restaurant any day, acting on a whim. I'm not shadowing her involvements twenty-four seven."

Serena peeled the wax paper from around her burger, showing amusement at his up-against-the-wall predicament.

Marvella scrunched up her brow. "While I'm right here in front of you, go ahead and ask her out for dinner. That'll help me get over my frustration with you, Rait Danner."

Serena turned to face him and lowered her burger. A most pleasant smile swept her face. A few seconds ticked by, heightening the anticipation.

He laid his burger on the chip bag. "The Branding Iron Grill has a special menu on Saturday nights. Plus, my sister is off on weekends, so she wouldn't be there to meddle. Would you like to go to dinner with me Saturday night?"

In his peripheral vision, he saw Marvella press her hands together as if praying. Well, if this had any chance of working out, the Good Lord would have to take over in a mighty way. For the moment, eternity stretched before them.

"Thank you, Rait. That sounds really nice. What time would you like to pick me up?" She locked gazes with him a hesitation of a second, but it seemed genuine.

A wave of doubt crashed over him, short-circuiting his good senses. Too deep to retract, he squared his feet to broaden his stance. "I think straight up six o'clock will do. No need to rush into things, after all. Are you at the Fairview Apartments?"

"Yes, number forty-three. Great, I'll look forward to it." Serena smiled before biting into her lunch.

"So will he, darlin'. He's just too tongue-tied to admit it." Marvella gestured for removal of his hamburger.

Rait took his lunch in hand and dropped deep into the shop to collect his thoughts. He'd keep the perfunctory dinner date to get Marvella off his case. With any luck, Serena wouldn't show up in some clown outfit, looking like something the bull had dragged into the arena.

When he glanced up, he'd stopped in the Christmas area, an angel staring at him dead in the face. "What part of heaven did you fall out of, little cherub?" He thumped her with a finger, and a tiny bell rang beneath her full skirt. The sound of laughter echoed from the front as he took the last bite of his hamburger. The grilled taste lingered, while the empty feeling inside backed off a considerable bit. Maybe a touch of clutter wasn't so bad now and then.

~

Serena checked the clock as she fastened the slender gold chain around her neck. Each time she'd seen Rait later in the week, she had expected a retraction on the dinner date. The mirror reflected her only solid colored dress, a demure navy knit that wrapped gathers against her left hip, evidence that he hadn't declined. Call it the first date that wasn't one, since Marvella had forced the whole thing. Still, it might be nice to look into his blue eyes across the table without other distractions and pretend romantic involvement could be possible.

A rap on the front door sent her stomach tumbling off a ledge. She bent to tuck the low-heeled slings on her feet and hurried to the door. After straightening her hair one last time, she threw the deadbolt lock and pulled the door open.

Rait stood in the doorway, still as a statue. Wearing a royal blue windowpane checked shirt, his eyes shone like the ocean on a sunny day. A muscle in his jaw flinched, which led to a trace of a smile. "I might be a minute or two early."

Her palm felt slick against the door knob, so she released it. "No, that's fine. I'm ready to go. I hope you didn't have any trouble finding the apartment."

"No trouble," he replied, his tone smooth like supple leather. He extended his hand to lead her out and the smile grew.

"Wait. Let me grab the key." She dashed to the kitchen bar and chose the key ring, but left her phone and purse behind. Joining him on the landing, she made quick work of locking up.

Rait held his ground. "You look like an extravagant accessory against my plain old ordinary, if you don't mind my saying so."

"I tried to tone it down with navy tonight. You can let me know if I managed that or not."

He reached for her shoulder and directed her toward his truck. Once he tucked her into the passenger seat, he paused. "I never had to live under a hog-tied rainbow before."

Serena adjusted her hem while he crossed and got into the driver's seat. She fully understood his reference. For smooth sailing, her flamboyant flair would have to take the night off. A small price to pay, she decided to be totally upfront about it. She waited until he settled into his seat and quelled the seatbelt's warning. "In truth, I bought this for a funeral dress. I somehow knew it would come in handy."

He propped his arm above the seat back and began to reverse from the parking spot. Once he had the truck wheeled around, he shifted gears but held his foot on the brake. "Guess that makes me the dead man." At the admission, he gave a hearty laugh and glanced sideways at her, his eyes twinkling slits of enjoyment.

Thank God for solid colors. The evening lost its clumsy dread as they drove toward the heart of Silverdale, a shimmering color by name and destiny. Tonight it would be their blend, a new shade she'd never experienced. After a week of matching stain tints to historic buildings, she looked forward to the distinct palette of possibilities that might be birthed.

Chapter 4

After replacing some rotted trim around the front plate glass window, Rait had the apothecary building nearly stained. In the process, he'd turned into an olive pickle spear, with stain dripped up his forearms. The drugstore's lettering would need a touch-up, but the façade held new charisma with the makeover. Wonder why they hadn't thought of this before?

He tucked his brush into his painting pail and wiped the grit from his face. For late May, they had made all kinds of progress. Assigning the refurbishment of built-in display cabinets to several craftsmen in town had been a stroke of genius, one he'd credit to Serena if given a private moment to do so. The trouble was, they never seemed to enjoy any privacy. Even their dinner out two weekends past had been a re-acquaintance promenade with half the folks in town.

Melissa's wedding last weekend left him straddling an awkward line. Truth be told, he dragged his feet so long thinking whether to invite Serena or not, the deed was left undone. Brandy Jo had brought that up a time or two at the reception, which only added more vinegar to his sour mood. Only B-Jo's little dancing jig at having caught the bridal bouquet lent him any merriment at all. Most of the time, he'd sat moping between Noah and Wyatt, a real gentleman's club of marital bystanders.

Movement across the street caught his attention. Serena had unloaded something heavy from her trunk, which clattered against the elevated walkway in front of the old saloon. Ready for a break, he trotted across the street to get a closer look. "Hey, what do you have there?"

She brushed her hair from her eyes. "Hi, Rait. Marvella found these stuck under a table in the rear of her shop. Do you think they could be original to the saloon?"

He examined the arch-topped louvered panel. "A batwing door? Wow, I'd never thought about that before. Do you have both sides, by any chance?"

Her face lit up like a kid being offered a candy bar. "Yep, the opposite panel is lying in the bottom of my trunk. If you could help me hold them up, we could determine if they might have fit the door opening. If not, they're likely not original to Silverdale Saloon."

"Since I never like an unsolved mystery, let's take a look right now, okay?" He hefted the remaining door from her trunk and walked it over to the door facing. "You hold the right side in place, and let's see if they meet up."

She shoved the panel with her foot and then braced it against the door frame. "Here we go, for a quick comparison. These babies are on the heavy side for me." She hoisted it with a grunt and held it at the same height his panel stood.

"Well, now. Look at that," he remarked with a whistle. "I think we might be looking at authentic push-open doors. Go ahead and ease yours down." He watched her kneel gracefully while guiding it to the porch planking. "Would you want these up for the Old Settlers' Days celebration? They might be a ticklish sight for sore eyes."

She dusted off her palms, her answer beaming from her face. "Sure. I'll refinish the louvers, if you'll research getting the hinged mounting rigged up. I'd love for these to swing to and fro when the kids venture inside for sarsaparilla libations during the event."

"That sounds perfect. Tell you what, if we can get someone to repaint the lettering on each building, I guarantee this would make one fine photo spot for the event. You could add that to your list of activities—authentic Old West dioramas." He let the door panel slide down his jeans until it rested against the toe of his boot.

"That's a great idea, even if it comes from a cowboy looking more like a chameleon."

He gave her a questioning glance while guiding the door panel flat.

"Your hands have turned green—as if touching the building caused your coloration to change. The apothecary looks amazing from here. You do quick work."

"Thanks. Guess I was so busy keeping drips off the porch planking, I sacrificed myself in the process. I have a small section on the far corner to knock out, and then I'm done. Let me haul that batwing door over to the workshop for you in my truck."

"That would be great. Plan to stay for lunch. I made an extra rolled turkey sandwich, in case I had a loyal volunteer to work with this afternoon." She smiled and tucked her hands into her back pockets.

He studied the delicate lace trimming her T-shirt, which she wore right-side out and normal. Maybe the way she dressed didn't bother him so much, after all. Plus, when she dazzled him like that with an unprovoked smile, who noticed her clothes anyway? "I'll be over there in fifteen minutes, so don't start without me. I'll finish the corner, and then dry my brush out on any bare cracks I find in the coverage. You would not believe how thirsty these old wood planks are to receive this weatherproof coating."

Her smile turned coy while mischief played across her face. "Oh, I might believe it. I think I recognize drought conditions when I witness them. Some things are plenty overdue around here. Maybe that's why I came to town." With a hitch of her brow, she turned and headed down Main Street toward the restoration workshop.

Forcing his focus elsewhere, Rait turned to the apothecary shop to lend his work a sharp assessment. It stood out against the other weathered buildings, a testament of revitalized color. "I might be in a drought—or I may just be coming out of one," he mused, giving his chin a rub. Only fifteen minutes stood between him and lunch, a perfect time to test his new theory.

~

Serena stood over the utility sink, guiding the knife around a large pit in the avocado that would turn their rolled sandwiches into a California treat. "Marvella mentioned a set of antique canisters to put in the mercantile. Since she has an eye for that kind of thing, I'm giving her the go-ahead on anything she wants to change in there. It doesn't hurt to spruce up now and then."

Rait opened the cracker-chip hybrids. Perched on a stool that boasted a metal tractor seat, he looked right at home. He extracted a chip and examined both sides. "I have to focus on the big projects and let the little details slide. I figured someone could come behind me to tackle those." He threw a chip in his mouth and let it crackle a time or two as he chewed.

"I called in the free ad for a sign painter and made the deadline for Thursday's Silverdale Shopper newspaper. We could have help by next week, which makes me want to start the saloon façade this afternoon."

"Is that building slated to be painted the rusty nail color?" He fingered out another chip and made it disappear.

She sliced the avocado right in the shell, and then dropped some on the sandwich wrapper. "Yes, rusty red. I thought that made a statement for the saloon's reputation."

Rait slapped his knee. "One year, we hired a troupe of showgirls that performed a dancehall review. It turned out a touch risqué for the plain folks of Silverdale, so that particular skirt-tipping outfit never got invited back. Whew, I trust we don't get down another blind alley such as that."

She handed him his lunch feast on a paper plate, complete with a sidecar of salsa. A perfect tease came to mind. "Does that mean I have to cancel the appearance of the Colorado firefighters' calendar models? I saw them advertise availability at an online entertainment site."

He picked up his sandwich, tipping it one way and then the other. "Does it matter which end is up?"

"Try the end with the sprouts sticking out. Yes, that one. That way the fold will catch any extra dressing trying to drip out."

He almost had the sandwich to his lips before retracting it. "That's a no for the prancing firefighters. They're non-authentic for the Old West, and of questionable good taste for a family fun event." He bit off about a third of the sandwich and pinched his eyes closed.

The conversation needed to take a turn, so she summoned up her courage. "Marvella told me that Brandy Jo caught Melissa's wedding bouquet on Saturday, so I guess that means she's the next Danner in line to get hitched." She scooted onto the work bench near his stool and shook a few chips onto her plate.

Rait worked the bite of turkey and saucy accompaniments into his cheek. The mention of Melissa's wedding made him look a bit uncomfortable. He reached for his drink, which drew out to be a stall tactic.

She would have to lead further. "Anyway, at the backyard barbeque, Brandy Jo hinted that things were heating up between her and Dane, so I wouldn't be too shocked to see them make an announcement soon. Lots of couples get married during the summer, when the options for honeymoon destinations seem endless."

He shook his head. "I cannot possibly lose two sisters within one quarter of the year." He drove a chip through the salsa and popped it into his mouth. A humming noise soon accompanied his chewing. "Umm, this is good salsa. The fresh cilantro sets it apart, for sure."

"Thanks. I made that from scratch with a few secret ingredients. All I'm saying is that I'd make friends with Dane, if I were you. And you might make mention of Old Settlers' Days being July twentieth and twenty-first. She would need to steer clear of those dates."

"You are incorrigible." When he reached to tap her knee with his knuckle in playful exchange, he stopped short of the tear in her jeans. He swallowed to make an inquiry. "Is this rip a fashion statement? If so, it seems a might subdued for you."

The workshop held a cozy ambience, one she hadn't expected. With his attention fixed on her like that, she should make the most of it. "No, that's authentic Old West, as you like to call it. I had a wrangle with the batwing door panels, getting them loaded into my car." She shrugged her shoulders to dismiss the minor damage.

"You gotta promise to let me get those from now on. Part of being honest with one another has to include knowing our limits. If you promise to ask for help, I'll make sure the committee gets you the assistance you need. Is that a deal?"

She fidgeted a bit on her perch, but nodded before she took a bite of her lunch.

"I'll get the panels up on the work table before we go back out to start the saloon. You can sand and refinish them up there. When you're done, I'll transport them back to the saloon for mounting. We still need to be able to lock the existing door behind them, once they're in place. That reminds me. Locking up should be part of your daily protocol."

"Done, done, and done, Chief," she replied. "I always lock up."

He tilted his head. "Please don't call me Chief, as I'm a volunteer helper. You're the director, so I could call you Chief—"

"But you won't" she replied, a threatening finger pointed in his direction. More than anything, she wanted to keep the ground level between them.

He stirred a chip through the salsa piled on the plate's rim. "Okay. I'll search for another nickname that fits. How do you like Kneehole Nellie?"

When he poked a chip through the crack of the denim jeans, she gave a tiny kick. "That depends. Is she cousins with Whoa Nellie from the stop-where-you-are family?"

He stood, appearing restless. "No, I don't believe so. I think she's a member of the go-ahead clan, if I'm not mistaken. Take your time finishing your lunch. I'll get those door panels in next. When you're ready, we'll head back to Main Street to paint Old Town red."

"That sounds like a party I don't want to miss. I'll teach you how to keep your paintbrush from getting so saturated this time." She waggled her brow to heighten her offer.

"What's wrong with this technique?" he posed, lifting his arms to display the olive green overruns that decorated his elbows.

"Ugh. You're headed for a mineral spirits bath after this next project, Mr. Danner."

He tugged his hat brim down and glanced at her from the back entrance. "That sounds mighty fascinating, Nurse Kneehole. It might prove to be the cure-all for what's been ailing me."

146

She gasped as he disappeared from sight. Having painted herself into a corner, she might have to relinquish with an actual scrub-down. Whether it would be pleasurable or not would be the only consideration. That could depend on their afternoon at the saloon, of all places to weigh one's deliberations. She sighed and hopped down to leave room for the batwing door, made to open with a mere push. Too bad hearts weren't like that, or the end of a prolonged drought.

~

Rait assumed the spread-eagle position, his palms pressed up against the siding behind the workshop. He froze when Serena ducked between his arms to get the inside of his elbow wiped clean. "That's going to be tender," he predicted.

"Relax, Mr. Danner." She scrutinized the drips before she touched the first square of skin. The pressure soon advanced from fairy wing brush-by to cat-paw soft.

"Don't worry about hurting me. Just scour off the stain, so I can be on my way." With her up close like this, every word out of his mouth felt like a betrayal. In no hurry whatsoever, he leaned on the shop wall and took his medicine, sweet though it was.

Intent on her work, she bent to get the tip of his elbow swabbed and arched her back right against his chest. "Sorry, I've got to get the right angle here."

"No harm done." His blood pressure kicked up a notch as her blonde hair cascaded with every turn of her head. The burning stench of mineral spirits almost caused him to miss the soft vanilla scent of her hair.

"Can you make your forearm go straighter? That way the excess cleaner can drip straight to the ground." She looked at him over one shoulder, and a flash of blue signaled him closer.

He pressed in like doing a push-up against the building. "How's this?"

"Yes, that's what I meant. I'll use more pressure along your wrist where there's so much stain. Let me know if the pressure gets too abrasive." She began to wipe in rapid fashion, eradicating the drips. Twice she stopped to reapply more mineral spirits to the rag. "You're custom-coated all right," she muttered, absorbed in her work.

When she migrated up to the top of his elbow, he flexed his bicep to remind her that a real live man remained attached to that forearm. "Hey, we got two buildings done today. That's worth a little cleanup woe and possibly my being late for supper."

She exhaled sharply and turned inside his arms to look at him eye to eye. "If you come in to volunteer on Thursday, please plan to stay in town for dinner. I'll make something Italian, so you don't have to rush

147

right back to the ranch."

He crimped the space between them by doing half a push-up more. "Now that sounds pretty cozy, Serie. What color would a man have to turn to take advantage of that deal?"

A tiny smile perked up her lips before she turned back to get the last line of drips under submission. "I think we should tackle the turquoise to get the post office painted. Remember to bring the longer ladder to town. Maybe with Cole's help, we can rig some scaffolding and both paint the upper level from it."

He tumbled against the workshop wall, leaving his right arm in place to receive the last rubbing sequence. "Was that Italian dinner invite for just any volunteer who happened by, come Thursday night?"

She glanced at him while rolling up the rag. "No, that stands as a private invitation."

Like the rise and fall of a distant tide, he felt drawn toward town with unmistakable magnetism. "Well, in that case, you can color me turquoise." He borrowed the rag long enough to scrub a rusty smear from her arm, whistled a cat call, and left her standing in the alley all alone. That break-away tactic might work to his advantage on Thursday night, akin to granting the shaker of parmesan cheese permission to roam the table.

Chapter 5

June seared the high plains with sun-birthed heat. Serena signed off on the repair work in the apothecary and had Rait install the antique set of scales onto the rebuilt front counter. With Marvella to take on restocking the canned foods and dry goods now that the carpenters had left, she became satisfied that particular stopover on the Old Settlers' Days tour would be a big hit. Maybe she could think up something the role-playing merchant could dole out as a treat.

She strolled down the raised sidewalk considering what her role might be that Saturday of the event. Inclined to work the ticket booth, she still wanted to be in costume like the other Old Town residents. Again, her quirky wardrobe posed a problem, as nothing in her closet would double for 1880's authentic. Footsteps followed her along the planking, and she turned to find Brandy Jo chasing her down.

"Hey, Serena. You're just who I'm looking for. Take a look at this news flash." She held up her hand and made a diamond ring twinkle in the broad sunlight.

"That's awesome, Brandy Jo. Congratulations." She locked elbows with the bride-to-be and swung her around the planking in a do-si-do, square dance style.

"The wedding is scheduled the weekend prior to Old Settlers' Days. I came to ask you to help me with makeup for the bridal party, as yours always looks so perfect. What do you say?"

"I'd be ecstatic to help, Brandy Jo. Thank you for including me. Have you planned your colors yet?"

"The bridesmaids are wearing turquoise dresses with gold accessories. I'll repeat the turquoise and gold gilt in the ribbons around our flowers. I found a new gal in town willing to twist our hair into up-dos. Her name is Jade."

"Thank goodness, as I'm a klutz with hair, but I'd love to do the makeup. Let me try to order some sample-sized cosmetics, so I'll have some color choices to match skin tones."

"See? I knew you were the right one to ask." She jumped up and down like a giddy girl.

"Do your brothers know about this pending hitch-up yet?" She furrowed her brow to impress the point on the flighty woman.

Brandy Jo grabbed her arm and laughed. "Yep, I made the announcement last night at the dinner table. Nobody made a blessed peep after that. Dad looked a touch forlorn, so I kissed his head before running out to meet Dane. We've got so much to do. I never even thought about a gift registry."

"Maybe you could include Marvella's shop. She has some nice things hidden among the junk over there." She let a tiny wink chase the suggestion.

"Wow, I like that a whole lot better than asking for gift cards to department stores where we have to drive sixty miles to shop. I'll stop by to get an idea of what could go on a registry, so I can recommend something specific to Dane."

"Guess I'll need a new dress—no, make that two new dresses. I don't have a pioneer dress for Old Settlers' Days, and I don't have anything traditional enough to wear to your wedding."

"It sounds like I need to take you over to the Second Go Round Shop. Nan tries to stock some nicer dresses in her back room. I get off lunch duty at two. Let's plan to head over there. Maybe I won't have to mail order bridesmaid dresses, after all."

"You only have a month to plan all the details, so my hat's off to you."

"Six weeks actually, which Dane thinks is a luxury. You don't see him scurrying around town trying to drum up groomsmen, do you? Ha."

"I suppose your brothers are all in the wedding party—"

"Yes, they are, the scoundrels. I cannot abide by their complaining. They'll match Dane's cowboy style or else." She squinted to add emphasis.

"Okay. Let me meet you at the restaurant at two. In the meantime, I'll try to find some restoration work that doesn't require a messy coat of stain to keep me occupied. Thanks for giving me something to look forward to, Brandy Jo. You are my first friend in town, and I couldn't have asked for a nicer one."

"Aw, shucks." She wrapped her in a fleeting hug and then turned to hurry on her way. "Come to the grill's back door off Windrow Lane. I'll be out as quick as I can."

"Got it. I'll be glad to drive us over, if you can navigate."

Back to her, the bride-to-be jutted a thumb into the air.

Serena crossed her arms over her chest to try and preserve the feel-good moment. Brandy Jo would be happily married in July—representing the second Danner to walk down the aisle. Remembering the sorting work Marvella had left for her at the mercantile, she headed across the street to the broad turquoise-stained building.

If she used the ochre stain to coat the window ledges, it might reflect Brandy Jo's color selections for her wedding. A subtle gesture, it would be her secret gift to the married couple, one she wouldn't ask permission to make. Rait would summarily dismiss the color choice, but she was all about making that man see beyond the obvious.

Maybe she'd keep that nugget of truth in mind while selecting her dress for the wedding. She needed to match the bridesmaids' turquoise, but in a cut that demanded some masculine attention. Her fate hung on the racks of a secondhand shop, a tenuous thread that drew a sigh. She proffered the key ring and entered the mercantile to sort folds of calico, a mindless task that suited her restless mood.

~

Fed up to high heaven with the heat, Rait reclined against a slanted rock to share the ravine's shade with Noah. The cattle had been particularly stubborn in moving to the next pasture on rotation, despite the lure of greener grass on the other side of the fence. He snatched off his hat and tapped it over his bent knee.

"Stay a spell," Noah said without opening his eyes. The cottonwood leaves rattled overhead as a cooling breeze blew through.

"No worries. This shade is worth a million bucks to me right now."

Noah grunted and turned toward him. "Dad wants a word with us." He wiped his top lip against his shirt collar and stared out across the grass.

"About Brandy Jo's hitch-up?"

"Most likely. I'm trying to make my peace with it. What about you? Nobody's closer than you two."

Rait licked his teeth, feeling drier than a bone. He'd like to admit the hurried-up wedding grated against the grain of his slow-and-steady disposition, though it would come across as the ornery brother attitude, should he voice it. Brandy Jo had been his confidante as long as he could remember. He'd bailed her out many a time from some half-baked shenanigan she attempted to pull. Those bygone days of childish pranks and last-minute rescues had to give way to what the future held. While he hadn't been watching, his sister had grown into a comely young woman.

Noah's brow wrinkled. "I mean, we trust Dane, right?"

"Yes, that man is straight-up sincere. I'm wondering if I trust Brandy Jo." A bottle of water hurdled toward Rait's chest, He snagged it midair. With a twist of the lid, he slaked his thirst until the plastic nearly caved in. When he glanced up at the benefactor, his dad stood on the opposite bank, planted solid as an oak tree.

He removed his hat and wiped his forehead on his sleeve. "You boys got a head count to report?"

"Eighty-six," Noah replied, tipping his water bottle to drain the last swallow.

Rait dug a boot heel into the dirt and considered his answer. "I was riding along mid-herd, so my count came in at one hundred-sixteen."

"Good enough. Despite chasing a couple of strays, I got a count of one thirty-six, so I'm betting we've got the entire herd. Let's move forward. Noah, when we get to that next rise, I need you to ride ahead to get the double gate open. Rait, you stay on the west flank, and I'll ride up the east side. Keep 'em moving until the last head trots through the gate."

"We really ought to reconsider hiring some help out here," Noah replied, his voice as vacant as the wind.

"Maybe for the fall roundup. We're hiring a cook to feed us in the meantime. Her name is Consuela. She's done some duty at the Branding Iron Grill and came heartily recommended." He fanned his face and settled his hat back on his head. "I wanted to speak a word to you boys about your sister's wedding plans next month. I know she'd appreciate your selfless cooperation. This is something Dane and Brandy Jo decided for themselves, so we need to stand behind their decision. Is there any reason not to?"

"No, sir," Noah replied.

Rait rose to his feet, so he couldn't blame the hard ground for chafing him. "I understood Melissa and Nate, since she'd finished up school and needed to find her place. I don't get Brandy Jo's impulse to head down the matrimonial aisle." He fingered his hat, reluctant to wear it.

"Honor lies down the far end of that aisle, Rait, a sanction from God above. I don't want grandchildren without that signatory blessing. Sometimes, the protracted courtship breeds its own problems. Either a man knows a woman's heart—or he doesn't. Just so you two holdouts know, Dane Bronson approached me some time ago, making his intentions clear and asking for Brandy Jo's hand in marriage. The three-month wait seemed appropriate to me, so I gave them my blessing."

"I'll stand as a witness for them," Noah replied, "as long as I don't have to wear a cussed necktie."

Rait fit his hat in place and scanned the distant horizon beyond the grazing cattle. Somewhere, a peaceful answer abided. He wished he could stumble upon it sooner than later.

"Rait?" His father's tone demanded a response.

"I'll stand with them," he replied. Betrayed by coercion, he'd follow through to keep the family peace for the sake of appearances. The war inside would continue, amplified by the loneliness of long nights. He backtracked to find his horse, thankful for the open horizon of the high plains that left a man free from being hemmed in.

~

Serena tried to shift the dress up to cover her exposed flesh. Though the teal silk offered a perfect coordinating color for the turquoise bridesmaid dresses, the style proved a bit more daring than she typically sported. Worse than that, the back had a cascading scarf dotted with shiny sequins. Some high school girl had gotten a good night's wear out of this dress for prom before sending it to the recycle shop.

"Look what that color does for your eyes, Serena." Brandy Jo strutted a full circle around her on the mirrored platform. "The tea length is perfect for an evening wedding, too."

The shop proprietor stepped closer to make her assessment. She pulled up the cascading scarf and draped it across her shoulder. "I'd detach this train and make a stole out of it, possibly even a bolero jacket."

"Good idea, Nan. This party dress needs the update," Brandy Jo said. "Still, the silk fabric is pretty special."

Nan nodded. "It truly lends the woman wearing it permission to look gorgeous. Serena, how does it feel to wear silk?"

She brushed a hand over her hip, a heady sensation. "It's outright wonderful—where it covers me. It's where it doesn't cover that has me concerned."

"So for one night, plan to be beautiful," Brandy Jo replied, a challenge in her tone.

Unsettled at being the center of attention, Serena stared down at Brandy Jo. "Maybe if you tried on that peasant-style wedding dress, I'd have more time to think this over."

Brandy Jo threw up her hands and headed for the changing stall, whistling a cowgirl song. Once the door clicked closed, that changed into a full-out solo.

Serena smiled at Nan. "Could you clip off that train to help me decide? If I could give it some modern flair, like twisting the shawl into a figure eight around my bodice, I might be more interested. Thanks for the twenty percent discount this month. That will come in handy."

"Hold it right there and let me find my scissors. Try to imagine the people who'll see you in this dress at the wedding. One thing's for sure, it will look stunning in the pictures." She scurried away on a mission.

While rustling sounds came from the try-on booth nearby, Serena turned sideways to examine her profile in the triple mirror array. Form-fitting, the dress left little to hide. Maybe just once she could celebrate her slender figure instead of hiding it under layers of draped-on couture.

"Here we go," Nan called, returning to the dressing room.

Serena shifted to the platform's edge and offered her back. The sound of snipping sheers sent prickles up her arm. Soon, the mirror revealed a detached length of sparkly fabric in the shopkeeper's arms. She turned sideways to examine the difference.

"So ladies, what do you think?" Brandy Jo gathered the full skirt of the gown and stepped barefoot onto the platform.

Serena clapped both hands over her lips. The gathered neckline graced the woman's shoulders with bejeweled embroidery like a fairy garland. From her tiny waist, a cascade of woven vines trellised down to floor length, making a veritable garden scene against an ivory satin backdrop. "Oh, Brandy Jo. You look out-of-this-world beautiful. Come look in the mirror."

The bride-to-be took center stage, turning in a complete circle to examine the dress from every angle. At one point, she gathered her hair, twisted it into a top bun, and clamped it in place with a plastic clip.

"Here, Brandy Jo, try these," Nan insisted. She shoved a pair of white sandals at her. "You need to wear heels. Watch the hem lift off the floor with these on."

Like a reveal at a magic show, the flowing dress complied with the adjustment. Now, the end embroidery made a scalloped edge as the hem whisper-touched the floor. Brandy Jo encircled the platform two times before approaching her. "I want Dane to see me wearing this dress, pledging to be his bride forevermore." Her eyes misted at the confession.

"You look like the very breath of a wildflower, carried to him by the wind," she replied. "I think you should definitely wear your hair up. It makes you look winsome."

"Like she walked out of a storybook," Nan added. "Would you wear a veil?"

"I'm planning to wear mother's veil, unless the years have yellowed it."

Nan winked and fussed over one of the sheer puffy sleeves. "If it has, bring it to me. I know a trick or two that will restore the white."

"Okay, here's my decision—yes to the dress and no to these

pinching sandals. I wanted to wear cowboy boots anyway." Brandy Jo pulled her shoulders back and took one last lingering look in the mirror.

"Did you see the white pair of cowboy boots in the front window?" Nan unfastened the lower back buttons while peering at her in the mirror. "They're size seven."

Brandy Jo passed her bottom lip between her teeth. "Run go get them for me, Serena. I might as well try them while I have this dress on to figure out if they'll work or not."

"Be right back." She skipped down the trio of steps, thrilled to get the bride what she wanted. The silk shift seemed to move with her, aiding her every movement. Lithe and free, she spotted the boots in the storefront display and snatched them up in haste. When she looked up, Rait Danner stood outside the window, transfixed on her every move.

She backed away from the window. Her next hope was dashed in short order when he reached for the door. Lord above, he couldn't see her dressed like this, and barefoot, too.

"Excuse me, Serena. Several of us volunteers are waiting for you to show us what to do next down in Old Town," Rait said, his gaze riveted on her.

Hoisting the boots to hide her middle, she tried to develop a clear thought. "Uh, start with the horse hitching posts at the livery and the saloon. There's one more, so you guys decide where it goes."

"Fair enough." He nodded ever so slightly. "Are you planning to buy that get-up?"

She drew the boots up higher. "Maybe I will, and maybe I won't." She raised one defiant brow and slunk away into the recesses of the shop. By the time she stepped into the dressing area, the mirror revealed her plight. She'd turned white as a ghost.

"Did you have some trouble up there?" Nan asked.

"Just a Peeping Tom, that's all." She handed the boots to Brandy Jo and came up the platform steps to hold her steady while she finagled them onto her feet.

"Must have been some Peeping Tom," the bride quipped. "Take a look at your chest."

A red blush fanned its way up to her collarbone from beneath the revealing dress. What a mess Rait had made of her immediate contemplations. Now, the purchase would be ruinous. "Your middle brother did this to me," she whispered with plenty of blame attached.

Brandy Jo snickered and began to two-step across the platform, lifting the dress's hem as she went to gauge the cooperation of the new boots. Once she'd danced back around to her spot, she leaned in with a twinkle in her eyes. "I didn't think Rait had it in him. Most of the time, he wants us to think he's asleep behind the wheel."

"Listen, Serena dear," Nan said. "Buy the dress if you like it. You truly look regal in it. That's my honest opinion."

The bride tapped her shoulder to solicit help with the higher buttons.

Serena stood sideways to the mirror, imagining attending the bride on the day of her wedding. As the pearl buttons mesmerized her fingertips, one thing became clear. No other dress would do for the occasion. "I'll take this dress—and the sash with it."

Brandy Jo gave her an impish grin. "Atta girl, Serena. Go get him with both barrels."

"Or he can find me, the lady in waiting all dressed in glamorous silk." She glanced in the mirror one last time, unsure of every stitch.

Chapter 6

Rail rolled the punch glass in his fingers, circumspect as the reception unfolded like a whirling dervish all around him. On his fifth glassful, he'd begun to wish the bowl had been spiked, to help put him out of his lone buck misery. Duly warned by their father to keep the pranks to a minimum, he'd only been able to help Dane's buddies decorate the getaway car. Cheerios in the cup holders represented his best off-the cuff idea, and it sure made a mess.

He scanned the dance floor to find his older brother giving undivided attention to the new hairdresser in town. More expressive than he'd seen Noah in a while, maybe the exotic beauty possessed some genuine charm. He sipped the sweet lime punch and tried to locate Wyatt next.

"Hey, you should look happier," Serena teased, crossing behind his table.

He gestured to the chair opposite his. "Come sit a spell, so we can commiserate."

She tucked her pink-glossed lips a bit before conceding. "My feet are starting to hurt a bit in these heels."

A vintage brooch anchoring her sash glinted in the low lights when she took her seat. Wearing more makeup than usual, she made a sparkly addition to his table. "Oh, that's so much better. Now, I can last through the reception."

Wyatt swept by and gave them a dashing wink, leaving a full glass of punch for her.

He raised his glass, in the mood for a bittersweet toast. "Here's to another sister lost."

She lifted her glass and gave him a keen look. "And another brother-in-law gained." She sipped without taking her eyes off of him.

"Who are you hiding from, Serena?" His burning question tumbled out at last, one he didn't trust the answer for, yet had to ask. When she looked at him questioning, he swirled a finger around emulating her circling sash. "Your layers of camouflage...the ones you call fashion. You're either hiding from someone or trying to hide behind something. So which is it?"

A woman laughed from several tables down the way. A white-clad milkweed seed floated by on the dance floor, marking the bride's jubilation. All of it seemed mocking in a remote way.

"I'm not hiding from some angry former boyfriend, if that's what you're getting at." She straightened her spine as if to protect her dignity. The punch glass rose to cover her expression.

"That leaves the possibility that you're hiding something, doesn't it?" He leaned toward her, held by magnetic tension. When her hand flitted to the brooch, it validated he'd struck on a hint of truth. "Take it off, then, and prove you have nothing to hide."

The chair beside him moved, its cushion soon hosting ten little toes with brightly painted nails. The gesture somehow made him relax. He dropped his left hand down and began to massage the closest foot.

Across the table, a fingering of the brooch caused it to slip off. She made quick work of containing it in her tiny purse. A dip of her shoulders caused to wrap to loosen in mesmerizing laxity until it fell completely from sight. Her hair shimmered in the low lighting, touching her chin while drawing attention to her pink lips. "Is this the openness you had in mind, Rait?"

He switched his hand to the other foot and ran his thumb down the curve of her arch. "Yes, I like it when there's nothing between us. Just bare honesty."

She twirled the glass in her fingers. "Okay then. Be honest." She leaned closer. "Do you like my dress?"

He stopped rubbing toes for the merest of seconds, trapped in a web of his own making. "I like you—in that dress. In fact, you look amazing tonight."

A hand patted his shoulder. "Head's up," Wyatt warned. "Brandy Jo wants everyone on the dance floor for this next song. I suggest you not cross the bride on her wedding day." With a testy smile, he disappeared to deliver his message down the banquet table.

When the toes dropped out of his grip, their intimate moment began to shatter. Faltering, he rose from his seat and locked gazes with Serena. "May I have the honor of escorting you to the dance floor—at the bride's insistence?"

"I suppose one dance wouldn't hurt," she replied. With a shrug, she shed the wrap and stepped into her high heels.

Rait skimmed past the table's edge and held out a hand to guide her. Missing her elbow, his hand landed in a luxurious patch of silky fabric fitted across the small of her back. Once on the parquet floor, she turned into his arms. In the blink of an eye, they were slow dancing, hand in hand. So sure he had dreamt it all, Rait had to shake his head while the singer crooned his raspy questions that echoed truths from the depths of love.

"Why the melancholy tonight? Having a hard time with yet another Danner wedding?" Her lips teased the skin of his heated neck as she formed the words.

A magnetic draw held him close, a strong influence that captivated his every motion. He bent to nuzzle into her hair. "I don't understand this love thing," he confessed, intoxicated by the smell of her. He maneuvered them into a darker spot near the rear corner of the dance floor.

She pushed back to look him in the eyes. "That's because you're trying to make sense of it here." A delicate finger tapped his temple. "Instead, you have to feel it from here." Her finger trailed down until it rested on his chest. Her eyes looked iridescent in the low light, eclipsed now and then with a sweep of her curvy lashes.

The undertow of attraction held him full force. "Why didn't someone explain that to me before now?" His whisper barely hid the huskiness in his voice.

She placed her cheek against his and let the music attempt any further explanation. Her hand soon left his and encircled his neck in a trailing caress that turned up the heat along its path.

The crooner repeated one last wish in the repetitive chorus, leaving Rait short of time. He led Serena off the dance floor where it opened into the darkened back hall. Now in private, he'd risk a taste of what could be. The second she looked up, he trapped her in a fluid kiss that slid across her glossy lips and returned for full contact. An eternity of elation transfixed him to the spot as she made it impossible for him to be anywhere else.

A blaring announcement followed the song, and the adjoining room brightened with full lighting. Unready for the intrusion, Rait eased back and ran a finger along the curve of her bare shoulder. "Let's not hide from each other, Serie."

Her chest heaved under the daring cut of silk. Blushed, she looked the image of innocence, wide-eyed and angelic. "I have no idea how to hide, even if I wanted to."

A hand clamped his shoulder. "Time for family pictures on the stage," Noah said above the party noise. "Didn't you hear the announcement?"

Rait shrugged off his grip and straightened his string tie, trying to become an upstanding Danner again. Hurried, he fished for Serena's hand and brushed a kiss across her knuckles. "Wait for me to take you home afterwards, okay?"

"No, I have my car in the rear lot."

Noah hooked an arm around his neck and forced him toward the photo shoot. He flashed four fingers in her direction, withdrew them, and flashed three more. When she clapped, he knew his message had gotten through. The night was young, and he no longer had any need to hide.

~

Somewhere between unsure and stir-crazy, Serena lit the candles across her coffee table and waited for what seemed like an eternity. She'd straightened and dusted the front room in the interim. A fleeting thought to change into workout clothes led to turning on the radio for mellow jazz instead. By every stretch of the imagination, it had been a lengthy, drawn-out day. Why her blood still raced through her veins posed a real enigma.

A single knock at the door brought the unfinished matter to a crescendo. She opened the latch to find Rait standing on the front stoop, her sash pressed against his nose like a bloodhound still on duty. She touched a shoulder, having completely forgotten the stole's whereabouts. "Please come in."

He unfurled the sash to its full length, revealing a tantalizing smile. "Only for some late-night conversation, mind you." Once inside, he draped the sash around her neck and gave the nearby candle array a sweeping glance.

A high-pitched scream started to sound from the back, which Serena imagined to be her conscience reporting in the pressure change with a good-looking man standing in the room. She tried to say something clever, but couldn't speak.

"Make that conversation…and a cup of hot tea. Thanks for thinking of that touch. It sounds like the perfect wind-down to a fever-pitched day."

She picked up a slender candlestick and saw the flames reflect in his intense blue eyes. "Right this way to the cozy kitchen for two. Or it will be, once I get the kettle silenced."

"I like the sound of that," he whispered from several steps behind.

Glancing back, Rait held a candle, bringing it forward like a sentinel in the night. Within moments, a cloud of steam turned the image into a dreamscape, saturating her heart.

Chapter 7

By noon on opening day, the crowd had swollen past the attendance mark set for Old Settlers' Days last year. Rait scratched his chin, recognizing the difference Serena had made with her expert leadership. Her online marketing blitz paid dividends that required little extra work.

No doubt the trickle-down effect would be felt around town. Brandy Jo texted that the Branding Iron Grill had a waiting line for seating, which hadn't happened in forty years. Serena added a map of sponsors for the event and places for visitors to explore on the back of the event flyer. Once kids had the stamp from each of the fourteen buildings, they could report in for a candy prize. Begging off a designated station, he'd played go-pher all morning and enjoyed it.

Spotting the mayor having his picture taken by the saloon entrance, he ambled over to strike up a conversation. "Not hanging out with the incorrigibles are you, Mayor Hastings?"

"I tipped up a sarsaparilla with a group of rowdy boys and caught a song or two on the player piano. How's life treating you, Rait?" He grabbed his lapel and showed off his fake sheriff badge for the camera's benefit. The photographer captured the shot, nodded, and moved on to the next customer waiting by the saloon's gold gilt sign.

Rait stepped toward the raised sidewalk, admiring the public servant's willingness to participate in the fundraiser. Though he had avoided pulling strings to get upper level support, the gesture boosted his spirits. "Life's been pretty rosy for me this summer. Having a director on board that really knows her business has taken the pressure off of me, for sure."

"Is that the perky blonde in the ticket booth, by any chance? I may have seen her at Brandy Jo's wedding." He waggled his brow a time or two to covey an additional message.

Rait chuckled and nodded. "Yes, sir. That's our director, Serena Thornton. She and Brandy Jo made friends her first day on the job. It's funny how things work like that."

"Old Town looks sensational with its face lift. Those colorful stains really bring the place back to life. Be sure to take plenty of pictures today, so Ray can have his choice of shots for the newspaper next week."

"Okay, then how about one of us over by the post office? I particularly like how that building turned out. The turquoise and burnished gold lends that federal building a regal air it lacked before." Rait led the way across the street and pulled out his phone to take the picture.

The mayor leaned on the hitching post and tucked a thumb in his pocket, looking pretty touristy. "Shoot long-ways and get the second story roofline. Maybe that optical illusion will make me look slimmer."

Rait spotted Cal Prang passing by on the sidewalk. "Hey, Cal. Come take a picture of me with the mayor, will you?"

Cal skimmed down the steps in a heartbeat, a smile on his face. "Afternoon, Mayor. What do you think of the Old Settlers' celebration this year?" He took the phone and stood in the street to get the right perspective.

"Top notch job, in my estimation," the mayor replied.

Rait put his arm around the public servant's shoulders, grateful for their affiliation. Thinking to hide his volunteer nametag, he flattened his palm over his vest pocket and gave Cal his best smile. Noticing his face remained shaded, he tipped up his hat brim.

After taking several shots, Cal returned his phone with a slap on his shoulder blade. "I'm heading for the marble tournament, boys. See you around."

Rait scanned the bustling street, trying to gauge the crowd. Lost in his assessment, he'd almost forgotten his companion, until a fatherly hand cuffed his forearm.

The mayor cleared his throat. "Your mother would have loved such festive goings on, you know that, don't you?"

Rait bowed his head at the mention. "Yes, sir. I think she would."

"Her spirit lives on in you. Well done, son." With a touch of his hat brim, the town leader sauntered toward the apothecary shop where a huddle of locals greeted him with a spirited welcome.

"Not just for visitors, is it, Mr. Mayor?" He chuckled at the recognition that the whole town needed the restoration, and a cause to celebrate its heritage. His phone beeped, so he glanced at the screen. "What? Those guzzlers are out of ice again."

He pocketed the phone and headed for the coolers stashed behind the saloon, privileged to be needed after all the picture posing and dignitary reflections had been accomplished. A man of action needed to stay on the move, which is why he'd opted out of building duty in the first place. His stomach growled to protest the clock's advance. Seeing a line at the ticket booth yet, he concocted a plan to pick up two boxed lunches and pay a call to the bonnet-wearing blonde anchoring the ticket booth.

~

With the evening shadows lengthening, Serena kicked off Brandy Jo's hand-me-down cowboy boots and rubbed her aching feet. After depositing the gate proceeds in the bank's drop box, she had retreated to the workshop to hide from the others and attempt an ounce of recovery. She shimmied up the endless blue calico skirt that had overheated her lower extremities all day and gave her legs a breather. Leaning back against the workbench drill press, she closed her eyes to relive the passage of a thousand nameless faces from the confines of her booth. Goodness, what an opening day.

Time slipped away as a breeze played through the open shop door. A songbird called from a nearby perch, lulling her into a deeper rest. The day's aches became nonexistent as her safe haven became a cocoon for a much needed rest.

A clang at the door startled Serena awake. When a cooler lid flew inside the shop, she remembered her whereabouts.

Bent low, Rait peered inside. "Whew-y, if those legs aren't a sight for sore eyes, Miss Thornton." His tease came chased by a slush of water being freed from a cooler. "I thought I might find you back here."

She hastened to return the calico past her knees to become presentable. With little energy for sparring, she opted to stay put on the bench. He could work around her. "Hey, Rait. I'm just trying to recover from eight hours of continuous standing. Note to self—find a bar stool for tomorrow afternoon."

"Good survival skills, Miss Director. What a gangbuster day. All stations reported in record sales." After pouring another cooler free of melt-water, he entered the shop and stood in the natural light filtering inside. "I ran into the mayor. He was pleased as punch. I took a photo with him by the post office. He wants us to send some shots to the newspaper editor."

"I like that idea. Too bad I stayed trapped in my own little prison all day and couldn't accomplish any picture taking—or anything else, for that matter. Thanks for bringing me lunch. I hadn't thought that far ahead."

"That's what go-phers do, migrate around the crowd and take care of odd jobs that come along." He took off his hat and fanned his face, his expression turning serious. "You gave our town an incredible day today, Serena. By knowing how to draw in the crowds, you doubled our attendance and made Old Town come alive again. Let me give credit where it's due, as we couldn't have done it without you."

She beckoned him closer with a wiggle of her fingertips. Soon, his warm palm covered hers, filling her with a life-lending current. "Being part of a team means so much to me. In college, it was all individual work. I prayed to God real life wouldn't be that isolating, and he's answering that prayer right here in Silverdale. You promote that team approach better than anyone, Rait. That made you the best candidate for being the go-pher today, though I wanted to change places with you a hundred times."

He tugged her hand to his chest. "I appreciate being left to roam. I spoke to folks I hadn't seen in years. That made for a great day, by any standard. Can you gather your things, so I can walk you out? We should close up shop here and get some rest. Tomorrow will be another run at the record, as soon as church lets out."

A tall figure darkened the doorway. In uniform, Cole Davis seemed agitated, staring at the ground. "Excuse me, Rait. I saw your truck out back and needed to get a hold of you."

Rait dropped her hand. "What's up, Cole? We're about to close down shop in here anyway. Can I help you with something?"

"It's Mayor Hastings, Rait. He's suffered a major heart attack. They've airlifted him to Colorado Springs, but it doesn't look good."

At the bad news, Serena shifted off the bench and stuffed her feet into the boots. "What needs to be done? Should we start a prayer vigil?"

Rait's face paled as he stood motionless, lost in the turn of events.

Cole glanced between the two of them. "I need to escort Rait to the town clerk's office for his swearing in. He serves as mayor pro-tem, just for such an instance as this. I hate to break up your plans for the evening, but this is a priority. Erlene is already waiting for us, Rait."

With his chin hanging low, Rait followed the deputy out of the shop and straight toward extra duty. Two vehicle doors banged shut. A car soon sped up the lane.

Serena approached the light switch, stiff from her rest on the wooden bench. A few questions came to mind, pointed ones that needed answers. She knew a junk dealer that might have a revelation, or two, hidden among her stash. She bolted the door and headed straight for the

Junktique Shop, more determined than ever.

Marvella stood clearing the register of the day's sales when she popped in the door. "Hey, Serena. What a bounteous day for Silverdale. I can actually walk the aisles of my shop now, I moved so much merchandise."

"That's a bonus, for sure. I'm afraid the day has ended with some somber news, though. Cole stopped in to tell Rait that Mayor Hastings suffered a major heart attack this afternoon."

"Mercy me. Is Al going to be okay?" She lowered the stack of bills, her expression laden with concern.

"I haven't heard his current condition, but the local hospital flew him straight to Colorado Springs, so it must be serious."

"Oh, dear. That doesn't sound good. Tell me. How did Rait take the news?"

Serena shook her head. "Not so great. One second he's high in spirits, commending me for a record opening day, and the next, he's downcast as he can be."

Marvella stuffed the money in a zippered bag and reached across the counter to pat her hand. "The Good Lord knows this one's going to be tough for that young man. Too bad, because I thought he was moving past all the grief at long last. I give you some credit for that healing."

Serena circled her hand with her fingers and squeezed it. "Cole escorted Rait to town hall, so the clerk could swear him in as acting mayor. I get that Rait is servant-hearted, but why the grim demeanor? Some things don't add up."

"That's because you're just learning the background story, honey. Rait's beloved mother was a Hastings. The mayor is his uncle, the last of the siblings in her birth family. If Al passes, then they're all laid to rest. That leaves Rait empty-handed. He's so much like that side of the family, I declare." She shook her head, looking tired.

"Should we hold a prayer vigil? There's power in prayer."

Marvella pulled her hand away. "First, let me get this deposit dropped by the bank vault, before I forget it. I'll call the prayer chain at my church when I get home and get the link started. You could call out to the Rockin' D and let the Danner family know, since Rait is tied up. Every church in town will be praying for Al by morning services tomorrow."

Serena gave her a weak smile and exited so the old woman could lock up. "I hope to see you tomorrow at the mercantile volunteer station."

"I'm looking forward to it. All this junk starts getting to me after awhile. Penny candy will be a nice break."

"Take a look at that calico to make sure I displayed it like you wanted. Feel free to fiddle with it, if necessary."

She took a few hobbled steps and grinned. "You'd think I would grow tired of such fiddling, but it runs too deep in my blood to give it up."

"Have a good rest tonight, Marvella. I'll see you after church tomorrow." She slinked into the driver's seat, totally spent and weary to the core. For the closing afternoon of Old Settlers' Days, she'd gain Marvella and hopefully not lose Rait.

The call to the Danner ranch weighed on her mind next. With Brandy Jo still on her honeymoon, she'd have to contact one of the brothers. Her side caught a stitch at having to be the bearer of bad news, but it somehow made her feel part of the family. A commitment with a silver lining, she'd relay the situation and let them know the community joined them in prayer.

As she pulled into the parking lot, she noticed several trucks—but none of them Rait's Silverado. A longing to share his travails birthed in her heart. Left on the sidelines, she would carry his burdens to the Lord and ask for grace during his tenure as mayor, however brief it might be. She exited the car and tromped up the stairs to her apartment, hoping he might call.

~

Unseasonably mild for the first week of August, Rait stared at the Hastings tombstone and felt every bit as granite as the family marker. His uncle had lingered two weeks before his cousins had honored the man's final wishes not to be maintained via life support. The church service turned out to be a somber affair, with a majority of the town's citizens in attendance. The procession to the cemetery had been agonizingly slow. Wyatt had driven his family, remaining uncharacteristically tight-lipped the entire way. Now, graveside service had no glimmer of hope.

Standing in line to be seated by the officiant, Rait scanned the attendees, unsure of what he might be searching for. Requisite tasks awaiting him at the mayor's office tried to steal his focus, but he turned his head as if to toss them aside. Someone stepped through the line in front of Noah. Out of the emotional blur, he recognized Serena in her navy blue funeral dress.

She walked to his side and looked up through the mesh veil of her stylish hat. Her eyes reflected a calm spirit. Her hand entwined his as she moved close enough their shoulders rubbed.

When his father shifted forward, Noah followed. Feeling the obligatory tug, he marched down the row, bringing her with him. Once seated, his unease began to abate.

Linking her arm through his, Serena leaned toward him, her head downturned. "God has promised to never leave or forsake us on our journey through this life. I hope that surety can bring you some comfort today, as I hold God's word to be the absolute truth. I'll be here for you, Rait, if you need me to stay close by." The last few words trailed off in a whisper.

With her earnest pledge, all the bone-deep hurt began to leak from his frame. Instead, the glimmer of hope he'd deemed impossible short minutes ago, now blossomed like a light dawning on a far horizon. The strength he needed became available on loan from a source he hadn't counted on—until that moment. In a fumbling move, he located her hand and gripped the lifeline she offered for the duration of the burial service.

Chapter 8

Serena rode in the passenger seat of Rait's truck, welcoming the three-day weekend Labor Day promised. A picnic basket rested between them. She didn't recognize anything along this winding road, though the late summer wildflowers held a quiet riot on the landscape at every turn. "It's like a secret show back here, with the prairie so full of flowers."

"Glad you're enjoying the ride." Without turning to regard her, a tiny smile curled his lips. "Not too much traffic out this way." As if to prove it, the road grassed over straight ahead.

To her surprise, they took a sharp left turn and soon traveled two ruts that served as the primary road. "Oh, my. We're headed far off the beaten path now. Should I be dropping breadcrumbs in hopes of finding my way back?"

"No, you'll have me navigating your return, no worries." He tapped the steering wheel and began humming.

The gable of a relict structure poked above the tree line along the hedgerow. She blinked to make sure she'd seen it. Once they traveled past the entrance drive, an open yard afforded a breathtaking view. An old church with weathered green shutters sat in a flower-filled lawn. A graceful steeple topped the white siding, lifting the eye skyward. What a restoration project it would make. The idea spurred her to action. "Can we stop, Rait? I feel compelled to stop."

He downplayed a smile and pointed ahead. "Here's the picnic spot I had in mind. Let's eat first and walk back to explore the church afterward." He slowed the truck and drifted into a grove of tall trees.

Serena spied a railing up ahead. "Is that a bridge? I'm going over to check it out. I may even have to get in the creek." She slid from the vehicle and ran through the grass. Where the trees ended, the meadow spread for miles, dotted with golden wildflowers. A wandering creek cut an undulating swath through the middle of the grassland, its surface reflecting the sun's glimmer. So beautiful, it stole her breath away.

"So, do you like it?" Rait lifted the basket while he tested the sturdiness of the ancient bridge. When he reached the crown of its arch, he sat down and let his feet dangle just above the water. "You're welcome to come join me—unless you want to play in the water first."

"I sure want to splash around, but maybe later, after we eat. I'm hungry, which means you must be starving." The thrill of being attuned to his habits compelled her up the bridge. It seemed to shake each time she planted her foot, but the planking held fast. As she laced her feet under the railing, a shiny green dragonfly welcomed her to the wilderness.

"This crossing is known as Hastings Landing." Rait took out a bag of chips and gestured over his shoulder. "The remains of the original Hastings homestead can still be seen off the western edge of the woods there. Turns out, the spot was too low-lying, so the family migrated the width of a pasture closer to Silverdale. That's over half a mile, as the crow flies, but still walking distance to this creek."

She chose a sandwich and rested it in her lap. "Did they help start the old church back there before we turned?"

"Yes, that's Cross Creek Church. To my knowledge, it hasn't held a church service in over fifty years." He tilted his head and his gaze skittered across the creek.

"But if someone did the restoration work, it would make a phenomenal special event venue. The grounds are so scenic, the photography would be outstanding."

He unwrapped his sandwich. "The woodwork inside will surprise you. It looks Gothic to me. They must have had an Orthodox influence, somewhere along the line." He pinched the corner of his bread off and tossed it to a turtle whose head appeared below. In a gulp, the treat disappeared.

"Look along the shallows down there—those silver minnows. Maybe they've never seen a human before." She leaned out beyond the rail to give them a good look. The movement along the surface rippled her reflection below, mesmerizing her with its running water sound.

"Go ahead and eat your lunch, so we can head off on our exploration."

"Fine, have it your way for now, but my exploration is going to end at that church. Promise me you'll save some daylight for that stopover."

He swallowed and reached for his drink bottle. Apparently, something she'd said made him happy. A grin flitted from his face before he took a long drink. "Anything you want, Serie. The day is plenty long."

Affection rose to elevate her high spirits, until she thought she might float off the bridge. "Have I mentioned how much I love our time together?"

He pretended to check his watch, although his wrist was bare. "Not today, I don't think." Instead of taking his next bite, he bent to her and waited.

"Thanks for making it so easy," she quipped in a coy tone. Lost in his steady gaze, she kissed him with sincerity as the waters tumbled by beneath their feet.

Afterward, he pressed his forehead to hers. "Hmm, that's a great way to start an adventure, even if I hadn't planned that part."

"You mean the best way." She shucked the sandwich wrapper, ready to get the exploration going. To hasten matters, she became a generous benefactor to the turtle below, much to the enjoyment of the minnows.

~

Rait allowed Serena to enter first, hoping he wouldn't regret it later, whenever he retold his story. When a floorboard creaked underfoot, it made him second-guess his chivalrous approach. "We can stop right here, if you want."

She turned and gave him a questioning frown. "What? No, we're going in all the way. I want to examine the pulpit and see any ornamentation they may have incorporated. Remember, this construction was made as unto the Lord, so it's not a spit-shine saloon bar. Didn't you once say flashy is phony?"

He blew out a breath. "Oh, yeah. That was me, back in the day I thought I knew more than you did about restoration. Good job making a believer out of me." When she eased right to head straight down the center aisle, he chose a left trajectory and walked forward along the wall.

Serena's arms floated up as though in praise as she made the ceremonious passage to the platform. She pointed out an alcove on his side that divided the open stage. After testing the platform with one foot, she stepped onto the elevated planking.

He examined what appeared to be an alcove for a piano. The instrument had long since been removed. Only the router-edged wood trim remained to lend any distinguishing feature. Still, the interior space held a hallowedness that defied description.

"The windows are definitely Gothic-inspired." Serena started facing the far wall and rotated around in a complete circle. "God most certainly dwells within these walls. I feel like he would desire us to worship him, even though we came in to explore."

He regarded her for a quiet moment, standing amid the dust and cobwebs while letting her faith light shine. The arching windows formed a cathedral around her, guiding him on his intended purpose. "Since God's Word says to worship in spirit and in truth, I'll start with the truth that's foremost on my heart." He took a couple of steps toward her, his hands clutched behind his back. "My world hasn't been the same since the first day you drove into town and turned my life upside-down, Serena. Even though I brought you here for your restoration expertise, I believe God had something more designed for us. To thank the Lord for watching over me, I come as a humble cowboy with one more question from his altar." He knelt and brought his clenched hand to rest on his knee.

Serena's hands trembled and tucked under her chin. Her gaze held love inexpressible as she looked down at him. A tiny sob broke her silence.

"So I ask you, Serena Thornton, would you become my lawful wife, that I might have you and hold you from this day forward? Please note that you would become a Danner by marriage and by name. You never said that you liked big families, so you'd better give it some serious consideration."

"That's such an easy answer, Cowboy." She knelt beside him and held out her left hand. "Yes, I want to be a Danner, Mrs. Rait Danner, that is."

An explosion of outright joy came next. How he got the ring onto her finger, he'll never know. But he most certainly found her lips, and put that fleeting bridge kiss to shame. Everything was better when undergirded by the Lord, even if the floorboards remained a bit shaky. He picked up Serena and carried her down the center aisle to begin the process of two hearts becoming one in God's sight.

"What if we got married in the newly renovated Cross Creek Church?" she asked, her tone landing like a caress.

"Sounds like you're in for a lot of work."

"Oh, no. It's a joint project. I'll get the High Plains Restoration committee to approve it after the holiday."

"Maybe you'd better check in with the Hastings family heirs to get their consent first." He lowered her to the top step and drew out his phone to snap her picture in the arched doorway.

"Evidently, I already have one of the main heirs wrapped around my little finger, my darling Mr. Mayor."

About the time she showed off her new engagement ring, he took her picture, or maybe two. Elation took over from there as he kissed his bride-to-be on the threshold of a new future, one planked with old wood and lots of new ideas.

Epilogue

The sun began to set on October fifth, framing the steeple of Cross Creek Church in a rose-colored hue that suffused the horizon across the entire stretch of meadow. Serena trembled as her ribbon-trimmed boots made quick work of the red satin runner unfurled from the church's steps. From inside, soft organ music filtered out past Brandy Jo, who held her bouquet. Determined to get the show started so her trembles didn't magnify into a quake, she put one foot in front of the other and approached the renovated structure.

Brandy Jo bent to press a kiss onto her cheek. "Here, take these flowers, and whatever else happens in there, don't let go until you have that man hooked on your arm." She gave her the Hollywood wink that had become the feisty woman's flamboyant trademark.

"Look at me, shaking like a leaf." She accepted a helping hand getting up the next step. Maybe this narrow-cut gown had a few limitations. Fortunately, she'd gone for a traditional style this time, not Bohemian, which always managed to get her into trouble.

In lieu of her own father, Bill Danner had requested to walk her down the aisle. Once she turned to the church's middle, there he stood waiting for her. Slowing her pace to appear more graceful, she took his elbow and aimed for the big turn at the center aisle. She pivoted and drew a deep breath, staring at her flowers. For a tender moment, the stargazer lily kept her spellbound.

"Okay, your train is ready," Brandy Jo whispered from about floor level.

When the organ hit a prolonged note, Serena took her first step. As rehearsed, members of the Danner family lined the aisle all the way up to the platform, but would be seated for the ceremony to begin. What looked systematic on paper now presented a huge blockade. Two steps away from the front, she still hadn't seen Rait. *Is he even here?*

Noah pulled Wyatt aside with a wink and backpedaled to sit on the front row. The next moment, the preacher came out from the far side, clutching a black leather Bible. Rait trailed his steps, looking more handsome than ever. His dark suit made his blue eyes all the more intense.

Serena waited for them to get situated before she ascended the first step. Bill froze in place, waiting for the appointed bestowment question. Serena locked her gaze on Rait and reveled in his focused inspection.

The preacher opened the Word of God. "Dearly beloved, we have gathered today in this most extraordinary place to wed this man and this woman in holy matrimony." He looked down on cue and nodded at her fatherly escort. "Who gives this woman to be lawfully married?"

Bill stiffened. "On behalf of the Thornton family, I so present her for marriage." He gave her a hug and departed.

Serena steadied her foot on the next step while someone got the giggles on her left, likely one of her younger sisters. Determined to leave it all behind, she ascended the top step and drew up opposite Rait. Such a dreamy destination, she took pause to remember the moment and the way her groom looked at her.

The preacher began to extol the virtues of making vows, the lead-in to their exchange of commitment. Sure of the text, he recited a Scripture and asked the audience to reflect on it.

Though only midway of the lead-in, Serena knew it had to stop. "Please hold it right there, pastor." She redirected her gaze at Rait. "Go ahead. I know you want to. Take my sash off, if you want me to be shed of it. I don't have anything to hide."

Rait tucked a tight grin into his cheek and moved closer. With his arms around her waist, he worked at the buttons above the bustle until he freed the excess fabric from her ensemble. He tossed the train toward the front row with a little extra spite. Someone in back let out a raucous cowboy whoop. Rait nodded at the clergyman. "Go ahead with this hitch-up, Mr. Preacher."

"Very well," he replied. "We will commence with the exchanging of wedding vows."

Serena raised a brow once Rait graced her with his full attention. She came to him on equal footing, and this time, the boots belonged to her. After a brief duration, she would step off this platform as his forever wife, what a major work of restoration.

When she mouthed "love you" over the preacher's wordy set-up,

Rait's blue eyes grew misty with emotion. The tiny tremor of his bottom lip was captured only by his bride, who immediately tucked it in her heart to treasure all their days of togetherness. Before she knew it, Rait repeated his full name at the preacher's prompt, pledging to be her lawful husband. She drew a breath, hoping to God above that she still had a voice to commit the same.

The End

AUTHOR BIO

Cindy M. Amos enjoys writing romantic fiction from her real-life experiences ranching in the Flint Hills of Kansas. From a background in field ecology and endangered species conservation, she captures the natural closeness of man living on the land. The author lives in Wichita, Kansas, with her engineering husband and two college-aged sons. She actively serves in the women's ministry of her home church and acts as secretary for the South Central Kansas chapter of American Christian Fiction Writers. Her hobbies include gardening, home canning, pie baking, and riding her bicycle along a section of Rails to Trails without regard to the time of day.

Find her available books on her website:
http://cindymamos.wixsite.com/natureink

Visit her Amazon author page at
https://www.amazon.com/author/cindymamos

OTHER BOOKS BY CINDY M. AMOS
Landscapes of Mercy Series
Redeeming River Rancher
Saving Bicycle Man
Justifying Sound Strider
Sanctifying Ace Aerialist

Lifting Lock Runner
Salvaging Doctor Junk

National Parks 100th Anniversary Romance Collection
Everglades Entanglement
Mesa Verde Meltdown

Christmas 3-in-1 Collection
Running Out of Christmastime

Taming the Cowboy's Heart Collection
Warming Stone Cold Lodge
50 States Collection
Secondhand Flower Stand (Kansas)
Red Cloud Retreat (Nebraska)
Tidewater Lowlands (North Carolina)
Canyon Country Courtship (Utah)

John Denver 20th Anniversary Collection
Calypso Reimagined

Loving the Town Hero Collection
Cascading Waterworks

America's Fabulous Fifties Series
Oil Field Maven

Falling Hard

Christina Rich

CHAPTER ONE

Noah Danner pulled off the gravel road and draped his arms over the steering wheel. The symbolic ride toward the Winter's ranch a few nights before Melissa and Nate's wedding continued to leave an ache in his chest, and he had a deep suspicion Brandy Jo and Dane would be heading toward the altar soon. He was happy for his sisters and Nate and Dane, but the birds jumping the nest made him feel as if something big was missing in his life and he was falling short of the Danner standard. And since he'd received word of Sgt. Mooney's death, a man he mentored at the VA, Noah felt it even more.

He blew out a discontented sigh. He'd served his country, and although he'd seen things he never wanted to see again and missed so much of his family while doing it he'd do it all over again. His only regret was being singularly focused. A major flaw in his character. Once he set his mind to something he kept on with dogged determination until the task was complete. Like with the junior rodeo. He hadn't cared about championships and belt buckles, but he had cared about beating Air Bucks. Once he accomplished the goal, he walked away.

And that's what he'd done with the military. A little more than eight years of his life. He would have gone another twelve if he hadn't been sent home. Resting his chin on his hands, he stared out at the expanse of land neighboring Rockin' D. While he'd been in Afghanistan returning fire, or taking cover, this place kept him focused. Kept him alive, even, but he couldn't shake the feeling he'd let his men down, like he'd left them behind when he should have made sure they all returned home before he hung up his camo. Not his choice. Still, it was hard to swallow knowing several of his buddies remained in the Middle East. Volunteering at the VA filled some of the void.. His experience in combat and the on-going therapy meant he could relate to most of the soldiers suffering from PTSD.

A bald eagle launched from the small mountain proudly perched near the northwest boundary giving way to a rocky crag near the southern line of the property where Melissa now made her home with his best friend Nate. Soaring through the air, rising, and dipping with the wind, Noah longed for the sense of freedom the bird displayed. If only he could break the chains binding him to combat and grief. If only he could grab hold of love, settle down and have a large family like he'd always wanted, something Melissa assured him was still possible. Noah, just didn't know, especially after his earlier conversation with Marvella. One he tried to push to the back of his mind, but it kept finding its way back as a focal point of his thoughts.

An endless ocean of tall grass molded the hills, beckoning him to become lost in their depths. The only recent tracks marring the land were from Cassidy's hooves. The land had belonged to Granny Danner and became Noah's when she passed away. He'd been five at the time, and he was certain the expectations of turning this land into a successful ranch like Rockin' D by himself had sent him running to the recruiter's office after he'd heard about Jade Bentley's marriage to a wanna-be rodeo clown from Denver with a reputation worse than Hank Halverson. Noah adjusted his ball cap and leaned back against the torn upholstery of his beat-up truck. He hadn't thought of her in years, and for good reason. At least he no longer felt the raw ache in his heart at the thought of her. Probably because he grew up and realized he'd never told her how he felt. He would take care to learn from his own mistake as well as his siblings. Too many misunderstandings and assumptions. If he ever found the right woman, he'd tell her straightforward what was in his heart.

Maybe Silver Lining would fill the void he felt growing bigger by the day, maybe it would give him purpose. It was close enough to Rockin' D to help Dad with the ranch, but far enough from the chaos of his siblings moving on with their lives. Maybe tomorrow he'd pack his gear and set up camp near the creek running through the valley. It was time bury his roots in the land left to him by his grandma. Warmth spread throughout his chest and he smiled. The more he thought about building a home the better he liked the sound of it, except his ideal home had been drawn up by a teenage girl he'd thought himself in love with at the time. How would his future wife take it if he built a house designed by a former crush? He suspected not too well, but he couldn't envision anything else nestled in the rugged land.

Turning in his seat, he drew the ball cap over his eyes, and resting his head against the arm rest, he propped his feet out the window. The scent of country pushed through his truck with the wind and sense of peace washed over him. Silver Lining, beautiful in its untamed ruggedness seemed like the answer to his dilemma, at least until he decided what he wanted to do with the rest of his life. As Marvella had reminded him earlier this evening, he was pushing thirty and well past the time to marry and have kids, but what woman in her right mind would want to attach herself to a broken man scarred by combat?

Sure, there were females vying for his attention, but they chased the Danner name, and the Danner good looks. They didn't know the real Noah, the bruised and battered Noah. The Noah who paced the floors at night because he couldn't sleep. The Noah who preferred the silence of nature over a crowded room. The Noah who jumped at a hammer smacking a nail. The Noah who hid from himself and never looked in the mirror because he was afraid of what he'd see. The Noah who was consumed with guilt over Mooney's suicide. There was no easy way around the truth of his friend's death. It was what it was. Noah wouldn't pretend it wasn't, but he'd seen Mooney the day before he'd taken his life and he seemed happy. They laughed. Mooney shared pictures of his wife and their two kids. There was no hint of depression, in fact, according to Mooney things had been looking up for him, but Noah supposed a man only let another see what he wanted to see. If only he'd spent more time with him, or called him more often, then maybe his friend would still be alive.

Noah closed his eyes beneath the ball cap before he let loose the grief residing inside his chest and forced images of his sister and Nate as they rode toward the Winter's ranch into his mind. The obvious love between them, the joy and serenity, gave him a thread of hope to cling to. He knew he couldn't have picked a better man for his sister or a better wife for his best friend. He honestly believed God had predestined them to be together, and maybe, just maybe God had someone in mind for him as well. He smiled to himself as an image of the girl he'd been sweet on back in high school came out of nowhere. Well, not exactly nowhere since he'd thought of her more than once since cutting his truck engine. Funny how he hadn't thought of Jade Bentley in years, but now he couldn't stop thinking about her. Maybe because he'd spent the evening with Marvella, Jade's grandmother. Man, he hadn't seen Jade since the summer of his senior year. Rumors that she'd fallen in with a bad sort after her mother's death had circulated the rodeo circuit for a time, but since Marvella hadn't said anything to him about her granddaughter and

Cole hadn't said anything either, he paid them no attention. Still, he couldn't help but wonder what had happened to her. Maybe he would ask Marvella next time she came out to Rockin' D for dinner. He drifted off to sleep as he replayed the last time he'd seen her ride in the high school rodeo.

The sound of tires digging against the gravel road tugged at him, but in his half-sleep state he conjured up a small convoy of trucks as he ducked behind a ridge. He peeked over the bank and tugged at the vision, fighting to see the approaching enemy when a barrage of bullets sprayed his truck. *His truck?* Had the enemy followed him home? Heart pounding, Noah jerked awake and scanned his surroundings. Silver Lining spread out before him like a welcome mat, Rockin' D lay to the east. Not an enemy in sight. He blew out several breaths and counted to three when he saw a vehicle sliding down the hill on the gravel road. Brake lights blinked at him through a cloud of dust, swerving back and forth. Was the person crazy driving like a fool on this back road? The engine rumbled as the driver downshifted, and even lower when the engine hit first gear. The driver wasn't acting a fool on purpose but was in trouble. He started his truck and pulled onto the gravel road. Holding his breath, he white knuckled the steering wheel as he watched the pink Volkswagen Bug make a one hundred eighty turn, nearly tipping over, and then flying off the road onto his land where it stopped.

Noah stopped his truck and jumped out as a woman climbed out the window of the Bug. She looked under her car, and then rose. Blonde hair cascaded over her shoulders as she jerked the Stetson from her head and slapped it against her thigh. She kicked the tire with her bright pink, jewel studded cowboy boots.

"I don't think that is going to help." He received a glare, and for a moment he thought recognition, but she settled for a glare as she jammed her hat back on her head. "Are you all right?"

"Sure thing. Too bad, my car isn't going anywhere." She leaned into the car, pulled out a duffle bag and slung it over her shoulder.

"You lost?"

"Not at all, Cowboy. You?" She glanced at him from beneath the rim of her hat. Her eyes shadowed. She slipped her phone from her back pocket and stomped across the grass until she reached the gravel road where she dropped the phone to the ground and crushed it beneath her heel until it broke into several pieces.

He shoved his hands into his pockets and shrugged. "Not exactly, just wondering who drives a subcompact car out here if they aren't lost."

"Obviously, I do." She waved at him and trekked down the road. The glittery jewels on her back pockets drew his gaze to dangerous territory.

The Bug made a popping sound causing Noah to jump. White smoke rose out of the windows. A delayed airbag. The driver was fortunate she hadn't hit a fence post or worse, rolled her vehicle.

"What about your car?"

"What about it? Nothing I can do about it now."

"I can give you a ride."

"No can do."

"Stubborn much?"

She halted and spun around. He couldn't see her eyes, but he sensed her gaze drawing a line from his feet to his head and back to his face. "Just cautious, Cowboy."

He held up his hands. "I'm harmless, I promise."

Laughter tumbled from her beautiful lips, about the only part of her face he could see. "I doubt that."

She swiveled and started walking again. Noah jumped in his truck and pulled up beside her. "I can't let you walk out here alone."

"Sure, you can. Just turn yourself around and go back to where you came from."

"My daddy would skin me alive, lady."

He thought he heard her mumble something about Danner chivalry as she glanced over her shoulder and toward the car she ditched, but that was impossible given she wasn't from around here. He sensed she was running from something, or someone. He got that. Knew what it was like to run. Before he knew what she was doing, she strode to the passenger side of his truck and jumped in. "What are you waiting for? Let's go." She looked out the back window as he eased his foot on the gas. "You got a phone on you?"

He slid the phone from the ashtray and handed it to her. "Where am I taking you?"

~

Jade Bentley punched in her grandmother's number and chewed on her thumb nail as she waited for it to pick up. "Come on. Come on."

"Everything all right?"

"No," she said, panic pushed tears to the edge of her lashes. Swiping the red phone icon, she disconnected the call, dialed her cousin's number, and waited for the ring. If she could trust anyone it was Noah Danner, but she didn't want him fixing her problems. She didn't want him knowing about her problems at all. The perfect Danner brood had no idea what it was like to royally screw up life. Another time and another place, she could have been a Danner. Mrs. Noah Danner. She had dreamed of it. Even carved into her journal with red ink. Noah & Jade. Mrs. Noah Danner. She'd even had a notebook filled with possible names for their future children. If the notebook still existed, it was packed in a box somewhere at her grandmother's along with her mother's belongings.

"Hey, Noah, what's up?" Cole asked from the other end of the line.

"It's me. I'm in Silverdale."

"You're calling from Danner's phone. That was quick, Cuz."

"Not the time. My car's sitting off Silver Lining road across from the pits."

Noah shifted his gaze, surprise clearly on his face. How would he feel if he knew just how well she knew the territory? How well she knew him? Or at least the youthful Noah from their junior rodeo days.

"What happened?" Cole asked. By the sound of his voice he wasn't surprised.

"Not sure. I don't want to speculate, but it's hard not to. I think someone jacked with my brakes."

"Someone or Micah Cane?" Cole asked.

"Like I said, I don't want to speculate."

"I know, Jade, but he's made threats and he's done this sort of thing before."

"I know." She didn't need to listen to all the things Micah had done. She'd lived it, and somehow she believed she could continue with life in Denver running her successful career as a cosmetologist at a high-end spa and salon and that Micah would forget about her while he was in prison. She'd been wrong.

"Now that he's out of jail, Jade, it doesn't take a seasoned officer to put two and two together."

Jade chewed the inside of her cheek. Cole was right, but it only made her fear the man she'd been married to even more. Not for herself. She'd survived so far, but she feared for Maw and Cole. The only family she had left. "Maw called me in a tizzy. She's not answering her phone."

Noah's dark blue gaze pierced her from beneath the rim of his ball cap. She'd spent most of her youthful summers crushing on. her former friend. He'd been good looking then, but now he was breathtakingly gorgeous in a rugged sort of way. She tried hard not to notice. She wouldn't notice because noticing would make her long for the impossible. She was done with relationships, and men all together, except Cole. He was her best friend. Her only friend.

"Let me speak with Noah."

"I don't think so."

"Look, Jade. Maw's house was broken into. She's not answering her phone because she's with me."

"Is she all right?" Jade sat up straight and looked over her shoulder, something it seemed she'd done every few minutes since Micah barged into the spa making more threats. If it hadn't been for Carlos and Monte her ex would have dragged her out of there by her hair. Unfortunately, Micah escaped before the police had arrived.

"Shook up, but fine. Before you get any strange ideas, the house is off limits until a unit can be dispatched. Let me talk to Noah."

Jade clenched her jaw. "Cole wants to speak to you."

Noah's dark eyebrows formed a V. "Cole?"

"Told you I wasn't lost."

Frustration gnawed at her gut as she listened to the one-sided conversation which consisted of nothing more than a few yeahs. Noah disconnected the call and before she could ask what the conversation was about, he was making another call. "Hey, Bro, have you unloaded the Moore's truck, yet?"

Draping her Stetson over her face, she crossed her arms and leaned against the headrest as she listened to Danner.

"Yeah, there's a pink bug by the pits." Noah laughed at something. "No, man. A car, you know a Volkswagen. A bit of an eyesore."

Jade shot daggers from beneath her hat. Danner could take his opinion and stick it under his saddle. She loved her car and drove it proudly in honor of her mother. She wasn't going to lie to herself, she was a bit peeved about Noah taking over, but with her car out of sight Micah would have a difficult time finding her. If he was in Silverdale.

"You definitely can't miss it." Noah's phone thumped onto the seat. "Do you want to tell me what's going on and why you didn't say a thing to me back there?"

"No."

"All right, not my business." Silence hung between them for several long seconds. "Melissa will be excited to have you back in town. And Brandy Jo, too, just in time for her wedding."

Jade snorted. From her experience, marriage was a crapshoot. "What do you know about the groom?" She sensed Noah's eyes on her and nudged her Stetson with her finger. "What?"

He turned his attention back to the bumpy road. "Nothing."

"Well? Who's the groom? Not Halverson, I hope." Hank's reputation with the women who followed the rodeo circuit had made the Denver gossip columns last year and he wasn't even from Colorado, but some of his conquests had been. Brandy Jo was a smart girl, but Jade had been smart too, or so she'd thought until she'd fallen victim to Micha's smooth cowboy ways. Her ex-husband made Hank look like a choir boy. Sweet, kind, and innocent. She slid a glance at Noah and wondered if the years had turned him sour, too.

"You've grown cynical. What happen to Miss Rodeo Congeniality?"

"Life," she said as she hid back beneath the Stetson. She rested her boots on the dash and noticed they'd passed the turn to her cousin's house. "Did Cole move?"

"No."

Dropping her feet to the floorboard, she sat up straight. "Where are we going?"

"Rockin' D, sweetheart."

"No." He'd lost that endearing accent that used to set her toes curling, but she'd be thrown from a docile goat if he still didn't make her melt like chocolate in the Arizona desert. Panic gripped her stomach and all the air left her lungs. She'd spent nine months watching her mother waste away when she'd been a junior in high school. Dropping out her senior year, she hooked up with Micah. A mistake she'd spent the last eleven years regretting. A mistake she would never again make. Not even with a man like Noah Danner, if he was still as authentic as he had been. The last thing she needed was his family roping her up and hog tying her with their friendship and affection while the town gossips tarred and feathered her for being a floosy. She gripped the armrest, her fingers touching the cool metal of the door handle. "Noah Danner, you better turn this truck around."

CHAPTER TWO

Noah claimed a dark corner on the front porch while Jade, Cole and Marvella discussed their business inside the ranch house. His feet propped on the rail and the chair titled on the back two legs, he couldn't help but think about how much Jade had changed since he'd last seen her. She was closed off, sarcastic, and angry. Far from the smiling optimistic girl he'd known in his youth. What had happened to her? How much truth had there been to all those rumors passing through town years ago? Besides the fact she'd lost her mom to cancer years ago, he really didn't want to know. He had his own issues to deal with. Including survivor's guilt on seven levels to Sunday. He tried to get over it. Tried to forget and put a smile on his face for his family's sake, but inside he ached, and no amount of therapy seemed to get him out of his head.

"Are you, all right, son?"

Noah dropped his feet off the railing and landed the chair on all fours. "Right as rain in a drought."

His dad placed a booted foot on the bottom step and leaned his arm across his thigh. "You want me to ask Cole to find somewhere else to take them?"

Scrubbing his palm over his face, Noah breathed slow and deep. In through his nose and out through his mouth, just like his therapist had coached him. None of his siblings knew the extent of his PTSD, but Noah could see it in his father's eyes, as if at one time he'd battled his own demons. "No, Dad. Rockin' D is the safest place for Marvella and Jade."

"That it is, son." His dad narrowed one eye and considered him.

"You don't need to say it, Dad. I already planned on camping out at

Silver Lining. I need to get the feel of the land again."

"I'm sorry, Noah, I'm not sending you off. I could use you around here for a while. At least until Marvella and Jade are safe."

His father rarely asked for anything, but if Noah was feeling the toll of Melissa and Brandy Jo's weddings, no doubt his father was too. As much as he needed space from Rockin' D, and from the emotions being stirred by Jade's return, Noah couldn't tell his father no. "All right."

"Are you certain, Noah? I know it hasn't been easy since you came home, and you have your own stuff to work through, but Marvella is a handful by herself. I imagine that granddaughter of hers is another. I can't run the ranch and keep the ladies in line, and I'm not sure how much help your brothers will be outside of branding cattle."

"I've got your six, Dad." The house had separate wings. One for the girls and one for the boys, easy enough to keep his distance and know Jade's activities.

"I know, son, but it's not my back I'm concerned about. It's Jade's." His father adjusted his hat on his head as his frown deepened. "What I'm about to ask you goes against my code, but, son, she's a runner. She'll leave at the first opportunity, and this Micah scoundrel is as bad as they come. It isn't my story to tell and Marvella swore me to secrecy, but you need to know the sort of situation you're getting into before you say yes. Jade's ex-husband knocked her over a good one a few years back, nearly killed her and he threatened to finish the job once he was released from prison. Will you watch out for her?"

Noah clenched his fists. Why hadn't he known about this? Why hadn't he been there? Because he had been caught up in trying to break free the past. "I may need to sleep outside her bedroom door to keep her from running."

"I expect you to and I will ignore the *no boys in the girls' hall* rule this one time."

Noah schooled his emotions. He didn't want his dad to see his irritation at having his plans to hide out at Silver Lining interrupted.

"You might need to sleep in the bed of your truck, or did you forget about that time she climbed out the window?"

He wanted to laugh at the memory, but the seriousness of the situation kept him sober as well as the fact that he wouldn't be sleeping underneath the stars tonight out at Silver Lining. "I remember, Dad." How could he forget? He'd been feeding the horses that night when he came out in time to see Jade and his sister skirt along the roof line, then shimmy down the trellis. He'd been scared for them, amazed at their daring, and pure angry at their tenacity. "If you recall it was me who marched them into your study and demanded they be whooped. They could have fallen and broken their necks."

Dad laughed. "Yep, I also recall someone else doing the exact same thing a few months before and was fortunate enough to walk away with only a broken arm."

The corner of Noah's mouth turned up. "In my defense, your sons—"

"Your brothers."

"Woke me up from a dead sleep yelling the barn was on fire. The window was the fastest route."

"Am I interrupting anything?" Jade slipped through the screen door.

Noah jumped to his feet and jerked his ball cap from his head. "Not at all. Did you all come up with a solution?"

She shoved her hands into her back pockets and leaned her hip against the railing. "Not that I like, but for Maw's sake I'll agree to it temporarily. At least until I can find other arrangements."

~

Jade didn't need a babysitter. Especially in the form of Noah Danner, but she wasn't about to disrespect Mr. Danner. He was as gold as a man came. The real deal, and his sons were cut from the same cloth.

"Cole will get the situation straightened out and you and Marvella will be home in no time," Mr. Danner said as he gave her shoulder a reassuring squeeze.

"Thank you, Mr. Danner. For everything." She watched a look pass between father and son before Mr. Danner disappeared inside. "I know your father means well, but you don't have to keep watch over me."

"You're serious, right?" Noah arched an eyebrow.

A herd of horses trampled through her stomach and she felt like she was seventeen all over again. "Have any of you told your father no? Ever?"

Noah shifted his gaze around the yard until something caught his attention in the distance. At first she thought he was going to ignore her question, but he leaned his palms against the railing, and then looked her in the eye. "Yes. I did when I joined the military."

"Oh." She chewed the inside of her lip. She'd heard from Maw Noah had gone off against his dad's wishes, not because his father was anti-military, but because he wanted him to wait until he finished college. It was obviously a sore spot, and not one Jade wanted to pick open. "I'm sorry, Noah. Sometimes my mouth runs off before I think."

"I noticed." Noah jammed his hands into his back pockets. "Look, I didn't expect us to pick up where we left off."

That was impossible. Noah was some sort of hero returned from the Middle East, she had a record. Not a long one, once was more than enough for her, but the one bad choice she'd made had snowballed into multiple bad choices until her life had become a chaotic ball of broken shards of glass. Anyone close to her eventually got cut. Friends, and family, which is why she was contemplating doing something that would probably get her killed, but it would be worth it if Maw and Cole were safe.

"A lot has happened in ten years, Noah."

"Eleven, but who's counting." The corner of his mouth twitched. "That's how long it's been since I enlisted."

"Why?" The question blurted out before she could think about it. She wasn't here to dig into Noah's head. She had her own problems and didn't need any more on her plate. And she definitely didn't want to remember any of the feelings she'd felt for Noah Danner.

He looked at her from beneath his ballcap and held her gaze for several long moments as if he were choosing his words carefully. "Honestly, I don't know, Jade. Maybe I was running."

Running. She knew all about that action, she'd been doing it ever since high school, but what did Noah have to run from? He grew up in a wonderful family. A functional family. All the kids on the rodeo circuit wanted to be a Danner because they wanted parents like the Danners. Jade didn't even know her father's name, and Mom did the best she could with what she knew, in between her sober stints. The summer and Christmas breaks she spent with Maw, and her time barrel racing had given her something to look forward to during the school year. Her mom had finally seemed to beat her addictions. Three years sober, and then the cancer invaded, and Jade was back to caring for her mom. This time, instead cleaning up beer cans and things a child shouldn't have to, she was wiping her mom's brow, giving her sips of water and helping her to the bathroom until she couldn't move from the bed. Then she watched helplessly as life shriveled from her mother's body.

"You've never been a runner. Maybe you were just looking to find yourself outside of the Danner name."

He shrugged. "Maybe. Look, Dad asked me to keep an eye on you, and I'm going to do just that, but I don't want you to feel like you're a prisoner."

She'd felt that way all her adult life. First, in her marriage, then the week she'd spent in jail waiting to see the judge, and then the years since her divorce looking over her shoulder, waiting for Micah to come after her for testifying against him.

"I want to trust you, Jade."

She bristled like she did every time someone brought up her past. "I'm not asking you, too."

His eyebrows formed a V. "Well, given your track record of climbing out windows and sneaking off, I'd say I have good reason to be cautious."

She flinched and then burst into laughter. She'd expected to mention her criminal record, not silly childhood pranks. "Really? I was a kid."

"Have you outgrown your impulsiveness?" He arched an eyebrow when she didn't respond right away. "I didn't think so. I'm not an easy pushover like I was back then."

She crossed her arms in front of her. Noah had been easy going unless someone horsed around and endangered themselves, someone else, or an animal. "As I recall, you weren't a pushover then either." She'd been so scared standing in front of Mr. Danner while Noah demanded she be spanked for breaking the rules and almost breaking her neck. "I can promise you, Noah, if I decide to leave Rockin' D, I'll use the front door."

"That's what I'm afraid of," he mumbled. "Can you at least sleep on it, tonight?"

"Like I said, for Maw's sake, I will." She pushed from the railing and swung the screen door opened. She hadn't expected them to pick up where they left off either. In fact, she had hoped to avoid Noah all together when she drove passed Silverdale's welcome sign, but she didn't expect the distrust and disdain he had for her. She had never expected Noah Danner to become a judgmental Pharisee, but obviously her past bothered him. A lot. She'd do what she could to keep out of his way until she made a deal with Micah. She was tired of running, tired of the people she loved getting hurt, and she'd ride the meanest bull on the circuit before she'd let Micah hurt anyone of the Danners, which is exactly what he'd do if he found out they were giving her shelter.

CHAPTER THREE

Noah's lids jerked open. He held still as he peered into darkness until he gathered his bearings. His tense muscles relaxed when her recognized the walls and decor. He sat up. A quick glance at his watch told him he'd slept for a couple hours. A rarity. Especially without his team keeping watch. Narrowing his gaze at the door beside him, he found the silence disheartening, but perhaps she'd fallen asleep as well. He shook his head. Why, when he was supposed to keep watch over Jade, had he fallen into a deep sleep? Pulling his knees into his chest, he ran shaking fingers through his hair and internally chided himself for falling asleep. He was half tempted to barge in the room to make certain she remained inside, but given the early morning hour and the promise she'd made last night, he opted to trust her, even if it did go against the grain.

He rolled up his sleeping bag and tiptoed on his socked feet as he crept away from the guest room occupied by one of the stubbornest women he'd ever met. He'd laid awake most of the night listening to her one-sided argument as she paced. Occasionally, he heard the bed creek and muffled cries. He knew what those tears cost her and tried to ignore the warring emotions emanating from the other side of the door. Her tears tugged at that part of him that wanted to race in demand she buck up because he would take care of everything, but then he'd thought that about Mooney. As if just being a friend to him would fix his dilemmas. Just as it hadn't worked with his friend, he knew it wouldn't work with Jade. His best option was recon. Observe and patrol, like with any other mission. The problem with the plan was, Jade wasn't another mission. She was a friend. Or at least they had been once. Maybe even on the verge of something more. And given the myriad of thoughts racing through his mind last night, there was no way he would be able to keep his emotions toward her tucked behind a bullet proof vest.

He believed in providence and predestination as long as the will of God was at the center. It was no accident Jade Bentley was in Silverdale just as he was thinking about the future. Now, all he had to do was figure out if their reunion was nothing or if they were being given a second chance.

Slipping downstairs, he tucked the bag into a closet beneath the stairs and caught a whiff of coffee coming from the kitchen. Once again, he glanced at his watch. Four AM. His dad quit getting up this early when Mom passed away, and Consuela, the new cook had been given a few days off after all her work on Melissa and Nate's wedding.

Walking into the kitchen, he found the coffee pot hot to touch. Memories of waking up early to find his mom and dad sitting at the table holding hands and praying while steam rose from their coffee cups ambushed him. His parents had set an example for their children at what marriage should look like, even when they didn't know they were being watched. Noah poured a cup of coffee and leaned against the counter. Rait must have had another sleepless night and set the pot on. His brother had been restless since losing Melissa to Nate Winters, but he had a feeling something else snagged his brother's hook. Question was would Rait keep her or cut her loose? There wasn't a better time to pick his brother's brain than while the entire house slept, and he had a feeling he knew where to find him. Pushing away from the counter, Noah strode across the kitchen floor and opened the door leading out to the back deck. The lights Brandy Jo had strung for Melissa and Nate's dinner glimmered against the early morning sky, illuminating a figure sitting at one of the long benches lining the deck, and it wasn't his brother. His jaw tightened. He should have been more vigilant and sat outside her window.

Afraid he'd disturb her if he moved and end up saying something stupid, he focused above her head. It was a good idea at its conception but poorly thought through as the outline of her profile drew his gaze like a magnetic forcefield. He hadn't allowed himself to consider what a beautiful lady she'd turned into. Back then she'd been a knockout, and the fact she could ride a horse just as well if not better than most of the guys on the circuit had given her an allure that kept him up at night. Then there was the friend thing. She'd been his confidant. He'd told her things he'd never confided to any other, not even Nate or his brothers, not even Melissa, things like his hopes and dreams.

Turning sideways, she curled her leg beneath her. "Are you going to stand there until the sun rises, Cowboy?" She must have sensed his irritation as she took a long draw on her coffee, and then said, "Circumstances in life have forced me to be hypersensitive to my surroundings. I knew the moment you thundered into the kitchen."

"I don't thunder," he growled. He should have known the moment she left the guest room, but the fact he hadn't been aware of her movements as he should have left him less disturbed than her words. He knew what it meant to let his guard down in warzones. For her to be on spot with someone like him who'd been known for his light footing and stealth, made him furious. How was he going to protect her if he wasn't alert? "How did you get down here?"

"Truth?"

"I wouldn't ask if I wanted you to lie, Jade. Of course, I want the truth."

"You're not going to like it," she said and turned back to skygazing. "I stepped over you."

That's what he'd been afraid of. He may not trust her, but somehow he knew she'd keep her word. "I'm sorry."

She glanced over her shoulder. "For what?"

The tension knotting his neck relaxed. He strode across the deck and sat on the bench. "For not doing my duty."

"Always the golden boy, huh?" Her mouth twisted into a smirk.

What happened to the young lady who captured attention with her energetic and bubbling laughter? "If you knew the truth you wouldn't say that with such conviction."

"Well, if you want to compare apples to rotten potatoes, you win in the golden boy department. I think you forget how well I know you."

"Knew."

Her scrutiny had him shifting in his seat.

"Deep down, Noah, I don't think you've changed much, if at all. That boy who followed all the rules and gave his sandwiches to those who didn't have any hasn't changed. Grown a little taller and added a bunch of muscle. Learned from life, possibly. But you still aim to please, you still follow the rules, and I have no doubt you put others' needs before your own."

The picture she painted was black and white and far from the truth. He had followed the rules where she was concerned and lost her. That was the truth of why he joined the military, but he wouldn't tell her that, or anyone else. He'd waited patiently for the day he could ask permission to court her, because that's what Danners did. They courted by making their relationship goals clear from the get-go. They didn't just date, they dated to marry, but not until both parties were at least seventeen. He'd followed the rules and kept quiet as they spent endless hours together off and on the rodeo circuit. They'd shared their hopes and dreams as they gazed out at the stars while they were surrounded by their friends, his siblings and father. She wanted a large family like his and live in a cabin in the country. When she'd spoken her dreams to him all those years ago he knew he wanted to be the one to make them happen. Of course, Jade never knew about his desire to make her happy. No one but his dad had, because Dad knew everything. Except when Noah had decided to join the military. His dad hadn't seen that one coming. Noah hadn't even seen it coming until he pulled his bike in front of the recruiter's office.

He ground his teeth together. If he'd been a people pleaser he wouldn't have gone against his father's wishes and enlisted when he had, if he hadn't broken protocol he and his team might not have been ambushed, and if he had put Mooney's needs first instead of being distracted by Melissa and Nate's wedding and Brandy Jo's recent relationship with Dane, maybe he would have seen the signs a little clearer and been able to save his friend's life. He furrowed his brow, unsure whether to be offended or not. "Not that your description of me fits but you make it sound like those are bad qualities."

She shook her head. "Not at all, it's just when someone like me stands beside you, my faults are more glaring."

How could she think that? From what he gathered she was a fighter and survivor.

She dropped her feet to the deck and stood. The gray sweats and the oversized t-shirt had him wanting to curl up beside her on the couch to watch a movie. He inwardly hissed. Twenty-four hours ago, she hadn't even been in his scope. Now that she was, he couldn't seem to the possibility of them together out of his sight. The images running through his mind would prove just how much of a golden boy he wasn't. He should be dwelling on all his faults. He should be thinking about Mooney's family. Not thinking about kissing her full lips. Before he could pull his thoughts from the lady standing next to him and address his lack of golden goodness, she said, "Cole texted me earlier. Maw and I can go back to her house today."

"They arrested someone?"

"Yeah." She ran her hands through her blond hair and sighed, making him wonder what she wasn't saying. He made a mental note to drop Cole a message. He had no reason to believe she was lying, but her hesitation put him on high alert.

"So, what now?" He wasn't sure he wanted to know her plans. All his ideas about predestination and second chances with her began to shake at the root. She re-entered his life like a dust storm and it looked like she was about to leave in the same manner. He popped off the bench and shoved his hands into his pockets. Just as well. He was broken and in no shape to fix her problems or anyone else's. He should have left the question alone and just let her go.

"I haven't talked to Maw, yet, but after yesterday, I think I'm going to hang around Silverdale a few weeks. Just until I make sure she is all right."

Something inside him smiled, and he nearly released the air trapped in his lungs. He wished his bipolar emotions would jump off the pendulum and decide if he wanted to renew their acquaintance or if he wanted to shove her back into the recesses of that deep, dark cavern where he'd kept memories of her unseen and far from his heart.

"And who is going to make sure you're all right?"

~

"Oh, would you look at that." Maw swept across the floor in her broomstick skirt and picked a ceramic unicorn off the shelf. "Do you remember this, Jade?"

After receiving word of Micah's arrest in Westdale, a town west of Silverdale, Jade had convinced Maw to leave Rockin' D by asking to see Junktique Shop. Her grandmother's mashed up antique and second-hand store was a favorite stop for locals and tourists. The few hours she'd stayed at the Danner's had brought too many memories to the surface, leaving her nerves raw. Any longer and she'd turn into that silly goose of a girl who practiced writing Mrs. Noah Danner in her journal and had his initials tattooed inside of an arrow on her shoulder. Maw didn't spook easily, which meant her reluctance to leave Rockin' D had more to do with matchmaking than fearing another break-in, especially since her grandmother continually fought the smile beaming on her face. If she didn't know better, she'd think Maw had concocted the entire break-in, but Micah had left his mark at her grandmother's home. She was thankful Maw hadn't been home at the tim. She had no doubt Micah would have done more than ransack the house. She had the scars to prove it. Noah's words from early this morning clawed at her stomach. If he had been around he would have protected her, or he would have ended up dead. That was a thought she couldn't bear.

"What are you doing with that, Maw?" Jade took the statue from her grandma and inspected it. "I made that in third grade."

"You would be surprised at the things I've kept."

Since she stood in the middle of the ancient brick store filled with items from old barnwood and 1920 tin tiles to curling irons and frying pans, she didn't think she'd be as surprised as her grandma thought she would. "But why is this here, Maw? Nobody is going to buy a piece of harden clay that slightly resembles a unicorn with a frayed purple bow." Jade turned it over and gasped. "Not at five hundred dollars!"

Maw plucked the ceramic piece from Jade's hands and sat it back in its place. "Some things are priceless, dear. I'm just thankful the store wasn't broken into and that all this mess is finally behind us."

"Me too, Grandma." However, she'd been running from Micah for a long-time, she wasn't ready to breathe yet. Even when he'd been incarcerated, he'd found ways to get at her.

"I know we haven't discussed things, but Betty Semple is leaving Silverdale. Her daughter wants her to move closer now that she's been diagnosed with Alzheimer's. If I start wandering down Main Street in my unmentionables, promise you'll save my dignity and put me in a home of seniors."

"You're as sharp as they come, Maw, and stubborn to boot. You'll probably out live me and Cole."

Her grandma waved her off. "Silverdale needs a hairdresser and you're in need of a salon. What do you say about kicking off those boots of yours and staying awhile?" Maw raised her hand. "Before you say no, I've already worked out a deal with Betty and her family."

Jade bristled at her grandmother's type A personality. Her life had been controlled by her mother's addiction, the cancer, Micah, and fear. She needed to figure out how to gain control of her own reins. "I don't know, Maw."

Her grandmother sat at a 70's style table with a yellow Formica top trimmed in silver metal and patted the chair beside her. "Come sit."

Jade sat on the bright red, yellow and green palm tree print and considered how to tell Maw no. She didn't want to start roots only to have them ripped out when Micah made good on his threats. Sure, he was locked up for a parole violation, but how long before he got back out? Would they release him until another trial was held? The restraining order she filed earlier this morning at Cole's instance was only a piece of paper. Very little protection against Micah's tenacity and fists. Something she learned several years ago. The police officers responding to her 911 calls could do nothing more than document each incident. Eventually they began to look at her as if Micah was nothing more than her imagination. She did, too. She stopped calling for help and endured the hell Micah trapped her in. "I don't know if I want to do hair anymore."

"What are you talking about, Jade Marie Bentley? You've always wanted to do hair."

She did, even as young as kindergartener she knew she wanted to make girls' feel pretty with ribbons and bows. "I don't know. I guess I'm tired of running and looking over my shoulder. I'm tired of losing things like my business and my home because of a mistake I made when I was grieving."

"There's no better place to call home than Silverdale, and folks here care. They'll watch your back and protect you."

Noah's question came back to her. She knew when he'd asked it that he was offering to keep her safe. Running like she'd done for so long kept her from creating bonds, it kept her isolated and free from heartache. It also kept those she could possibly care for safe from Micah's destruction. Problem was, she was lonely. She wanted friends, like Brandy Jo and Melissa. Noah, too. But she'd never be able to be just friends with the man she crushed on so badly when she was a girl and she wasn't about to date again. Boyfriends, fiancés and husbands were scratched off her list. She'd done it all once and lived to regret it. She wasn't going down that road again. "I have nothing against Silverdale, but everyone knows the salon is the place to gossip. I think the town gossiping about their hairdresser would be counterproductive."

Maw smiled. "It may benefit you, Jade, but only if you're seen with a Danner. They're always the talk of the town, and I have it on good authority that Brandy Jo is getting married."

"Maw, you shouldn't listen to gossip." It didn't matter that Noah had confided in her already.

"I don't consider first hand sources gossip." Maw picked at some dried hot glue with her fingernail. "I bought the building from Betty a few years back when her husband died. She needed the funds. It was a steal, with the promise that for as long as I owned the building it would remain a salon. So, I either find a hairstylist or I sell it."

Jade's jaw dropped. "Why?"

"History, dear. It was a barber shop before it was a salon, and as long as I have a say it will remain a salon. Of course, it needs a bit of updating, which I'll leave to you, but you can see my dilemma. So, what do you say?"

What could she say? Her grandma had always been there, always supported her and loved her even at her lowest. She'd do anything for her, even attempt to make a small-town salon as successful as the one she'd worked at in Denver before her past destroyed it all.

CHAPTER FOUR

Noah dismounted Cassidy, leaving her to explore the ravine now that he'd finished counting heads of cattle for the third time. The day had turned blistering hot and he was glad for the cool rock he leaned against, and much happier to finally focus on the wayward thoughts that kept him from concentrating on counting.

He slid his ball cap lower on his brow and closed his eyelids. He'd had a feeling about Brandy Jo and Dane, and now that the announcement was official, the restlessness eating Noah up on the inside seemed more prominent than it had a few weeks ago. Maybe because he had yet to make good on his plans to rough it out at Silver Lining for a few weeks. Every time he rode out, he came right back. All because of Jade Bentley and his lack of cell service when he reached his destination. Not that she'd called him for help, she was too stubborn, be he wanted to be reachable if she needed him. He didn't want to force his help, but that didn't mean he didn't check up on her several times a day. He was beginning to feel like a stalker, but he needed to know she was doing okay. Even Cole seemed to be getting irritated with the twice a day phone calls.

Why don't you go check on her yourself, and while you're at it ask her out? Cole obviously didn't know his cousin really well. Asking Jade out would be like jumping in a cage with a lioness and trying to steal her cubs. One thing was for certain, he couldn't keep going on as he'd been. He needed to see her and to talk to her. It was the only way to really access the situation. He adjusted his ball cap, his fingers brushing against his hair. It'd been a few months since he'd buzzed it. Maybe he'd go in to Jade's salon and get a haircut. Of course, he'd have to endure his brothers' harassment if they discovered he wasn't cutting his own hair, but it'd be worth it.

The clop of hooves reached Noah's ears before Rait rounded the bend and before he knew it, his brother sat beside him. Like old times. It wouldn't be long before Dad joined them. Rait had been in a rare mood these last weeks and Noah wasn't certain it was due to Brandy Jo's upcoming nuptials. More likely it the sour mood had something to do with the young woman Rait had hired to direct the restoration committee.

Rait moved to turn away. Had his brother hoped to come here to gather his thoughts too?

"Stay a spell," Noah said, hoping to get to the bottom of his brother's irritation.

"No worries. This shade is worth a million bucks to me right now."

Noah groaned when the muscles in his lower back rebelled as he sat up. He needed to spend more time riding Cassidy and less time driving, especially if he intended on building a cabin on Silver Lining like he wanted. "Dad wants a word with us."

"About Brandy Jo?"

"Most likely. I'm trying to make my peace with it. What about you? Nobody's closer than you two." Not even him and Melissa. Somewhere along the way she'd replaced him with Nate, but it was his own fault for not returning her letters. So much of what he'd done had been classified, and it was best to say nothing at all rather than risk the lives of soldiers. Rait and Brandy Jo were different. They were two peas in a pod, always fighting, but always watching out for the other. They knew each other's secrets, something Noah sort of envied since he didn't have anyone to share his thoughts and deepest longings. Noah squinted at his brother and wondered how much Rait's tantrum had to do with Serena and how much it had to do with Brandy Jo keeping her feelings about Dane to herself.

"I mean, we trust Dane, right?" Noah furrowed his brow.

"Yes, that man is straight-up sincere. I'm wondering if I trust

Brandy Jo."

Dad appeared on the opposite side of the ravine and tossed a bottle of water at Rait. His brother's reflexes were quick. Another bottle hurtled toward Noah, the quick movement startled him, and he ducked to avoid the projectile. It bounced of his shoulder and tumbled to his lap. He tensed as he waited for Rait to harass him over the incident, but thankfully his brother held his tongue.

"You boys got a head count to report?" Dad lifted his hat and wiped his arm over his brow.

"Eighty-six," Noah said, and then downed the half of his water.

Rait kicked his heel into the dirt. "I was riding along mid-herd, so my count came in at one hundred-sixteen."

"Good enough. Despite chasing a couple of strays, I got a count of one thirty-six, so I'm betting we've got the entire herd. Noah, when we get to that next rise, I need you to ride ahead to get the double gate open. Rait, you stay on the west flank, and I'll ride up the east side. Keep 'em moving until the last head trots through the gate."

If his brother hadn't noticed, his father had. Riding in last had always been Noah's job, and the gate had been Rait's. His brother was more of a white-collar business type. He could ride and handled the cattle well, but when it came to chasing the stubborn ones, Rait wasn't as quick as the rest of the Danners. At least he hadn't been.

"We really ought to reconsider hiring some help." Noah hated broaching the subject, but with Melissa gone and Brandy Jo about to leave, they'd need help. Ranching was in all the Danner's blood, but Rait was destined for other things, like Silverdale's City Council and eventually mayor if Uncle Cal ever retired. Rait might even run for governor one day. He was a natural politician like their uncle.

"Maybe for the fall roundup. I wanted to speak a word to you boys about your sister's wedding plans next month." Dad waved his hat in front of his face before dropping back onto his head. "I know she'd appreciate your selfless cooperation. This is something Dane and Brandy Jo decided for themselves, so we need to stand behind their decision. Is there any reason not to?"

"No, sir," Noah said, knowing he hadn't known a more

honorable and good man than Dane. The man was a perfect fit for his younger sister, but he prayed Brandy Jo didn't run him over with her gusto.

Rait jumped to his feet and clenched his fists. "I understood Melissa and Nate, since she'd finished up school and needed to find her place. I don't get Brandy Jo's impulse to head down the matrimonial aisle." He shoved a finger against the rim of his hat.

"Honor lies down the far end of that aisle, Rait, a sanction from God above. I don't want grandchildren without that signatory blessing." His father removed his hat and leaned against the pommel. They'd all been taught from the nursery that marriage was sacred and an honor, and that children were a blessing, a blessing Noah longed for, but with only one stubborn woman capturing his attention he wasn't sure he'd ever make it to the end of the aisle.

"Sometimes," his dad continued. "The protracted courtship breeds its own problems. Either a man knows a woman's heart—or he doesn't." Did Noah know Jade's heart? Did he have the stamina and the time to figure it out before she tried to take off again? "Just so you two holdouts know, Dane Bronson approached me some time ago, making his intentions clear and asking for Brandy Jo's hand in marriage. The three-month wait seemed appropriate to me, so I gave them my blessing."

That was good enough for Noah. "I'll stand as a witness for them as long as I don't have to wear a cussed necktie." He chuckled, hoping to ease the tension radiating from his brother.

Rait adjusted his hat and stared past the grazing cattle. Their father's words, no doubt struck a chord with his brother, just like they did with him.

"Rait?"

Noah snapped to attention at his father's tone, feeling like he was ten again.

"I'll stand with them." Rait pulled his shoulders back as if he was preparing for a battle and stalked toward his horse. The pair disappeared in a cloud of dust. Noah prayed his brother would come to terms with losing another sister, and if he didn't, he prayed the director Rait hired to help restore Silverdale would distract him, just like Jade was distracting him whether he liked it or not.

Noah climbed to his feet and dusted his jeans.

"He never did transition well. Neither did you, if I recall."

Noah's lip twitched. "You were always there to guide us and help us through, Dad. When Mom died, you gave us an example of how to not be owned by grief or any rotten circumstances in general but navigating those waters as adults are a little murkier than what you made it look."

"Are you still seeing your therapist?"

Noah nodded. "I'm starting to sound like one, huh?"

"Seems to be doing you some good, Son. I'm sorry for what you've endured and about your friend, Sergeant Mooney. Life seems to spin faster the older you get. It's why a man needs a good woman to love him and keep him balanced." His father's eyes began to water. "I miss your mom, and I never wished more than I do now that she could be here to see each of you find your life mates, to help your sisters with their weddings and to encourage the future brides of my sons, which is why I need you boys to be on board for your sister, to support her and Dane. He's a good man, cut from a gentler clothe but one like ours. He'll treat her good and he loves her. That's what is important." His dad shifted in the saddle. "You know, your mom and I didn't start off on an easy road, but we knew God was in it and we trusted Him, even though our families didn't exactly approve of our marriage. We loved each other, and they supported us because they loved us and that is what I'm asking of you boys. Support Brandy Jo and Dane because you love her. They won't always have an easy time of it. Your sister is as stubborn as any Danner, but he'll make her happy."

"I know, Dad."

His father looked down at his hands. "Noah, what I'm about to say may be a little more difficult for you to hear, but I want you to listen up."

Noah swallowed the knot in his throat and wished he would have gone off with Rait. "Yes, sir."

"I want you to be happy. Life is fickle, there is no other way around it. It is what it is, but if you keep yourself guarded and from taking chances you could miss out on the greatest blessings of your life." He drew in a long breath as he gazed out across the endless stretch of land. "When I married your mom, I never once imagined life without her, and the more days I spent with her the more I fell in love with her, she completed me in every way possible. When God took her, the pain was unbearable, but I knew I had to live by the words I'd taught you kids and continue to trust God's plan even if it didn't line up with how I'd planned it.

"I have the blessed assurance that one day your mama and I will be reunited, but even more, I'll be in the presence of Jesus and that is why I was able to walk peace in front of you kids. Losing a friend hurts, no matter how that friend is lost, but don't let your losses keep your head down. You've got to pick yourself up and dust off your britches, just like when you got knocked off bulls."

"Yes, sir. I'm trying." It was why he wanted to be out at Silver Lining, to gather his thoughts and find a starting place.

"Do more than try, son. You've got to live life, Noah. Find yourself a good woman, someone like Jade and chase your dreams. Be intentional. You always did like her. She's stubborn and been through a long rough storm. If anyone can reach her, you can. Now, that I've got that off my chest let's get back to work before your brother rounds up all the cattle himself."

Noah covered his irritation at how well his dad could read him with laughter. "I'd chop all the wood we need for winter if Rait was that quick. Sitting behind a desk the way he does has softened him and slowed him down a little, but don't tell him I said so."

Noah climbed into the saddle and raced his dad toward the next rise. He smiled and slowed as his thoughts traveled back to Jade and his father's forthrightness where she was concerned. They'd been friends, and at one time he'd even told his father he was going to marry her one day. That was before she'd left Silverdale and didn't return, before she married another man. His smile turned downward, and he sat taller in the saddle. He could give Jade grace because they were young at the time, and after having lost friends in combat, he understood the wave of emotions and confusion, but he couldn't get over the sting, the fact that she'd turned to someone else in her greatest time of need. It should have been him comforting her after her mother's death. It should have been him who waited at the end of the aisle. That's why he joined the army, because all his well laid plans had been rerouted by her decision to marry another man, and he hadn't been able to abide the thought of making Silver Lining his home when all his dreams had included her by his side. Now that she was back, would today be any different?

Maybe his dad was right, maybe he should chase the dreams he'd shelved when Jade chose a different path. Now that she was available and back in Silverdale, maybe he should be intentional with pursuing her, or at least discovering if the Jade he'd known and loved still existed inside the brick walls she'd erected. It wouldn't be easy, he'd seen that when she'd stayed out at Rockin' D with Marvella, but he'd tap into the Danner stubbornness and at least give it a try. Starting tonight, if she'd let him.

CHAPTER FIVE

Jade swept her last client's hair clippings into the dust pan when the cowbell chimed. Her gaze flitted to the wagon wheel clock on the wall, and then she dumped the hair into the trash can. . "We're closed."

"I was hoping you'd have time for an old friend."

Jade's heart lurched to her throat and she turned around to see if her ears had deceived her. Standing inside the glass door, Noah took her breath away as he slid his Aviators from his face and into his shirt pocket. The black T-shirt stretched tight across his chest with the movement. She thought creating distance between them would remove him from her mind. She couldn't have been more wrong, especially since she'd seen him ride by on his motorcycle and in his truck several times in the last several weeks. Of course, she hadn't known that at first and she'd become paranoid, thinking Micah had gotten out already and was stalking her again, until she asked Cole, who had assured her he hadn't. Then one of the older ladies cooed over how good Noah Danner looked on his motorcycle, and another mentioned how she wouldn't mind dating his truck. Jade had laughed at that, because she wouldn't mind dating Noah's truck either, especially since the parts needed to fix it had yet to be delivered. Besides, it wasn't conducive to living in the country. The roads here weren't quite the same as the ones in Denver. Even then she had difficulty getting around, but only in the snow and ice. Here, she just didn't get around and settled for driving Maw's old white safari looking Jeep. She glanced out the window to see which vehicle he'd brought with him today and grew weak in the knees at the sight of his dad's beat up truck. The same truck he'd pick her up in on the way to their rodeos.

"Whatcha need, Noah?"

"A haircut. In case you haven't heard, my sister is getting married in a few days."

She laughed and motioned for him to sit in the chair. "I don't think there is a soul in Silverdale who hasn't heard about the next Danner wedding. I've heard through the grapevine that there is even a pool going on to see who is next. I have to say, from what I hear of the ladies, Rait has you beat."

"The odds?" The room seemed to disappear until all that was left was him. His eyes, the warmth of his presence in the air-conditioned room. The pungent smell of dye from her last customer finally abandoned her sinuses and was replaced by horse, hay, outdoors and Noah's spicy cologne. He hung his hat on a rustic nail and gazed into her eyes long and hard.

"Ten to one." Gravity grabbed hold of her and tugged her toward him like a magnet until the corners of his gorgeous mouth lifted, breaking the connection.

He winked and then plopped into her chair a brush of air filled with his cologne bathed her skin. "Hmm, you know how I feel about losing."

Yes, she did know how he felt about losing, but she didn't know how she felt about him winning. The fact that he was even being considered as a competitor against Rait for the next Danner wedding meant the ladies of Silverdale believed he had someone in mind to meet him at the altar. And she didn't like that idea at all. She kind of liked his daily drive-bys and actually looked forward to them. His attention made her feel safe and cared for, she even began to forget about Micah and started sleeping through the night, something she hadn't felt since the last summer she'd married Micah. Noah's future wife wouldn't appreciate his attentiveness to another woman, especially one with Jade's reputation. Releasing her fists from their bawled state, she jabbed her fingers through his hair.

"Hey." He grimaced.

"I'm sorry. I wasn't expecting the thickness or the length." She gentled her touch as she combed through his hair. The soft dark curls sliding in between her fingers sent her stomach into a full roil. If she kept this up she might forget she'd sworn off men. She pulled her hand back and snatching a clean cape from the small whiskey barrel acting as a shelf, she clipped the cape around his neck. "What are we doing?"

He caught her gaze through the mirror. "I thought I'd take you to the Branding Iron, tonight. Word is steak is on the grill and I know how much you like your steak."

Whoa! Dinner with Noah? Her emotions dug heels into the cement. If seeing Noah marry bothered her, having her be his target bothered ten times more. She'd learned a tough lesson with Micah and she wasn't about relive it. "I meant with your hair, Noah."

"I know. Will you?"

"Danner's don't date, remember?" She said, slipping her scissors from their case. Dinner was a date, right?

"An old rule meant to be broken. See, I'm not all golden, Jade. But if you don't want to call it a date, let's call it catching up."

She narrowed her gaze. "Is this a ploy to change the betting pool? I know you don't like to lose, but I'm not going to be your pawn just so you can beat Rait."

"Considering I didn't know about the ladies' betting books until a few minutes ago, no." He spun his chair around, took her hands in his, and looked up at her. The rough callouses against her palms weakened her knees. And her resolve to keep Noah at a distance.

"If you're worried people will talk we can take a picnic basket out to Silver Lining. I have a basket in the truck already."

She tugged her hands from his and smacked his arm. "Noah Danner, you are sure of yourself."

He spun back around. "If you knew how nervous I was about asking you out, darling, you'd take pity on me. I was hoping you'd say yes."

"It took you this long to get up the nerve to stop and ask me out?" Her hand shot to her mouth. She wasn't known for thinking before speaking and she regretted her question for the flirtatious way it sounded. She didn't want him to ask her out. No way. No how. Not even if she did sigh every time she discreetly watched his vehicle crawl by the salon.

"You saw that, huh?"

Before she considered what she was doing, she pointed at the tally marks written in black eyeliner on the mirror in the upper right-hand corner with capital letters M and T beside them with her scissors. It didn't take her long to realize he preferred his motorcycle in the evenings and his truck every other time of the day.

"I drove by that many times, huh?" He seemed shocked by the revelation, and then laughed. "I think you might have missed a few. By my calculations I drove by at least four times, sometimes six a day, and let's not forget the times I drove by Junktique before you opened the salon. Why didn't you ask for help with the renovations? Rait is a pro at this stuff and I'm not too bad myself. We have some old barn wood that would look great in here."

Jade's jaw dropped, and she shook her head at his intentional rambling. He was sinking his hook into her heart and reeling her in. She needed him to stop before she swallowed the bait. She didn't want to be hurt again. He wouldn't hurt her physically like Micah had, but Noah had the power to crush her in ways her ex-husband never could. And she definitely didn't want to ruin his life, if Micah came after Noah. She tucked the scissors into her back pocket. "Do you know how long it took me to realize it was you and not my ex-husband?"

"I'm sorry about that. I honestly drove by just to check on you, to make sure you were okay. I think Cole was getting irritated with my calls and texts and I decided to change tactics."

Her feathers ruffled because she could take care of herself, but they quickly soothed when a vision of the hospital room Micah had put her in slammed into her mind. She'd nearly failed at caring for herself and it was to have someone care enough to watch out for her, but that was dangerous for Noah, especially when Micah got out, and he would. He always did. "I'm fine."

"I can see that, but I rest easier seeing it with my own eyes."

She slipped the scissors from her back pocket and laid them on the table before sitting in the chair at the station next to him. Releasing a heavy sigh, she rested her chin on her fist and considered him. There had been a time when all she thought about was being Mrs. Noah Danner, but all that changed because of bad choices she'd made. She could have moved in with Maw after the death of her mother, but she'd been scared and hurt. She didn't want to experience that kind of pain again, which meant isolating herself from the people she truly loved. Like Maw, Cole and even Noah and his family. "Noah, you have to know I'm damaged goods. I always have been. It's just when we were kids, I honestly believed I could be someone else other than an addict's daughter."

His brow deepened. "What are you getting at, Jade? It's not like I asked you to marry me."

"No, you didn't. But I'm being up front with you, right here, right now. You're the marrying kind of guy and you wouldn't ask me to dinner if you didn't have intentions to explore a relationship with me. I don't want you to waste your time *catching up* with me when there is a good woman out there for you. A woman who won't bring baggage with her."

"What if that woman is you, Jade?"

Her heart literally stopped, and then sped up like she'd drank a thirty-two-ounce coffee in ten minutes.

"One night catching up won't hurt us, Jade. Besides, there is something I want to show you."

One night might not hurt him, but it would her if she caught a glimpse of all she'd miss in life by marrying Micah, and even though they'd been divorced for years, she wasn't free of him, he'd made that clear when he'd broken into Maw's home. She should tell Noah no, but she was a gluten for punishment, and she'd like to completely forget about the fear cloaking her shoulders for just one night. "All right. I'll go, after I cut your hair."

~

Noah's palms moistened against the old steering cover as they pulled through the gate branding Rockin' D and he wondered what in the world he was doing. His father's pep talk had made him feel as if he could conquer the world, and then ask Jade out, but after her little speech back at the salon, he felt as if all his raw wounds were about to be exposed, and he didn't know how she would take it, knowing the man she'd placed high on a pedestal was just as damaged as she claimed to be. "Here we are."

She looked over at him. "Horses? Do you know how long it's been since I've ridden?"

"Would you rather we didn't?"

"Are you kidding?" She jumped out of the truck and climbed onto the fence. She scratched the nose of the grey spotted Appaloosa, a horse he'd specifically chosen for her knowing how much she'd gushed over the dappled horses whenever she'd seen one. "She is beautiful."

"I thought you might like Misty." He wouldn't tell Jade that he'd only purchased the horse a few weeks ago because it reminded him of her. "She's a little feisty, but nothing you can't handle."

Noah grabbed the brown paper bags and the rolled blanket from the back seat and closed the truck door. He held the paper bags up for her inspection. "I hope you still like PB and J."

She flipped her hair over her shoulder and tossed a saucy smile at him. "It's not steak, but I much prefer the company out here than Branding Iron's."

"I agree. Tell you what, if we survive this excursion and I don't scare you off, I'll make you dinner."

She hopped onto the fence and into the saddle. "Another PB&J?"

He climbed onto Gabe, his black and white paint. "I'll have you know, I'm considered the grill master around here."

"All right, then. I rarely turn down a good steak." She clucked to Misty. "Let's see if we survive."

They rode toward Silver Lining, neither of them saying a word. She seemed content taking in the landscape and fresh air, and he was content riding beside her, watching her. She'd changed out of the white lacy top, denim capris, and pink strappy studded heels that had made her almost as tall as him and into a T-shirt and a pair of jeans, and she exchanged her heels for a pair of hot pink cowboy boots with black straps decorated with studs. "What's with the pink?"

She glanced at him like she'd forgotten he was there. "What?"

"The pink car, the pink shoes." He pointed at her feet. "The boots."

"Breast cancer awareness."

"Is that what your mom had?" At the turn of her mouth, he said, "Never mind, we don't have to talk about it."

She shook her head and slowed Misty's pace. "Actually, nobody has ever asked me about her. Not even Maw, and whenever I bring her up the subject quickly changes. It's like talking about cancer and her death is contagious. It's kind of weird, if you know what I mean."

He hesitated, checking to see if his armor locked in place, it didn't. He didn't know if he liked that or not, he didn't like being vulnerable, but if he was going to try to win her over he was going to have to be. "I do." He adjusted his ball cap. "I lost friends in combat, and it was like that. If we talked about it after the debriefing it was like we were setting out to curse the next mission, but recently." He halted, his jaw tightening against the emotion welling in his chest. He cleared his throat. "Right before you came back, a friend of mine took his own life."

She stopped Misty and reached over to touch his arm. "I'm sorry."

His brow wrinkled. "Thank you. It's hard to process. I dealt with a lot of survivor's guilt from the Middle East, but nothing like this. I keep trying to figure out what I could have done differently."

"You know there is nothing you could have done, right?" When he kept silent she slid her fingers down to his hand and squeezed. This was right. Being here with her, confiding in her. It was right. Good. Perfect. Predestination. As difficult as the conversation had turned, he knew in that moment that he would do everything in his power to convince her that they were meant to be together. "It's not your fault, Noah."

"That's what my therapist keeps telling me." He clamped his mouth shut. He wanted to move, to race across the terrain and feel the sting of the wind against his face, anything to out run the words that had just spilled from his mouth, but he didn't want to break the connection between them. "Are you surprised?"

Her lids blinked over her blue eyes. "About what?"

"That I'm broken, too?"

"Because you see a therapist? No, I applaud you for not letting your pride get in the way and having the courage to seek help. I can't imagine what you saw over there, Noah. The things you had to do while serving our country. Thank you, for your service."

Some of the heaviness weighing down his shoulders ever since he'd returned home lifted. Being the oldest of all the Danner siblings, he felt a certain sense of responsibility to model perfection in front of them. For months, he'd been faking it. Pretending to be put together when he wasn't. With a few words, Jade uncovered him and put it all in prospective. "I can't say pride didn't get in the way. My father is the only one who knows."

"You haven't told Rait or even Nathan?"

"No. I didn't want them to think less of me."

"Noah, they love you. All of your siblings do. They would never think less of you."

He wanted to ask if she loved him, too, but she'd only been back a few weeks, and this was the first time seeing her since she'd left Rockin' D. He needed to give her a little more time to come to terms with what was happening between them, and he needed to be sure himself. A man pushing thirty should know better than to fall so easily after all the years of absence. "Shall we keep going? We're almost there."

CHAPTER SIX

Jade lifted her chin and breathed. She'd forgotten just how different country mountain air was compared to the congested city. Noah's saddle creaked as he dismounted and walked their horses through a bright red gate.

"Welcome to Silver Lining."

She swung down from Misty and stood next to Noah. A vast sea of grass waved at them. A small mountain stood like a castle turret overlooking the land. If they climbed it they could probably see Rockin' D and maybe even Silvedale. Leading down from the mountain, her eyes followed a hard line of majestic gray stone, like a castle wall. "It's beautiful, Noah. I can see why your grandma wanted it."

"It's not the size of Rockin' D or the Winter's spread."

She shook her head. "No, but there is enough grazing pasture if you wanted your own small heard. And it looks like the creek won't run dry."

"Come on," he said, taking her hand in his. "I want to show you something."

The walked for only a few minutes, but it was enough time for her to think about how nice her hand felt resting in his, even if it was a little scary at the same time.

"All right, close your eyes."

Odd how she instantly did what he asked, as if she trusted him, and she did. More than anyone outside of Maw and Cole. She never would have closed her eyes in Micah's presence, not unless she was dodging a fist or blocking out the pistol shoved in her face. She sensed Noah's movements and knew he untied the blanket from his horse. Air whooshed past her face as he unfurled the quilt with a snap and she barely flinched. That was a good sign, right? Or was she allowing too much of her guard down?

"Keep them closed." His hand engulfed hers once more as he led her a few feet, and then he turned her around. "All right, sit."

"Noah, this is silly," she said as she crouched, and then fell onto the blanket.

He chuckled, the sound warming her insides. His shoulder brushed hers when he sat next to her. "I know, but it's fun. Okay, you can open them."

She gasped when she caught sight of the vista. Even though they'd only walked a short distance and up a slight incline, the view had changed dramatically. "Oh, Noah! It's breathtaking."

Instantly she forgot all about her fears and Denver, and even Micah. It was as if Micah had never existed in her world. Noah had always talked about Silver Lining when they were kids, but she'd never seen it beyond the boundary of Silver Lining Road. It had been another piece of land nestled in the mountains, but this, this was amazing. It was almost like standing on top of the world. She jumped to her feet and took in as much as she could. Miles and miles of mountain tops kissed clouds. Sunlight bathed parts of the hills while white puffy clouds blanketed other parts, leaving the hills in the shadows.

"I know." He tugged at her hand, motioning for her to sit beside him. He handed her a brown paper bag, and then laid back on the blanket with his hands folded behind his head. The evening sun bathed his skin, giving him a glow of contentment.

"You love it here, don't you?"

Noah peeled one lid open. "I do. It is peaceful. Somehow, when I am here, I remember there is a loving God."

Laughter bubbled over. "Noah, your family always goes to church."

Sitting, he pulled his knees up and rested his arms on them. "Going to church and believing in God are two different things, sweetheart."

"I guess I never separated the two. I always believed people who went to church believed in God."

"I think there are a lot of people sitting on pews who don't even know who He is, but just the same, there are people who haven't been to church who do know Him." His lips flattened. "I've seen a lot of things, Jade. Things that have made me question God's presence, like when my friend took his own life. Where was God in that?"

Her heart lurched. She'd been so caught up in being angry at the world that she hadn't considered what others were going through. She never thought anything bad happened to the Danners, except losing their mother, and even then Mr. Danner had soldiered on. She recalled him once telling her youth group at summer camp that circumstances in life should never dictate God's goodness. God was the same yesterday, today, and forever. Loving, forgiving and self- sacrificing. "I guess that is where true faith comes in, huh? I mean, if we say we believe in Him, we can't stop believing in Him because life throws rotten tomatoes at us. Just look at my life, it's been rotten. I don't need to remind you who my mom was, but when she got cancer, she started begging God to forgive her, not so she would be healed, but she knew she was about to stand before Him.

"I was angry and hateful toward God and everyone. Marrying Micah was a bad choice. I guess it was my way of throwing myself in the pig sty because I felt that was all I deserved. I deemed my circumstances as a lack of love from God, but I shouldn't have. My circumstances don't dictate God's goodness, just like what your friend did doesn't dictate God's goodness. God was faithful to your friend every day, and I believe God saw his struggle. I can't believe all this is coming out of my mouth."

He blinked. "I can't either. You sound like my dad."

She smiled. "He's a wise man. Aren't you going to eat?"

He dropped back to the blanket and propped his head on his hand. "Would it make you feel better if I did?"

She nodded. "You didn't bring me out here to eat alone, did you?"

"You're not alone, but," he said, sitting up and unfolding his brown paper bag. "I did bring you out here for a picnic. Shall we pray."

She stared at him from beneath hooded eyes as he closed his and thanked the Lord for all of his blessings and for her and the truth she'd spoken. An ache formed in her chest. How long had it been since she'd thanked God for anything? Since before her mother's diagnosis. She scanned the horizon, proof of a loving and giving God, who obviously created the bountiful beauty before her and silently apologized for being neglectful, and then thanked Him the gift of sight and the words of wisdom He'd given Noah through her, words that stirred life in her spirit.

"Amen," Noah unwrapped his sandwich. "It's not much, but it was spur of the moment."

"And what would you have done if I said I wanted steak?"

"Then I would have had lunch for tomorrow." He grinned. "Nice choice."

"Yeah, I would eat peanut butter and jelly every day if I could sit right here and enjoy this view." She unfolded the brown paper bag and reached inside. Her fingers brushed against a piece of paper and she pulled it out. "What's this?" she asked as she pulled it out, and then smiled. "We're a little old for notes, aren't we?"

"Never."

A wave of delight slammed into her stomach. If she wasn't careful she'd find herself head over heels in love with Noah Danner again, but then she had a feeling it was too late and she was already cartwheeling down that road. She unfolded the aged, crisp paper and her heart skipped a beat. It was a rough architectural sketch of a cabin she'd drawn at sixteen. She narrowed her gaze at him. "You kept this?"

"I added a few things, like the mountain and the trees and the creek." He leaned close enough to touch her and pointed at the space marked living room. "I thought to expand this area and place a breakfast nook here and add a deck there."

"You're going to build this?" She turned her head as she asked the question and found his blue eyes intently gazing into hers.

"Yes." His gaze dropped to her mouth, and then lifted to her eyes.

Her heart pounded in her chest. What were they doing? What was she doing? She shouldn't want this, but she didn't want anything more. Just one taste of the kiss she'd imagined as a teen girl to see if it had been all she'd thought it would be. He cupped her neck and drew her to his mouth. The soft warmth beckoned her, teasing and tantalizing as he nibbled and tasted. A slight gasp from her and he deepened the kiss. Her hands slid along the curve of his honed pecs and around his neck until her fingers curled into his hair. She hadn't kissed a man since Micah and his kisses had always been rough and demanding. Before she knew it, she'd pulled Noah down onto the blanket, drinking in every bit of him. Noah eased back, his heavy breaths matching hers. Her heart thundered against her chest. His lips left a trail of heat along her jaw, to her brow and then her ear. She dug her fingers into his biceps as tears burned the backs of her lids. She'd been a fool to marry Micah. She hadn't loved him, not like she had Noah. She'd known it the day she said her vows, which probably added to her ex's insecurities. She wouldn't take the full blame, though. After their marriage she'd discovered a trail of abused women he'd left behind. If she'd known it before... What? Would it have changed her mind? Probably not considering she'd felt as if she deserved the punishment Micah was willing to dish out. Hot tears streamed from the corner of her eyes as wrapped her arms around Noah's neck and silently apologized to Noah and the young girl she'd been for not making better choices.

"Shhh, sweetheart," he whispered. "I want to be with you more than you know, but I won't dishonor you."

His words hit her like a glass of cold water. Her hands fell to the ground as she stared at him in horror. She rolled from beneath him, jumped to her feet and stalked to Misty. Her cheeks flaming hot with embarrassment.

"Jade," he beckoned. "Wait. I'm sorry. I shouldn't have kissed you."

She flinched like she was ducking one of Micah's punches, only this time she wasn't being blamed. She shoved her boot into the stirrup and swung into the saddle. Even though Noah was taking responsibility for their shenanigans, she couldn't help but hear Micah's demeaning words ringing in her ears. How could she have behaved so badly? Like the rodeo floosy her ex accused her of being.

"Jade!"

All she wanted was to know what it felt like to be loved by Noah, even if only for a moment, and Lord help her if she didn't get away from him now, she'd jump off this horse and kiss him again and agree to everything he offered. What would Silverton think of her then, a divorced rodeo floosy tempting a Danner saint. A woman like her would never be good enough for a man like him.

His hand slid over hers on the reins and she caught an unfamiliar emotion in his eyes. Empathy? Hurt? Pity? Whatever it was it wasn't anger and she didn't know how to deal with it and it almost frightened her more than facing Micah. "Yah," she hollered, nudging Misty to race back toward Rockin' D in the hopes she'd find a ride back to town before Noah caught up with her.

~

Noah waited a few seconds before he chased after her, partly from the shock of what had happened and partly to give her time to cool her heels. He hadn't meant to kiss her, not yet, not today. He'd hoped to dance with her at Brandy Jo's wedding and swoop her out into the moonlight where he'd gaze into her eyes until she agreed to marry him. A little rash, and too soon after their reunion, but after her reaction to Silver Lining and that kiss, he was confident she was the one for him.

Convincing Jade of that fact might be more difficult than he'd planned. He prayed he hadn't spooked her back to Denver. If he did, he'd follow her until she understood just how he felt about her. He rode into the corral and found her brushing Misty. The saddle hung over the fence. Relieved, he slowed Gabe's pace, dismounted and removed the saddle. Jade handed him the brush, patted Misty's rump, and then climbed over the fence.

The corner of his mouth twitched in irritation. He'd been a fool to kiss her. She stalked toward a shadowy spot of the barn and leaned against the faded red wood with her arms crossed. Confident she wouldn't attempt to walk back to Silverdale, he ran the brush over Gabe and then released him. He hefted the saddle onto his shoulder and disappeared into the barn where he found Rait hiding in the shadows. His brother held his finger to his mouth and motioned for him toward a stall at the opposite end.

"I saw Jade riding hard and didn't have time to slip into the house. Is everything, all right?"

"I don't know." Noah checked the open doorway. "Would you mind finishing up here while I take her back home?"

"Not at all. You might take your bike."

"That's a little much, don't you think?" He didn't want to push further, but the thought her arms wrapped around his waist as he chased the wind cemented into his being. His six-pack shivered.

"Since dad took the truck and Wyatt has yours, I don't think you have a choice unless you want me to take her back in Serena's European tin can." Rait shrugged at Noah's obvious look of horror. He couldn't imagine his little, big brother shoved into Serena's car. "Hey, my truck was filled with materials for Settler Days and I needed to grab something from here."

"How long do you think you'll be?"

A grin curved the corner of Rait's mouth as he glanced at his watch. "Oh, another hour or so."

"Thanks."

Rait clapped him on the shoulder. "What are brothers for, man?"

Shaking his head, Noah shoved his hands into his pockets and found Jade in the same place he'd left her. "Look, I'm sorry."

She lifted her chin, the tear stains had dried, but the redness around her eyes told him he'd made her cry. "Can we not talk about it, please?"

"All right. How do you feel about motorcycles?"

She blinked. "What?"

He explained the vehicle situation to her. "It's either that or you wait for Rait to head back to town. He'll be awhile though, so either way, you're stuck with me." He forced his lips to remain flat. He didn't want his victory smile sending her home on foot, and knowing how stubborn Jade was, she'd walk a hundred miles if she knew how badly he wanted to feel her arms around his waist. He motioned for her to follow him to his private sanctuary, the original Rockin' D barn, not even an eighth of the size of the newer one, and a place often invaded by his siblings when they needed advice. He swung the barn door wide and flipped on the lights. Her pink VW nestled in the back waiting for parts. "You can sit over there while I find another helmet."

She opted for leaning against the door.

All right, so her stubborn walls were back in place. Good thing he knew a thing or two about improvised strategies. He snagged a black helmet from a hook and tossed it to her, and then climbed on his bike. "Are you ready?"

Her shoulders slouched, but after inspecting the inside of the helmet, she put it on and tucked her hair inside before securing the straps. His motorcycle purred to life and she climbed on behind him. His stomach muscles tensed with expectation as he waited for her to wrap her arms around his waist, but the stubborn lady kept her hands on her thighs. Revving the engine, the motorcycle lurched forward. He smiled when her arms swung around him. His smile only deepened when she leaned against his back and held on to him as if her life depended on it.

CHAPTER SEVEN

"Are you ready to go?" Maw poked her head through the open door and sucked in a sharp breath. "Jade Marie Bentley, what are you thinking?"

Honestly, she was thinking about packing up her pink Bug and driving back to Denver, but as desperate as she was to get as far from Noah as possible, she couldn't leave his sister hanging on her wedding day. Besides, the VW still wasn't working.

"You can't dress like that to a Danner wedding."

Jade peeked at herself in the mirror. Her favorite red top and skinny jeans along with her red, yellow, and white comic book heels fashion was more for a day of shopping at the mall in the city, but it wasn't like she'd planned on attending a wedding while she was in Silverdale and she had nothing else. "I don't have a dress. Maw."

Maw snagged her hand and marched her out the front door. "Come along. I'm sure Nan is still open and if she isn't I have a key."

Her grandmother dragged her over to a quaint little shop called Second Go Round. "Oh look, there's Nan, now. We're catching her just in time." Maw pushed through the door just as Nan turned the open sign to close. "Sorry, Nan, but as you can see we have an emergency. My granddaughter can't attend Brandy Jo's wedding like this."

"Of course, not, Marvella. I have just the dress." Nan disappeared behind a curtain

"I wasn't exactly planning on staying after I finished the bridal party's hair, Maw."

Maw spoke to Nan as she followed her into a back room. "I don't know what happened between her and Noah, but she's been in a snit ever since he brought her back on his motorcycle last night."

"Maw, I'm right here. Nothing happened."

"Well, just the same. Brandy Jo will expect you to stay after you do her hair. Oh, Nan, this is perfect."

The pair returned holding a floor length white and floral spaghetti strap dress with a high neck-line.

"Uh, no."

"It won't hurt you to try it on, Jade."

"Please do," Nan added. "I've been waiting for someone of your slender figure and height to pull this off."

Jade rolled her eyes and took the dress into the fitting room. She slipped out of her shoes and clothes and slid the dress on over her head. One tug and it all fell into place, straight to the floor. A slit at her thigh revealed a lot of leg. Thankfully, she'd shaved last night. She pulled her hair off her shoulders and glanced at the back. The crude basement-sketched permanent ink of Noah's initials glared at her like a bright beam of light, but it was the scar from one of Micah's bullet that repulsed her. The tattoo had been a constant source of Micah's irritation and she supposed he'd thought to remove the ink with lead. Good thing he'd been a bad shot, not because he'd missed the tattoo, but he'd missed vital organs when he'd tried to kill her. It took her a few years to realize the near-death experience wasn't because of something she'd done on a whim right after the news of her mother's cancer and months before Micah had entered the picture. He didn't need a reason. She let her hair fall to cover the initials and the scar. The dress was perfect, even if it made her feel vulnerable.

"Jade, let us see."

Jade slipped her heels back on and drew in a breath before slipping out the door.

"Oh, darling. I'm afraid all eyes will be on you and not the bride."

Jade offered a hesitant smile. "Thank you, Maw."

"Your grandmother is right, Jade." Nan lifted Jades hair off her shoulder and quickly dropped it back in place. "The shoes will have to go, of course."

"I have some clear heels at home that will wear nicely with the dress," Jade said.

"You don't have time. Change. I'll run home and grab them and meet you at the chapel. You mustn't leave the bride waiting on her special day."

Jade caught her grandmother's enthusiasm, even though she wasn't looking forward to running into the bride's brother. Maybe she could hide in the bridal chamber and nobody would notice, and then skip the reception all together. She hastily changed clothes, and after grabbing her supplies from the salon, she raced to the chapel in hopes she'd beat the wedding party, especially Noah. No sooner had she pulled into the parking lot and cut the engine of her grandmother's jeep than Noah appeared out of nowhere and opened the door for her.

"Do you need any help carrying things?"

"Sure," she said as she stepped out of the jeep. Opening the hatch ,she crawled in to reach a runaway can of hairspray.

"What are those?"

"What?" She climbed out of the back and noticed his line of sight. "My shoes? You sure comment on my shoes a lot."

"Well, you wear some interesting duds worth commenting on. Do all the ladies in Denver wear such interesting shoes?"

"I happen to like shoes. Boots, heels, sandals, and flip flops. You should see my collection of house slippers."

"I would love to see your slippers, bright and early in the morning as we watch the sun come up while sipping our coffee together," he teased and offered her that smooth Danner grin.

She shoved the larger tote into his gut and received satisfaction at his grunt as she ducked back inside for the smaller tote.

"Hey, what was that for? You need a Ka-Pow warning with those shoes."

She stood less than a few inches from him and all she could think about was pulling his head down for another delicious kiss that continued to curl her toes, but she knew the danger as the warning bells jangled in her head. "One kiss and you have us hooking up."

"Not just hooking up, darling. Danners don't hook up. They get hitched as in forever."

She gaped and took a step back. She swallowed the nausea building in her stomach. "I did that once. It was a disaster and I won't do that again."

He smoothed a strand of her hair behind her ear, and she was well aware of cars pulling into the parking lot. "That's because you married the wrong man. I promise you when we marry, it won't be a disaster."

She side-stepped him and hurried across the parking lot. Her heels clapped on the pavement and she felt the warmth of his gaze on her back. What had she gotten herself into? Another time and she would have melted at his feet. She nearly had. Her legs still wobbled beneath her.

~

Noah watched as Jade ascended the stairs and as soon as her hand touched the handle, he hollered across the church parking lot. "I will marry you, Jade Bentley."

Her shoulders pulled back and she lifted her chin as she entered the church.

"What are you doing, Noah?" Rait came up beside him.

"Pursuing my future bride."

"Looks like you're scaring her," his youngest brother Wyatt said. "Hey, where's your neck tie?"

"He's not wearing one."

"Why not?"

"He scared poor Dane into believing the neck-tie was a deal breaker for taking our sister."

"And it worked?"

"Yep, but don't you get any ideas, little brother." Rait ruffled Wyatt's head. "You're already stuck with the tie."

Noah pulled his attention from Jade and focused on his brothers. "Did you get the Cheerios?"

"Yep," Wyatt said, sounding pleased with himself. "Twelve boxes."

Noah furrowed his brow and snapped his attention to Wyatt. "Twelve?"

"Sure, the way Danners have been dropping off like flies at the onset of winter, I figured I better be prepared, especially since you and Rait seem to be racing each other toward that matrimonial state."

"Now, wait a minute," Rait protested. "I've never mentioned marriage. That was Noah."

"I better not find a single loop in my truck," Noah added. "Looks like you'll be eating Cheerios for a long time, little brother."

"Aw, come on, guys. Why did you have me get them for Dane?"

"We're just welcoming him to the family, that's all." Rait wrapped his arm around his brother's shoulder.

The church door swung open to reveal a fiery mad Jade with her hands on her hips.

"She doesn't look happy, Noah."

"Nope. Mad as Misty when you rescued her from the horse mill and broke her in a few weeks ago."

Noah pierced Wyatt with a look. "Don't you be flapping your jaw. No one needs to know I just acquired her."

"I don't think he'll break Jade."

Noah elbowed Rait. "She's not a horse, she's a lady, and you'd get much further with Serena if you remembered that."

"Noah, if your sister is late for her own wedding. It's your fault." Jade glared. "I need my bag, please."

"I see your progress, Noah," Rait teased. "At least she's polite."

Noah left his brothers in a fit of laughter and swaggered toward Jade. He almost wished he'd worn that cussed neck tie as an added layer of armor. He'd just have to rely on his charm and not his good looks in a suit and tie to get back into Jade's good graces.

CHAPTER EIGHT

"Are you sorry you got stuck with me?" Noah rested his hand on the top of the passenger door after he opened it for her.

"No, I'm still doused in the awkwardness of being the only non-family member in attendance."

He leaned in, closing the space between them. She'd looked good in the jeans and the Ka-Pow heels she'd worn to the church, but this slinky floor length dress with the slit teasing his eyes was driving him crazy, and it wasn't just the memory of the kiss they'd shared yesterday. It was her response to Silver Lining, her words of wisdom to help him see love would trump the shame he felt at not being all put together as he thought he should be. He'd even had a heart-to-heart with Rait last night, and just like she'd said, his brother's love for him was evident. Rait even helped him realize that he hadn't had any nightmares since Jade had returned, maybe because he'd been focused on her and not the trauma he'd experienced. Everything about her tempted his self-control. If he had it his way she'd be a Danner soon, but he'd spooked her enough for one day. "Marvella was there."

"She's practically family."

"And so are you."

"Noah," she whispered his name as her lashes brushed across her cheeks.

He crooked his finger beneath her chin. "I will make you see your worth, Jade Bentley. You deserve good in this world and I'm determined to give it to you."

"I'm damaged goods."

"So am I, sweetheart. Sometimes I wake up in a pool of sweat

224

because of a reoccurring nightmare. Sometimes I can't sleep and pace the floor. Most of the time. I don't want to share that baggage with anyone, especially someone I love, but what if you are the key to my healing?"

"Your past won't ever cause me harm."

"Is that what you're scared of, that Micah Cane will hurt me?"

She didn't say a word but stepped onto the running board.

"Here," he said, grasping her elbow. "Let me help."

Driving the black beauty to the wedding had been a no-brainer since it was a special occasion, but he hadn't intended on escorting Jade to the reception, even though he'd wanted to. Her shoes were no match for the chrome running boards. "I'm sorry Marvella's vehicle won't start. I'll look at it when I'm not so gussied up."

"It's all right, I'm sure it is something simple. I have a feeling Maw is behind it."

He was surprised that she responded to him. "I'm not seeing it. The manipulating part, maybe, but outside of disconnecting the battery, which I checked, I doubt she wouldn't know how to disable the jeep."

"One of your brothers?"

"I think they'd know better but maybe Brandy Jo's wedding has turned their practical joker personas up a notch." He backed out of the parking lot and caught a glimpse of an unfamiliar white cargo parked across the street. The hair on his nape stood on end, and he made a mental note to find Cole as soon as they arrived at Barton's Big Red Barn. "I'll get Rait to help me tow it home after the reception, and then I can take a look at it."

Lost in thought, she stared out the window and absently nodded.

"Is there anything you need before we head over?" He flipped on the blinker. "Jade?"

She slowly turned toward him.

"Is everything, all right?" he asked wondering if maybe she saw the car too.

"Yeah, I think so. I just had a weird feeling, that's all."

"Are you sure?"

She nodded. "Let's not miss Brandy Jo and Dane's entrance."

He hid his relief and didn't share his own concerns as he headed toward the Big Red Barn. The sooner they arrived at the reception, the sooner they would be surrounded by people who cared for them. He hated the possibility of bringing trouble to Brandy Jo's reception and putting a damper on her big day, but he knew his sister wouldn't have it any other way. In fact, if his little sister knew anything about the situation she'd probably stomp right over there and confront whoever it was in the van.

He pulled out on the road and checked his rearview mirror. As he suspected, the van followed. "Do you want some music?"

"Sure."

He commanded the radio on, hoping the noise would keep her from picking up on his tension. She wrinkled her nose at his choice of vibes. "I didn't take you for the classical sort."

"I learned to like it overseas. It helped calm me down after an intense situation. You can change it if you would like."

"No, it's kind of nice, besides I caught a glimpse of Brandy Jo's song list and I can guarantee Mozart isn't on it." She slipped off her shoes and propped her feet on the dash as she scooted down in the seat. "You don't mind, do you?"

Any other time he wouldn't have, but he couldn't afford to become distracted by the designer nail polish on her tanned toes. "Not at all, sweetheart. Are you feeling better?" He shifted his gaze from her toes to the van in the mirror as he rolled up to the stop sign.

"I'll feel a lot better when I have more comfortable clothes on. I don't wear dresses often."

He stole a glance at her and then turned left. "Really? You wear slinky shoes and gemstones on the back pockets of your jeans, but you don't wear dresses?"

"I don't know. I always feel awkward wearing them, like a clown."

"Trust me, darling, when I say you don't look like a clown. I don't want to come off sounding like one of my sisters, but you look amazing." Stunning.

"Thank you. I feel exposed."

At the moment, he understood. It wasn't often the enemy was behind him. As soon as they turned on the highway, Noah accelerated a few miles over the speed limit. Enough to place some distance between them and the van, but nothing more than any other lead footed cowboy. "I hope Brandy Jo doesn't get her feelings hurt when all eyes turn to you when you walk in."

"I'm sure you'll keep them from looking." She smirked.

"What's that supposed to mean?"

"Well, you've been hovering and brooding ever since I entered the sanctuary and the closer we get to the barn, the darker you look."

He reached across the seat and squeezed her hand. "I'm sorry. I don't mean to come off possessive. I guess I want to keep you all to myself."

"You're serious about dating me?"

"Not dating, Jade. I love you and I want to marry you." He pulled in front of the barn and parked near the double front doors. He put the truck in park and leaned his arms over the steering wheel as he drank her in. "I always have. I told my dad that very thing that last summer you were in Silverdale, but you left and didn't come back."

"That's a big step, Noah, and I haven't even been back but a few weeks. Once you get to know me again, you may not like me."

"I know all I need to know right here." He thumped his chest. "And we'll take it as slow as you like."

She picked at a chipped spot on her fingernail. "Can I think about it?"

He jumped out of his truck and ran to the other side. Opening the door, he smiled at her and held his hand out to her. "I'm not going anywhere. Why don't you go check on Brandy Jo's hair and I'll catch up with you in a minute."

She nodded, and as she ducked into his truck for her bag her hair parted over her shoulder revealing an obvious gun shot wound. He touched the scar with his finger. She flinched. "Jade, what happened?"

Her shoulders slumped. Turning toward him, she looked as if she was going to ignore his question or start an argument, but she blinked and looked into his eyes. "A memento from my marriage."

He clenched his fists, and then tugged her into his arms. "I am sorry, Jade. You know I will never hurt you. Ever."

"I know, Noah. That is not what scares me."

"He won't ever come near you again. I promise," he whispered near her ear.

"I believe you believe that, but he's hurt so many I love. I couldn't bear it if he hurt you too."

Noah leaned back and gazed into her eyes. "You love me?"

Her gaze fell to the ground and she nodded. "I do."

He grabbed hold of her and swung her around. "Woo who!"

"Noah!" She squirmed until he settled her back on her feet.

"Will you marry me?"

"I need to check on your sister."

He grabbed hold of her fingers as she slid from his embrace. "Jade, will you at least save me a dance."

She slipped inside the barn without saying a word just as the white van that had been following them entered the parking lot. Noah pulled his phone from his pocket and called Cole.

"I'm on it," Cole said before Noah could tell him why he called. "We've had a tail on him since he left Westdale."

"You knew he was out of jail and you didn't say a word?"

Cole pulled in the lot. Several patrol cars surrounded the van. Officers jumped from their cars and held the driver at gunpoint. "Sorry about that. Everything happened so fast. Why don't you see to Jade.

We've got it covered from here."

"Thanks." Noah nodded at Cole from across the lot and slipped his phone into his pocket.

~

The small of her back tingled from Noah's palm as he swayed her back and forth to the music. His gaze, filled with all the love, held hers.

"I know it's been a short time, Jade, but I know what's in my heart. I will ask you everyday until you give me an answer."

She knew the answer she wanted to give, but she wasn't ready. Not yet. Not until she was certain Micah wouldn't be a problem for them. "I hope your patience doesn't wear out."

"I've waited this long for you, Jade. I'll wait another decade if I must. However, I hope you keep in mind that we aren't getting any younger."

She smiled. "No, we aren't as, as Maw keeps reminding me."

Noah bent his head and briefly touched his lips to hers.

"What was that for?"

"With Rait massaging Serena's feet, I thought to turn the betting pool into my favor."

Jade laughed. "You're terrible."

"I know, but you love me anyway, right?"

"Yes. Yes, I do, Noah Danner, and I believe I've fallen hard."

"That's all that matters."

EPILOGUE

True to his word, Noah asked her to marry him every day since Brandy Jo and Dane's wedding. Rait and Serena had a beautiful wedding in October, but Noah had given the ladies of Silverdale a run for their money with his varied marriage proposals. From newspaper articles, and soap on her windows, to a billboard with him on bended knee. Each one made her fall more in love with him.

She stared at the newspaper stained with tears in her hand. Disbelieving what she read. The cowbell sounded, and she glanced at the door and smiled.

"What's wrong, Jade?" Noah strode toward her.

Shaking her head, she threw her arms around his neck. The paper crumpled in her hands. "Nothing. Nothing at all."

"I don't understand." He pulled back and dried her tears. "Why are you crying?"

"Ask me?"

His brow furrowed. "What?"

"Ask me to marry you."

"Okay." The furrow deepened. "Jade Bentley, will you marry me?"

"Yes! Yes! Yes!" She peppered his jaw with kisses.

"Do I want to know what has caused the sudden change?"

She showed him the article. "Micah is going away for a long time."

After scanning the paper, Noah said, "I should be irritated that he is the reason you haven't answered me all these days, but I'm not. I'm very thankful I don't have to wait another seven months." He grimaced. "Please don't tell me you want to plan a big wedding."

"I would marry you today if possible."

"Why not, today?"

"Maw would have a fit."

"Tomorrow?"

"Are you anxious, Cowboy?" She reached up and kissed his lips.

"I'm just ready to make you my bride and take you home to our cabin."

"Our cabin? I like the sound of that. All right, then, do you think the court house is still open?"

"What about Marvella?"

"Oh, I think my grandmother will understand. Besides, since she's the one who gave me the paper, she's probably waiting for us, along with your family."

"Our family."

"Our family." She rested her head against his chest. "I love you."

"I love you, too. Now, let's get hitched."

The End

Dear Reader:

I realize there is a lot going on here. First, Jade is one in four women who suffer from abusive relationships. I've been fortunate enough to have been saved from that trauma, but I have loved ones who weren't as fortunate. This story is dedicated to them. I love you. I'm proud of you for taking steps to remove yourself from the volatile situation. I'm excited to see what God has instore for you and your future.

Secondly, while writing this story, an acquaintance of mine took her life. She was important to one of my daughters and I believe was instrumental in helping her through the grieving process after my husband passed away. Survivor's guilt is real. I've experienced it more than once, and I hurt for my child and her co-workers as they tried to process what happened.

My prayer, is this: if you are in an abusive relationship, seek help. If you are depressed and feeling suicidal, seek help. There are resources available and people willing and ready to lend a hand.

Blessings,
Christina

Books by Christina Rich

Historical
Love at Twenty Paces (A Coaly Creek Novel)
Love in the Midst of Scandal (A Coaly Creek Novella)
Quinn McCall Gets His Bride
Dear Author (A Hopper Falls Novella)
Thread of Hope (A Hopper Falls Novella)
The Lady's Companion and the Detective
Saving Miss Ryan from the Bootleggers

Steampunk
An Unlikely Governess (A Harris-Spotchnet School of the Peculiar Kind)

LASSOED BY LOVE

Rose Verde

Chapter One

Chrystolle 'Crissy' Spencer gulped down her coffee, and her eyes smarted. She didn't realize the brew was still hot. She set the mug down, grabbed her purse and stepped out of her apartment. Her phone rang, and she almost missed her step trying to fish the offending instrument from her bag. *Not the time for it.*

She was already late, by a good ten minutes and her boss would sure have a fit. She chuckled at the thought. Luckily, Crissy had never been at the receiving end of his ire in the six months she'd been with the company as a professional writer. Though she'd studied journalism, but fresh from school, this was what she got and it paid the bills.

The ringing ended and started again before she finally pulled it out of the hole in her bag where the phone always chose to hide away.

Her cousin, Pam's smiling face showed up on her screen. Crissy swiped the phone and placed it to her ear. "Pam, good morning, can I call—?

Pam sniffled.

"Are you okay?" Crissy asked, frowning.

"No." She sniffled again.

Crissy hurried on her way to Rocky Mountain Magz her heels beating out a staccato on the sidewalk. "Pam, calm down and talk to me. What's wrong?"

The short inhalation came again. "It's Fred."

Pam's husband again. Poor guy. He'd had a rough past two years dealing with leukemia. Crissy's pulse raced. "Is he all right?"

"He's stopped responding to treatment."

Crissy closed her eyes briefly. *Not again, God.* "I'm so sorry, dearie."

Despite the cool spring temperature, Crissy's chiffon blouse was plastered to her back by the time she shouldered her way through the company door and into the large office they called *the pit*.

The huge space was partitioned into small cubicles with white boards. The incessant tapping of keyboards filled the place. She scrunched her nose at the cigar smell still hanging in the air. They operated a no smoking system, at least only for the employees. When her boss, Nick binged on one of his cigars, the smell stayed for the day like an unwanted guest.

She waved to her friend, Becca, their copy editor, who sat in front of her computer typing, and then stepped into her cubicle.

By that time, Pam had broken down for real and Crissy ached for her. Fred was diagnosed with leukemia months after their wedding, four years before. His health had been more of a concern than starting a family.

Crissy set her bag down, phone still to her ear and turned.

Nick stared at her, disapproval written all over his face.

Her shoulders slumped. "Sweetheart, I got to go. My boss is giving me the look. I'll call you back as soon as I can," she whispered.

Letting her cousin go when she needed Crissy made her belly turn, but what choice did she have?

Nick jerked his thumb towards his office and walked away.

Sighing, Crissy went after him, her four-inch heels clicking across the floor. Her pencil skirt did nothing to ease her walk. What a day to choose that kind of outfit.

"Be careful. He woke up on the wrong side of the bed today," Becca whispered.

Figures. He smoked when he was grumpy. Ignoring the look of pity from Dana and Jones, who worked in advertising, she stepped into the office.

"Were you not aware of today's meeting?"

Crissy's shoulders slumped for the second time that day and she had to keep from slapping a hand to her head. "I'm so sorry, sir. I totally forgot."

He glanced pointedly at the clock that ticked merrily away behind her. Crissy didn't dare look. She knew by how many minutes she was late. It was unlike her to sleep past her alarm, but she needed to get her materials ready for him today. Slave driver that he was, he wouldn't appreciate her saying it was the need to finish up the due work that kept her up for the better part of the night.

"Where's the article you were supposed to get to me?"

"I'll send it to you right away."

She turned to go.

"I haven't dismissed you."

Crissy stopped, hiding another sigh. His black irises stared daggers at her for a moment, his lips drawn in a thin line as though fashioned by pencil on paper. All his handsome looks disappeared when his face took up the look like a baby's smacked bottom. Crissy almost giggled at the thought. But, if what Becca said was any indication, he'd show her the door. Crissy couldn't afford that.

"We're going to upscale the company by the end of next month."

Crissy frowned. It was on her lips to ask what he meant but as though reading her mind he said, "Starting two weeks from today, we have to increase our subscribers by fifty percent. Otherwise, I may have to let a couple of you go. That means we need some top-notch feature articles. We've been seeing a lot of voracious readers, especially with the western column."

"Ok, sir."

"I already told the others. Keep your act together; stay on your toes—twenty-four-seven—or you're out of here! The next two weeks will determine who stays and who goes."

He was kidding, right?

The look in his dark orbs said he was serious. Crissy couldn't help but be grateful that she missed the meeting. Becca would fill her in. He relaxed in his seat. "You can leave."

She pivoted on her heels. Hopefully, she'd escape before he changed his mind.

"Get that article to me. Remember, if you come late after today, you better have a good reason."

"Yes, sir." She placed just a little emphasis on the sir. He was the boss.

Crissy was just so glad to be out of the office. She couldn't afford to lose her job. Not now that her only help, Pam, had so much going in her life. Crissy's father— She applied mental breaks. No use going there.

Becca mouthed, "We'll talk later," and went on with her typing.

After Crissy sent the document to Nick, she started on the next installment. She loved working for RMM. The magazine's special features provided new challenges each day and helped broaden her horizon on a wide range of subjects. It also ensured they had quite a number of subscribers. Almost a million, as of the previous year. Wasn't it a little crazy to want half a million subscribers in a month?

Dropping in her seat, she grabbed her phone and sent a message to Pam. *Will call you at lunch break.*

By the time twelve rolled around, Crissy's back and fingers ached, her brain deplete of glucose. Turning her head one way and another to ease the kink in her neck, she rose. "Becca, are you ready?"

"Give me a sec," she said without looking.

Nick was lucky to have this measure of dedication, Crissy thought, looking at others hard at work. Was his statement a veiled threat to her? After all, she was the youngest on the team. The article that won the last Pulitzer prize, Crissy submitted it. If Nick didn't get his desire, would he really let her go?

Becca stepped out of her cubicle. "What's with the face?"

"A number of things. I need to return a call."

As they walked out of the office and headed for the food court, Crissy dialed Pam. "I'm sorry I had to cut the call earlier. I was late and my boss was already upset."

"I hope you didn't get into any trouble?"

Trust Pam to be concerned about Crissy when the woman had her own troubles to bear. "No, I didn't." If Crissy thought Nick was threatening her, it wasn't something she wanted Pam to worry about. "How's Fred?"

"He's...deflated by the news but he's hanging in there."

"I'm so sorry to hear that he's no longer responding to treatment." Crissy slipped into a chair at their fav food court while Becca went to place their orders. "Did they say why?"

"The medical terms are nerve wracking." Pam's voice caught.

Theirs was the kind of love that stood the test of time. The last two years had been crazy. If there was anything like for better, for worse, that was their commitment to each other. Not the low lying... "I get that," Crissy said taking her mind from the direction it wanted to go. It had been a year and she was done with relationships.

"Are you still going on vacation soon?"

"Not likely. My boss came up with some crazy expectations today. I doubt anyone's going anywhere, any time soon. You wanted me to do something?"

"I was wondering if you could stay at the ranch house for two weeks. We're going for some trial treatment and his parents want him home."

Crissy could imagine how Fred's parents would feel with their only child battling for his life. "I don't think I can get away. Plus, I have to come up with new articles over the next couple of weeks."

A sigh filtered across the line that punched Crissy in the gut.

"I could always find someone to help with the animals. My concern is Kitty. She needs assistance."

The twenty-one-year-old tabby was a fond pet for the family and needed care by virtue of her age. She was deaf and partially blind.

"We'll find a way," she said after a moment.

Pam's usual upbeat personality was absent today. It was quite understandable. "I'm so sorry. You know I would've gladly come to help, but I'll definitely visit when you return."

"Sure." There was silence. Pam's name was called in the background. "Fred needs me. I have to go."

"Huge hugs, dear. And extend my regards to Fred. I'll be knocking on heaven's doors for both of you. Love you."

When the call ended, Crissy slipped her phone away. "My cousin," she said to Becca.

She didn't feel like eating with this recent news but Becca already bought her food. Besides, she had another four hours before work ended and needed her energy. Pulling it close, she bowed her head in prayer. But all she could think was, *God, please.*

~

Wyatt Danner knocked on the Moore's door and waited. He glanced around at the small porch. Light spilled from the angled door of the old farmhouse, warming the remodeled porch with a splash of gold.

He loved what the couple had done with the place in the past year. The door opened and Pamela Moore smiled at him. "Thanks for coming. Come in."

Wyatt stepped out of his cowboy boots and followed her on stocking feet through the mocha-scented kitchen.

Her husband, Fred lay on the sofa in the living room, a heavy comforter covering him. "How are you feeling today, Fred?" Wyatt asked.

He raised himself up, and grimaced. "I'm fine."

He didn't look fine. He was pale and appeared much slimmer. But, Wyatt kept his observations to himself.

"Can I get you coffee or anything?" Pamela asked.

Wyatt shook his head. "Thanks, anyway. You wanted to see me?"

"Yes." She was quiet for a moment, her fingers stroking her husband's hair. The look of love that passed between them was unmistakable. It was like his parents'. No wonder Dad took such a hit with Mom's death. The years had not lessened the pain.

"We have to be away for a couple of weeks while Fred gets assessed for another treatment. I was wondering if you could assist us. All our arrangements have fallen through—my cousin can't get away. Dickson, he's a friend. We were planning to have him help us, but he can't either. I still have plans to find someone, but if you could help with a few days, that'd be great."

Wyatt shrugged. "What would you need me to do?"

"I've cleared out all the horse stalls so they can go a few days without. All you need do, is feed and water them morning and evening."

"I can do that."

"I'd normally not ask this of you but I've run out of options. I appreciate your pitching in and helping."

"Sure, ma'am."

She kissed her husband lightly on the lips and rose. "I'll show you the feed if you don't mind."

"Not at all," Wyatt said, rising. After exchanging greetings with Fred, Wyatt followed Pamela outside.

The earthy smell he associated with horses and manure tickled his nostrils. The barn had been redone too from when Wyatt used to come to play with the former owner's kids, much bigger than when the Craigs' owned the place. They'd let it fall into disrepair but the Moores' seemed to mean business with the dude ranch they were building. If only the man enjoyed a bit of good health.

A large loft with fodder probably left from winter took all of the front area of the barn. The stalls were huge. Wyatt did a quick count. "You have ten horses."

"Yes and two mini. Their stalls are the ones at the end." Pamela pointed to the bags of grain on top of a shelf. "Whatever you need is here. Supplements are in the cabinet underneath."

He nodded. She stepped in through a small door and waited for him. Chickens were held in several large crates. "Their food is that way. The measuring cup is in the sac. A couple of scoops will be sufficient for the morning until you come in the evening."

"All right."

"I'll definitely make another arrangement."

"Two weeks is fine. I can do it."

A look of gratitude slipped into her blue eyes. "You don't know what this means to me." She touched his arm briefly. "Thanks."

Pity for the couple stirred in Wyatt. It wasn't much to do. "How about walking the horses? Two weeks is a long time. I could do that if they are manageable."

She thanked him one more time. As Wyatt headed back to their family ranch, he thought about how he'd fit this schedule into all the things that pulled at him. But there was no way he would let the Moores' down. They'd been very good neighbours in the past year. Not just that. Pamela also served in the church's hospitality team with Wyatt.

Yeah, he had a lot to do, but one day at a time, he told himself.

Chapter Two

Crissy hit send on the document she'd been editing all morning. It was almost lunch break. Today's meal was sandwiches and some hefty research. Hopefully, she'd get something Nick would like. Everything else she'd suggested—fashion, travel, business, he'd shot down the moment she gave it voice.

Not that she was surprised. Of course, you didn't expect anything beyond the gruffness. And God help you, if he woke up on the wrong side of the bed like Becca said, then, all hell was let loose.

Becca poked her head around Crissy's cubicle. "Going for lunch?"

Crissy's gaze ran down the computer screen. "Nope." She pointed to her lunch pack. "I've sentenced myself to a meal of sandwiches until I come up with something Nick thinks is worth his time."

Her friend stepped in and perched on her table. "Anything interesting yet?"

Crissy looked up. "No. My creative juices are drying up by the minute. I'm thinking of finding some not very well known facts and trivia about Colorado—wildlife areas, sports, rodeo. I don't know."

"Rodeo would be a good one. You could feature a cowboy, rancher, or even a bull rider. Find someone who wants you to tell his story. The prospects are endless."

Crissy held Becca's hazel gaze. How did her friend get her glossy honey blond hair in such classy coiffures fit for a queen?

"Well, say something."

"Where would I find any of those?"

Becca seemed to think for a moment. "How about your cousin's neighbors? She's good friends with them. Maybe she could hook you up with one of the kids or the rancher himself."

Crissy's brain began to click on all cylinders but then she remembered Pam's need to travel and her shoulders slumped. "Pam's not going to be around. You know how I told you about her wanting me to stay over at her place until she returned?"

Becca's eyes were as wide as saucers. She jumped up. "I thought my friend would grab an opportunity when she saw one. Go talk to Nick. If he buys the idea, you could ask for time away. Voila. You help your cousin and get what you need for your article."

It wasn't fine print yet. She couldn't possibly sashay to the ranch and ask to interview someone for her write up. Becca held her by the shoulders, guided her out of her seat and led her to the door.

Nick's disapproving look stopped them in their track and Crissy swallowed. Had a monitoring spirit suddenly possessed him? How come he showed up—?

"Crissy has a great idea for you, sir."

Being Nick's copy editor and longest serving worker, Becca had lost her fear of their boss.

He didn't appear convinced. He never seemed persuaded by anything. If it was a ploy to keep them on their toes, he was doing a good job of it.

"In my office," he said shortly.

Crissy gave her friend a what-have-you-gone-and-done look.

Becca smiled sweetly. "See you after break."

Nick sat in the swiveling chair behind his huge mahogany desk covered with every imaginable clutter from magazine clippings, books and a basket overflowing with odds and ends. He preferred it that way.

The shelf behind him didn't fare better. Mementos and plaques of different sizes sat there in no particular order. Heaven helped anyone who tried to fix his office.

"Shut the door," he said in his usual grumpy voice.

When she came back from closing the door, he gave her a go-ahead look with one raised brow. The dratted man didn't offer people seats.

Crissy rattled off her idea. Deafening silence descended in the room. If he wasn't dismissing the thought in a flash, was that a good thing? That remained to be seen.

"You couldn't possibly just walk up there and get whoever it is to talk to you."

My thoughts exactly. "Yes, but if I can get two weeks off, that would afford me time.

"Two weeks? For what?" His tone was incredulous.

He wanted the job done and she needed time. "I could shadow

whoever agrees to talk to me, get a firsthand experience …"

He thought for a moment. "And if you don't get anything meaningful in two weeks, you understand your job is toast."

"Uh." *That wasn't in the plan.*

"Are we agreed?"

"Uh, yes sir." *Not really.* Her breathing shallowed. She'd heard of people suffering from panic attacks. Was she about to suffer her first episode? *Breathe.*

He glanced at his calendar. "You are expected back by the end of April. Give me feedback every other day."

He turned to his laptop in dismissal. Had she just handed him the ticket to fire her?

Maybe her cousin had found help and didn't need her. She made the trip back to her cubicle on near dead feet.

"You surely haven't seen a ghost," Becca said, the moment she entered Crissy's office, two snack sacks and a steaming Styrofoam cup in her hand. Crissy could bet it was Becca's favorite chocolate. She wasn't one to worry about weight. Plump and curvy, she ate what she wanted. Becca sat one of the sacks on the table. "I thought you might need this and after seeing you, I know you need it. Shoot. What did he say?"

"He agreed but thanks to you, my dear friend, if he isn't satisfied, I'm back on the job market again."

"Nick has a short term memory," she said in a conspiratorial whisper. "Whose article won the prize not so long ago?"

"What if Pam doesn't need me anymore?"

"One way to find out." Becca gestured to the phone. "I'm sure she won't forbid you from staying at her place. Call her."

Crissy tucked her bottom lip between her teeth. She definitely couldn't go back to Nick to say she changed her mind. He was a move-forward-never-backward kinda guy.

Dialing Pam, she held the phone to her ear. "Hey, Pam."

"Crissy, how are you? I'm in the middle of packing."

"How's Fred? Have you found someone?"

A small sigh filtered across the line. "Fred is hanging in there. He's trying to be strong for me. About the ranch, our neighbor is going to pitch in until we return. He's a bull rider, you know how that is? I'll hate to be the reason he can't travel if he needs to. Plus, they have their own ranch to handle. I may have to take Kitty with us."

Could lady luck be smiling down on Crissy? "I'm thinking of coming so you don't have to worry about Kitty. Finally got to take two weeks."

"You did?" There was relief in her cousin's voice.

"Yes. I'm hoping I can get one of your neighbors to interview for an article." She needed feelers on knowing how to proceed.

"You could ask Wyatt. He's nice and approachable but if he knows you're publishing it, he might not agree."

Crissy frowned. "Why?"

"I don't know the entire story, but he injured himself recently and his girlfriend broke up with him when she thought he'd never walk again. She apparently talked to the media and they made a big deal of it. "From what he said, he had to threaten to sue them."

That was a fat hole in her plan. Wasn't it? "I'll be there later tomorrow."

"Thanks. You know where I keep the keys."

By the time the call ended, Crissy dropped the phone and watched it clatter to the ground.

Her job may be toast for real.

~

Wyatt parked his truck in front on the Rockin' D Ranch. His back ached as though someone was splitting wood inside. It had been four months since his accident, a month since he regained good use of his legs, which had been a big miracle.

His doctor would break out in hives if he knew Wyatt was back on a bull already. But he needed to be ready by the time summer rolled around. He had a long way to the top. And riding bulls had always been his best way to prepare.

At that moment, he wanted to crawl into bed, but he needed to feed the Moore's animals before heading off to bed. Leaving them hungry wasn't a way to start something he'd consented to doing. If the excruciating pain in his back hadn't kept him he would've been there earlier. Was he testing fate in going back riding so soon?

He climbed out of his truck and winced. Following the back track to reach the Moores', he walked into the barn and located the grain bag. Pouring grain into the feeder, he filled the trough with water for the horses. Each task, one excruciating work after another.

When he stepped into the smaller room, the chickens erupted in a cacophony of noise. "Hey, quiet. I'm not an enemy."

They kept on. They should've been fed earlier, not past eight. But there was definitely no way he was going to leave them through the night without something to eat. He poured food into each trough, changed out their water amidst the noise that threatened to break his eardrums. He planned to give them only a little since he'd be there to feed them again in the morning.

If only they'd be quiet…

A horse's whinny caught his ears. He better get out of there. It sounded again, only this time it was more than one. What was upsetting them? Setting the bag down, he walked towards the door to check.

Smack!

Before he could react, an object swung at his head. He grabbed for it but his attacker was faster. He had just a moment to look at the blond blue-eyed spitfire before she swung again. This time he was prepared. He wrenched the bat out of her hand.

She turned for the main door, whipping her phone out of her pocket.

Wyatt didn't have time to find out who she was. He went after her and grabbed for her knocking the phone from her hand. They went down in a tangle of limbs. When she opened her mouth to scream, he clamped a hand over it. "Who are you?"

Blue eyes wide with fear, she stared at him, a wild pulse beating on her neck in time to his racing heart.

He eased his weight from her but not enough to allow her to escape. He had enough pain for one night and he wasn't sure how much damage she could do. But there was no way she'd be able to answer with his hand over her mouth. "I won't harm you. Promise you won't scream." Not that shouting would do her much good. Their ranch was the closest and there'd hardly be anyone home yet. She didn't have to know that. "I'll let you go."

She nodded. He waited a moment, then took his hand away, prepared, if she changed her mind and decided to yell.

She raised herself on her elbows, a suspicious look in the eyes that stared up at him. "Who are you?"

"Wyatt Danner. Ms. Moore asked me to take care of her animals. Who are you?"

Her cheeks stained with color. "Chrystolle. Chrystolle Spencer. Pam's cousin."

He raised his eyebrows. The same cousin who couldn't get away? She looked to be in her early twenties.

Wyatt stood up and reached out his hand. She looked at it, then back to his face and took it. Hers was soft against his calloused one. He pulled her up.

"Uh, I wasn't sure what was disturbing the birds…"

If not for her deepening color that showed she was embarrassed, he would've laughed. "And I guess you thought you could take down whatever that was with a bat."

She scrubbed her hands down her pant legs. Hopefully, she'd seen the stupidity of her action. "I'll advise you call emergency in the future. Silverdale is peaceful but you don't want to take a chance."

She nodded. An awkward silence followed.

For a moment, they stared at each other. She stood up to his shoulder for his five feet eleven. Wild looking blond hair escaped its ponytail confines. But for her slight frame bordering on skinny, she was a sight for sore eyes. He mentally rolled his eyes at the cliché his mind came up with. "I'll leave you. Have a good night."

He limped back, put out the light in the small room and went past her. The fall seemed to have unhinged his bones.

"I'm sorry for attacking you. I thought someone had broken in."

"That's so late in coming, your apology." He smiled at her. "I'll have to decide if I'll forgive you."

"Uh..."

Turning, he strode out the door. He definitely wasn't flirting with her. Was he?

Not by a long shot. He had a focus—get back to riding. That didn't involve another woman.

He'd been down that road before and didn't plan on traveling it again, he thought, as he made the short walk back home, every step sending fiery darts along his nerve endings.

Chapter Three

"What did you say?" Pam's chuckle filtered across the line. Same reaction Becca had the previous night

"How was I supposed to know he'd be feeding animals that late?"

Pam went into a fit of laughter this time. Even though Crissy's cousin was cackling at her expense, she could only be happy Pam was laughing again.

"I wished I were there to see it."

"Very funny."

"You know how those romantic movies start. Your encounter could make for one."

"He looks too handsome for his own good. Men like that think too much of themselves and have an ego the size of Kilimanjaro. They think they're the best thing to happen since sliced bread."

"Isn't that a little too harsh for someone you just met?" Pam's voice turned serious. "Not everyone is like Mark."

Crissy heaved a sigh. She remembered Wyatt's body pinning her down on the barn floor, his warmth seeping through her clothing. A good thing she hadn't changed into her pajamas. Her cheeks flamed at the thought. Pam had always warned her about investigating things first ... "It's just hard to get over that kind of betrayal."

"Especially with someone you call your friend. I get that. The Danner kids are wonderful. Wyatt for one, is a great guy. The women love him because he makes them feel special."

Crissy's mind brought up Wyatt's features—rugged, boy next door dimples and those blue, blue eyes— "Thanks for the info. I'm not shopping for a boyfriend." Not someone as good looking as Wyatt,

246

anyway. "How's Fred?"

"He's great. I've hardly had time with him since we got in with his mom doting on him. I'm not complaining. He needs someone besides me."

"Yeah, I understand. So, he goes in for the evaluation tomorrow?"

"Not right away. We have a boatload of tests to run. The plan is have him rest tomorrow, and we'll get started the day after. How's Kitty?"

The cat in question strolled into the living room bumping the legs of the center table on its way towards Crissy. She apparently had found a way around her visual impairment. "She's just waking up. I better go feed her." The sound of a truck filtered into the house. "Talk to you later, dearie."

She picked the cat up stroking her fur. "Let's get you fed, lady."

Crissy walked into the kitchen and peeked through the window in time to see Wyatt heading towards the side of the house. The grey of dawn had started to lift. He was dressed in faded jeans and a buttoned-down checkered shirt, the cream color set off his blond hair that was several shades darker than hers. Heat rose in her face remembering the fiasco of the night before.

Setting the cat down, Crissy retrieved her bowl and poured some milk in it. "I'll be back, buddy."

She wanted to apologize is all.

Yeah, sing that to the birds, a small voice taunted. Ignoring it, she stepped out and closed the door. She owed him to find out if he was okay. To avoid a repeat of yesterday's episode, this time against her, she made a noisy entrance. If his strength was anything to go by, she wouldn't go unscathed if he attacked her.

"Warrior," he said when he poked his head through the inner door. *How come the chickens are quiet now?*

"I'm not a warrior. I was defending myself."

He smiled displaying cute dimples. "I beg to differ. Who attacked who?"

Crissy flushed. "I hope I didn't hurt you?"

He waved off her concern as he poured some oats for the horse in the first stall. Crissy stepped closer. The smell of horse, feed and old spice that Mark used stirred her nostrils. One more thing to remind her of the cheating low life.

Perfectly shaped eyebrows arched. "Should I be worried?"

"About?" she asked frowning.

"Last time I got this close, I had the daylight beaten out of me."

"Very funny." Swallowing a chuckle, she said, "I'm sorry."

"I still haven't figured out how you will pay for your crimes. Beating up an upstanding citizen is not acceptable anywhere in the world." He chuckled. "That's some mighty wild swing you got there, by the way. Thought of it for the better part of the night and kept laughing."

He did? The whole thing had kept her awake for a while, too. Embarrassment at her missteps and fascination— She cut the thought. She was there to get information. "You're the Danner's bull rider, right?"

Surprise lit his blue gaze and he flicked his blond bangs out of the way to get a better view of her.

"How did you know?"

Crissy shrugged. "Media, duh. You guys are celebrities."

He snorted. "We're just pawns in their hand. People who help them make brisk business. They forget we're normal human beings with flaws and all. They end up making merchandise of us."

His tone was bitter. For moments, the jovial guy had snuck behind an emotion she couldn't name—anger or just bitterness. She remembered what Pam had said. "You got into their hands?" He just gave a curt nod. "What can I help you with?"

He took in her dress. "You city girl won't know what to do."

"You think. I grew up on Pam's family farm in Michigan. I'm not your regular city girl."

"Where's your family?"

"Don't have one."

"Sorry I asked."

"No worries."

She followed his lead and over the next half hour, they fed and watered the animals. "You want to come in for coffee?"

"If you promise not to attack me." Humor danced in his eyes.

Crissy slapped a hand to her forehead. "Will I ever hear the end of this?"

"Not likely. Unless you pay up what you owe."

"Coffee good enough pay? I make a robust brew that would keep a cowboy perked all day long."

"You think? That would be too easy. I'll keep thinking of something that would give you as much pain as you gave me."

"You're mean."

"That's not what family and friends think." He extended his arm. "After you."

She turned and headed for the house. Once inside, she grabbed the coffee pot and located the ground beans. Moments later, she poured him a mug full of coffee.

"Thanks." He sipped it and nodded. "No kidding. Where did you learn to make this? Most females don't take strong coffee."

"I told you." She poured hers and took a sip welcoming the jolt of caffeine in her system. She wasn't much of a morning person and relied on her never failing highly caffeinated brew to perk her up. "As a teenager on Pam's family farm, I needed something to keep me going with school and farm chores. I'm not a morning person. So, I figured if I was going to earn their love, be good enough…" Crissy stuttered to a stop. She didn't know this guy and here she was baring her soul, something only Pam's family knew about.

"Have you been here before?"

Grateful for the change in subject, she said, "Twice, the day Pam and Fred moved in and when I came to celebrate my job. Getting one straight from college was a big deal for me?"

"What do you do? Pamela told me you couldn't get away. Imagine my shock when my attacker turned out to be you."

She rolled her eyes. "You sound like a broken record." She liked his banter. "I work for a magazine company for now as one of their professional writers. I'm a journalist, though. My boss came up with some crazy project and I never thought I'd get the chance to get away." She propped her chin on her knuckle. "What's life like as a bull rider?"

He stared at her for a moment. If it was mock suspicion, she didn't know. "Hmm. Just the kind of person I should stay away from." He drained his cup and stood." I better get going. We have some cattle branding to do."

She nodded. Maybe, she was too hasty.

But, time wasn't her friend.

~

He walked to his truck and pulled the door open. "What plans do you have?" he asked before he could stop himself.

She lifted her shoulders. "Writing."

"That must be boring."

She laughed. "Not quite, even though I'd rather be out with my friends kayaking."

"You're into crazy sports too?"

"Not anywhere close to bull riding, but yes."

"I just figured a way for you to pay up your debt."

Her expressive blue eyes regarded him from the porch. "Unless you prefer I lodge a complaint. I have a bruise on my belly to show." Her eyes widened. Wyatt chuckled. "I was just joking. If you pay up, I promise never to bring it up again."

She contemplated for a moment. Wyatt didn't plan to examine why he was inviting her. "Anyway, if you're not interested, you'll hear from me." He climbed into his truck.

"Hey, I'll go change." She bit her lip. "Uh, I need to watch Kitty."

"Good. Bring the cat along. Our housekeeper will be glad to help."

She turned and entered the house. Minutes later, she walked out in form fitting jeans and a body hugging tee shirt, the big tabby in her arm. For someone so slim, she was curved in the right places. Wyatt pushed open the passenger door, appreciating the scent that preceded her. He wasn't shopping for a girlfriend.

So why did you invite her along? Good question.

And a bad idea. His siblings would tease him mercilessly.

He pulled out of the driveway.

"You're sure your housekeeper wouldn't mind? Kitty needs a lot of help."

"She won't. Just tell her what assistance Kitty requires. We'll pick her up when we return."

Few minutes later, they turned into the Rockin' D just as horse trailers headed out. He looked at her. "Do you even ride?"

"Enough to save my life, yes. And I can rope a calf."

He searched her gaze. Was she kidding? "Definitely not the ones in your magazine."

"No," she giggled. "Real life ones. I used to have a friend whose dad owned a ranch. They were neighbors with Pam's parents."

"Can you get yourself out of there?" Rait asked.

Her startled gaze went to Rait. "My older brother. Let's get the horses out." She climbed down, uncertain. "He won't bite," Wyatt said with a wink.

Rait waited until they reached him. "Everyone else is gone."

"We'll be there in no time. Rait, meet Chrystolle, Pamela's cousin. Chrystolle, Rait."

"The one who almost killed you last night?" Amusement lit his eyes.

Heat fanned his neck and Wyatt willed it not to burst into his face. Talk of putting one's feet in one's mouth. He raised his hands in surrender. "It's not every day a guy gets beat up by a woman he doesn't know."

"I guess he needs that sometimes."

If his brother wasn't married, Wyatt would've been jealous at the smile he gave Chrystolle as he shook her hand. Jealous? Him? That would be the day.

"Everybody calls me Crissy."

She slipped her hands in her back pockets. Was she nervous? "This way. We need to get the horses ready to go."

"See you around," she said.

"Sure."

After handing over Kitty to Consuela, their new cook, Wyatt led Crissy toward the barn. "How come I don't get to call you Crissy?"

"Do I owe you a response? Not only do you beat me over the head for attacking you, you tell your brother."

He stepped in front of her. Better to be upfront before another sibling told her. "We had a family dinner last night." This time he was sure the flush had made an appearance on his face. "I actually told everyone." He scratched his head.

Crissy's eyes were as wide as gold coins. She stopped. "How many people were there?"

"My dad and five of us." He didn't mention the in-laws. Couldn't.

She blushed a deep red. "I'm so not going with you."

She huffed and turned tripping on a stone. Wyatt grabbed for her, steadying her. "Crissy, I'm so sorry." She stopped but didn't turn. "I hadn't planned that you'd meet them. But that doesn't excuse me."

"I guess I'll have to decide if I forgive you. Won't I? One more word from you and I might just attack you again."

"Not one word, I cross my heart."

She fought a smile as she followed him back into the barn. Within minutes, they led his Azteca mare and an Arabian thoroughbred into the horse trailer and latched it. Crissy got into the cab. "Are you in for a full day?"

"We'll see." She flashed him a big smile.

He liked her enthusiastic spirit, her... what?

Something in her called to him but he better keep his likings under wrap. Did that have anything to do with what she said about needing to earn love, be good enough? Yeah, she was nothing like Chelsea, but getting himself back into the tours was the most important thing now.

Chapter Four

Wyatt pulled up beside six other horse trailers. It looked like the Danner branding was a huge affair. There were—she did a quick head count—twenty-five people walking around the huge pasture putting things in place. A spot she assumed was the cooking area was already set up beside the chuck wagon. The mooing of cattle filled the air amidst human chatter. More like shouting to be heard above the discordance.

"Are you coming?"

Her gaze flew to his. *What am I doing here?* "Uh, yeah."

"If you don't want to, you could stay with Grey by the chuck wagon. Except that you'd still owe—"

She pointed at him in warning. "We're even in that regard. Not one word. Thanks to you, I have to deal with your family thinking what a crazy woman I am."

He laughed, pushing her door open. His woodsy cologne invaded her senses but was soon replaced by the combo of cow dung and urine. She screwed up her nose and climbed down.

She wished she was with her writing pad, but then, it would be glaring that she was writing for her magazine. She'd have to put her mind and memory to good use. "Can I take pictures, something to remind me of your punishment?"

He laughed. "Sure." Wyatt led the horses out while Crissy took pictures on her phone. When Wyatt was done, he came over to her. "I'll introduce you to Dad."

"Not gonna happen."

"You're blushing."

When she glared at him, he looked away but not before she caught a glimpse of those dimples that said he found the whole thing funny.

"Dad is coming. But, don't worry. He's nothing like my brother."

Mr. Danner reached them. "You're late, son. Who is this lovely young woman?"

"Crissy, meet my dad. Dad, Crissy. She's Pamela's cousin."

Crissy willed herself not to blush. The man's blue eyes crinkled at the edges. Was he amused? "Call me Bill. Nice to meet you."

"Same here, sir." His handshake was firm. Though slightly shorter, Wyatt got his good looks from his dad.

"We have everything set up, let's get it going. Wyatt, I think it's better you brand than roping."

"I'm fine, Dad."

"I know. Humor me, all right?"

Wyatt didn't answer, his face pinched as though angry.

"I could rope if you can't. I mean, I'm not the best and haven't done it in a while, but I could try."

His look didn't thaw. "I'll introduce you then." He handed her a Stetson. "You'll need this."

His gesture touched a chord in her. Crissy slapped the Stetson on. "You look angry."

"I don't want to talk about it."

"Okay. I'm sorry."

He made introductions, got Princess saddled for her. "She's gentle. You should be fine."

Without another word, he turned away. Whatever his dad's reason, giving him branding duties rubbed Wyatt raw. Crissy didn't want to see this part of him or anyone's for that matter. His action shaved off the years back to when Crissy was a little girl cowering under her dad's wilting anger while Mom drowned her sorrow in the bottle. Not something she cared to experience, ever again.

Rait glanced in Wyatt's direction as he went towards the branding section and then walked up to her, leading his horse. "Have you done this before?"

"Yeah, long ago. I can give it a try."

He looked at her for a moment. "We'll work together. Just follow my lead."

Crissy nodded. She swung onto the saddle and accepted the rope he handed her. She glanced in Wyatt's direction and he turned his gaze away.

Well, whatever. Turning, she followed Rait. Two other riders were in the big corral. Apparently, the cows and their calves had been herded there and now they were being sorted.

"Stay here." Rait pointed to the entrance of a second corral separated from the other by a small door. "We'll direct the calves as they send them this way."

"All right." Princess seemed to know what to do, because as each calf ran their way, Princess urged them into the pen.

A half hour later, they had two hundred calves separated from their mamas. Their disapproving lowing rent the morning sky.

"You ready, Crissy?" he asked, smiling in encouragement.

She smiled in return. "Yes."

Rait cornered a calf, swung his rope in the air and it slipped smoothly over its neck. *Whoa, not the guy she should be working with.* With her skill, she was bound to slow him down. She mimicked what he did but instead of the rope catching the calf's leg, it hit him causing him to flee. But not so far with Rait's rope around his neck.

"Try again."

His encouragement gave her a boost. Two tries later, she got the legs.

"Good job," he said giving her a thumb up. They led the calf to the branding area. Wyatt held her gaze for a split second then gave her a small smile that said 'I'm impressed'.

She smiled back.

Once the calf was branded and vaccinated, they turned him loose.

Subsequent ones got easier with each calf they caught. She might just have another article that might interest her boss.

~

Hours later, Wyatt headed to the food stand. He wiped his brow on his shirt sleeve and gagged at the rancid odor of scorched hair. For midday, it wasn't too hot.

Rait was just getting his own lunch, too. The aroma of steak and stew clashing with the stink of burnt hair was not the greatest combination. Wyatt loved branding, especially the roping. Nevertheless, Dad was right. With the measure of pain he had following his bull ride yesterday, he wasn't fully healed. Yet, it rankled all the same.

His brother walked up. "That's some lady you got out there. I could see her rope going around your neck."

"How so?" he asked feigning nonchalance. Even though Crissy's talent surpassed his expectations, he hoped she didn't work so hard to win their approval. Samantha, their neighbor's daughter, had started after Crissy and had been replaced after a few calves.

"Only a strong woman's love will rope you. You think because Chelsea left you when you needed her, you're done?"

"She's only here briefly so stop getting ideas. The fact that the

254

Danner's kids are all heading down the aisle doesn't mean everyone is cut out for marriage."

"Noah's next in line. And you're next to Noah. We'll see, right?"

Someone else stepped up to get his food. Rait winked and walked away. After filling his plate, Wyatt went to where Crissy sat alone eating. "Hey, you did good," he said sitting beside her on the grassy shade made by the horse trailer he'd driven.

"Thanks."

They ate in silence for a few minutes. "I'm sorry about earlier. Dad was right."

She didn't respond, just kept eating.

"Are you upset with me?"

She shrugged.

He set his food down and angled his body to face her. For the first time he noticed a few freckles on her nose. They added to the beauty that stirred something in the region of his heart. He shoved away the unwelcome feeling. He didn't know her. Period. "I injured my back four months ago. Dad thinks I'll worsen it by roping calves. I get that. It's just that it's something I've always done."

"Do you get violent when you're angry?"

Her voice was so quiet but the same question reflected in the gaze that held his. He hadn't imagined it. He frowned. What was she driving at? "No, I don't."

She nodded and continued eating. There was a lost girl look about her, raising a protective instinct from nowhere. "Why did you ask?"

"It scares me."

Her face pinked and she averted her gaze. Was it from the realization that she was telling him things she shouldn't. "You've dealt with an angry person before?"

She nodded. He shouldn't be asking, but he did all the same. "Your boyfriend?"

"No, my father."

Wyatt frowned, taken aback. "I thought you said you didn't have a family?" *Wrong question.* "He hit you? How old were you?"

"Six. He hit me all the time." She rose, plate in hand, gave him a sad smile and walked away.

What father abused his child? Wyatt thought about their growing up years and was grateful for the kind of parents he had.

Her words came floating into his mind. *As a teenager on Pam's family farm, I needed something to keep me going. I'm not a morning person. So, I figured if I was going to earn their love, be good enough...* Was that what she thought? That she hadn't been good enough and that was why her dad hurt her?

Did she still feel she had to earn people's love? That would be a huge burden to bear. He dug into his food. Lunch would soon be over. But, the more he thought of it, he wondered what he'd say to her to make her think differently.

Chapter Five

It was six-forty-five when they arrived at the Rockin' D. Wyatt had talked to her like there was no big deal to her confession. In fact, he hadn't mentioned it. What was it about him that made her want to bare her soul? In less than twenty-four hours, she'd hinted at the secrets hidden in the basement of her life. She showed people what she wanted them to see, a happy, vibrant go-getter, not the insecure girl she was inside.

Giving her heart to the Lord helped some. The first few years, she'd tried to earn God's love. It was still a constant struggle, a part of her accepting that God loved her irrespective but the other part not fully grasping it. When Mark cheated on her, she'd thought—

"Earth to Crissy. Are you okay?"

"Uh, yeah. Just tired." The concern in his gaze sent her heart into a cartwheel.

"Get Kitty and we'll go over to your place. You can rest while I feed the horses."

"I can manage that. You don't have to worry."

"I assured Pamela I would, so get going." He cut the engine.

Crissy opened the door and went towards the ranch house, Wyatt behind her. The awareness he was stirring in her had her throat drying up, her belly flip-flopping like no man's business. She swallowed.

Consuela's bubbly singing came from the direction of the kitchen where she'd been in the morning. The short Spanish woman with a few gray streaks of white in her dark hair looked middle aged. She seemed like a happy person.

"You're here."

"Yes. Thanks for taking care of Kitty."

"She wasn't any trouble at all. I'm thinking she may not be feeling well. Only had milk and wouldn't eat anything else you brought."

"She is old. I think that's the problem."

"Anyway, keep an eye on her. Just in case."

Crissy thanked her again, then picked up Kitty where she lay inside a box.

"You need help?" Wyatt asked.

"No, thanks."

When they got back, Crissy excused herself and went to put Kitty down to rest. By the time she returned, Wyatt had reached the third stall. "I'll be by early tomorrow. We can let the horses out for a few minutes and get them back in. We can take advantage of that and clean out the stalls."

"Aren't you stretching yourself thin when you still have to work at your place?"

"I get to work beside a beautiful woman who, though unsure of herself, is witty and smart."

He was staring, the sincerity of his words reflected in his eyes. Did he really think so? He didn't know her, or her past. If he did, would he still think her smart? Blurting out what she said about Dad had been stupid. Mark had showed pity but then his true color manifested weeks later.

"You've heard too much negativity that makes you doubt yourself. Whose report will you believe? Theirs or God's, who says you are fearfully and wonderfully made? I sense a beauty in you that comes from the inside. Don't let people short change you," Wyatt said.

The air between them crackled. Crissy searched his gaze. Nothing to indicate that he was patronizing her. All Mark had spoken to her were derogatory words. She'd thought telling about her past would win his affection, which somehow she knew was lacking, yet, she'd expected would change things… Why was she comparing the two men, anyway?

"Let's finish up here. I bet you want to rest."

When they finished the chores, Wyatt said good night at the door and headed out.

Disappointment unfurled in the pit of her stomach, she couldn't say why. Her emotions were getting mixed up. Bad idea.

She went inside, checked Kitty and then grabbed her laptop and went into the kitchen. Setting it on the tabletop, she booted it. Crissy opened up a word document and typed in *THE NOVICE RANCHER*.

Deciding it was best to make her calls first, she grabbed her phone and dialed Pam. She stared at the screen while she waited for her cousin to pick up.

Better to keep her focus on the reason why she was there in the first place. She and Wyatt had separate lives. At the expiration of two weeks, she'd be back to hers.

She sighed. Why did her heart feel bad about it?

~

"How's Crissy?" Noah asked.

Wyatt slipped a pole into the hole. Rait and his dad worked a distance from them. "You've been talking to Rait."

"I missed seeing the woman who had the gumption to take on my kid brother. Rait had very good things to say about her, by the way. His words not mine. He thinks you'll be heading for the altar soon."

Wyatt laughed. "We'll definitely be the talk of the town. Last year alone saw three of us married. You just took the leap, and it isn't even six months, yet. Not joining any time soon. I barely know this girl, remember?"

In a way, but, he knew things he could bet not a lot of people knew. He'd gone all spiritual on her yesterday about who God meant her to be. Those things took time to sink in until it's no longer head knowledge, but a thing of the heart. "Chelsea used my accident and the likelihood that I wouldn't walk again as an excuse. The main thing was the fact that I was gone much of the time. She didn't care for what I did for a living, didn't care for the long travels."

"Does Crissy know that you're a bull rider?"

"Yes."

"Then you've got nothing to worry about if what Rait tells me is true."

"And that is?"

Noah glanced towards Rait and back. "He thinks she's smitten." He pretended to whisper but anyone within a foot of them would pick his words as clear as day.

"Don't hold the thought. You both are sure running ahead of yourselves." If this got around to his other siblings, he'd be getting an earful.

"You don't like her?"

"It's got nothing to do with like. Have you been listening to anything I said?"

Wyatt couldn't hide the exasperation from his voice. Crissy stirred feelings in him but where did that lead them. Besides, he didn't believe in love at first sight.

"I heard and the fact that you sound frustrated tells me more than what you are saying."

"Shut up and let's finish up here. I have a wedding rehearsal to attend."

Half an hour later, as they rounded up the stretch of fence, his phone rang. Unknown number. Wyatt considered ignoring it but when the call ended and started again, he swiped the screen.

"It's Crissy. Sorry to bother you. I saw your number by the phone and thought to call you."

Wyatt willed his pulse to slow. "Are you okay?"

"Yes, but I think Kitty may be coming down with something."

"Did you call Pamela?"

"I don't want her to worry. Can't seem to see any vet's number and wanted to find out if you could recommend someone."

Wyatt glanced at his wristwatch. Almost four. The wedding rehearsal was at seven. They had time to be at the vet's and back. "We have one we use. You know what? Watch for me in ten minutes."

"Don't put yourself out on my account. If you just point—"

"It's nothing. Get ready."

Wyatt started packing up the tools. "Pamela's cat is sick."

"And you want to take her to the vet instead of telling her where to go."

"Meaning?" Wyatt gave him a cocky grin.

"Just saying. Maybe not only Crissy is smitten after all."

"You're entitled to your opinion, brother."

After telling Dad about his destination, he waved to Rait. He didn't miss the knowing look his older brother gave him.

Wyatt drove to the house and took a quick shower. He surely didn't want to be in the truck with her, smelling of sweat. *You're definitely putting in a lot of effort to impress her,* a small voice taunted. Wyatt rolled his eyes. By the time he got to the Moore's place, a good fifteen minutes had passed. "I'm sorry—"

"Don't worry about it. I knew you were busy." He took in the worry in her face and then glanced at the cat. "You have an idea what is wrong?"

"No. She's been restless for the past half hour. Pam will be so devastated if anything happened to Kitty, especially with all she's going through."

Wyatt led her to the truck and opened the door. He waited for her to get in, closed the door and rounded the hood to get in. "Kitty will be fine. Dr. Ben is the best in Silverdale."

She nodded, her hand stroking the cat. Crissy was feisty, yet, gentle. She was an interesting mix of spunk and spice.

He pulled out of the driveway and soon headed down Main Street.

"Did you ever have a pet?"

"No. Mom was allergic."

What was her childhood like? No loving parents, no pet.

"What about you?"

Wyatt contemplated what to tell her in the midst of her worry. "We used to have a dog. Died five years ago on my nineteenth birthday. The dog had been sixteen at the time. He passed peacefully in his sleep. We hadn't seen it coming and my kid sister cried for days. We haven't had one since Jack."

Taking her mind off the sick cat was the best way to go. He rummaged through his CD collections. "What kind of songs do you listen to?"

"A wide range. Dad loved those pulsing beats, mom couldn't stand them. Pam's parents, on the other hand, listened to country. I guess I'm hybrid." She chuckled.

Wyatt selected a Jazz singles and slipped it in. "I can say I'm hybrid too. Mine depends on mood."

Silence descended as they made the fifteen minutes' drive to Ben's Animal Place.

"I don't have her history."

"Chances are that Pamela uses this place, you know small town and all," he said pulling into the driveway and parking beside another truck.

A young lady probably in her mid-twenties walked up to them as they cleared the double doors. "Who do we have here? Is that Kitty?"

Wyatt didn't miss the relief in Crissy's gaze. "Yes."

"Is she here for her annual exam?"

"No. Is she due? She seems to be refusing to eat and I noticed a restlessness that wasn't there yesterday."

"I might have to check about her due date. I'll give you some paperwork and we'll call you in a bit."

"Thanks."

"Let me help you." Wyatt took Kitty to allow Crissy grab the papers. Thankfully, there was just one person who was already leaving.

Half-hour later, physical examination completed, Dr. Ben said, "Do you have drugs, rodent poison or anything around the house?"

"No, actually, I just came in two days ago. My cousin is out of town. You think she ate something?"

"That would be my guess. Not every poison manifests immediately. We're going to do some tests and if it's confirmed, we'll initiate some treatment but that will mean keeping her overnight?"

"Will she be okay?"

"Hopefully."

When they got back to the waiting area, Crissy glanced at her wristwatch. "You should go. I'll find my way home."

"I hate to leave you."

"I understand."

Wyatt held her gaze. "You're worried."

Crissy nodded. He took her hand. He loved the small feel of her warm palm against his.

"What will I tell Pam if Kitty doesn't recover?"

Wyatt ran his thumb over the back of her hand. "We'll believe for the best. I'll be praying for her. Besides, whatever is wrong with Kitty probably started before yesterday."

They sat in silence some more. "I was thinking of inviting you for the wedding rehearsal. But, you'd want to know more so you can communicate with Pamela."

She nodded. Minutes later, finally running out of excuses to hang around, he rose. She looked like she was close to tears. "Can I give you a hug?"

She gave him a watery laugh and nodded. Wyatt leaned down and held her close. He inhaled her scent. "I want to stay, but, Dustin needs me. We've had this scheduled for months."

He let her go and held her gaze again.

"Don't worry. Go on."

"I'll call you."

As he walked out the vet clinic that evening, he asked himself the one question he'd been dodging for days. Was he falling for Crissy?

Chapter Six

Crissy made chocolate and opening her laptop, she sat at the kitchen island. She didn't have an appetite. Leaving Kitty at the vet was a hard decision but if the cat ran into problems in the night, what could Crissy do to help?

Her phone rang and Pam's smiling face came on the screen. Crissy groaned. No matter how she dreaded it, she couldn't put off talking with Pam about her cat.

Swiping the screen, she said, "Hey. How are you and Fred?"

"Tired. Had his tests today. We'll see the doctor tomorrow."

"That's good. Is he close by?"

"No, he's sleeping. How are you coping? Wyatt told me you both walked the horses today."

"Yes. We also cleaned out the place."

"I told him you know what to do and not to bother coming but he says he wants to. He's just nice that way."

"Yeah." And he was tearing down her desire to keep her heart under lock and key.

"How's Kitty?"

"She's fine. I actually just got off the phone with the vet tech—" A short gasp filtered across the line. Crissy rushed on. "She was refusing food, and then I noticed she wasn't very comfortable, so I took her in. Have you had any poisons around?"

"Is that what the vet thinks?"

"Uh, something like that."

"She escaped into the garage a few days ago. We have some weed chemicals in there. If she had contact with it, I didn't know. It's hard to figure out what problems are due to her age or not. Poor baby. By the time we return, I'll have her in for routine check."

"Dr. Ben did all that."

"Thanks so much. I'll reimburse you when I come."

"Nah, take that as my little contribution for all the years you've helped me."

"Aww, that's so sweet. Thank you. But, you know I'd do it again in a heartbeat." There was a pause. "How are you getting on with Wyatt? No more attacks?"

Crissy laughed. "Definitely not. After the price I paid."

"Whoa, what price?"

"A whole day roping calves."

"You're kidding, right?" Pam asked.

"No."

"I'm seeing prospects."

"Of?"

"Just saying. You've always been good with animals. I remembered when Cole was teaching us to rope, you got the hang of it faster than any of us." She laughed. "Poor animals suffered at my hand. Besides, you don't want to keep working for that boss of yours who doesn't value you."

"He's more bark than bite." *Hopefully.* She wasn't anywhere near fulfilling the reason she came.

"So, have you talked to Wyatt about your article?"

"Not yet. Like you said, he's media shy. I may have to do some snooping on my own. I met his brother. Maybe, I could talk to him about it."

They talked a little more. As soon as the call ended, another one came in.

"Wyatt?"

"Finally. I've been trying to reach you. Who have you been talking with for so long, lady?"

"Pam. How's it going?"

"Great. The rehearsal is done. Friends are just hanging around. Have you eaten?"

"Lost my appetite."

"I can fix that. Mexican or Chinese?"

"What do you mean? You're not staying to chat?"

"I have a better option. I'm buying us food. Make your choice."

Was he saying she was a better alternative than his friends? "Mexican."

"I was sure you'd pick that."

"You read minds?"

"Nope. Just a lucky guess. I'll be there in a few. By the way, I called the tech. Kitty's fine."

"Thanks. I know."

"Great. So, we can celebrate that. See you soon."

Crissy set the phone down. She shouldn't read any meaning into Wyatt's gesture. He was Pam's friend, that's all. But, what if... She shook her head. No what ifs.

She spent the next ten minutes working on THE NOVICE RANCHER: My personal experience. After composing an email to her boss suggesting the article for western themed column, she hit send.

The sound of Wyatt's truck came to her ears. The butterflies in her stomach chose that moment to take flight. Willing her pulse to slow down, she went to the door.

Wyatt had a broad smile on his face as he climbed down from the truck. Crissy's fingers itched to smooth the bangs on his forehead out of the way. Instead, she slipped her hands deep into her jeans pockets.

He glanced up at the twinkling stars.

"Grab a jacket, let's stay out. It's beautiful."

"Good idea." She went back in. By the time she returned, Wyatt had the truck tailgate down. He patted the spot on the other side of him, their food in between.

"You thought of this?"

"No. I'm spontaneous by nature. I like to say I prepare for every opportunity."

"Hmm." He helped her up into the truck bed. "What did you get?"

"See for yourself"

Crissy opened the food pack and the smell of the herbs and seasoning in the Pozole sent her stomach rumbling and her digestive juices flowing. Wyatt smiled. "Told you I'd fix your loss of appetite. Dig in."

Crissy started to eat. The burst of flavor on her tongue had her groaning. "This is good."

"Yeah. One of my favorites on the circuit. I have a small freezer in my trailer where I stock a variety of Mexican food. Our cooks have always been Mexican until Consuella. Go figure."

They talked about random things. After having their plates cleared away, Wyatt stretched out on the truck bed. Propping a hand behind his head, he stared at the stars.

"What was it like the first time you climbed a bull?" she ventured.

He was quiet for a moment and she thought he wouldn't answer.

"Scary, exhilarating, adrenaline pumping through my body. The feeling is always the same for me because every bull is unique. You're not always sure what one bull brings to the arena. You just get on his back and do your thing." A small smile played on his lips.

"You almost won your second buckle last year." He turned and looked at her. The porch light reflected the surprise in his eyes. "Pam's parents were rodeo lovers back in the day. I've been to a number in my lifetime. Somehow, I find myself following the PBR seasons. What was it like to win the first time?"

Wyatt linked their hands and stared at it for a moment. "A dream come true. Then I found out it wasn't as easy as just winning and that was it."

"What do you mean?"

"Every buckle won was just the beginning of a desire for another. It's a tedious competition, requires focus, but I love it. My priorities are God, my family, bull riding, in that order." He chuckled.

Before she could stop herself, she said, "Has your injury set you back greatly?"

He nodded. "I want to show you something."

He rose and hoisted himself down. Crissy sat up and moved close to the edge. But before she could climb down, he picked her up like she weighed nothing and deposited her beside him.

After latching the tailgate, he led her to the passenger side and opened the door. "We're just going over to our place. When do you go to bed?"

"Ten, eleven. Depends."

He glanced at his wristwatch. "A few minutes past nine. You'll be back in plenty of time."

He climbed in, grinned at her and then pulled out.

Her heart rate had gone up making it double time. She was falling for Wyatt. But what happened when she left?

~

When they arrived, Wyatt placed a hand on the small of her back, leading her to his practice barn. He flipped the light on.

"A mechanical bull?" He could hear the awe in her voice.

"Yup. A gift from a friend after my accident. You'll see him at the wedding."

"Are you inviting me to your friend's wedding?"

"Uh, yeah and I'll be glad if you agreed. It's nothing dressy. Cowboy themed."

"Jeans and shirt? Because that's all I came with."

"I could pick you up at four tomorrow and we'll go pick out something for you."

266

"Nope, but thanks."

"Why not?"

"Kitty's bill has made a dent in my savings."

"I'm not asking you to pay for it, just believe for it." He winked. "The thing is, I invited you and I'm paying. Please don't say no."

She stared at him with those blue eyes and he felt as though he was drowning in their depth. The air between them crackled. For a moment, they stood transfixed. Then Wyatt took a step towards her, then two.

He reached out and tucked a strand of hair behind her ear. She held his gaze, a wild pulse beating in her neck. Would she pull away if he kissed her?

He swallowed a sigh. How long had he known Crissy. Chelsea didn't have this kind of effect on him. Should he be worried? He didn't believe in love at first sight, yet from the day he met her, more like trapped her on the barn floor, he'd known he wanted to get to know this woman standing right in front of him.

Wyatt brushed his thumb across her lip and stepped back. Was that disappointment he read in her eyes? He pointed to the Rodeo bull. "Wanna try?"

She laughed, the sound breathless, from fear of getting on the bull or from what they both knew almost transpired. If he kissed Crissy, there'd be no going back. Was he ready to take the risk?

"No, I'll stick with kayaking and mountain climbing."

"Which is scarier? I'd take bull riding over mountain climbing any day. So?"

She shook her head again.

"Come on. If you don't want me to turn it on, I won't. Plus, I can put it at the slowest speed and turn it off before it throws you." He bent down and touched the padded flooring. "With this you're safe." He faced her. "You'll love it."

She swallowed visibly and nodded. Wyatt almost laughed. The woman who wasn't afraid to come out at night to rescue animals, who, through determination, roped more calves than any other female, was afraid to climb a bull.

He took her hand and helped her on the bull. "You want to have stories to tell, right? As long as I'm not in it, though." He placed her left hand on the horn of the saddle and winked. "Slow, or no."

Her eyes lit with a smile. "Slow."

"Hold on a sec." Wyatt whipped out his phone and took several snapshots of her. She made crazy faces at him and had him chuckling. "Very photogenic."

"Can I see it?"

"Not now."

Slipping the phone in his pocket, he stepped over to the motor and set the speed and spin direction.

Crissy held her hand in the air mimicking a real ride.

"There's nothing to it."

"Yeah, some bulls are nice that way, but then you meet mean ones…" Without warning, he adjusted the speed a little. "Like this."

She shrieked, finding her balance but couldn't. Wyatt pressed the stop just before she hit the padded floor.

"You okay?"

She held a hand to her chest, giggling. "You could've warned me."

"I'm sorry," he laughed. "You should have seen your face."

She smacked him. "You're not nice."

"I know." He held out his hand to her. She took it. Instead of getting up, she jerked his hand. The element of surprise worked against him and he fell forward narrowly missing her.

She giggled. "How's that for a taste of your own medicine?"

Wyatt laughed but the pain that seared his back chopped of his breath. He winced.

Crissy turned on her belly, concern marred her features. "Did I hurt you? I'm so sorry."

"I'm okay. Don't worry." But his back was telling a different story. "I'll just catch my breath for a moment."

He closed his eyes for a moment. Crissy's hand brushed his hair out of his eyes and he looked at her. His gaze dropped to her lips and she swallowed visibly.

Eyes staring at him with so much worry and her flowery scent wrapped around him were two dangerous combinations. Swallowing a wince, he got up. This time when he gave her his hand, she took it gently and he pulled her up. He led her to a bench and they sat down.

"This is the closest I'm getting to any bull. I don't know how you guys do it."

"Yeah. You don't think about it. If you do, you won't get on."

"And you do even when you know you could get injured."

"Every bull rider knows he's playing his hand when he makes the decision to ride bulls. It's not *if* he will get injured but when and how bad. Isn't that the same every time you go mountain climbing or any of those extreme sports?"

"True. How did your family accept your choice?"

"Mom and Dad were always supportive of whatever we chose to do, as long as it was good."

"I'm envious." She was silent for a long time. Just when he thought she wouldn't continue with what was on her mind, she said, "It was hard to figure them out. They both acted like I was unwanted, a mistake. Even when Mom and I are in the same room, she looked right through me without seeing me. For the better part of my life, I felt like I wasn't there. And she'd spend her days in drunken stupor."

Crissy talked in very detached tone. But after her words about needing to earn love, he knew better. Wyatt ached for the little girl she used to be.

"Dad was always mad about something." She stared at the back of her hand for a few seconds, then gave him a bitter smile. "I never knew what I'd do to earn his wrath. He'd hit me…" Her voice caught.

Wyatt draped his arm over her shoulder and held her.

"Nobody found out? Your teachers in school, maybe?"

"He swore me to secrecy, made sure I didn't have marks that people could see."

"And you said you were six. How long had this been going on?"

"I think a year or more. It just escalated with time."

Wyatt's anger rose swiftly. Why did some people have babies they didn't want? He held her close rubbing his hand up and down her arm. "Where are they now?"

"I don't know. Pam's father is Dad's older brother. He came visiting over one summer break. He took Pam and me swimming and saw the marks on my body. He pressed me for information. I don't know what he said to my parents but they never made trouble. They didn't want me, anyway?"

Wyatt wrapped both arms around her. "I'm so sorry."

"Thanks. It was a long time ago."

"I know." What he also knew was that the impact still remained. They stayed that way for minutes. Wyatt kissed her head. "Let me see you home."

When Wyatt climbed into bed later that night, the things Crissy told him stayed with him. She turned out well in spite of her past. With the emotions that roiled in him—anger against her father, compassion for Crissy—as she told her story, he realized he was falling for the blue-eyed lady. And somehow, he felt he could trust his heart to her and not be betrayed.

Chapter Seven

The smell of new leather wrapped around Crissy in the Everything Cowboy Mall. The place was packed with anything anyone could want—jeans, Wranglers, belt, sturdy boots, Stetson, in all sorts of color and sizes. Bouquets of assorted flowers lent their scents to the atmosphere.

The sales girl handed Crissy a pair of boots. "That boyfriend of yours really cares about you."

"He's just a friend."

The young girl's eyes almost popped. Her brown hair was piled on top of her head as smoothly as Becca always had hers. Why did people succeed with their hair better than Crissy did with hers? Pulling her messy curls in a ponytail perpetually was the easiest way to go. Especially when she managed to conquer them with a brush.

"Then I want that kind of friend, sweetheart."

Feeling self-conscious, Crissy emerged in a slightly above the knee sundress. The background was mainly cream with multiple flowers. She loved this one. Would Wyatt like it? All six dresses she'd worn in the last fifteen minutes, he'd rejected. Even though he seemed like a difficult to please person with her choice of clothes, he was a good sport about it and... it was kinda romantic.

She flushed at the thought. Thankfully, his gaze was buried in whatever he was doing on his phone.

She reached him. "What are you doing?"

"Checking my email. I..." The words died in his throat.

He did a slow appraisal from her Stetson, down to her dress and cowboy boots. Crissy tried not to squirm.

"You take my breath away."

"You like it?" she asked. Heat crept into her face. After telling him about her past, she hadn't expected him to show up today. Yet, instead of leaving, he treated her differently. Like she was someone special.

"You're kidding me? I love it." She stopped a foot from him. "You'll steal the show from the bride."

She laughed. "Not likely. I'm never the belle of the ball."

"I beg to differ." He stepped closer and adjusted her hat. "You could grace any western magazine."

He brushed her cheek with his knuckle leaving fire in its wake. Crissy swallowed, her legs threatening to cave under her.

The door opened and Wyatt blinked. He scratched his head. "Uh, I'll pay for this and we'll leave."

Crissy nodded trying to shake some semblance of function into her mushy brain. She didn't doubt Wyatt would've kissed her this time. The thought of his well sculpted lips on hers sent her blood pressure skittering off the chart. She swallowed a groan. What was wrong with her?

He made her feel special, stirred her heart like no one ever did, but she wasn't here for a two week fling. He didn't strike her like that kind of person either.

Her cell phone rang just as Wyatt joined her and they walked to the truck. Bossy Boss, the name she used for Nick flashed on the screen. Crissy almost ignored it but that would be rude. She hadn't heard from him since she sent the document last night.

She accepted the call. "I saw the article you sent. I must say that's pretty creative." Nick praised her? Crissy almost fell out of the truck. Wyatt chuckled, a hand thrust out to help her. "Have you started on the main work? The western corner is a good idea and will just fit right into the magazine."

"I'm working on it, sir."

"What had you almost tumbling out?" Wyatt asked as soon as the call ended.

"Nick praised me for once."

He frowned. "And Nick is?"

Crissy narrowed her gaze at his tone. "Don't tell me you're jealous."

"Should I be?"

"Maybe." He fell silent as he pulled out of the parking lot and headed down the street. "You shouldn't be," she said taking pity on him.

"You're kidding me? Don't do that again."

"I got you there, right?"

"A little."

He held her gaze for one heart stopping second. His smile sent her heart picking up a staccato beat, making it double time.

What are you doing to me? She wanted to scream.

Wyatt slipped a CD into the player, this time a soft blues declaring love that had just come home. "You think Kitty's okay?"

"I'm sure she is, otherwise Consuela would've called us. But if you prefer to check in," he pulled his phone from his pocket, took his eyes briefly off the road to pull up the number, he hit dial and handed it over to her. The woman's voice came immediately.

As soon as Crissy mentioned her name, Consuela said. "Not to worry. Kitty's fine."

Crissy thanked her and handed the phone back to Wyatt.

"Satisfied now?"

She nodded.

Soon he turned into an area with fields after fields of greenery. A couple of ranches dotted the distance. So different from the bustle in town. Serene, the environment called softly to her.

After a few minutes, he turned into a narrow road.

"Is this your first western themed wedding?"

"Yup. Thanks for inviting me."

"That's late in coming." He grinned and she swatted him.

He entered a gate with the inscription Lazy D Ranch. There was a row of trucks parked to one side of a huge red barn. "Who gets married in the evening?"

"Meghan." He chuckled. "That's what she wants."

A big guy walked towards them. Crissy climbed down and waited for Wyatt to join her.

"Just the man I've been meaning to see."

They shook hands vigorously and did the shoulder thing guys did.

"And who is this gorgeous lady with you?"

Wyatt took her hand. "This is Chrystolle. My friend Luke. The one I told you bought me the bull."

He shook her hand, his brows raised at Wyatt. Crissy wasn't sure how to interpret the body language.

"How was your trip?" Wyatt asked. If he saw his friend's look, he chose to ignore it.

"It was great. I'll be around for a bit before I'm off again."

"Luke owns the highest number of bulls on the PBR circuit," Wyatt said in explanation.

"Don't pay him any mind. I'm just a small fry in the pan. Wyatt likes to exaggerate." He favored Crissy with a smile and then turned to his friend. "I guess you're ready to jump back in the flow?"

"Yeah, rode this week. Had a beast of pain. But, it's not stopping me. Plan to join the circuit once it kicks off for the season."

"Good for you. By the way, I saw Chelsea. She's getting married."

Wyatt's grip tightened on Crissy's hand. "Ouch!"

Wyatt's gaze jumped to hers and he let her go. "I'm glad for her," he said through clenched teeth. Apparently, he was anything but. "We'll go greet the couple before the ceremony."

Did Luke realize he'd upset Wyatt with the piece of information he passed? Not likely, because he moved onto how happy he was that Wyatt was back on track.

"Sure." Luke shook hands with Wyatt again, waved at her and went away.

As they cleared the door of the big ranch house, they heard a raised near hysterical voice saying, "Everything that could go wrong has gone wrong today."

Other voices tried to soothe her.

"What will I do for a bouquet?" she continued.

Wyatt tapped on the door. The voices fell silent. A middle-aged woman peeked through the door and her face brightened. "Wyatt," she said apologetically. "We're having a mini crisis."

She waved them in. Then she said to the person Crissy assumed was the bride judging by her smudged makeup. "We'll figure this out too."

"When?" The girl that looked like she hadn't even finished high school whined.

"Hey, Meg. Who's troubling you?" Wyatt asked.

She blushed and came to hug him. "Everything is going wrong, just a few minutes to my wedding."

"Where's Dustin?"

"He's sorting some things out." She apparently had cried with the red eyes and veins popping on her forehead. Not a good look for a bride.

"What kind of flowers do you want? I saw somewhere we went shopping." All five pairs of eyes turned on Crissy.

"Any will do at this rate," Meghan said.

"Great. We'll be back in no time. How long do you have?"

"Half an hour."

"We'll be back in twenty." She grabbed Wyatt's hand and dragged him out of the house.

By the time they returned, someone was waiting to get the flowers—a gorgeous blend of spring colors, including yellow billy balls, chamomile, peach roses, peach and red ranunculus.

The sound of the organ started in the big barn.

"Time to get in." Wyatt said, taking Crissy's hand.

273

They slid into the barn as the wedding march started to play. Wyatt located a bale of hay at the back and gestured for her to sit. His friend sat a few rows from them. He turned and smiled at Wyatt. Or was it at her? Crissy frowned and then quickly smoothed her expression.

Wyatt plopped down beside her. "Were you planning on apologizing for almost fracturing my fingers earlier?" she whispered.

"Are you kidding? You sure know how to hold a grudge." His eyes lit with humor as he took her hand and kissed it, spreading warmth in its wake. "I'm sorry."

Ignoring the glance of the young lady on the other side of the aisle, she said with a huff. "That's so late in coming."

He chuckled quietly. "Sounds like our national anthem. Why did you ask then?" His warm breath fanned her neck and her heart fluttered like a kite in a blustery wind.

~

"This is really cool."

Wyatt took in the over two hundred people in attendance, amidst fairytale lights, Mason jar flowers, wooden signs, chandelier and string lights that offered some romance to the atmosphere. He wasn't one to pay attention to decors but this wasn't bad if he said so himself, different from other barn weddings he'd attended. He'd consider something this picturesque when—

"The bride is here." Crissy's voice sounded breathless and Wyatt turned to look at her. There was awe on her face.

Meghan walked in on her father's arm in a sheet of satin that looked like she'd been poured into it. Cowboy boots like the one her bridal train wore completed her outfit. She held the flowers Crissy had picked out. Whoever did her make-up had covered every telltale sign of her tears from earlier. "The flowers are pretty. You have good eyes."

"Thanks." She smiled and Wyatt wanted to kiss her. In the midst of the confusion, no one had thought of dashing to the store. How would he not fall for this caring woman? She didn't know Meghan from Adam.

When Meghan reached Dustin, he turned with a smile and mouthed "You look beautiful."

Crissy wiped her eyes. Wyatt took out his neatly folded bandana and handed it over to her. She gave him a watery laugh and accepted it. He could see the bride's mother too wiping her eyes. Why did people always cry at weddings, anyway?

Wyatt had missed everything else in between. Next he knew, they were sitting down to hear the message. The pastor, a middle aged man with salt and pepper hair mounted the podium. He had a huge smile on his face that lit his dark eyes. His cowboy ensemble sat well on his tall slim frame.

"You know why I love weddings?"

There was a chorus of "No".

"Jesus performed his first miracle at a wedding. He must love weddings."

That earned some laughter.

"We'll go straight to the point. This is just going to be a charge for everyone here, single, married for a day, a year, whatever."

He slipped his glasses on. "Let's turn in our Bibles to Mark 10 verse 7 and 8"

A rustle of papers followed and then he began to read. "For this reason a man will leave his father and mother and be united to his wife and the two will become one flesh. So, they are no longer two, but one flesh."

He took off his glasses. "This scripture is an echo of Genesis 2 verse 24. I'll just examine the word, become. There are different meanings—to arrive, to come about and begin to be. Let's take a look at *begin to be*. If we slot it into the passage, it says the two shall begin to be one flesh, the principal word being "one". It means what hurts you hurts the other. When you slight the other person, you actually slight yourself because you're what?"

"One flesh," came the chorused answer.

Wow. Wyatt had never looked at it that way.

"Wedding is just a ceremony. The real deal is the marriage and it takes work. It means we throw away our selfish inclinations to have things our way. We find ways to merge our wills, deal with our emotions in a way the other doesn't feel lost in the maze. It's hard work."

He laid emphasis on the hard work.

He turned to the couple. "Cathy and I have had a good marriage not because we never offended or upset each other, not because we never said hurtful things to the other. Not because we never slammed doors or gave the other person the cold shoulder until our hearts healed. We wanted the relationship. We loved, despite our differences, agreed to disagree. We worked at it."

"Ask yourselves today. Is this what you want, five years, ten years down the line? If it is, you're going to apply yourselves to make it work, love in spite of everything. None of you is perfect." He was silent for a moment as though allowing the words to sink in.

"Just like the wedding at Cana in Galilee didn't fail, because Jesus was there, He's the third in the three fold cord. It cannot be broken. Will you give him room? In your own strength, you will fail but with Jesus in your boat, no matter the storms that rise, you will come out on the other side victorious. Shall we rise?"

The vow taking passed in a blur but the man's word of wisdom stayed with Wyatt. When he married, he wanted it to last a lifetime. *That's my desire, Lord.*

They moved out to the reception area, a huge catering tent. "Are you all right?"

"Yeah." Her voice was a small whisper. He took her hand and squeezed it but didn't let go.

It was getting dark. The ceremony would end soon. As the DJ started the program inviting the couple to the dance floor, he whispered to her, "Wanna get away for a bit?"

"We could dance first."

"Nah, I have two left feet when it comes to dancing. Bull riding is my thing." She covered her mouth and giggled. Wyatt pulled her hand. "Let's go."

"To where?"

"Just out to the truck. We'll be back to eat. I'll definitely not miss that."

"You love food, huh?"

"You bet."

When they got to the truck, Wyatt opened the door and let her get in, then circled round and climbed in.

"Beautiful ceremony."

"Yeah." He was silent for a moment. "Everyone seems to be getting married these days."

"You have a thing against weddings?"

"No. Just that it's crazy. I had four of my siblings marry in a little over a year."

"Wow. How many siblings do you have?"

"Five."

"That's cool. Growing up an only child was quite lonely." she seemed to catch herself. "If you meet someone you're crazy about, why wait?"

"You haven't found that one yet?"

She blushed. "I'm not going to tell."

"Hmm. I think your face says you have."

She swatted him and he grabbed her hands and held them. Her smile froze and she held his gaze. Did he dare think that he was the one she found, because he'd been thinking in that line lately, that he might just have found the woman for him.

He let go of her right hand and stroked her cheek with his knuckles. "You're growing on me, Crissy." His voice sounded husky, alien to his ears.

His gaze dropped to her lips as her tongue sneaked out to wet them. He cupped her neck sending her Stetson flying. Wyatt stretched across the console, his heartbeat making it double time. Their lips were mere inches from each other when a sharp rap on the glass had them springing apart. Wyatt closed his eyes. *This person better have a good reason.*

He turned pasting a smile on his face. It was the groom's younger brother and Wyatt's circuit partner.

"Hey bud. I just got in and was told you were around." He looked between them. "Was I interrupting anything?"

He definitely knew, but trust Owen to act all nice and innocent. Wyatt gave Crissy a we-have-business-to-finish look and climbed out of the truck.

Chapter Eight

Wyatt followed her to the door. "Wanna come in for a sec?"

"Nope. Just being a gentleman." He lingered for a minute. Deciding against what he wanted to do, he stepped back. "Good night."

She didn't answer. He turned to look at her. Crissy stood just at the door, Kitty cuddled in her arms.

He could see questions burning in her gaze. "What?"

"Who's Chelsea?" He'd expected that long before now. He retraced his steps, his gaze holding hers captive. "My ex. Crissy, we had a great night out. Can we not talk about her now?"

She shrugged. "Why not? Because you still love her?"

"You're not... She left me after my injury when she thought I was never going to walk again. Told the media things—"

She swallowed and nodded. Something flickered in her gaze and was soon gone. Guilt? Over what? He stepped towards her and she moved back. For every inch he moved, she did the same.

"Good night," she squeaked.

"Not so fast." He took Kitty and set her on her feet. Watched her walk to her box and climb in, then he turned his attention back to Crissy.

They continued their two step forward two steps backward dance until the back of her legs bumped against the sofa. He grabbed for her before she tumbled backwards and hurled her to himself.

"If it's because you want me to shut up—"

"You think?" Wyatt's heart pounded. Did she hear it? She swallowed visibly, wetting her lip, something he'd come to associate with nervousness.

278

Wyatt took off her Stetson and dropped it carelessly at his feet. Then he reached out, pulled the band from the perpetual ponytail and watched her wild blond curls cascade down to her waist. "Where have you been all my life, Crissy?"

She reached out and pulled his head down. Wyatt found her lips, just as glad to oblige her.

When they came up for air, he smiled. "Better than I imagined."

"Huh?" Her breathless voice showed she was just as affected.

"I've been thinking about doing this all day."

"Wyatt?"

"Shhh." He dropped a light kiss on her lip. "If you regret this, tell me tomorrow, next week, not today." He kissed her again, this time long and slow. When he broke the kiss, he hugged her allowing the cadence of their hearts to speak the things they couldn't put into words just yet.

Dropping a light kiss on her head, he stepped back. Her eyes glowed. "I'll go feed the animals and be on my way. Good night."

When he got to the door, she said, "Wait."

He stopped and looked back. She came up to him and hugged him again.

"I had a great day today."

"Me too." He pressed her close for a moment and let her go. "How about dinner tomorrow. Seven."

"That will be great."

"It's a date."

"How about today?"

"It hardly qualifies for a date with someone knocking on the truck window."

She blushed, giggling. "You looked like you wanted to strangle him."

"For a moment I considered it." He grinned. Wyatt kissed her on the cheek. "See you in the morning."

He lingered a moment more, then opened the door and stepped out.

Maybe this was it.

How about your reaction to the news about Chelsea? A small voice taunted.

Good question.

~

Wyatt's truck had long gone. Crissy felt like she was floating on bubbles as she walked over to the place where her laptop sat on the kitchen island. After talking with Pam, she dialed Becca. It was good to hear that Fred was starting treatment in the new week.

"Runaway friend. So, you remembered me today."

Crissy laughed. "Goes both ways."

"Yeah, but you've got it easy. No Nick breathing down your neck. The office is quiet with three of you out there. I've been working with the publishing team, tweaking the layout of the magazine. I thought I didn't want your jobs but with this new glamour to it, mine seems so meh."

Crissy laughed. "Poor baby. But at least you're not afraid of losing your job. Mine is on the line and I'm not sure where to start. Wyatt is not making things easy."

"Are you on a first name basis already? Girl, dish."

"It's insane. I mean I've only known this guy, days and…"

"You've fallen for him. Love is stranger than fiction. Alexa met Tom on a blind date. Six weeks later, they were married. And dare I say they are doing well, girl." She ended on an inflection. "That makes your work easier."

"Not exactly. He hates the media." Crissy explained what she knew which wasn't much. He didn't even talk about his injuries apart from mentioning it during the branding. "Whatever I write will be what I gleaned on my own but that still puts him smack in the middle of it, otherwise it's no story."

"So, what do you plan to do?"

"I'm going to write it and have him read it. Hopefully, he'll like it enough to give his consent. Or I might as well kiss my job goodbye."

Kitty sidled up to Crissy's legs and she picked the cat up. Crissy was glad that Kitty seemed to have fully recovered.

"Maybe, you could just tell him why you need to write it?"

"And have him feel I'm manipulating his pity."

"If he's in love with you like I think he is, then—"

"A few kisses don't equate to love."

Becca shrieked. "Wyatt Danner kissed you? I'm swooning, girlfriend."

Crissy flushed at her slip and groaned. "I'm not going to hear the end of it. Am I?"

Becca guffawed. "You're so not. Let me be the first to see your write up. Take lots of pics, all right?"

"Yeah."

When the call ended, Crissy dropped the phone. "Kitty, want some milk?"

The cat meowed. Taking that as a yes, Crissy poured some milk for her, watched her lap a few times. She powered on her laptop and opened a fresh document.

She stared at it for minutes. And then typed a heading *WHEN THE CURTAINS ARE DRAWN*

She wished it were so easy to just say, "Hey, Wyatt, I want to do a series on you. What's your life like out of the bucking chute?

Sighing, she closed that and decided to do a writing session on her experience on the mechanical bull. Something to get her creative juices flowing. Who knows, she'd need it.

Chapter Nine

"You're skipping dinner. Where are you going to this time? You've somewhere to go every night now. What gives?"

Wyatt turned to his brother-in-law Nathan, his oldest sister, Melissa's husband. "Does she still ask this many questions? I thought marriage changed people."

Nathan chuckled, his eyes crinkling at the edges. "I'm afraid not."

"I'd be staying out late until she sleeps," Wyatt teased. His sister laughed, not fazed.

"Who sleeps?" Dad asked, walking into the living room.

Wyatt rose.

"Not so fast, kiddo." Melissa blocked his path. "Wyatt is hiding someone from us."

"Would that be the same girl from the neighbors?" Dad asked.

"The one who beat him up. One and the same." Humor gleamed in Melissa's eyes.

Wyatt swallowed a groan, heat filling his collar. Dad chuckled. What possessed him to tell his family? "Can you all stop already?"

"Not until you tell us where you're heading out to." His sister could be persistent. Since Mom passed, Melissa had taken on mother role for everyone, made it her duty to know when everyone was happy or sad. He missed her at the ranch house now that she was married. She was happy, which mattered to Wyatt.

"Still waiting, buddy. Where are you going and with whom?"

Wyatt could feel all eyes on him. He was a grown man not a teenager for crying out loud. But his best bet was to give her what she wanted, get out of there before his other siblings showed up. "Dinner with Crissy. Can I go now?"

Melissa smiled triumphantly. "Yes you may. You should bring her to dinner next week."

"No thanks."

Laughter trailed him and he heard her say. "You might just start preparing for another wedding, Dad."

Maybe, Wyatt thought. If he got the part of his emotion that stayed hung up on Chelsea dealt with. He climbed into his truck. Moments later, he pulled into the Moores' driveway. He grabbed the red single stem rose and walked up to the door. Before he could knock, a smiling Crissy pulled it open.

"You're early."

He kissed her lightly on the lips. "I need to feed the animals. How's Kitty?"

"She's great."

"Good." He handed her the rose appraising her shorts and shirt with the Stetson he bought for her. "You'd look stunning in a potato sack."

She giggled, holding the rose to her nose. "You have a weird way of giving a compliment."

"Yeah? I'll be back."

"You need help?"

"Nah."

Half-hour later, they were on their way. "What did your family think about not having dinner at home today?"

"Got an earful." He smiled. "By the way, my sister wants me to bring you to dinner next week." She was already shaking her head. "Don't worry. You don't have to impress anyone. My family is as down to earth as they get, if I say so myself."

"But they remember me as the lady who beat their brother up."

"They think it's funny. I think it is too." His grin widened. "Imagine that I'd just had myself shaken up by some bull and had the most god awful pain this side of Silverdale and you jumped right at me. I didn't know what hit me."

She burst out laughing. "Very funny." When her laughter subsided, she said, "As a kid, I was always investigating sounds. Pam had a fit when I told her."

"You ever took fighting lessons?"

"Pam's older brothers. They had like eight and ten years on us— Pam's the baby who just happened along when she wasn't expected. Joey and Lucas taught us. But what happened that day with you was more of a habit. My heart was pounding in my ears while I waited for whoever it was to show up." She started laughing again.

"If I was a criminal, what would you have done?"

She shrugged. "I don't know."

"Hmm." He swung into the parking lot of his favorite Mexican restaurant."

"I've heard you can't get in here without reservations. And it's usually booked to the teeth."

"I'm a cowboy, remember? We got our ways."

"That's impressive."

"Oh yeah?" He grinned. He held out his arm and she linked hers through it.

The moment they stepped through the door, a brunette met them. "Wyatt Danner?" There was awe in her voice.

"Yes."

"This way."

Wyatt unhooked their arms and placed his hand on the small of Crissy's back, leading her to their table. He held out the chair for her and then took his. The waiter handed them menus.

"What would you have while you wait for your dinner?" Her question was to Wyatt.

"Ask the lady. I'll take whatever she's having."

He didn't miss the look of displeasure on the girl's face. *Whatever.* She soon went to get them their sweet tea while they perused the menu.

"What are you eating?"

She pronounced one of the foods and laughed. "They're tongue twisting and as a rule, if I can't pronounce it, I don't order it."

"Have no fears. Anything you eat here is amazing."

"I better leave you to choose then."

The waiter returned and Wyatt placed their orders of Arroz con Pollo and cheesecake for dessert.

"You eat all these and you don't gain weight?" Crissy asked when their meal was delivered.

"It's in the genes. High metabolism."

"Lucky you. I have to practically starve to keep the fat off."

"You look good."

She searched his gaze. "Thank you."

"So late in coming."

She giggled. For a woman who looked so sure of herself, it was an obvious armor. Yet, he somehow understood why she would feel so insecure.

He and Crissy talked about anything and everything while they ate. He loved how easily they could connect on every level.

~

Crissy swiped the last of her cake and hid a burp. "You were so not kidding."

"Oh yeah. You want to catch some fresh air?"

"Yup."

Several other trucks had filled the parking lot since they came. People trooped in and out of the restaurant. The noisy chatter from within, the music blaring from the mounted loudspeaker, the aroma that hung in the air, all added novelty to the night.

When they got to his truck, Wyatt lifted her up and deposited her on the warm hood. He hopped up beside her.

Pushing the wipers out of the way, he rested against the windshield. She did the same. The wiper on each sides meant their bodies were in close proximity. Wyatt's body heat seeped through her shirt turning her system into Jell-O. She'd fallen for this guy. That she knew without an iota of doubt.

Wyatt took her hand and linked their fingers.

"Reminds me of one time I was going to one of the rodeos. I'd just started out then, hadn't made a lot of friends, so, I didn't have any traveling buddies. I'd just finished a ride and I was running to catch the next one. My truck packed up in the middle of nowhere and I had to pass the night there. It was late and no vehicles around. The closest motel was an hour away, by car."

"Were you afraid?"

His chest rumbled. "There're very few things that scare anyone who mounts the back of a bull for a living. We live for the thrill, love the risk."

He traced the back of her hand with his thumb, each circle sending ripples of warmth all over her body, robbing her brain of the ability to think. Did he know he had this kind of effect on her?

"The year before last, I rode in over a hundred rodeos, spent days on the road from event to event. I made good money and then won the championship. I hope to be able to retire by the time I'm 30. Don't plan on becoming a washed up bull rider."

"Before the last injury, have you had any serious ones?"

"More than I could count. Broken ribs, fractured collar bone, broken arm, you name it." He chuckled. "It's crazy, huh? Most times, once you can walk out of the arena on your feet, you just sucked it up and got back on. I've been knocked out a few times."

Her heart raced. She did extreme sports, mountain climbing, bungee jumping a couple of times, kayaking like no man's business, but... "Does your family watch your rides?"

"They used to. Mum stopped watching after one of my knockouts in the first year I started riding professionally. She begged me to stop throughout that year. I couldn't. I dreamed it, talked about it, ate it. It was all I knew. So, I promised to call her after every ride and I did. I'd grab my phone and call. Soon as she answered, I'd say I'm okay, Mom, love you. It was always great to hear the relief in her voice." He fell silent.

Crissy didn't need to ask. He missed his mom and she envied the relationship they had. It was always hard to not have any of her parents come to the school shows. Pam's parents did their best. It just wasn't the same.

She rubbed her hand up and down his arms trying to imagine the ache in a mother's heart.

"After she died and dad took it so badly, I started to listen more, be more careful—yeah, I know careful has got nothing to do with getting off a bull alive." His voice was serious. "I didn't want to cause Dad any more pain."

"That was why he kept you from getting on the horse to rope calves?"

"Yeah, the doctors didn't think I would walk again but God had mercy on me. It was a very difficult time of physical therapy and all. Luke got me the bull to keep me out of the arena when I started making progress."

"How long did it take?"

"Four months. I'd wheel myself into the barn when Luke came to visit me and would pull myself on the bull, sweating and panting in pain. He'd set the speed and... I continued that for another two months. The rest is history."

He didn't mention anything about his girlfriend's desertion. Was that to mean he still felt something for her?

Pushing the thought away, she lifted their joined hands and kissed his. He draped his arm around her and pulled her close, his woodsy scent stirring her senses.

"What's the medical help like at the events?"

"It's improving, especially with recent deaths. It's not there yet. But, a lot depends on the honesty of the rider. Injuries like broken bones are apparent and they heal easily so most people just discount them and ride anyway. The silent killers are the head injuries."

"So, the rider ultimately has to decide to sit rides out?"

"Yeah. Which I used to think was weakness, not any more. I've seen guys leave loved ones behind, hurting, because they knew they shouldn't ride, but did. Anyway, if the medical team suspects concussion, they give you a test. You fail it, you sit out."

"Looks like someone has to protect you from yourselves."

"Yeah. I learned one thing as I began to recover, though. I'd set my heart on getting better, so I applied myself to everything my therapist said to do and more. If we're determined to do something, with God on your side, we can achieve it. I had those down moments of near depression when I wanted to give up. I feared the head injuries I'd had a couple of times despite helmets were impacting me. I had friends, family who wouldn't let me stay down. They prayed for me, believed in me. Through that time, one scripture kept ringing in my head like a record on replay. 'I can do all things through Christ which strengthens me.' I did with His help. I'm ready to return again. It's a long way to the top 35 but we'll see."

He slipped his arm from underneath her and slid down from the truck. Crissy raised herself up but remained seated.

Wyatt stood in front of her, his hands against her hips. He stared into her eyes for a long moment. She tucked her hair behind her ears, swallowing at the intensity of his gaze.

"I'm going riding on Friday. Will you come? I'd like to have you there cheering me on."

Crissy swallowed. Hard. Could she really sit there somewhere on the bleachers and watch him ride knowing he may not be fully recovered from his injury?

"What do you say?"

"Sure,' she choked out.

If he noticed her fear, he didn't give any indication.

"Name your price. What can I do for you in return? Something that will make your day."

She grinned. "I want to ride the Soaring Eagle at the Royal Gorge again."

His eyes widened. "No, no, no, something else. I hate heights."

"Yes, yes, yes. Only that will do. I support your crazy sport, you support mine." She giggled. "Besides, you said there are only a few things that scare a bull rider."

"Not nice."

Wyatt tugged her closer. When their lips met, it was all she could think about.

Chapter Ten

Wyatt winked at Crissy where she sat behind his chute. She grabbed her phone and took pictures of him. Her excitement had rubbed off on him. When he'd asked her yesterday, Wyatt thought he'd glimpsed fear in her eyes. But today she talked animatedly about taking pictures before the ride and he made sure they came early to afford her the opportunity. She was supporting him by coming and he wanted to do the same—be a part of whatever she was doing.

Wyatt turned his attention to the announcer as he called the next rider. The bull Wyatt was riding tonight, *Die Hard,* was restless, like he couldn't wait to go. Unfortunately, he spewed riders like lukewarm tea. Anyway, Wyatt didn't get to where he'd been in his career by worrying about those things. The rider before him barely made five seconds before the bull threw him. The fact that all the four riders before him hadn't made their eight seconds filled him with hope and trepidation in equal measure.

Minutes later, his chute was called.

Wyatt Danner. You would recall that Wyatt won the previous year's championship and was gunning for last year's before his injuries.

Wyatt said a quick prayer, settled on the bull and tuned the rest of the announcement out. Once he signaled that he was ready, the chute gate was thrown open.

The beast charged onto the dirt floor and swung wildly one way and another, spun like crazy, it's heavy hoof pounding the ground beneath them. Spittle flew as he grunted and jumped. Wyatt lost count of the swinging and spinning but he hung on. On and on it spun, jumped and swung, all in a bid to unseat Wyatt. Just when he thought the animal would unseat him, the dratted buzzer went off. Wyatt jumped clear of the bull and missed his step.

Die Hard charged after him. He had to jump for the chute bar just as the bull-fighters chased the animal away. His heart pounded from the ride and his escape. He climbed down, and his gaze met Crissy's. The fear in her eyes was quickly replaced by excitement. She clapped just as the announcer screamed out he'd gotten 92 points.

By the time Wyatt was done greeting friends half an hour later and stepped out into the night, Crissy was standing by the truck. She ran into his arms and he twirled her round. When he set her down, he winced. Alarm reflected off her eyes.

"Are you okay?"

"Yeah, a little pain but nothing a couple of pills won't fix."

She didn't look convinced but held her voice.

He kissed her temple and opened the truck door. "You know, I had a better ride than last week. Nerves I guess."

"I always thought I was an adrenaline junkie but it's nothing like you guys do. First time I had someone I l... um someone I know on the back of a bull that acts like it's demented."

Though he couldn't see her face very well in the dark, he could bet his buckle she'd blushed. Had she wanted to say love?

He didn't press it because he wasn't sure he was ready for the word just yet even though Crissy had crept past his defense. "They're trained to buck. The people who rear them trace bloodlines like they do for thoroughbreds, give them special food and care." He chuckled. "It's actually in their best interest to buck."

"Interesting. Do they get injured in the rides too?"

"Never seen any. It's a competition between beast and man where the man is disadvantaged. An average guy weighs one hundred fifty pounds and is pitted against a bull weighing a ton or close to."

They settled into the six hours plus drive from Wyoming. They talked over his plans to hit the circuit once the season kicked off. If she had reservations, she didn't say.

"I'm sure you'll do well after tonight."

Wyatt glanced at Crissy. Her encouragement meant everything to him and he told her so.

"So, you need a lot of money to go from event to event?"

"Not so much. I've made a lot of friends over the years and can travel from state to state without needing to lodge in a hotel and that means I don't have to buy food."

"What's a typical day like?"

Wyatt was just glad to tell her what he did from sunup to sundown on the circuit. They talked back and forth for a while as the truck ate up the distance. The fact that she wanted to know what he did pleased him. He opened the console of the truck, took out his diary and handed it over to her. "I keep track of things during my down time."

That was a part of him he never shared with anyone. Crissy took it, her gaze holding his. Then she turned her attention to the journal.

What would she think? Crissy would know more about him than he'd told her from his writings, more about his injuries and his recovery. He realized he didn't mind. Chelsea had never read his diary. She didn't care for what he did anyway and never bothered asking. How had they lasted those three years? He'd looked good on her arm for a while and then not so good, especially after his injury.

"Can I read this later?"

"Sure. Tired?" he asked.

"Yeah."

He squeezed her hand. "Go to sleep. I'll wake you up when we get home." Yeah, home. He bet she wasn't used to doing a thirteen-hour ride to and fro. He was.

She leaned over, kissed him on the neck and settled back in the seat. He loved Crissy, no doubt. Was he just fixated on Chelsea's betrayal?

~

Other than watching bull riding, Crissy didn't know much about the extreme western sport. She copied the URL of the document she'd been reading and pasted it in a file. Sometimes Nick liked to verify information. Crissy had learned to pay more attention. Of course, that was something Professor Juan always stressed while she was in school.

She glanced at her write up. Would Wyatt like it enough to consent to publication? Hard to tell. She just wouldn't show him right away.

THE LIFE OF A PROFESSIONAL BULL RIDER
By Chrystolle Spencer
About W. Danner

W. Danner is one of well-known faces in the famous western sport and one of the top 35 bull riders in the world, at least, until his injury. The 24-year-old travels all over the country riding at various events, competing on the Professional Bull Riders (PBR) circuit. The season usually spans January to May then picks up again from August all through October, culminating in the PBR World Finals. During these months, Danner travels from place to place riding almost every weekend. It's a taxing schedule with little to no sleep. Yet he loves what he does with   a   passion.
Picking up the interest at an early age, he said. "I really had no other

choice than to be a bull rider. I dreamed it, lived it, it's all I know."

This is his sixth tour, though set back by his injury, he's eager to make a comeback. He has made good money riding bulls at PBR events and from sponsors. His plan is to have enough money to retire by the time he turns 30.

He jokingly says, "I could probably keep going, but I don't want to be broken and not enjoy life. I don't plan on becoming some washed up bull rider."

Crissy picked up Wyatt's journal. She'd spent all of the early hours of the morning reading, after they got in. The more she read, the more she realized that only passion and determination could make anyone choose this kind of life.

A knock sounded at the door. Crissy already knew who it was. She walked over and opened the door. "Hey." She smiled at him.

"Hey you too."

She stepped back for him to enter. "Were you able to get a little rest?"

"Enough to keep body and soul together. You?"

"I'm good. Want some pasta? I made some."

"That'd be great." He glanced at her laptop. "You're working?"

"Uh, yeah." She shut the laptop. When she turned, she encountered his raised brows.

"Something I shouldn't see?"

She busied herself retrieving dishes.

"Since you're not answering, should I be concerned."

"No." Heat fanned her face.

The suspicion didn't leave his eyes. "Good to know, but I won't be eating. Thanks for the offer. The animals are settled for the night."

Why hadn't she thought of shutting the laptop? Now she looked bad in his eyes. What if she showed him? Not yet. She hadn't even finished. Crissy could literally see her job floating away. Could she even show him knowing how he felt about the media?

He backtracked. "Wyatt wait."

"Crissy, I think we should take a break." He gestured between them. "I feel things are going too fast."

"Because?"

"I don't know. I won't keep you from your work. Have a nice night, Chrystolle."

Her heart wrenched. He hadn't called her that since the first day. When the door shut quietly behind him, Crissy stood there for minutes unable to move. What just happened? What changed between the time he got in....

Back on the stool, she opened her laptop and the document. For a few seconds, she contemplated deleting the write up. She could just write generally, but that wasn't her agreement with Nick.

Since she got involved with Wyatt, it was as though a part of her had been waiting for the other shoe to drop. It did, but sooner than she expected.

Crissy grabbed her phone and dialed Becca.

"Hey, girl. Three more days."

"Yeah, and I think I should be preparing my resignation."

"You're kidding, right?"

Her throat tickled. "Wish I were."

When she told Becca what had happened, she ended with, "I have two options—show him and then he refuses to let it be published or scrap it. Judging by his reaction, I'd rather take the second."

"And lose your job."

"Rather than make him feel I've betrayed his trust like his ex."

"I get your point. But I'd love to read it anyway."

"I'll send it tonight, but it's between us."

"You can count on me."

When the call ended, Crissy contemplated calling Wyatt. But what would she say?

Chapter Eleven

Wyatt helped Melissa carry the last cooler into her husband's truck. Nathan had gone ahead.

"Are you going to pick Crissy up?"

"I didn't invite her." That was what he wanted to do yesterday. But then he'd thought he'd glimpsed his name in the document before she'd shut the laptop. He shook his head.

"Someone's lost in thought." Melissa put her hands on her hips. "You've been acting all strange. Even Noah commented on it."

"I'm fine." He closed the tailgate.

His sister didn't look convinced. "In the last week plus, all we heard about was Crissy. Now you won't invite her to the potluck knowing she leaves in two days."

"We've decided to take things slow."

Melissa opened her mouth and snapped it shut, then she climbed into her truck. "Don't be long."

"I won't." He took the back route to the Moore's ranch. It looked like the animals were used to him now. Even the birds didn't make any noise. He fed them and changed their water. He'd cleaned out the stalls yesterday morning and didn't have to. His plan had been to make room for them to have a nice day at church but all that—

Wyatt finished the chore and took the back route to his place. After a shower, he got dressed and prepared for church.

Still, he couldn't shake the morose feeling that hung on him like a wet rag.

~

Crissy hit send on the document to Becca's email. The more she

293

thought of having written about him without his consent, the worst she felt. Anyway, she'd made up her mind she wasn't sending it to Nick. If Pam returned tomorrow night, Crissy could leave first thing on Tuesday. What had looked promising ended up being a waste.

The sound of a truck filtered into the house. Heart in her throat, Crissy went to the door. Disappointment clawed up her belly. The rational part of her brain knew she and Wyatt were done before they started.

She opened the door and stepped out.

A young woman probably in her late twenties climbed down from the truck.

"Crissy, right? I'm Melissa, one of the Danner kids."

Crissy reached out a hand. "Nice to meet you. How may I help you?"

"We have a potluck in church. Actually, I'd reached when I thought I would've invited you. I thought Wyatt would. Seeing you're dressed, were you going to church?"

The woman talked a mile an hour. "I was thinking of going to one down the street."

"Then I'll be disappointed. I promise you'll have a great time." She raised her hands as though in prayer.

"Okay, I'll just grab my bag."

"Great." She clapped her hands.

Not something Crissy wanted to do. Wyatt would definitely be there. She bit her lip, staring at her bag. Melissa honked and Crissy jumped. Snatching the bag from the table, she hurried out.

Melissa soon pulled out of the driveway. "I've heard a lot about you." Crissy flushed. "Don't worry. All good things."

"Thanks."

"Nice to finally meet you. Heard you're leaving this week. I was hoping you could have dinner with the family, but my naughty brother preferred to keep you to himself."

Her face heated. What would she say to that? Melissa didn't require any response as she continued moving seamlessly from one subject to the other.

"Wyatt's grumpy. His face looks like a baby's smacked bottom."

Crissy couldn't help laughing. She loved this woman already. Crissy would've expected Wyatt's sister to be upset with her.

Melissa turned into a parking spot in front of a building, an old cowboy church near Hastings. The rustic-styled red barn turned sanctuary looked relatively new.

To one side, they had tables set up. "We'll eat after the service. Oh, that's Pastor William."

The man in his forties dressed in shirt, Wranglers, and Stetson came towards them.

"Melissa, I was just asked about you from Nathan. He said you went to bring a friend."

"Yes." Melissa held Crissy's hand. "Crissy, meet Pastor William. Pastor William, our friend, Crissy."

"Pleased to have you here, Crissy." The pastor's handshake was firm, his grey eyes lit up with a smile.

"Thank you, sir."

Wyatt came from the back of the church. He seemed to be in a heated discussion with a young lady. He hadn't seen them.

Crissy stopped with her hand on the door.

"That's Chelsea. His ex. Don't pay her any mind. She did him much evil. Good riddance when they broke up if you ask me."

That was what he feared she was doing to him.

He turned, his gaze encountering hers for a heart stopping second and then he strolled away.

The organ struck a tune.

"Let's go. Service is starting."

She'd have to talk to him later, clear the air before she left. She didn't expect his forgiveness anyway, especially since he'd told her time without number how much he hated anything to do with the media.

The worst thing was that she knew. Too late. Their love was too good to be true...

Chelsea brushed past them, her cloying perfume wrapping around them.

"Ours is not a regular church." Melissa said as they walked in. "It's open to everyone—cowboys, non cowboys, large city or just plain country folks who've seen the ups and down life's trail. No barriers to keep people away like in traditional churches. Our leaders are called vaqueros. Interesting, huh?"

"Very." Crissy let her eyes roam. The small choir was decked out in hats and boots. A cowboy played an acoustic guitar, while a lady played the piano. Melissa slid into one pew and introduced Crissy to a quiet looking man on her right. "Nathan, meet Crissy. Crissy, my husband."

He reached across and shook her hand. "Pleased to meet you."

"Same here."

The church service was nothing fancy, just a couple of simple hymns before the message started. It was...a laid-back atmosphere. That's the word she was looking for.

As the service proceeded, Crissy tried to concentrate instead of dwelling on what she needed to do by the end of service. But with Wyatt sitting just a few pews away, Crissy had a herculean task focusing. Not a good thing.

Chapter Twelve

Wyatt surveyed the delicious looking homemade dishes laid out on the tables. His stomach rumbled. He'd skipped breakfast so as to be able to do justice to the food. Mom, bless her soul, always said there was some competition involved in their annual potluck. The aroma of each casserole—his fab Tex-Mex flair, brunch, vegetarian, squash and pineapple had his juices flowing in no small measure. The foods were supposed to be crowd pleasers and they were.

Wyatt waited for the couple in front of him to move on. He filled his plate and went to join his brother and friends at their table. His senses hummed with the fact that Crissy was just a few tables away.

He hadn't known Melissa would invite her. She laughed at something his sister said and his pulse stuttered. What he said was true, no matter what his heart thought. Trust wasn't built on emotions and they'd had lots of those.

How come his heart didn't agree?

"You two got into a fight?" Rait asked.

"Chelsea?" He didn't want to talk about what the manipulating woman said to him. Who did she take him for? A puppet on a string? If she hoped the announcement of her wedding would make him jealous, then she had another think coming. But he was jealous, a bit. Anger at her was more. She ruined what they had.

"Are you listening?" Rait whispered. "Crissy. She keeps casting longing glances at you."

Wyatt chanced a glance in her direction. Their gazes met and held. One second. Then two. Her smile froze. She looked away. Dressed in a knee length dress that hugged her trim waist, her hair in a low bun, she was beautiful.

Swallowing, he returned his attention to his food. "Not really. We decided to take things slow. I don't need distractions right now."

"That wasn't the impression you gave us all of last week. I mean she followed you to Wyoming to ride. You couldn't get over it."

Wyatt continued eating. The food tasted like dust on the arena's dirt floor.

"Talk to me, man."

"I'm not sure what to say."

"Who made the decision?"

"I did."

"Did she think so? From the way she's looking at you, I assume otherwise."

Wyatt didn't answer. What if it wasn't what he thought? His face heating, he said simply, "I just told her and walked away."

"That's fear talking. You're afraid to let yourself fall for anyone because you've been betrayed. Lucky you, Chelsea only used the press. My friend's girlfriend, Yvonne had an affair with his best friend. He actually caught them red-handed on the day he was planning to propose. Thank God, he found out. It was devastating but he's married today and doing well. Don't punish a woman for something that is no fault of hers."

Wyatt glanced in Crissy's direction. This time, she snatched her gaze away so fast.

Maybe he'd just come out and ask her. But that would be later.

~

Crissy hit submit on the third job application for that day. She massaged her neck to ease the pain. Pam and Fred were slated to return by evening. Crissy already had her things packed.   She'd been listening for Wyatt to come feed the animals. Her phone rang.

"Becca, how are you?"

"I'm fine." She was quiet for a spell. "Crissy I don't know how to say this. I mistakenly forwarded the document you sent with the ones I'd been working with for Nick."

"You're kidding, right?" Crissy covered her mouth, her belly dropping to her feet.

"Wish I were. Didn't realize it until he asked this morning. I just stepped out of his office to give you a heads up. I'm really sorry."

Crissy sighed. A beep sounded. "I think he's calling already. Talk to you later." Nick's nickname, Bossy Boss, popped on her screen. Swallowing, she swiped the screen to accept the call.

"Why did you not send the article straight to me," he said without preamble.

"Uh…"

"Its great. Your last articles with the pictures have generated quite some positive response. This will nail it."

"Sir, unfortunately, we can't publish it."

"Why not?"

"Because I don't have consent."

"So, how did you get this information?"

"He shared it but he hadn't meant it to be something that went out to the media."

For the first time, Nick seemed to be short of words.

"I'll give him a call then." And the phone went dead in her ears. Why hadn't she made better effort at talking to Wyatt yesterday? Was it because she'd been jealous about seeing him with Chelsea or how popular with the women he was.

Better to get dressed properly, if she had to show up at their ranch to warn him.

She ran into the visitor's room and grabbed a brush. After hurriedly pulling it through her hair to put the tangled mess in a semblance of order, she came out of the room.

The doorbell rang and she jumped.

Her belly churned, whatever was left of her breakfast threatening to make an appearance. How was she going to tell him?

The chiming came again and Crissy tucked wisps if hair behind her ear walking over to the door. She yanked it open as the doorbell rang a third time.

For a moment, they stared at each other. His blue eyes blazed. Had Nick called him already? He must've been on the property to be here this quick.

"You said I'd nothing to worry about."

She closed her eyes briefly. "I'm so sorry." She wasn't sure what else to say. She could pretend not to know what he was talking about, but to what intent? Nick was tenacious that way.

"Which is it? Going ahead with writing things about me when you know how dead set I am against it or lying to me about it."

"Want to come in?"

"No. I just came to find out something."

Crissy gulped, her pulse drumming in her ears. "Okay."

"Was I just a pawn in your hand to further your career? Was this some calculated effort on your part?" he asked tightly.

The heat from the scorching inferno in his eyes, fanned over her. Her shoulders sagged. Calculated aptly described her coming, but not in the way he thought. *What did it matter?* "No. There's nothing I can say that will make things better. I'm sorry."

He shook his head and without a backward glance, turned towards the back of the house probably heading back to his. She should've seen the handwriting on the wall.

She closed the door, leaned against it and slid down until she was on her haunches.

What to do now.

Chapter Thirteen

The chute flew open as soon as Wyatt gave the signal. *Bullet* swung his powerful body against the chute gate shifting Wyatt's momentum. Righting himself was no use because he was soon sailing over the bull's head. Wyatt narrowly missed the three-foot-wide sturdy horns. Momentarily, he fought to push air into his lungs.

The mighty hoof clipped him on the side before the bull fighters sent the animal off. His ribs burned. Within split seconds he was helped to his feet.

Wyatt pulled off his helmet and grimaced at the move. He held his side. He knew his ribs weren't broken—he'd had a couple of those to know. But he'd be sporting a huge bruise.

He needed to shake the feelings that held him bound all week. Crissy had just let him have his say and apologized. She hadn't pretended not knowing what he was talking about, neither offered any defense. *Yeah, because she had none.*

Why did he not feel better cutting her out of his life? The melancholy he felt when he'd first said they should take a break had only intensified over the week.

"What happened to you, buddy?" Cory, his closest friend, asked when they got to the locker room.

If he was going to get back on the circuit, he needed to get his act together. As it were, this weekend was a waste. He'd messed up the days, his rides. "I'm good." When his friend's eyebrows rose, Wyatt said, "Really."

"You might want to reconsider if you're fully fit to make a comeback just yet. I understand the feelings, but if you're not ready, it's okay to wait. Rule number one is to stay alive. At this rate, I'm afraid for you."

The doctor walked in and Cory stepped out. By the time the doctor was done with his assessments, Wyatt had an icepack over the huge discoloration on his side, he was ready to hit the road and head home.

But Wyatt couldn't make himself get up. What was it with him, anyway?

Crissy betrayed his trust. He gave her his journal out of trust, bared his soul to her…

"That girl loves you," Melissa had said after the potluck.

She definitely had a great way to show it.

If it didn't show in her support for you, following you several hours across states, what shows?

The times during the branding, the shopping, the wedding that had chosen to play in his mind in relentless slow motion in the last few days, started again.

He groaned and leaned his head against the backrest, closing his eyes.

Her face sneaked into his mind and his eyes shot open.

What was wrong with him?

~

"I can't believe he let you go." Becca huffed.

"We had an agreement I couldn't fulfill and that's okay. Hopefully, I'll hear from the companies I applied to within the new week."

Losing her job didn't compare to the heavy ache that had settled in her gut since Wyatt turned his back and walked away.

"You think he saw the mail? Why not just give him a call?"

"And say what? I sent him the article on Monday. Today is Sunday. What if he just doesn't want to know what I had to say?"

Melissa had been gracious to send her his email address. What if that ticked him off too?

"You really liked him?"

"Crazy, right? I know. We seemed to have…" She searched for the appropriate word. "A connection. But, boy was I mistaken?" Crissy marveled that she was dry eyed when gloom had been her companion all week. She sighed. "For a moment there, he made me believe in me, but I guess he told me things I wanted to hear. One thing I'm glad for, is that I was able to help my cousin and things are looking well for them now. That's a good thing."

"I agree, but we miss you at work."

"I do too. I've never been claustrophobic but these days it feels like the walls are closing in. I can't seem to figure out why."

"I'd say you should go out but everyone you could visit will be at work. How about we go Kayaking like we wanted to do two weeks ago before you left for the ranch?"

"Great idea. By the way, I'm in the mood for some comfort food." The earlier she accepted that what happened between her and Wyatt was a passing phase, which was over before it began, the better.

Chapter Fourteen

Dinner was long over. Wyatt sat in the barn staring at the spot where Crissy had fallen days ago. Memory was cruel. He hated the way his mind re-lived everything he'd done with Crissy in those two short weeks. They were better than the three years he had with Chelsea if he told the truth.

Noah walked in.

"Aren't you supposed to be home with your wife?" Wyatt asked.

He dropped beside Wyatt on the bench. "I won't be long." He looked at Wyatt. "I hate to see you like this. I want to help. What can I do?"

Wyatt gave his brother a lopsided smile. "Nothing. I'll be fine."

Silence settled between them.

After a moment, Noah said, "How about you ask to see what she wrote about you? I've been checking their magazine lately. To the best of my knowledge, your story hasn't been published. I think that says something."

"Other than I could make a case out of it?"

"Chelsea knew and went ahead all the same. Think about that."

True. If Crissy had feelings for him like he thought she did, would she write anything against him? Not that he offended her in any way.

"Talk to her. Not sure you've looked in the mirror lately. Plus your bad rides... You've gone grumpy on all of us. Are you sure you really didn't hit your head last time you fell?" Noah's voice was teasing.

"Very funny."

Noah rose and squeezed Wyatt on the shoulder. "If you need me, just holler."

"Sure. My regards to your wife."

"She'll hear. And don't dash our hopes of another wedding."

Wyatt snorted and watched his brother walk away. It'd been two weeks since Crissy left. Would she even take his call. Her absence was like a hole in his heart.

When he'd stepped through the barn door earlier, memories had flooded in—Crissy on the bull, he changing the speed and suddenly throwing her, the kisses they shared. It broke down the walls of his anger.

Here he was sitting on the same bench where they'd sat that night and talked. Did he take his paranoia so far? Why did he not ask to see the document like Noah said? Did she even miss him? How had he thought he was better off without her?

He lay down on the bench as memory after memory poured into his mind.

He heaved a heavy sigh.

Undecided, he clicked on his Facebook page. Cory had expressed his joy at seeing him back to riding.

Wyatt responded with a tap dance Gif. He scrolled through a few pages and then clicked off. He'd never really been a fan of social media. Going through people's stories always had a way of exhausting him.

He signed off and decided to check the pile of email that had come in all week. He hadn't felt like checking them, hadn't felt like doing a lot of things in days. Most times, they were emails from things he subscribed for and never got to use.

True to words, e-mail after e-mail, he deleted each of them. The subject of the last one was in caps. PLEASE READ!

He clicked on it.

I hope this meets you well.

He scanned to the end. It was signed by Chrystolle Spencer. Not Crissy...

He went back to find his place.

I feel I owe you an apology. Truth is, I suggested doing a western feature for our magazine because my boss was hoping to increase subscriptions. He agreed but on condition that I interviewed someone for it. I had initially told Pam I couldn't come watch her house while she was away. Long story short, Nick gave me days to get the job done or lose my job. Except that I realized you were not amenable to media posts about you. I was hoping you'd like what I wrote and agree to its publication.

I take responsibility for everything that happened. I'd sent it to Becca because she wanted to read what I wrote about you.

Unfortunately, she sent it to Nick in error.

You were never a pawn in my hands. I care too much for you to have done that.

I just wanted to say I'm sincerely sorry.

Chrystolle Spencer

PS: Find attached the document. I've deleted everything about you in my system. Becca too. I think Nick may still have his copy but he won't publish it without your consent. I made sure of that. It was nice knowing you and spending those two weeks with you.

Wyatt wiped the moisture from his eyes. He tapped the document to download it.

When he opened it, he read the introduction that talked about him and his aspirations. In the body, she'd used a day in his journal.

He scrolled to the last part.

LIFE BEYOND THE ARENA: When the curtains are drawn

Every bull rider knows the risk he faces when he climbs on the back of a massive animal weighing a ton or close to. Only one thing keeps them going back again, passion for what they do.

W. Danner had suffered a setback injury that took him from the ninth position in the world standing to starting almost from the bottom.

But I see a man who overcame the odds even when they were stacked sky high to make a comeback.

He's also a contributory part of a team geared towards changes in the rodeo world. Because of his efforts alongside the family and friends of his late friend who committed suicide after a series of head injuries, every rodeo will have medical personnel on ground to attend to riders. Plus, they now have awareness programs to educate riders about head injuries and its aftermath in a bid to remove the stigma and help people speak up and get help.

Do you have a friend, a brother who would love us to tell his story from his perspective? Drop us a line at Crissy@RMM.com

Wyatt scrubbed a hand across his face.

What had he done?

~

"You're free to go. You'll hear from us soon."

Crissy thanked the lady, took her bag and walked out of the company. Her phone rang. She glanced at the screen. Nick? He better not be asking her to convince Wyatt to give permission to run the article. She'd do no such thing.

She accepted the call. "Good morning, sir."

"Can you come to the office?"

She stopped in the middle of the sidewalk, warmth seeping through her suit. "Is there a problem?"

If there was, Nick wouldn't sound so happy, but she needed to know. He hadn't called her since she left the company last week.

"I'll be waiting," he said.

The phone went dead in her ear. Trust Nick to behave like that.

She hadn't missed working with him at all. Luckily, his company was just a few block down the road.

She arrived minutes later, panting. A blue truck sat in front of the company's entrance. The plate number looked like Wyatt's. She frowned. What would he be doing here?

Her pulse sped up and she scolded herself to stop being ridiculous even though she knew it was impossible to have two identical plate numbers. Even if it was, he was probably here for something else. Had he read her email? She swallowed the ball of ache that rose in her throat every time she thought about the fact that he obviously wasn't giving her another chance.

She'd be fine, eventually. Time healed wounds. Didn't it?

Crissy pushed through the door and entered.

Becca gave her two thumbs up. The others also had curious looks in their eyes. Shrugging it off, she made a short walk to Nick's office.

She recognized that cologne anywhere. It seemed to hang over the clothes she wore the last couple of weeks. Or she imagined it. Standing at the door, she took in a couple of deep breaths to coral her runaway feelings then stepped into the room. "Wyatt, what are you doing here?"

She hoped her surprise didn't show in her voice. Thinking he was here and seeing him, were two different things. She didn't like the way her heart pounded away as his blue gaze held hers. His blond bangs had grown longer, hanging over his eyes. Handsome as ever. *Breathe!*

He rose, smiling. "I came to see Nick and to give my consent for the article."

"He's also agreed to get his friends to feature for us."

"Us? What do you mean? I no longer work for you."

He pushed her letter across the table. "Here it is. You have forty-eight hours to think about it."

"Are you giving me an ultimatum yet again? I'd rather not take it back. Since both of you have reached an understanding, what has that got to do with me?" she asked not looking at Wyatt.

His proximity was affecting her ability to think.

"Crissy, can we go somewhere and talk?"

She glanced at him then. The plea in his eyes was her undoing. She turned her gaze to Nick. "You wanted to see me?"

"He wanted to see you." He pointed to Wyatt. "Let me know your decision."

She nodded and walked out, Wyatt at her heels. He pulled open the passenger's door and waited for her to get in. When he climbed in, he said, "Your place or mine?"

"My place." She rattled off the address. Her insides were so mushed up she wondered if she wasn't going to lose her breakfast. When they got to her house, she opened the door and led the way in. Dropping her bag and key on the table in her studio apartment, she stepped out of her pumps.

"Why did you quit? Nick gave me the impression it was your decision."

Crissy had a few choice words for the man but kept them in. "It was my only option. You want something to drink?"

"After we talk."

Crissy dropped onto the only sofa in the room facing her small bed. Her room was organized, always was, but she hadn't thought of the close proximity the size would put them in. Hadn't been thinking, really. She scooted to the extreme far end of the seat to give him room if he wanted to sit down but didn't offer him a seat.

He looked around at her small apartment. She'd done some frugal decorations with splashes of pink, white curtains and trims. "I like this."

"Thank you. But I guess that's not why you came?" Hovering over her like he was doing, sent her pulse into overdrive. Maybe she should've let him sit instead. Yet, she couldn't make herself get up. Crissy licked suddenly dry lips.

"No." He held her gaze. For a heart stopping moment, they stared at each other. Crissy had to fight the urge to run into his arms. Only the thought that it may not be reconciliation that brought him, held her to the seat. She blinked against the ache that blindsided her, her lungs burning with the effort of pushing air in and out.

"I read your email and your write up."

"And ignored it," she couldn't help saying.

"It was last night." At her raised brow, he said, "I know. I check my email once in a while. I'm sorry I didn't hear you out or give you a benefit of doubt."

Crissy burst into tears. She covered her face. What was wrong with her?

Chapter Fifteen

Wyatt closed his eyes, inhaled and exhaled. He expected anger, not tears. That way he'd have felt better for what he did. At a loss, he sat beside her and gathered her into his arms. She didn't resist him. "I've no excuse whatsoever," he said into her hair.

She wrapped her arms around him and for moments, just wept.

Wyatt rested his chin on her head and held her. Seconds morphed into minutes.

"I've known misery in no small measure since you left. I know you'll be wondering why I hadn't called. I'm not going to excuse that either." Wyatt held her away. He tilted her chin so that she looked into his eyes. "I've missed you, Crissy. This weekend was a disaster for me because I couldn't stop thinking of you. What did you do to me, Crissy Spencer?"

She smiled amidst her tears. Her eyes were blotchy now, veins popping on her forehead.

"I...spent all week wondering why you didn't respond to my email. Thought you hated me that much."

Fresh tears slipped from her eyes. Wyatt thumbed them away. "Even when I didn't know what you wrote, I couldn't hate you."

"I missed you too."

"To think that you lost your job because of me."

"I don't know if I'm relieved or not."

"You have time to think about that, I don't. I can't wait to do this." He dipped his head and found her warm lips. Her perfume stimulating his sense. He pressed her closer as he kissed her. Coming up for air, he smiled. "Didn't realize how much I missed you. I love you, Crissy."

"Love you too, Wyatt Danner."

"Want to grab some lunch?"

"Not yet. Unless you're hungry."

"Whatever you want, baby."

"I just want you to hold me for some time."

"That's easy." He chuckled. "I can't imagine myself climbing a rock, but if that's what you want, I'd do in a heartbeat. Anything other than the sinking feeling I battled for days."

She cuddled against him. "I didn't fare better either. Here I was beginning to believe I was worth loving and the whole thing was gone like a puff in the wind."

Wyatt hid a wince. He kissed her on the head and wrapped his arms around her tighter. "I'm sincerely sorry I became an architect of doubt. The fact that I'd been pigheaded doesn't change the reality or God's truth about you."

She looked up at him as though to gauge his sincerity. Wyatt dropped a soft kiss in her lips.

He checked his wristwatch. "I have something to show you."

"What?"

"You'll see."

~

Wyatt held her hand, his eyes twinkling as he smiled down at her. Crissy smiled back, her pulse racing that Wyatt was right here with her. But for his plan to show her something, something they drove this far to find, she wanted to just stay curled up in his arms for the whole day.

The sun was warm against her back as they walked the deck south of Pizza at the Royal Gorge Park.

"Where are we going?"

"You'll soon find out, sweetheart. Patience."

"I don't know what that is. Not my strong suit."

Wyatt grinned at her. Through the two hours ride from Denver, he'd refused to tell her where they were headed. That was cool, though. She loved surprises. Knowing Wyatt, it would be worth her while.

The launch area of the Soaring Eagle zip line loomed ahead. "Is it what I'm thinking?"

"You need to stop talking before I lose my nerve and go back."

Crissy giggled.

"What's funny?" He stopped.

"You told me there's hardly anything a bull rider fears." She placed a finger at the base of his neck. "You're blushing and your pulse is racing."

He grabbed her hand and kissed it. "You're too smart for your own good." He winked. "Let's go."

He dragged her on and she swallowed another giggle and followed him. There were several people already waiting for their ride. Wyatt talked to the guy in charge. He told them there were two sets of people before them.

By the time it reached their turn, Wyatt spotted fine beads of sweat on his forehead. "We could always go back."

"I paid for it yesterday."

"How—"

"Your turn, Wyatt Danner."

Crissy didn't have the opportunity to ask how he guessed she'd forgive him, talk more of agreeing to go see whatever he wanted to show her.

Both of them were strapped on in no time.

Crissy had only mentioned it to Wyatt once. She'd loved it the first time she rode—the rush of adrenalin, the exhilaration, better experienced than imagined.

"Are you ready?" the guy asked.

"Not yet."

Crissy glanced at Wyatt. He was sweating for real. She reached out and squeezed his hand. "You'll be fine."

"I know."

He was fiddling in his pocket. Did he have a safety charm? Crissy giggled at the thought.

"You have your day, but I'll make you pay." He smiled apologetically to the man beside them. "One minute more and we're ready to go."

Wyatt produced a red velvet box, turned to Crissy and opened it. Crissy's gaze flew to his, her hand to her mouth.

"Crissy, from the day you tackled me, somehow, I knew my life wouldn't be the same again. I have a phobia for heights but chose to come here today knowing this is one of your favorite places. I've not been the best of persons, but I want to be your biggest support from this day on. You make me happy and I don't want another day to pass without asking you. Will you marry me?"

Crissy blinked to clear her vision. "Yes, Wyatt Danner. I love you to the moon and back."

He slipped the solitaire on her finger and kissed her amidst cheers and claps.

Her heart overflowed with joy as she held her hand out to admire the ring. Wyatt gave the man a thumbs up and their chair zipped backwards parallel to the Royal Gorge, below the aerial tram towards the ridge north of the visitor's centre.

Crissy lifted her face to the wind, enjoying its caress.

By the time they were zooming back to the launch area, Wyatt's death grip on her hands had eased some.

"Looks endless, down below."

She glanced beneath them as the beautiful scenery changed below and smiled at him. "Looks like someone has conquered his fear."

"With you on my side, I guess I can do anything, but don't count on me repeating this anytime soon."

She smiled at him, her heart welling up with joy. "You knew I would let you back in."

"I wasn't sure, but I always like to prepare."

The same thing he'd told her weeks ago.

Their chair came to a stop just then. One thing she had no doubt about was Wyatt Danner was full of surprises. There'd be no dull moment here on out.

God, I can't thank You enough.

Epilogue

Within minutes, Wyatt's siblings and friends had the barn cleared. Crissy glanced around at the faces surrounding them. One face filled her with joy. Fred. It was too early to know if his trial treatment was working, but the fact that he could come out for Crissy's wedding ceremony was a great thing.

She turned and encountered Wyatt's gaze. He winked at her and gave her a smile that always had the potency to make her legs weak. She returned his smile. Wyatt came over to her and reached out his hand. Crissy slipped hers in his and let him lead her to the makeshift dance floor. They'd practiced the moves a million times and Crissy hoped she'd do the dance justice. It didn't help that for Wyatt, country dance was like eating bread and butter. He'd laughed when she reminded him he was supposed to have two left feet as far as dancing was concerned.

The cameraman stepped forward and took a couple of snapshots.

Wyatt's friend and DJ, Luke, gave them a thumbs up and started the music. Wyatt wrapped his hands around her waist while Crissy kept hers around his neck. He stared into her eyes for a moment, then kissed her.

For a few seconds, they waltzed to the beat of *This is Home with You*.

"I've got you, baby?" he whispered.

Crissy smiled, her heart swelling at the thought that this was the man she was spending the rest of her life with. "I know that."

"Here we go."

Their guests erupted in laughter with claps when he spun her out and she came back into the sweetheart position. Crissy counted each move in her head-*spin out, spin in, pretzel.*

Wyatt dipped her and gave her a swoon-worthy kiss before righting her. Friends screamed and whistled. Crissy burst out laughing. That wasn't part of the script. But in the past few weeks, she'd learned to expect the unexpected.

He swung her out again and she returned in. For the first time, Crissy elicited the *trust fall* without tripping. His grin was the size of the Arkansas River.

A couple of moves later, the song ended.

"You did great."

"I learned from the best."

"Okay, everyone is dancing the next song," Luke announced. "Grab your partners. It's super easy. We'll do stomp, kick, triple steps, then eight counts of shuffle steps. Are we good?"

There was a chorus of 'yes'.

Within minutes, the dance floor was occupied to do the line dance to *With You Forever.*

Crissy didn't know anyone in the barn. Okay, minus Pam and her husband. But the support from Wyatt's family and friends brought tears to Crissy's eyes.

"You good?" Wyatt asked, apparently sensing her mood. He nuzzled her neck.

"Yeah."

The next song began and for a few minutes, they danced. When the song ended, everyone meandered to the buffet table. Crissy couldn't ask for a better day, especially with the man who seemed to sense her every need and emotion.

His brothers said he'd been lassoed by love. If anything, Crissy was the one caught.

"I love you, babe."

"Love you, Wyatt Danner."

His kiss promised the love of a lifetime. She couldn't have wished for a better ending.

Rose Verde is an avid reader and a writer of happily-ever-afters. Her stories explore real life issues and God's dealings with us through them. She writes of second chances and a chance to fall in love despite all odds.

When she's not writing, she's dreaming up the next story. Rose lives with her family in Toronto.

To get updates from Rose
    Other Books by Rose Verde
    His Thanksgiving Surprise
    A Time To Laugh
    A Time To Heal
    Spring Beauty Inn
    Christmas Wish

Rodeo Mix-Up

Martha Rogers

Chapter 1

"**Pops, I don't care** what you or those hard-headed brothers of mine think. I'm not going back to college, and this time they can't make me."

Kylee Danner crossed her arms over her chest and glared at her father. This time she'd show them she meant business. They'd already made her go to college for two years, and that was enough.

Those brothers still thought of her as the baby of the family. If they were here, all three of them would scold her for using her favorite nickname for her daddy even if Pops didn't object. They hated it and called it disrespectful. Her father remained silent, but the anger in his eyes said it all without words. She waited, tapping the toe of her boot on the floor.

Finally, he raised his hands with palms facing each other. "Why, Kylee? Why?"

"College isn't for me. I don't need a degree to work on this ranch or to barrel race, and all I want to do right now is race." That and being with Jesse Martin, the cowboy who'd roped her heart, but Pops didn't need to know that.

Her father stood and leaned his palms on his desk. "You can't barrel race all your life. I thought you wanted to be a teacher."

"I did when I was in high school, but I love riding Belle and competing. She's the best barrel racing horse around." Kylee raised Belle from the day of foaling, and the two understood one another.

"That may be, but what about five, ten years down the road?"

She puffed a breath through her lips. "I don't know, but I'll handle it. Besides with Missy and Brandy Jo married, Consuela needs a little help around here even if she doesn't have a houseful of Danner mouths to feed now."

Her father worked his jaw as he'd done so many times before when he didn't like her decisions. He continued to glare into her eyes.

She stepped around the desk and wrapped her arms around him. "You know I love you and this ranch more than anything, and now that the guys are married, it'll be good to be around here without them meddling in my life all the time."

"Who's meddling in whose life?"

Kylee spun around to find her brother Rait leaning against the door jamb. "You, Noah, and Wyatt, that's who. I'm twenty years old, have two years of college behind me, and you three still treat me like I'm five."

"Because that's the way you behave at times, little sister." He straightened and sauntered toward her with a smirk gracing his features. "What are you pestering Dad about now?"

"None of your business. It's between Po . . . Dad and me." She glared at her brother as she marched past him and out into family room.

Rait swatted at her backside as she passed. "See, you're acting like a little child now."

That only served to stir up her anger. Without looking back, she stomped her way toward the kitchen.

Consuela laid down her spoon and held out her arms to Kylee. "Oh, my little one, I see trouble in those eyes. Want to tell me about it?"

Kylee walked into the outstretched arms. Consuela may not have been with the family many years, but she had captured Kylee's heart. "It's Pops and Rait. Why won't my brothers let me grow up and make up my own mind about things?"

Consuela patted her back. "Honey, you're their baby sister, and you'll always be that to them. Your daddy loves you, too. With the others all married now, you're the last one in the nest."

Consuela spoke the truth, and even though Kylee understood that love, she still wanted them to let her be herself. "I just don't want to go back to college. I enjoy barrel racing more." She stepped back from the cook and perched on a stool by the island where Consuela prepared the batter for Pop's favorite cake.

Consuela returned to her mixing. "Remember, your dad only wants what he thinks is the best for you. Your mother has been gone only a few years, and he's worked hard to keep things going for all of his children."

"Well, Brandy Jo didn't go to college, and she's done just fine.

Besides, Belle is a great horse, and she's helped me win a lot of races." Kylee leaned in on the counter. "Consuela, it's all I really want to do . . . and . . . and I've met someone I really like."

Consuela's eyebrows shot up. "Kylee, the Miss Independent of the Danner family, has found a fella?"

Heat rushed into Kylee's face. "Yes, but please don't tell my brothers or sisters. You know how they are. Rait and Noah ran off every boy who came around while I was in high school. It's a miracle they let me go to the senior prom."

"Now, honey, they're just looking out for you, but I won't say anything. You just be careful about keeping secrets from your family." She finished pouring cake batter into the pans and set the bowl aside. "They'll be harder on you if they find out you're keeping things from them."

The concern in Consuela's eyes and voice touched Kylee who missed having Missy around to give her advice about guys even if did her older sister did get a little bossy and support their brothers about some things, namely going to college. "You know I don't like keeping things from people because it shows lack of trust, but this time I'm just doing it for now. I plan to invite him to come out to the ranch and meet the family soon, but I don't want them to get wind of anything until I do."

"It sounds to me as if you've thought this through, and that's a good thing. I'll be praying for you to do everything right."

Kylee came around the cooking island and hugged Consuela. "Thank you for your trust."

"What's this about trust?"

Kylee spun around to face her brother Wyatt. "Why do you all keep sneaking up on me? First Rait and now you."

"No one's sneaking up on anyone. You just didn't hear me come in." He removed his hat and stepped over to the counter to snag a cookie from the plate sitting there.

Consuela swatted his hand. "I know it won't spoil your lunch but stay out of those so there'll be plenty for the rest of the folks."

Wyatt gulped down the cookie, grinned and snatched another one. "I'll just eat one more."

Kylee grabbed the opportunity to leave. Before she reached the doorway, Wyatt called her name.

She turned to glare at him. "What now?"

He narrowed his eyes at her. "Are you really dropping out of college for barrel racing? Dad and Rait are in there discussing it. Is it true?"

"Yes, I am, and you better not try to stop me. I love barrel racing and want to enter more competitions, but school work keeps me from it, so

I'm not going back."

"Have you thought this all the way through, Kylee? Do you know what you're doing?"

"Yes, I have, and I do. This time you won't talk me out of it. Now, if you'll excuse me, I'm going in to town for lunch. Save me some of that cake, Consuela. I'll eat it when I get back."

Wyatt waggled his finger at her. "This isn't over, Kylee Danner, not by a long shot."

With one last glare, she left without commenting. Let them argue all they wanted. They wouldn't change her mind, and they couldn't make her. This time, she'd stand her ground. Kylee pulled out her phone and sent a text message to Jesse asking him to meet her at the Branding Iron Grill. At least someone would listen and not argue.

~~

Jesse cringed when he read Kylee's message. Not because he didn't want to see her, but because her dad must have given her a hard time about her decision. Did this mean he wouldn't get to meet her family yet? He pocketed his phone and headed for the grill.

When he entered, several heads turned to give him the once-over. All small-town people reacted the same whenever a stranger came among them. He'd seen enough of them, so he ought to know. He smiled and doffed his cowboy hat before taking a seat at a table.

A young woman approached him. "Hi. What can I get you today?"

"Nothing yet. I'm waiting on someone." He looked around. "Brandy isn't here?"

She frowned and glanced back at the cook, Marvin, behind a shelf separating the dining and kitchen areas. The man shrugged and shook his head. She turned back to Jesse. "Who wants to know?"

Before he had to answer, Kylee swept through the door. Those blue eyes darkened with anger until they were almost navy blue. This would be a testy lunch.

She plopped into the chair across from him and waved at the two men behind the serving shelf. She glanced up at the waitress. "Hi, Ella, I need a good chicken fried steak and lots of potatoes and gravy. Just tell Marvin I want it crisp and not greasy."

Ella peered down at Jesse, this time with curiosity etched on her brow. "How about you?"

"A sliced brisket barbecue sandwich and fries will be fine, and a glass of iced tea."

After writing it on her pad, she stared at him, then at Kylee, and back to him again. She shook her head and turned away. "Your order will be right up."

Kylee let her breath out in huff. "Now I've really fired up their curiosity, and I bet Ella will be calling Rait in no time to tell him his little sister is with some dude at the grill. I should have thought of that."

"I take it things didn't go well with your father." He's heard about Bill Danner from his own father many times. Dad called him an expert cattle man who also owned some of the finest cattle and horses around.

"They didn't go at all. Dad gave all sorts of reasons I shouldn't be quitting college. Rait and Wyatt were even worse. They all but demanded I go back."

Ella set two glasses of iced tea on the table. Jesse raised an eyebrow because Kylee hadn't included tea with her order.

"Ella knows I always have iced tea with my meals. That's another thing about small towns, not that Silverdale is so small, but everyone knows everyone else's business." She tore the paper from a straw and poked it down in her glass.

"Tell me what happened." He'd learned from his mother and his two older sisters that listening with no comment made a big difference in a relationship.

"Well, Dad asked me why I wanted to quit and what I'd do on down the road when I couldn't barrel race anymore. Rait said I acted like a child, and Wyatt asked me if I knew what I was doing. Sometimes my brothers can be a real pain."

Ella set their plates on the table and nodded toward Jesse. "And who might your friend be, Kylee. Never seen him in here before."

Kylee grimaced and scrunched up her nose. After a moment, because Ella still stood at the side of the table, Kylee answered her. "He's a friend, Ella, from Denver. I imagine you'll go right back there and call Brandy Jo or Rait so you can tell them everything. I wish you wouldn't."

"Honey, you know that won't make any difference. Just about everybody in here knows your daddy and will want to know who his baby had lunch with today."

Kylee sighed. "I know. We should've gone out of town to eat."

After Ella left, Kylee leaned forward. "I'm so sorry about this. I don't know what I was thinking. Guess maybe I didn't think at all. Missy is always telling me I'm too impulsive."

He reached over and grasped her hand. "It's okay, Kylee. I'd like to meet your dad and your brothers. After all, that is why I came with you."

She peered at him with a furrowed brow. "Are you sure? They can really be tough on guys who want to date me."

He squeezed her hand and spoke low so others, who exhibited obvious interest couldn't hear "Kylee, haven't we come far enough in our relationship that it's time for me to meet them? I care about you and want to be a part of your life in the coming days."

"And I care about you, Jesse." She bit her lip and nodded. "I guess it is time. I can't keep you under wraps forever. It's just that with all the weddings we've had in past months, I haven't had a great opportunity to say much about my own dating life, and nobody has asked anyway."

They ate in silence a few more minutes. Jesse wanted to tell her the truth about himself and reveal his true identity. He feared how she'd react if she knew his real name. She'd most likely back off. On the other hand, she may see his name as an opportunity to further her own career and say she loved him for all the wrong reasons. The thought of either one soured his stomach and vanquished his appetite.

Kylee worked her lips and wrinkled her nose as though she thought something through. She laid down her fork. "Okay, I've made a decision. Tomorrow is Friday night, and all of the family will be there including all the new in-laws, so I want you to join us and meet everyone at once."

Jesse mulled it over. He'd stayed out of the limelight of his father's career, and even though his father knew Mr. Danner, Jesses had never actually met him. Maybe none of them would recognize his face, and they certainly wouldn't recognize his name except as a rodeo bronco rider.

"All right, I'll come to the ranch for dinner. It'll be interesting to meet your brothers after what you've told me." Somehow he'd have to keep his identity secret and his background private until he could explain it all to Kylee. He planned to be a champion bronco rider on his name and not his father's.

Chapter 2

Kylee waited until Friday afternoon to tell Consuela to expect a guest for dinner. The less time she had before the dinner, the less time her brothers would have to grill her about Jesse. She sauntered into the kitchen where Consuela prepared the sides to go with the brisket smoking outside.

Pops put it on earlier in the day, and the aroma filled her head with visions of a plateful of meat with a smoky homemade sauce covering it. Next to her father's barbecued ribs, the smoked brisket ranked high among her favorite meals.

"Man oh man, that smoked brisket is making me hungry. Do I detect your baked beans to go with it?" Kylee propped herself on a barstool by the island."

"Of course, what else would your daddy let me serve? Your mom's potato salad recipe is in the refrigerator, too." Consuela sliced onions and placed them in ice water to be crisp later. She glanced over at Kylee. "What's on your mind? You didn't come in here just to visit."

Why did she have to be so intuitive? Kylee bit her lip. "No, I didn't. Remember that guy I told you I'd met? Well, I invited him to supper tonight. I figured he might as well get the gist of the whole Danner clan at one time, and I knew you always fix way more than enough for an extra mouth."

Consuela laid her knife on the counter and leaned forward, amusement in her eyes. "That was quick. Yesterday, you didn't want them to know, and now you've invited him for supper. I'm proud of you for not waiting, and yes, I have plenty of food prepared."

She reached up into the cabinet for plate. "You'll have to set another place at the table. It'll be interesting to see how your brothers take this."

"I know. Yeah, they'll bombard him with all sorts of questions which I think he can handle." So many times before, she'd brought boys out to the ranch, and after a few third degree questions from her brothers, most never asked her out again. Now everyone in town knew their reputation which left no hopes for a local boy in her future.

"Maybe you should tell Missy or Brandy Jo and let them corral your brothers." The timer on the oven beeped, and Consuela removed a chocolate cake.

"You baked that chocolate cake with cinnamon and a can of soda! I gotta' be sure to leave enough room for that." Kylee hugged Consuela. "Jesse will love it."

"Then let me go, so I can pour the icing on it while it's warm."

"Okay, I'm going out to the deck and check on that brisket." She resisted swiping a finger through the icing knowing she'd get a good swat on the hand if she did.

Pops lifted the lid of the smoker to check the meat. He grinned when he looked up to find her nearby. "How's my girl doing this evening?"

"My mouth's watering for that brisket to be done." She wrapped an arm around his waist. "I have something I want to tell you." Her nerves tangled themselves into knots, but she couldn't bring Jesse in cold with no notice at all.

Her father closed the smoker, checked the temperature gauge, and removed his hot mitts. "What's that? Did you decide to go back to school?"

"No, I didn't, and I'm not changing my mind. This has to do with something entirely different." She licked her lips and dug deep inside to find courage for her next words. "I've met a really nice guy, and I've invited him for dinner tonight to meet the family."

Her father stared at her for a moment before blowing out his breath. He placed his arm about her shoulders and led her to a chair on the deck. "So, my little one has a boyfriend. Tell me about him." He sat next to her and leaned back with his fingertips touching.

"His name is Jesse Martin, and he's from Denver. I met him at one of the rodeos last winter, and we've been dating whenever we appeared at the same rodeo event, and he's been over to the university to see me a few times."

"I see. What else do you know about him?"

"Well, he's a champion bronco buster. Wyatt's probably heard of him since Jesse won first place at a number of rodeos this past year. He grew up on a ranch and knows a lot about cattle and horses." Now, as she spoke about it, she didn't really know that much about him. She slumped in the chair. Her brothers would take care of that tonight. Why hadn't she asked him more questions?

"I see." He stared at her a moment longer. "What makes him special in your eyes?"

Good. A question she could answer with her heart. "He's good-looking, has a great sense of humor, makes me laugh, and he's a wonderful Christian. We've attended a few Bible studies at school, and he's come even though he's out of college. He's also kind to other people and likes to help others."

Anticipating the next question by the look in his eye, she said, "He's twenty-five, and has a degree in animal husbandry and business."

"That's five years older than you, Kylee."

"But—"

He held up his hand to stop her. "No buts now. I'll reserve judgment until after I meet him. I'm not sure I can say the same for Rait, Noah, and Wyatt, or even Missy and Brandy Jo for that matter."

"Thank you. I knew you'd be fair, and that's why I told you now. I do need a favor. Will you warn the others beforehand, so they won't be taken by surprise? Ask them to be nice to him until they can get to know him, too."

"I'll try, but I can't guarantee anything with any of them. So much has happened in the past year or so, and I don't quite have a handle on it all myself."

He stood and pulled her into his arms. "My little one is growing up. I don't like your decision about college, but it's time for me to let you make your own. You may make mistakes and have problems, but I'm always here for you." He kissed the top of her head. "This is one time I truly wish your mother was here."

Tears misted Kylee's eyes. She wished Mom could be here as well. Some good motherly advice would make this evening go so much better. Mom had been the one to control her son's antics and curb their teasing.

~~

Jesse turned into the drive leading up to the Danner ranch. The Colorado lodge-style home sat on a slight rise with out-buildings and a corral spreading out to the side. Most of the family must have arrived indicated by the number of vehicles parked in front.

He stopped the car before pulling up behind the others. With his nerves shot, a prayer would be the only thing to calm them. Gripping the steering wheel, he closed his eyes. "*Lord, I'm praying for You to make this a good evening for me and for Kylee. I know I'm not being fully truthful with her, but I pray You will help me protect my identity for just a while longer until I can find the right time to tell her. Is it wrong for me to want her to love me for who I am and not because of my family?*"

A dagger of guilt stabbed his heart. Who did think he tried to convince? He wanted to tell Kylee the truth, but that depended on how much she cared about him. If she loved him the way he had begun to love her, then his name would make no difference.

Uneasiness still blanketed his shoulders, but he drove on to park behind one of the trucks. If any of the Danner men recognized him from anywhere but the rodeo, it'd all be out in the open anyway.

Kylee must have been waiting for him to drive up because the door flew open and she raced out to his truck before he even opened his door.

"Jesse, I'm so glad you're here. Everyone's around on the deck, but I've been looking for you from the front room window." She stopped a few feet away and crossed her arms over her chest. He'd seen that move too many times not to know she wanted protection.

As soon as he stepped out of the car, she grabbed his hand. "I've told them you were coming, so expect a jillion questions."

Jesse pulled her into an embrace. "It'll be okay. You'll see." If only he could believe those words. Too many questions would lead to more untruths or hedging the truth, but he'd be as honest as he could.

He held her hand as she led him around to the deck where six men and five women congregated around a table spread with snack items. The heavenly aroma of smoking meat and barbecue filled the air. The oldest man stepped forward with extended hand.

"You must be Jesse. I'm Bill Danner. Welcome to the Danner ranch." He gripped Jesse's hand with great strength.

"Good to meet you, Mr. Danner. Kylee's told me so much about her family, and I'm glad I'm getting to meet all of you." Mr. Danner released Jesse's hand, and he flexed his finger. That man had strong grip for someone in his fifties.

Three other men, all dressed in western style shirts, jeans, and boots, stepped forward. He recognized Wyatt from his seeing him perform as a bull rider not long ago. They introduced themselves and gestured for him to join them for a snack before the meal.

The one he remembered as Rait, clapped him on the shoulder and didn't let go. "So tell me, how did you and my little sister meet?"

Jesse swallowed hard. This one he could answer with ease. "We were at a rodeo in Colorado Springs, and your sister won her race. After all the events were over, a few of us got together and went out." He held up his hand at Rait's frown. "No, not what you're thinking. It's a Christian group, and there're only a few of us, but we stick together, and we invited Kylee and one of the other girls to come with us. We went to a fast food burger place and had a late night supper. I asked her out again, and she said yes."

Missy nudged her brother's arm. "Now see, they went to eat burgers and fries. It's all perfectly fine." She turned her attention back to Jesse. "Kylee says you're from Denver. Where did you go to school?"

"Actually, we lived on a ranch in a small town not far from Denver. Usually people have never heard of it, so I say Denver because people know it." So far, so good with the questions. He could be honest with his answers. Still, he didn't like the glares from the brothers, especially Wyatt.

Brandy Jo flashed her smile at him. "So, you grew up on a ranch, too. Then this must all be familiar to you. Is that what got you interested in busting broncos?"

Jesse laughed and nodded. "You got me there. I was riding horses almost as soon as I could walk and loved them. I watched the ranch hands break in some of the wild horses they corralled, and decided that's what I wanted to do one day. I ended up getting plenty of practice on the ranch."

Kylee reached over for his hand. "And that's another thing that attracted me to him. We've both loved horses since we were babies." She squeezed his hand and leaned into him.

Wyatt stepped over to a foot or so from them. "Gettin' a little cozy there, aren't you, Kylee?"

Brandy Jo swatted Wyatt's arm. "Back off, big brother." She smiled at Kylee. "Come on, Dad's ready with the brisket. Let's go help Consuela bring out everything else." She walked away with Kylee, but turned her head back to give Wyatt a glaring frown. Jesse decided that was one gal whose bad side he didn't want to be on.

Wyatt poked Jesse's chest. "I recognize you from a few of the rodeos I competed in. I'm here to tell you, I know all about rodeo romances, and this had better not be one of those. If you hurt Kylee or break her heart or anything else, you have three of us to answer to. Understand?"

Jesse gulped but stood his ground. "I do, and this isn't a rodeo romance. I care about her, and I don't plan on hurting her either."

Wyatt leaned back. "Okay. Just so long we understand each other." He walked away to rejoin his wife Crissy, who shook her head and grabbed his arm.

He'd met the Danner family, and so far it went about like Kylee had warned it would. Now if he could get through the rest of the dinner, he might survive the brother's and their protective attitudes. Not that he blamed them, if he had a younger sister like Kylee, he most likely would treat any of her boyfriends the same way.

From their attitudes tonight, he had a long road ahead to loving Kylee Danner.

Chapter 3

Kylee pounded her pillow and glared at the clock. She'd spent a sleepless night all because of her brothers' relentless questions and curiosity about Jesse. He handled their probes well, but by the end of the evening, weariness grew evident in his eyes.

Her brothers smirked in smug self-satisfaction at their grilling. If Missy and Brandy Jo hadn't stepped in and changed the subject a few times, it could have been even worse.

She flopped over onto her back and stared at the ceiling. She did learn a few other things about Jesse she'd not known before, but there seemed to be a lot more under the surface. His rather vague answers about his family bothered her, but not to the extent it changed her feelings for him.

Finally, Kylee threw back her covers. Lying in bed and stewing over last night only served to rile up her anger against her brothers even more. Better to get up, get busy around the ranch, see Jesse, and put the other behind her. By now her brothers and Pops should all be out working.

She dressed in jeans and a knit shirt then pulled on her boots. With her hands on her knees, she bit her lip. Jesse hadn't kissed her good-bye last night like she hoped he would, probably because he thought or knew Rait, Noah, and Wyatt would be watching.

Before going to find breakfast, she pulled out her phone and sent a text to Jesse.

Come to the ranch this morning and go for a ride. I want
to show you our land.

Almost immediately he returned the text saying he'd meet her in an hour. She grinned and pocketed the phone. With a heart filled with joy, she sauntered down the stairs and into the kitchen. A plate of muffins and a note sat in the middle of the granite topped island. Consuela's handwriting let Kylee know the coffee carafe sat on the warmer, and if she wanted more than muffins this morning, she'd have to do it herself.

Laugher erupted from Kylee. Fat chance of her making anything worth eating. Her cooking skills fared only a little better that Rait's. She peeled the paper from the muffin and bit into it, savoring the sweetness of the orange-blueberry concoction. Bless Consuela. She'd made Kylee's favorite muffins because she knew Kylee would need a treat after the rough evening the night before.

An idea occurred to Kylee. She hopped down from the bar stool and went to the pantry. She pulled an old picnic basket from its place in the corner. She'd take some muffins along this morning and share them with Jesse. Coffee would be good, so she filled two thermal mugs. Maybe a sweet treat snack would take the edge off last night.

After packing the basket, Kylee gulped down the rest of her coffee and stuffed the last bit of muffin into her mouth. With a satisfied grin she headed out to the stables to saddle Belle and Morning Star.

The sun shone overhead through a few scattered clouds making it a perfect day to show Jesse her most favorite place. Since the renovations, she loved it even more. Maybe Jesse would realize how much she cared about him by sharing it now.

Her brothers may think her too young to know what she really wanted out of life, but two things were certain, ranching and barrel-racing. If the Lord made Jesse the man in her life, he'd move to number one with the other two close behind. She wanted what her siblings had found in their marriage partners.

After saddling Morning Lightning, she entered Belle's stall with a carrot in hand. "Hello, pretty girl. We're going out with someone special today." She brushed her fingers through Belle's mane. "I hope you like him as much as I do."

Belle gave her the best times in barrel racing and more than a few first-place awards. One of them had almost alienated her from her siblings. She'd missed Melissa's engagement party to race in a competition in Laramie. That had not set well with Wyatt or Missy, but she'd run the best race ever and took first prize that day. She couldn't help it if she'd paid the entry fee months before Missy decided to get married and didn't want to forfeit the money.

With a sigh, she led Belle and Morning Lightning out to the yard. Her family would never understand her need for independence. If they'd stop trying to control everything in her life, maybe she wouldn't have to try so hard. Marriage hadn't made a difference in them so far.

Once out in the yard, Kylee leaned on the top rail of the corral. She believed the Rocking D must be the most beautiful place in all of Colorado. With the mountains, the trees, and the wide-open skies, she could think of no place else she'd rather be. She missed her mother and their long rides and talks together. Mom had let Kylee be Kylee without any expectations other than she love the Lord above all else. That Kylee could do without hesitation.

The sound of a vehicle coming up the hill broke into Kylee's reverie and her heart jumped up a notch. Jesse would be here any minute. She scanned the area but saw no signs of her brothers or dad coming. "Thank you, Lord, for keeping them busy this morning."

Jesse's truck came to a halt, and she ran over to greet him.

He jumped down and wrapped his arms around her. "So glad you sent that text inviting me out. I planned on coming anyway but hearing from you is better." He kissed her cheek. "Now, where's this horse you want me to ride?"

She led him over to the corral where he spent a few minutes getting acquainted with Morning Lightning.

"She's beautiful." He ran his hands over her red flank, gave her a final pat, and picked up the reins. I'm looking forward to riding her. Where are we going?"

"That's a surprise, so mount up and follow me." Others may drive out to the meadows, but she preferred the horse trail which gave a much better first view of Hastings Landing.

~~

Jesse rode behind Kylee for a few minutes, admiring once again her horsemanship. She and Belle became one, and that's what made her a champion barrel racer. Her brothers may not believe it or encourage her, but she rode with the best.

When he trotted up next to her, she turned and grinned. "Isn't this a wonderful view of the mountains?"

"It is, and I can see why you love the ranch." He'd admired the view of a few moments ago much more so than trees, but she didn't need to know that.

He glanced around at the terrain, full of summer wildflowers growing in a rainbow of colors amidst the grasses swaying in the breeze. They crossed what looked like a rutted dirt road. "Is that how you get here by car?"

"Not now. You'll see when we get there. It's not much further."

They passed through a few trees and then came upon a spot straight from a travel magazine. A white church with windows sporting bright green shutters sat amidst a mass of flowers even more colorful than the wildflowers they'd passed. A towering steeple, with a bell visible in the center, lifted to the sky. A road led up to the area that appeared to be used for parking.

"What is this place way out here in the middle of nowhere?" He would never have believed such a meadow lay hidden among the trees. He even spotted a creek and an old-fashioned wood bridge to the side.

"This is Hastings Landing. It's the old homestead of my mom's family. Rait brought Serena out here, and she fell in love with the church. It was old and run down, but she had it restored, and had their wedding here. Now it's used for other celebrations as well." She swung down from the saddle and grabbed a bag hanging from the saddle. "Come on, I have a snack for us."

He jumped down from his mount and trailed after her to the creek. It sparkled like a sea of diamonds as the sun danced across the ripples. "This is a beautiful spot, and I can see why Serena wanted to restore the church."

Kylee chose a place on the bridge and set the basket there. "We can sit here and watch the water flow under the bridge. This one is new. The old one wasn't safe, but Serena made sure this one looked just like it. You can see why she's been so successful with her restoration projects."

She opened the basket and removed two insulated mugs from it. She handed him one.

"No cream and one sugar, right?"

"Right and thanks." He lifted the tab to expose the opening.

Then she handed him a muffin. "Consuela made these this morning. They're my favorite."

After one bite, they became his favorite as well. After the dinner last night and these muffins, Consuela had to be the best cook around. He savored the treat while observing Kylee. She stared out over the land with pure contentment written across her face.

"From the peace in your eyes, you must love this place."

"I do. It's my favorite spot. Mom and I used to ride out here and talk. Being the youngest, I had her to myself when the older ones were off doing their own thing. I'd come alone sometimes to think and work through problems. Sometimes I came to let off steam after my brothers made me so angry I could spit nails."

Jesse chuckled at that confession. After her brother's grilling last night, he understood why she might have to calm her anger. "What do they call the church?"

"It's Cross Creek Church, and someday, when I get married, it's going to be right there in that pretty building."

From the way his heart jumped all over the place whenever he was with her, he hoped he'd be a part of that wedding. Still too soon to go down that road, but he liked the idea more and more each time they were together. Only problem would be with his family and trying to fit his mother's ideas and her guest list into this small area. He stuffed the last bite of muffin into his mouth. That remained a problem for a day on into the future.

Kylee pointed off in the distance to what looked like another building under construction. "Over that way is the site of the original homestead of our great-grandparents. Rait and Serena are building their new home over there near it. That's why they're staying at the ranch right now."

"They picked a beautiful place, and it's not that far from the ranch." How fortunate to have family ties so close. He could be a part of it if . . . no, he couldn't go there yet.

Kylee set her mug back in the basket and hopped up. "Come on, we can wade in the creek, and then I want you see the amazing job Serena did with the church."

Once again, he followed her. She knew how to wrap herself around his heart, and he didn't mind one bit. At the creeks edge, Kylee removed her boots and socks then rolled up her jeans to mid-calf. He did the same, and in moments they stood in the middle of the creek as minnows darted about their feet like shimmering silver missiles.

She reached down and lifted hands full of water to splash across his face, laughing every minute. He splashed her back, and as she swatted at him, she slipped and fell against him. He caught her and stared down into eyes as blue as the Colorado summer sky.

Kylee gazed back, her face inches from his. His heart raced with an emotion he tried to bury but it could no longer be denied. He pulled her closer and bent his head to capture her lips with his. The sweetness of orange and blueberry muffin flavored the kiss as she leaned in to return it.

The waters swirled about their ankles in time to his beating pulse. The love squelched for the past few months, welled from deep within. The kiss deepened until his senses pulled him to stop. He leaned back and cupped her face in his hands.

"I think it best we head back now, or I can't guarantee I can resist the pull you have on me."

She said nothing but bit her lip and nodded then reached for his hand. He held it in a tight grip as they waded back to the bank and put on their boots. In silence Kylee gathered up the basket and mugs.

At the spot where they'd secured the horses, he held her shoulders and bent to touch her forehead with his. "I'm not sure what just happened back there, but it felt so right. I don't know where it may be going, but I hope you're along for the ride."

"I'm not sure either, but it's a ride I'd like to take as well." She tilted her head back, and her smile lit up her eyes. Her radiance burrowed deep into his heart.

He wanted to shout with joy but grabbed the reins of Morning Lightning instead. "Then let's get on with it. Want to race back to the ranch?"

Kylee grabbed Belles reins and swung up into the saddle. "You're on, cowboy. Let's go." Then she kicked Belle into action and took off across the meadow, her blonde hair streaming behind her like the flag in a rodeo parade.

He laughed and took off after her. One thing for sure, wherever this ride led, there'd never be a dull moment with Kylee Danner along.

Chapter 4

Kylee beat Jesse, but then Belle had always been faster than Morning Lightning. At the corral she dismounted and grinned at Jesses. "Anyone ever tell you that you're a pretty good rider?"

Jesse laughed and swung down from the saddle. "Yep, I've heard that a few times. Guess that's why I'm a champion."

That smile went straight to her soul. The kiss, only minutes ago, sent confusion tangling around her heart which still raced even after the one on horses ended. She hadn't shown him the church, but then there'd be other days they could take that tour.

Inside the stalls, Kylee brushed down Belle and fed her while Jesse did the same with Morning Lightning. One good thing about loving a cowboy, he knew how to do the same things she did and loved them as much as she loved him. Did her head say love? After only three months of being together, could that be what her heart felt? If so, she definitely wanted to explore it more.

Jesse leaned on the top of the stall. "Morning Lightning's all set for the rest of the day. How about Belle? You finished with her?"

With one last pat to Belle's golden rump, she nodded. "All done." She stepped out of the stall, secured the gate, and reached for his hand.

They strolled out to the yard where he'd parked his car. "I hate to leave like this, but I have to get back home. I talked to my folks, and Dad needs me at his ranch for a few days."

Disappointment sank Kylee's hopes of a nice, leisurely lunch without Pops and her brothers. Then again, they would probably return and interrupt it with more questions for Jesse. "I understand. Life can get pretty busy around a working ranch. Will you still be able to compete at the rodeo next week?"

"Oh, yes. I'm all ready for more competition. That means I'll see you Thursday if you're still planning to come."

She swatted his arm as they walked to his car. "Hey, I didn't give up my entry fee for my sister's engagement party, so I'm not about to give it up this time."

"Okay. Just checking." He held her hand as they stood by the car. "I'm going to miss you, Kylee Danner."

She lifted her head toward him and drew closer. "I'm going to miss you, too, cowboy."

He accepted her invitation for a kiss. He stepped back and laughed as he opened the car door. "I could get used to this real fast, so I'd better get out of here."

Kylee grinned and jammed her fingers into her back pockets. "See you next Thursday."

She stared after the truck as it made the turn onto the main road. At the same time, another car made the turn to come to the house. Kylee waved as Serena drove closer.

Perfect timing. Kylee needed some girl-talk time, and Serena filled the void left by Missy and Brandy Jo.

Serena parked and hopped out of her car. "Was that Jesse I saw leaving?"

"Yes, and I need some advice." Kylee glanced around. "I don't see any sign that Rait or Pops being back, so maybe we can have some privacy."

Serena looped her arm with Kylee's. "This sounds interesting, especially if it has to do with Jesse. Let's get a soda and find a place to relax before lunch."

In the kitchen, Consuela grinned when they walked in. "Well, I was wondering where you two might be. I see you got my note, Kylee."

"That I did, and thank you for the muffins." She slapped her forehead. "I left the basket out in the barn. I took some muffins and coffee out with us when Jesse and I went for a ride."

Consuela waved her hand in the air. "Don't worry about it. I can get it later."

Serena opened the refrigerator and pulled out two cans of soda. "Can we do anything to help with lunch?

Consuela shook her head. "No, it's going to be light fare today. I saved some of the brisket from last night, so barbecue sandwiches, chips, and some of my baked beans will fill the menu."

Kylee sniffed the air. "If my nose tells me right, that's peach cobbler I smell baking."

Consuela laughed and leaned toward Serena. "I never could fool that

girl when it comes to peach cobbler. She can smell it from miles away."
She waved her hand again. "Now, go on, shoo, get on with whatever you
need to do."

Kylee and Serena both lifted their cans in Consuela's direction before
sauntering arm in arm out to the deck. Late summer in Colorado, a brief
time between heat and cold, meant a perfect time to spend on the deck
admire the surrounding mountains soaring in majesty toward the
heavens.

Serena sighed and flopped into a chair. "I love this place. The air is so
clean and smells of wildflowers, livestock, and green grasses. I can
understand why none of you wants to leave this beautiful valley."

"Speaking of this beautiful valley, I took Jesses out to Hastings
Landing this morning. Your house is coming along."

"Yes, it is, and I hope it's finished before winter sets in. I have a lot of
ideas about decorating in the style that will compliment the surroundings.
It'll be modern but have a lot of the charm of an older place as well. I've
been with Marvella at Junktique this morning looking for some things I
might use."

"That explains why I couldn't find anyone around. That's when I
asked Jesse to come out and go riding with me." She set her can on the
table between them. "You know, I love what you did with the church.
Mom and I rode out there a lot when I was younger. We both loved the
place, as most of the Danner clan does, but it holds special memories of
Mom for me."

"Thank you. It was one of my favorite projects, and it was perfect for
our wedding." She swallowed a swig of soda then laughed as though
remembering something.

"You know, Rait proposed to me out in that creek. That's one of the
reasons I'm so happy to be building out there."

"Really? I didn't know that." Heat rushed up her neck at her own
memory of this morning at the same place. "Hmm, Jesse kissed me this
morning while we were wading in the creek. We've been together three
months, and that's the first time he's really kissed me."

Serena's eyes sparkled, and a knowing grin stretched her lips. "And
how did that make you feel?"

"Like heaven on earth. I've never felt anything like that before." She
lowered her head and picked at an imaginary spot on her jeans. "I think .
. . I think I might be in love with him, Serena. Whenever I'm with him,
my heart does crazy things, and I want to be near him every minute.
When he leaves, it's like a great void inside, and I want him back."

"Oh, my, you do have it bad. I'm so sorry for the rough time the guys
gave you at dinner last night. I could see how much you two care about

each other, and I think it scares them. You're their little sister, and they want to protect you from being hurt."

"I know that, and I'm afraid my reputation for going off on impulses and doing silly things while I was growing up may be part of the reason they're that way. I love them like crazy, but I'm so independent that I've always resisted their help, advice, or whatever they gave."

"That's why Rait thinks this barrel racing thing of yours is an impulse, but I've seen your love for it, and I believe it's not just a whim."

Kylee reached over and squeezed her sister-in-law's hand. "Thank you. I'm so glad you're a part of the family now. Missy can get so bossy, and Brandy Jo and I are so much alike that we get in each other's way. It's nice to have someone I can talk to who won't judge me and try to tell me what to do."

Talking with Serena taught her something else as well. If Kylee wanted to be treated like an adult, she sure better start acting like one.

~~

Jesse stopped his truck just outside the gate leading up to his family's ranch house. Late August meant the rounding-up cattle for fall auction would be in full swing. Jesse loved that part of ranching more than other. That and breaking in new horses made ranching life one he'd choose over any other.

His father aspired to loftier goals, and he'd made the first rung of the ladder in state senate when Jesse and his sisters were still teenagers. Now he campaigned for an even higher office after winning in the primaries.

Jesse earned a degree with a double major in poly sci for his dad and in business to have all the skills he needed to run the ranch. Someday it would be his, but Dad still held on. If he won in November, Jesse's life would change, and so might his relationship with Kylee. From the expression he'd seen today as she showed him the land, how could he ask her to give up her beloved ranch for what would soon become his?

How and what could he tell his family about Kylee? She possessed beauty, brains, and the skills needed to be a top rodeo performer. That part came easy, but as far as love went, they might have different ideas. Dad didn't like Jesse discarding the family name and choosing one of his own for his rodeo competitions, but he understood and accepted Jesse's choice to remain out of the Morris spotlight.

He glanced up at the sign over the gate. The Circle M brand in wrought iron stood out against the background of mountains and meadows under the Colorado sky. Jesse loved his home, and looked forward to the day he'd run the Morris spread. Being a rancher's daughter, Kylee would understand his plans for having the best horses and cattle in the state. He didn't plan on riding broncos in the rodeo the rest of his life.

With a puff of breath between his lips, he stepped on the gas and drove past the fences bordering the paved lane up to a driveway almost the size of a small parking lot. The two-story house set back from the drive in true Colorado ranch style. Built by his grandfather, the log structure grew through the years to accommodate a large family much like the Danner family. Now only his parents lived there, but he hoped to do so one day with a wife and family of his own.

He barely had time to hop down from his truck than the paneled door to the house swung open, and his mother ran across the porch to welcome him with open arms. Still as beautiful as the days she graced movie screens all across America, Arianne Martin had retired to be Hal Morris' wife and mother to their children. Now, as the wife of a state senator rising in political stardom, she wore her role in public with grace and beauty. Here at home, she remained simply his mom.

"Jesse, I saw you coming up the road. I'm so glad you're home for a few days." She stepped back and hooked her arm through his. "Carrie and Bruce are here with the children. She's out at the pool with them, and Bruce is out with your dad."

He walked back into the house at her side. "It's good to be home, and I have something to discuss with you and Dad sometime this evening."

"Oh, now, that sounds interesting. Dad said they'd be back mid-afternoon. He doesn't want to miss time with the grandchildren. You go on out to see Carrie, and I'll bring out some refreshments."

His sister greeted him with a hug. "Long time since you've been around little bro. I've missed you, but I haven't missed any of your rodeo appearances on TV. My little brother, the champion bronco buster." She leaned back to stare at him. "What do I call you now, Jesse or Connor?"

Before he had a chance to retort, his three and five-year-old nieces grabbed him around the knees, their wet swim suits soaking his jeans. "Well, if it isn't two of my favorite little girls." He reached down and hugged him, ignoring the soaked fabric.

Carrie reached for towels and handed them to the two girls. "You're drowning Uncle Connor's jeans. Here, take these and dry off."

The girls squealed and grabbed the towels. Carrie placed her hand on Jesse's shoulder. "Bruce and I went to the rodeo up in Laramie. Mighty cute little barrel racer you hugged after she won her race. Kylee Danner, I believe."

Heat flooded Jesse's face. "Yes, and please don't say anything to Mom and Dad until I can. I plan to do that while I'm here this week." He glanced up to see their mom headed their way with a tray of drinks and snacks. "Oh, and I guess you can call me Connor while I'm home. It might confuse the girls otherwise."

He reached out and grasped the tray his mother held. "Here, let me get that for you." He set it on the table and called the girls over. This weekend just became more interesting now that his sister had found out about Kylee before he told his parents.

Chapter 5

After one more argument with Pops last Sunday afternoon about dropping out of college, he told Kylee he'd think more about it. He didn't like the idea, but at least he'd consider her wishes. Her brothers still needed to be convinced, but she wouldn't worry about them.

During the few days before her next competition, she practiced with Belle around the barrels in the corral. On Wednesday afternoon, she made one last practice run before packing up and heading out to a rodeo in Carbondale.

When she finished the third round in one of her best times ever, her father leaned on the corral fence and clapped. She rode over to him and dismounted. "I see Rait's truck. Are you finished for the day already?"

"Yes, we are. Rait's gone on inside with Wyatt." He grinned and tipped his hat to her. "You're good. Wasn't that one of your best times?"

"It was, and how did you know that?" She stepped up on the bottom rail to be at eye level with him.

"Honey, I keep tabs on all your races and times. I have to admit you're getting better all the time. Maybe this will be good for you after all."

She reached over and swung her arms around his neck, her heart swelling with gratitude. "Thank you, Pops. I'm going to win some really big championships one of these days. You wait and see."

He hugged her back then grasped her arms and pulled back. "You go take care of Belle. I'm going in to join the boys, and I'm sure Consuela has some snacks on hand for us. If you want to join us, we'll be in my office." He pecked her on the cheek then headed toward the house.

Kylee's heart grew light as a feather as she led Belle to her stall. Now she'd get to ride in bigger competitions since she had his approval and wouldn't have to worry about missing class.

After unsaddling Belle, she wrapped her arms around the Palomino's neck. "We're going to have some real fun and win some big races because you're the best horse around."

Belle snuffled and shook her head as though she agreed. Kylee picked up a brush and ran it over Belle's side. She loved this horse, and the good Lord willing, they had some happy times ahead.

Tonight, she'd get everything packed and loaded, ready to leave early tomorrow morning. She'd get her dad or Rait to hitch the trailer to her truck. Rait nor Dad liked her driving by herself, but since he was married now, Rait couldn't take off with her like he once did.

When she finished with Belle, she stored away her supplies and headed for the kitchen to find whatever snacks Consuela may have out. A plate of cookies sat on the counter, and she found a pitcher of lemonade in the refrigerator. With a glass of the lemonade and a napkin full of cookies, she decided to drop in on Pops and her brothers.

The door to the office stood slightly ajar. Kylee reached out to push inward when she heard Rait say her name. She stopped still. Were they trying to talk Pops out of letting her drop out of school? She bit her lip and waited to hear more.

"I say we have to tell her before she leaves tomorrow. Who knows what that Martin guy will do?" Wyatt's voice carried a note of anger.

What were they talking about? Why would they have anything to tell her about Jesse? Anger boiled up, but she waited and listened.

Someone pounded the desk. "I can't believe you two. I thought Jesse to be a fine young man. True, he's a few years older than Kylee, but he cares about her. Even I could see that."

Kylee frowned at the anger in Pop's voice. Before she could push the door wider, Rait spoke. "Look, if Jesse is lying to Kylee and hiding his true identity, she'll find out. Let's see what happens with the competition this weekend."

What did he mean by Jesse's true identity? He was Jesse Martin from the Circle M ranch west of Denver.

Then Wyatt spoke up. "I'd be there to see what happens, but I can't. Chrissy and I have other plans. Why don't you go?"

Her father's gruff tone reflected his dissatisfaction. "I don't think either one of you should go, and neither one of you should say anything. Let Kylee find out for herself. He can't keep a secret like that."

Kylee had heard enough. Her anger now at the boiling point, she pushed through the door. "What do mean Jesse's true identity or his secret?"

Rait and Wyatt's faces burned red, and Pops stood with his arms crossed over his chest.

"What's going on? She set her snack on the table and fisted her hands on her hips. "What did you not want to tell me?"

"Okay, now you have your chance. Tell her what you think." Pops glared at his two sons.

Rait cleared his throat. "Hmm, um, we think you should break off with Jesse and not see him anymore. He's not who he says he is."

"What are you talking about? He's a rodeo champion bronco buster, and I've seen him ride." Kylee glared at Rait with her heart pounding.

Wyatt shook his head. "Sorry, Sis, but that's not who he really is."

"And how do you know that." She glanced from one to the other with fire in her soul.

They said nothing but looked at each other as if willing the other to speak first.

Kylee caught her breath as the truth dawned on her. "You looked him up and checked him out, didn't you?"

Rait blew out his breath. "Yes, and we found—"

"How dare you! You've done something like this every time I've brought someone home to meet any of you." Tears threatened to fill Kylee's eyes, and she bit back her fury, ready to hit one of them.

Rait reached out to her. "We're only looking—"

Kylee jerked back. "Don't touch me. I'm so mad I want to slap you, and I'm trying hard not to. You have no right to meddle in my life like this. Some things I can understand, but to check out someone's past just because I like him is not right."

"They're just watching out for you, honey. However, I do agree they've gone a little far this time."

"Yes, they certainly have." Kylee turned to leave, but her father's voice stopped her.

"Wait, Kylie." Pops narrowed his eyes and waved his hand toward her brothers. "Go on, tell her what you found."

She turned and glared once again at her brothers. "What?"

Rait held a piece of paper out to her. "Jesse Martin is a known felon out on parole for robbery. He may be a rodeo champion today, but he's dangerous."

Kylee snatched the paper away from her brother. "I don't believe you. He's—" she glanced at the paper and read what Rait had told her. Her hand trembled, and her throat closed. This couldn't be true. Not her Jesse. She wadded the paper into a ball and threw it at the desk. "I don't believe this."

Her brothers may love her, but this time they'd gone too far. She ran from the room, leaving her snack behind, and raced up the stairs to her room. Inside, she threw her body across the bed and grabbed a pillow. The tears flowed and soaked the pillowcase.

That couldn't be the Jesse Martin she loved, the Jesse who kissed her at the creek. She sat up, sniffed, and wiped her cheeks with her fingers. She'd been dating him for three months, and everything she knew about him gave her confidence in his character.

She'd get to the bottom of this. They'd be together tomorrow night, and she'd get some answers.

~~

Wednesday night came, and Jesse still hadn't told his parents about Kylee. Carrie had fussed at him twice, but then left him alone. He glanced around the dinner table at the family he loved with all his heart but having the Morris name in Colorado and his mother's stardom past meant being in the limelight with his parents. That's why he'd chosen his mother's maiden name of Martin and his own middle name to compete on the rodeo circuit. So far, no one made any connection in the names.

If people were aware of his Morris family connection, he wouldn't be sure if they supported him because of his abilities or because of the family name. Now, with Kylee in his life, he must make the choice and let things go from there. His time with the Lord this morning ended with the resolve to tell them tonight. He'd have no peace until he did.

Carrie nudged his arm. "You aren't eating. Thinking about Kylee?"

He nodded and shoved aside a mound of potatoes on his plate. With a glance at Carrie, he cleared his throat. "Mom, Dad, I have something to tell you."

At their raised eyebrows and questioning eyes, he laid his napkin on the table. "I've met a girl, and I'm falling love with her."

Now Mom's eyes lit up with excitement. "Oh, honey, that's wonderful. It's time for you to find someone to share your life. Who is she? What's her name?"

Dad held up his hand. "Just a minute. Does this mean you're giving up the rodeo?"

"No, it doesn't, at least not for now. She's a part of my rodeo life. Her name is Kylee Danner of the Rocking D ranch in Silverdale."

Now Dad's face beamed. "She's Bill Danner's girl?"

"Yes, sir, she is."

"Her father is a fine man and well known in the ranching circles for his excellent cattle. They bring top prices at auction. She's from a good family"

"When are we going to have a chance to meet her?" His mother smiled from across the table.

He shook his head. "I don't know, Mom. I'm hoping it will be soon." He frowned and chewed his lip. "You see, she doesn't know my real name or who my family is."

"Oh, I see." His mother sank back against her chair. "That's not good."

"I know it isn't, but she thinks I'm just another cowboy on the rodeo circuit. She also thinks I work for the Circle M." The time had come to give her the whole story, but at the moment he had no idea how or when that could be.

"Why don't you tell her your real name, bring her to dinner here, and we can all meet." His mother picked her phone from her pocket. "I need to start making plans now."

His dad laughed. "Well, you were telling the truth when you said you worked at the ranch. Not only do you work here when you're home, you're also going to own it one day."

His mother looked up from her phone with a puzzled expression. "Didn't her mother pass a few years ago? Seems I remember hearing that at the Cattlemen Wives Association when we planned our last event."

"That's right, she did. Kylee really misses her. She took me to Hastings Landing where her mother's family homesteaded. They have a true legacy here in Colorado."

Mom laid her phone aside. "I think I'll wait until you make things right with Kylee. It's not fair to have her thinking you're someone other than who you are. With your father running for the U.S. senate next election, it's best to get things out in the open."

"Thank you and I will tell her . . . soon."

Carrie squeezed his arm and smiled with a nod of approval. At least that was out of the way, but would his revelation to Kylee expose everything he'd work so hard to conceal?

Chapter 6

On Thursday morning, Kylee waited in the house while Rait and Pops hitched the horse trailer to her truck. She had stayed in her room for dinner last night, her anger still boiling against her brothers. If Noah, her other brother, and his wife Jade had been in town, he would have been right in the mix with Rait and Wyatt.

When she decided Rait should be finished, she picked up her duffle bag and headed out to the stables to help load Belle. Instead of the trailer being hitched to her truck, it sat behind Rait's.

With her eyes spitting daggers, she dropped her duffle bag. "Just what do you think you're doing?"

"I'm going with you, and we're taking my truck." He stood from tending to the hitch. "Don't give me an argument because you're not winning this one. Serena and I are riding with you or rather you're riding with us. I don't trust Jesse now, and I want to keep you safe."

"I'm perfectly safe with Jesse, and I don't need a caretaker." She spread her feet and planted her hands on her hips.

"Go get Belle, and we can get on the road." He turned and glared at her with the look that told her he meant business.

"You are so stubborn." She blew out her breath and raised her hands. "I don't know what Serena sees in you."

He picked up her bag to toss into the back of the pick-up. "Quit arguing and go get Belle, or I will."

Dropping her head in defeat, she stomped into the barn and over to Belle's stall. "C'mon, girl, you and I have a race to win." Still seething with her anger, she led Belle out to the trailer. Serena stood by the truck and shook her head.

Rait helped her settle Belle. "I'm sorry you don't care for this, but you know Dad and I don't like for you drive alone, and it's a long trip. So, we're going with you. The truck has plenty of room for you in the back seat. You can rest or read or whatever. This way you won't be so tired when you arrive."

What he said did make sense for the driving part, and her anger calmed to a simmer rather than a full boil. "All right but promise me you won't confront Jesse or anything like that until after I've had a chance to talk with him."

Rait furrowed his brow. Serena slipped her hand over his arm.

"That's not too much to ask of you, Rait. We'll be right there in case anything does happen."

"Okay, but Kylee, you'd better find out his story or I will." Rait yanked open the two passenger side doors. "Get on board so we can head out."

He marched around to the driver's side. Kylee reached over and hugged Serena. "Thank you. If he has to go, I'm glad you're along, too."

"You're welcome. I figured this was one time I needed to be around so he wouldn't mess things up for you and Jesse. I hope it's all just a big mix-up."

Kylee hugged her again before they both climbed into the truck and buckled up. This might end up being a long drive, but at least she wouldn't be worn out when they reached the arena. Jesse couldn't be who her brothers thought he was, but she had plenty of time to find out the truth.

Once on the highway, Rait glanced back at Kylee. "I've said all I'm going to say about this for now. So enjoy the ride."

"Okay. There has to be some mistake, but I'll talk to Jesse the first chance I get."

"Very well, Serena and I will be there simply to cheer you on in your event and keep an eye on things."

That eased her mind somewhat, but doubt and uncertainty still nudged at her heart. She pushed them away and concentrated on the joy of seeing Jesse again and barrel racing. One more thought crept in and underscored her uncertainties.

Her own skills had to be honed and improved before she would even think about becoming a professional. That may down the road, but for now, the smaller rodeos and county fairs gave enough prize money to keep her going. But as good as Jesse was at riding broncos, why wasn't he in more of the Professional Rodeo Association events. That's where the big money was.

After a quick stop for lunch on the highway, Kylee looked over the schedules for smaller rodeos the remainder of the summer and into the fall. One could be found just about every week. This particular one ended the last Thursday of this month.

With the rodeo events beginning at seven that evening, their arrival in early afternoon gave her time to take care of Belle and rest. Once she had Belle settled in a stall at the arena, she searched for Jesse, but he hadn't arrived yet. After checking in with all the credentials for herself and Belle, she went to find Rait.

She found him and Serena visiting with some of the other cowboys entered in various competitions. Serena's western attire brought a grin to Kylee. She looked good in jeans and boots and fit right in with everyone else.

Rait stepped away when she approached him. "Have you heard from Jesse again?"

"No, I haven't. Since he's not here, I guess you can go ahead and take me to the hotel."

One of the cowboys turned who had turned to leave turned back. "You mean Jesse Martin?"

At her nod, he shook his head. "Just had a text from him, and he's going to be late, but he'll be here in time to check in." Without waiting for a response, he walked away.

Kylee frowned. "That's weird. Why didn't he text me?" She pulled out her phone to find it dead. She slapped her forehead. "Oh no, I forgot to charge it before I left. I bet he tried to contact me. Let's go so I can get it charged."

Once back at the motel, she checked into her room while Rait and Serena reserved one. Waving her key at them she headed for the elevator. "I'll see you at six to go back to the arena."

She decided not to wait for the elevator and slung her duffle bag over her shoulder to head for the stairs. Once in her room, she dug her charger out of her bag and plugged it in. As soon as she had enough power, she checked her messages, and there was one from Jesse telling her he'd been delayed at the ranch and would let her know soon as he arrived.

After unpacking, she flopped into the chair by the window. With an hour before time to shower and change for the Grand Entry, she opened her tablet to check her email using the internet code on her motel key card carrier. Nothing from Jesse since last night, so she clicked onto her server and stared at the screen debating about a search for Jesse's name.

She'd prayed long and hard last night after Rait and Wyatt made their disclosure. The Lord knew the truth and would help her find it. Jesse professed to be a Christian, too, and they had even prayed together. He hadn't really tried to kiss her before they went to the creek, so he did have standards. What she did know about him made the information found by Rait and Wyatt all the more puzzling.

With a sigh, Kylee closed down the tablet and shoved it aside. She'd find out the truth this evening and prove her brothers to be wrong. With that decision, she moved to the bed for quick nap before meeting Rait and Serena, with the hope she'd hear from Jesse before then.

~~

After checking into his hotel, Jesse sent a text to Kylee letting her know he'd arrived, and he'd meet her at the arena before the parade. During the drive from the ranch, he'd run through several different scenarios in which he told Kylee the truth, but none of them satisfied. How could he explain his reasoning behind not using his family name?

Before he reached the rodeo site, his cell phone rang with the tone reserved for his sister. He punched it on where it rested in a holder on the dash. "What's up, Carrie?"

"We're on the way to the hospital. Mom's had a heart attack. Will you meet us there? We'll pay back your entry fee and whatever other expenses you have."

"That won't be necessary, and I'm on my way. I'll be there in an hour or so." He pulled off to the side of the road, checked traffic, and then made a U-turn to head back to Denver. He lifted his heart and soul in prayer as he drove. Mom had to be all right. With her being a celebrity not only from films, but also as the wife of a man running for the U.S. senate, this situation may be all over the news.

If so, he had to keep a low profile and stay out of pictures. If Kylee found out the truth before he could tell her, he had no idea what might happen, but it wouldn't be good. *Kylee!* She expected him to meet her at the arena for the parade.

He pulled over to the side of road once again and grabbed his phone. He typed in his message.

Headed home. Family emergency. Will call you later.

After hitting send, he prayed she'd get it before the Grand Entry and know he hadn't stood her up.

When he finally drove into the parking lot at the hospital, his heart pounded from all the scenes his imagination created. He jumped from is truck and raced into the building. He stopped first at the ER desk, asked for Arianne Morris, and told the lady she was the son.

The clerk wrote a number on a piece of paper. "She's been admitted and taken up to CCU. Here's the number."

He grabbed the paper and headed for the elevators. He punched the button to call it down when a woman stepped to his side. "Aren't you Arianne Martin's son?"

Jesse groaned. That's all he needed—a reporter. "I'm Connor

Morris."

"But Miss Martin is your mother, right?"

"My mother is Mrs. Sam Morris." The elevator doors opened, and he stepped inside. "If you'll excuse me, I'm going to see her."

A hand stayed the door. "Oh, Connor, I'm so glad I caught you." She turned to smile at the reporter. "I'm Rene Hammond, Connor's fiancée." She grabbed his arm and snuggled close

As if things couldn't get any worse, Renee had to show up. *Why now, Lord* ? Something clicked in the background and Jesse jerked his head toward the sound. A photographer and his long -ago girlfriend combined meant disaster in the making.

The doors closed as Renee grinned up at him with a death grip on his arm.. "I see you've finally decided to come home. I've missed you."

"Why did you tell that woman you're my fiancée? We haven't been together in over a year." He'd put her so far out of his mind that he'd forgotten her completely.

"Why, Connor, we were practically engaged until you decided to go off and compete in rodeos all the time. With your mother so ill, you won't have time for that, and I'm here to support you and help you." She batted her eyelashes at him and smiled in her coy way.

Jesse cringed remembering how she once used her wiles to get to him. It wouldn't work this time. "That was then, Renee. I'm still a rodeo cowboy and have no room in my life for you."

The doors opened, and he stepped into the hall where his sister grabbed him. "I'm so glad you're here. Dad's in with Mom now. She's going to need surgery, but we're not sure when." Her eyes opened wide and her mouth dropped when she realized Renee accompanied him. "What are you doing here?"

"To support Connor of course." She clung to his arm and leaned her head against his shoulder.

Carrie's lips formed a tight, straight line. "He doesn't need your support. He has his family." She turned to glare daggers at him.

Jesse shrugged. "She found me just as I was getting on the elevator. I didn't invite her."

He grabbed Renee's arm and pulled her back to the elevator. He jabbed at the button with his thumb. "It's time for you to leave. We have family stuff to discuss, and it doesn't concern you. Don't call me. If I need you, I'll get in touch."

"All I'm trying to do is be supportive." Crocodile tears he remembered from before welled in her eyes.

"Then do it from afar for now." The elevator doors opened, and he pushed her inside. "Good-by."

The doors closed on her pouting face, and he slumped forward against the wall. A hand touched his shoulder.

"I can't believe she tried to worm her way back into our lives." Carrie tugged on his arm. "C'mon, Dad's waiting for us. Mom's resting comfortably now, but we have some decisions to make."

He followed her down to waiting room wishing with all his heart that Kylee walked beside him. He could use her support.

Chapter 7

After the Grand Entry, Kylee sent Rait a text telling him that Jesse wouldn't be coming tonight. He didn't answer but wasted no time in finding her at Belle's stall.

"Okay, what's this all about?"

"I don't know. He sent me a text earlier saying he had a family emergency and wasn't coming. So, you and Serena made the trip for nothing." Belle nickered and nuzzled Kylee's outstretched hand, and Kylee turned her back to Rait.

"We still get a chance to see you compete, and it's been awhile since I've done that." He placed a hand on her shoulder. "Look, I know you care about him, but his not showing up tonight the day after we found out about him doesn't look good. Maybe he knows we're on to him."

Kylee's muscles tensed into a bunch. Care about him didn't cut it. She loved him. "And how would he know that? I think there's a real emergency, and I'm worried."

"Didn't you say he worked at the Circle M ranch? Let me text Dad. Maybe he can find out more about what's happened."

"Ha, good luck with that. Pops rarely texts me back." Kylee cringed and braced for Rait's scolding.

"I can't believe you're still calling him that after we told you it's disrespectful."

She didn't need to turn around to see the anger in his eyes. His voice said it all. "He doesn't mind it, so you shouldn't either. Go on back to your seat and let me get ready for my race. I'll let you know if I hear from Jesse."

When Kylee's race time came, she cleared her mind of everything and concentrated on guiding Belle around the barrels. When she crossed the finish, her heart jumped against her ribs. That had to have been her best time ever. Seconds later, her score posted, and the crowd cheered.

Her score landed her in first place, making hers the time to beat. Kylee blinked back tears and leaned her head against Belle's neck. "We did it, girl, you're the best." If her time of 16.50 held up, with the other wins she had, she'd have enough points to be the final rodeo at the end of the month have a chance for the Champion Buckle.

An arm slid around her shoulders. "That was amazing. I'm so proud of you."

Kylee blinked and jerked her head back. "You've never said that to me before."

Her brother wrapped his arms around her. "I don't think I ever realized how good you are at this. I can see now why you want to do it all the time."

"He's right, Kylee. That was amazing. I may not know all that much about rodeos, but I know a good ride when I see it." Serena stood next to Rait. A smile as big as all outdoors shone across her face.

Rait stepped back but still held Kylee's shoulders. "Have you heard anything else from Jesse?"

"No, but I'm not surprised. If it's a real emergency, he's too busy to talk or text. I'll hear from him eventually." She had to keep telling herself that in order not to break down and cry because she missed his being with her to share her victory.

"Let me know when you do. When this is over, we'll get something to eat and go back to the hotel. I'll let Dad know about your win." He paused. "Better yet, I'll take a picture and send it to him after you get prize money."

Kylee grinned at the image of her father's face playing in her head. "I think he'll like that. I'll meet you back here."

At the end of the evening, Kylee sat on her bed at the hotel. Today had been a good day. Pops congratulated her on her victory and said how proud he was of her. Next time he promised he'd be in the stands cheering her on.

The only thing to mar the entire day had been the text from Jesse. Still no news from him, and she feared bothering him in the middle of a crisis. With nothing else to do until the ride home tomorrow, she picked up the remote. The nightly news lit up the screen, but Kylee kept the sound mute. The only thing she wanted to hear would come on the sports news. Her Rockies were playing well and might even make to post-season.

A picture caught her eye and she gulped. That looked like Jesse. She hit the mute button to restore the sound in order to hear the reporter. "Arianne Martin, wife of Hal Morris, front runner in the campaign for

U.S. Senator, is still in CCU with an unknown heart condition. Earlier we were able to catch her son, Connor, and his fiancée as they boarded the elevator."

That was Jesse! He wore his favorite shirt and held his white Stetson in his hand. How could it be? The reporter said his name was Connor.

Someone banged on the door then Rait's voice called. "Kylee, open up."

She paused the show and dropped the remote.

When she and ran to open it, Rait barged in. "Did you see the news?"

"Yes, and I don't understand. That looks like Jesse, but the reporter says it's a guy named Connor Morris and his fiancée. She said something about Arianne Martin."

He picked up the remote. "If this is really Jesse, I'm going to string him up like a side of beef."

The news started again. "We're told that Arianne Martin suffered a heart attack earlier today at their ranch outside of Denver. Here's Dani Reeves at the hospital with the report.

"Thank you, Ed. Connor Morris, Mrs. Morris' son, arrived at the hospital this afternoon with his fiancée, Renee Hammond." A picture of a woman and Connor on an elevator played in the background as the woman reported.

Kylee stared in disbelief. It had to be Jesse unless he had a twin brother. She choked back a sob as the reporter called the woman his fiancée again.

"We spoke with Miss Hammond as she left the hospital. The scene returned to the reporter with the woman.

"I rushed here as soon as I heard about Arianne, Mrs. Morris. I'm on my way back to the ranch to get some things she'll need while in the hospital. I'd do anything for my future mother-in-law."

Kylee waved her hand in the air. "Turn it off. I don't want to hear anymore!" How could he have lied to her like that? He'd practically proposed at the creek, and she fell for it.

Serena came into the room. "I'm so sorry, Kylee. I would never have expected that from Jesse." She sat down on the bed next to Kylee and hugged her.

Kylee burst into tears and sobbed into Serena's shoulder. "He isn't a criminal, but I think I could have handled that better than whatever this is."

Rait stormed out of the room like a bull after a rodeo clown. "This is worse than being on parole for a felony."

"Serena, don't let him go off angry and do something that'll make us both look like idiots." Kylee sat back and swiped at her eyes with her fingers.

"I'll handle him, but there has to be some mix-up somewhere. The young man you brought to the ranch is either a good liar, or that girl on TV is lying."

Kylee squeezed her eyes shut. Why would a girl lie about something like that? She hugged herself while her heart broke into a million pieces.

~~

"Connor, you're not going to believe what I just saw on TV." Carrie picked up the remote to the waiting room TV and clicked it on. By the time she found the news, they had gone on to another story.

"What are you talking about?" Jesse grabbed the remote from her and muted the sound.

"I was downstairs meeting Bruce when I saw the TV news. That . . . that Renee was on the news introducing herself as your fiancée and telling them all about Mom and how she was going out to the ranch to get some things for Mom because she wanted to help take care of her future mother-in-law. They even had a picture of you and Renee getting on the elevator together."

"She did what? You've got to be kidding me." Anger rose in waves, and heat filled his face. "Who does she think she is after all?" He scrubbed his hands through his hair and began to pace.

"Look, I don't think Maria will let her in the house, but I'm going out there now to see if Renee did go there. I'll bring Mom's things back when I come. Try to get Dad to go home and get some rest as well. He won't be able to see her again tonight, and he needs to be fresh to talk with the doctors again in the morning."

He stopped pacing. "I'll try, but you know how stubborn he can be." A new thought occurred. He slapped his hand against his head. "What if Kylee saw the news? What's she going to think? She doesn't know my real name, and this will ruin everything I was going to tell her this weekend."

"Try calling her and explaining to her what happened."

"Yeah, but his isn't something I want to do over the phone. I need to see Kylee." He shook his head and frowned. "I didn't even send her another text explaining why I couldn't make it."

"Don't beat yourself up. You had other things on your mind. It may be too late to do anything about it tonight, but you can still try." Carrie kissed his cheek and squeezed his arm. "I'll be praying for you to straighten things out with her. And do try to get Dad to go home."

She turned and left him standing in the waiting room with his thoughts spiraling around in his head. He glanced over to where his Dad had fallen asleep slumped in a chair by the window in the CCU waiting room. Let him sleep for now, Jesse had a phone call to make.

He hit Kylee on speed dial, but her phone went straight to voice mail. He left a message for her to call him. When he ended the call, he sent a text for good measure.

If you saw the news, it's not what you think. Please call me so I can explain.

Now, he must wait until she called or sent a text back. He stepped over to his Dad and shook his shoulder. "Dad, wake up. It's time to go home."

His dad sat up and ran his hands over his face. "I can't go home and leave Ari here. I need to be here in case she wakes up."

Jesse sat down next to him. "You won't be able to see her until morning, and you need the rest so you can discuss future treatment with the doctor with a fresh mind."

"But what if something happens to her during the night, and I'm not here?"

Fear and love mixed in his father's eyes to create a sadness that weighed him down and added years to his age. It went straight to Jesse's heart.

"I understand, but we need to find a better place for you to get some rest."

"No, I'm fine right here. Maybe a pillow will help, but I'm not leaving."

The firm set of his jaw meant he wouldn't be moved, and Jesse had to accept it. "I'll get a pillow." He headed for the nurse's station on his errand. Did he really understand his father's need to be here?

Mom and Dad had a love that withstood the notoriety of her fame as an actress and his ambition in the world of politics. That's the kind of love he wanted with Kylee, a love that would always make her first in his life.

After securing the pillow and settling his Dad, Jesse ambled to the window overlooking the parking lot and leaned his head against the coolness. *Lord, I haven't been honest with Kylee, and now she's found out in the worst way possible. Please work on her heart and let her forgive me. I do love her, and I want her in my life forever. Forgive me for holding back the truth for so long.*

He blew out his breath and turned back to sit next to his dad. Here sat a man who loved God, his family, and his country. That's the kind of man Jesse wanted to be, and he prayed Kylee would be by his side to share it all.

Chapter 8

The drive home roared with its silence. Kylee had no words left in her to express the grief and heartbreak overflowing in her soul. She'd cried and prayed herself to sleep last night, but no relief came. She needed answers, but where and how would she get them?

Rait and Serena had expressed their words last night and somehow sensed Kylee didn't need more today. Even with Serena's assurance that this was a big mixed-up misunderstanding, all hope drained from Kylee, especially after seeing the picture on the front page of the paper this morning.

Jesse called again and again, and sent text messages almost every hour, but she couldn't bring herself to listen or read them. Kylee could think of no reason or explanation to account for what she had seen on the news report.

When they turned into drive leading up to the house, Rait addressed her from the front seat. "I sent a text to Consuela to let her know we'd be here for a late lunch. She'll have something for us to eat, and then we can sit down and discuss this situation as a family."

"No, I don't want to discuss anything right now. I'll take care of Belle and then come in to eat, but that's all. You and the others can discuss it all you want to, but it's not going to change anything,"

As soon as the truck stopped, Kylee jumped down and ran around to open the trailer to release Belle. "Come on, girl, we're home." She placed the bridle about Belle's neck and led her to the barn.

She may have won a big race last night, but she'd lost something far more important to her. How could she ever let herself trust a guy again?

Once she had Belle settled in her stall, Kylee picked up a brush and ran it over Belle's coat.

She blinked back tears as she worked. "You're the only I can trust, my Belle. You've never let me down. Those brothers betrayed my trust, but then I guess they had just cause to be suspicious of Jesse. Nothing was as it seemed." How could he have hidden something so important as another woman in his life? "I hope I never see him again."

Her tongue may have spoken the words, but her broken heart didn't cooperate. Someday she did want to see him again, but that day lay far in the future. She swept one last stroke across Belle and stepped back. "There, after you have a feed you can stay here and rest. You did a great job, and I'm proud of you."

"Talking to Belle again I see."

Kylee jumped and swerved around. "Brandy Jo, you know better than to sneak up on me like that."

"I'm sorry. I thought I was making enough noise for you to hear me." She wrapped an arm about Kylee's shoulders. "We saw the paper this morning, and Serena just confirmed our suspicions. I'm so sorry. I really liked the guy."

"Did she tell you what Rait and Wyatt did before we left?" Her lips quivered, but she steeled herself. She would not cry anymore.

"Yes, and that's despicable. They had no right interfering in your love life. I know they're just looking after their baby sister, but that was taking things a little too far even if it was the wrong person they found." She pulled Kylee into a strong hug.

"You're my little sister, too, but I understand how you feel about living your own life. They meddled enough times in mine."

Kylee leaned into the hug. Most often she and Brandy Jo didn't see things alike because they were both so independent, but her presence today gave Kylee comfort because somebody else understood. "I don't know how Jesse could lie to me like he did. When he kissed me down at the creek, I just knew we were made for each other. How could I fall in love with him?"

"I don't know. Wish I did, but I don't although I do know how you could fall in love with him. He's charming, good-looking, loves horses, and loves the rodeo as much as you do. He must have had a good reason for not using his real name."

"Yeah, he didn't want me to know who he really was and that he had a girl." Kylee glanced away and swallowed the lump in her throat.

"Could be, but I be there's more to the story than that." She stepped back and looped arms with Kylee. "Tell you what, let's go up and see what Consuela has for lunch then you can ride with me and Dane back to our house. Maybe if you stay there for a few days, we can talk through this. I can even get Missy to come, and it'll be like old times when we solved each other's problems when we were growing up."

"That sounds good." Then Kylee chuckled. "Reminds me of the times when the three of us ganged up on the three of them. I guess we did give them some grief back in the day."

They walked arm in arm back to the house and into the kitchen where Consuela had set food out on the island for a buffet lunch. When the cook saw them, she held out her arms to Kylee.

"I'm so sorry for all this trouble, dear little one."

Kylee stepped into the woman's arms, again forcing back the tears threatening. Danner girls didn't cry when the brothers were anywhere near. Showing emotions didn't set well in this household, and her anger with her brothers only a day or so ago proved it.

Mom should be here, but since she wasn't, Consuela was the next best. She'd come to love the woman who took over the housekeeping and cooking duties when things were so chaotic after Mom's death and Missy's marriage.

Consuela stroked Kylee's blond locks. "Maybe it's all a misunderstanding and everything will be all right. That's what I'm praying for." She stepped back from Kylee. "Now, let's get some lunch into you. I made barbecue sandwiches and your mom's potato salad."

Brandy Jo reached for a plate, frowned and put it back down. "I have a better idea. Let's get this fixed up and take it to my house. I'll tell Dane where we're going and to send Missy. We can go over in your car."

Not having to face her father and her brothers at the moment appealed to Kylee. She didn't need or want to hear their comments. "That sounds like a good plan. Let me go up and get a few things. I'll be right back down."

"Good and I'll get our lunch packed while you're doing that."

Less than ten minutes later, Brandy Jo followed Kylee to her car. "I told the guys we'd be at my house and to send Missy. I don't know what's keeping her."

Time with her sisters sounded like a wonderful idea. She wouldn't mind if Serena came along as well, but right now, she'd rather be with her two sisters. As much as she had disdained their help other times, she welcomed it today. One of these days maybe she'd learn to make wiser decisions and stay out of trouble.

~~

Jesse drove up to the Danner ranch house with his heart in his throat. With no idea as to the kind of reception he'd get, he stopped just inside the gate.

Lord, I don't know what is going to happen in the next half hour or so, but You do. I'm trusting You to give me the right words to say that will explain what I've done. I pray the Danner family will forgive me, and that I will back Kylee's trust. Amen

The prayer instilled courage into his soul as he parked. He didn't see Kylee's car anywhere, but maybe that was just as well. He needed to talk with her father and explain the circumstances of his name.

Consuela answered his knock on the door. "You! Young man, you better have some good explanation for what's been going on the past few months. Kylee's not here, and I don't think she'd want to see you anyway, but I'm sure her father has a few words for you."

She stepped back for him to enter. He removed his hat, walked into the entry hall then followed her to what he remembered to be Mr. Danner's office.

Consuela knocked on the door and opened it a bit. "Mr. Danner, Jesse Martin is here to see you." She nodded for him to go on in before she turned and headed toward the kitchen.

Bill Danner stood behind his desk. Dane, Rait, and Wyatt sat across from him and turned around to stare at Jesse when he entered the room. The only ones missing were Noah and Nate.

"I pray to God you have a good answer for changing your name, hiding the fact you have a fiancée, and creating havoc in Kylee's life." Bill Danner leaned forward, palms flat on his desk and his eyes blazing.

"I'd like to hear the answer to that myself." Missy entered the office followed by her husband, Nate.

Jesse gulped. The Danner clan had circled their wagons against him. "First of all, I don't have a fiancée. I dated Renee, but that was finished well over a year ago, and we were never engaged. She may have wanted to be, but she didn't like my participating in rodeos, and told me to choose her or bronco riding. You know which one I chose."

Missy fisted her hands on her hips. "Okay, so you say you're not engaged, but you and that girl looked might cozy. How can we believe you?"

Jesse shook his head and blew out a long breath. "I don't know what else to say about it. I'm not and never have been engaged to Renee. I think she simply likes to be a part of a well-known family and to get her face in the news."

"Well, she certainly did that, but when did you plan to tell Kylee about your name?" Missy took a chair beside Rait.

"I had planned to do at the rodeo Thursday night, but when I got the call from my sister, I had no choice but to go home."

Mr. Danner, the fire gone from his eyes, sat down and leaned over with his forearms resting on his desk. "I understand your going home, but not the ruse with your name. I know your father from auctions. I've worked with him in other cattle business, and I knew he had a son named Connor. I'd never met you, so I didn't know what you looked like. I would have welcomed you as Connor Morris, so why didn't you let us know of the connection and use your real name?"

"Sir, when your mother is a well-known actress and your father is running for the U. S. senate, all kinds of things can happen. I wanted to make a name for myself and not on the coattails of my parents. My middle name is Jesse, so I used it and Mom's maiden name for my own. That way I got no special favors from anyone." Jesse paused and gazed about the circle of men and one woman now staring at him with distrust and skepticism.

He breathed in deep and expelled it before he could continue. "I've fallen in love with Kylee. She's like a breath of fresh air with her optimism and charm. From what I've come to know about her, she's also a wonderful Christian and loves people. Even if she's never met someone, she treats them like an old friend. She's rather impulsive at times, but that only adds to her charm."

Rait nodded his head. "That's our Kylee all right, but she's a little young for you isn't she?"

"I don't think so. Five years isn't that much difference." He approached Bill Danner and stood before him, hat in hand. "All I know, Mr. Danner, is that I love your daughter."

Bill Danner stared at Jesse a few moments before he leaned back in his chair. "Well, at least we know you're not an ex-con."

Jesse's mouth dropped. "I'm not a what?"

A half-grin tipped one side Bill's lips. "These boys of mine did a search of your name and found a guy on parole with the same name. There was no picture, so they assumed the worst."

A guy on parole? That's the last thing Jesses expected to hear. "Whoa, I didn't expect that." No wonder hearing his spiel hadn't lessened their anger, but how could he gain their trust? He glanced around at the men whose expressions gave no clue to what they were thinking. He turned his gaze to Mr. Danner.

"Sir, I can assure you that I love Kylee, and I'd like to marry her, but I'd like your approval first."

Rait spoke up. "Dad, be careful. Think about Kylee and how this guy hurt her."

"I am son, but I also know your sister cares for Jesse."

Jesse's heart leaped with hope then fell. He had to regain her trust first.

Bill pointed a finger at Jesse. "I give my approval, but I don't like the way you kept the truth from Kylee. I can see your reasoning. It was wrong, but for the right reasons." He stopped and glared at each person seated around him as though daring them to disagree. "Kylee is the one you'll need to convince now, and that isn't going to be an easy job with my stubborn, independent, youngest girl."

How could he convince Kylee when she wouldn't even talk to him? He still had a long way to go before this could be resolved.

Bill Danner rose and extended his hand. "Good luck, son. Kylee is at Brandy Jo's house trying to mend her broken heart."

"Thank you, sir. If she'll have me, I promise to take good care of her."

"I'm sure you will." Bill Danner's firm handshake encouraged Jesse, but the looks on the faces of her brothers and the two brothers-in-law warned of their mistrust. Those four he wouldn't want to antagonize any further.

Missy jumped up. "Brandy Jo just sent me a text. I'm on my way to her house now, so let me do some smoothing of the pathway. I'll text you when you should come and explain yourself to her."

She leaned over and kissed her husband's cheek. "Pray it'll all work out for the good." Then she narrowed her eyes at her brothers. "You two need to think of Kylee as a young woman who can make up her own mind and not as your baby sister."

After she closed the door behind her, all of them, except Bill Danner, stared at Jesse with doubt and mistrust filling their faces. This group of men would be more difficult to convince, but he loved Kylee, and he'd prove it.

Bill shook his head and blew out his breath. "This is going to be an interesting afternoon." Then he motioned for Jesse to have a seat. "While we're waiting, tell me about your mother. How is she doing?"

Happy to change the subject, Jesse explained about the decision his parents had to make about surgery. The doctors predicted her heart would be fine again with the surgery. His own heart wouldn't be until he could talk to Kylee and restore what had lost.

Chapter 9

"Kylee, you have to eat." Brandy Jo set a plate with a barbecue sandwich in front of Kylee. "This is your favorite brisket and sauce."

"I'm just not hungry." She let the tears roll down her cheeks. Never mind the rule that Danner women don't cry because she didn't care about silly rules right now, and her brothers weren't around anyway. Her heart hurt with the stab wounds of betrayal, and food could do nothing to heal them.

Brandy Jo wrapped her arms around her sister. "I'm so sorry. This is a horrible situation, but there has to be some explanation for the way things are so mixed up."

"There is a good reason."

Missy breezed through the door with that determined look in her that eye that told Kylee she had no choice but to listen. Once Missy made up her mind, she wouldn't be turned back.

She sank into the chair across from Kylee and grasped her hands. "Okay, I want you to hear me out. I've come from the house, and Jesse was there with the guys and Dad. I think you should get in touch with him and tell him you'll listen to his explanation."

An icy chill ran down Kylee's back. "What in the world could he say to undo all that has happened the past few days? I saw what I saw and read what I read, and I don't see how any excuses he gives can change that." It would take more than words of apology to heal the hurts and fill the void inside her.

"Look, things aren't always as they seem to be, and what you saw isn't what it looked like, and what you read is not the real story."

Kylee narrowed her eyes and stared at Missy. "Then what is the real story? Pictures don't lie, and papers print the news."

Missy looked her straight in the eye. "Jesse needs to tell you that, and you need to listen. Please, Kylee, don't be stubborn about this."

Brandy Jo knelt beside Kylee. "You still love him, or it wouldn't hurt so badly. Please put away that stubborn Danner pride and listen to Jesse's story."

Kylee shredded the napkin she held. She did still love Jesse, but could she ever trust him again? If Mom were here, she'd know exactly what to do. Kylee glanced away, remembering her mother telling her that if she loved something worth having, she should fight for it and go after her dreams. She'd been talking about barrel racing, but did it apply here as well. As much as she hated to admit it, maybe she ought to listen to her sisters this time.

With a big whoosh of breath, Kylee nodded. "Okay, I'll see him and pray he has a good excuse."

Missy pumped her fist in the air before grabbing her phone and sending a text. "Okay, little sister, he's coming. So, it's time for you to wash away the tear stains and put on your prettiest face."

Kylee followed her sister to the bathroom and touched up her makeup. This had better be the right decision or she might never trust another man, or at least not for a long time.

~~

After telling them about his mother, the tension in the office had grown so thick Jesse thought he'd suffocate. He left the men and went to the stables to carry out his plan for when Missy let him know to come. After saddling both Morning Lightning and Belle, he led them to the corral.

Jesse stood between the two horses, one pale gold in color, the other a deep red. "Okay, girls, this ride is going to be the most important one I've ever made if I get the go ahead. Kylee loves you both, and I'm hoping and praying she'll love me, too."

Belle nuzzled Jesse's neck as though she approved of what he'd said. He shook his head and grinned. Horses were a lot smarter than people gave them credit for being, and he took Belle's actions as a good sign.

After sitting on the corral fence for fifteen minutes, the text finally came along with the directions to Brandy Jo and Dane's house. His heart thumping, Jesse mounted Morning Lightning and grabbed Belle's reins. "This is it. I just hope we don't get lost." Both horses tossed their heads and neighed.

Jesse laughed and nudged them to head out to the path indicated in Missy's directions. Within minutes he no longer worried about direction for both horses seemed to know exactly where they were going. With his spirits rising at every hoof beat, he couldn't get there fast enough.

In less than ten minutes, the house came into view. He rode up into the yard and dismounted. At the same time, Kylee opened the door and stepped onto the porch.

Jesse's heart thudded against his chest at the sight of her with honey blonde hair in one long braid down her back, and her favorite tan hat perched over it. He gulped and gripped the reins to still his shaking hands. Riding the toughest bronco in the state never made him this nervous.

"Care to go for a ride? I could use some company." He held Belle's reins out to her.

She grabbed them from him. "This had better be good, Jesse Martin. I don't want any more lies." A moment later she sat astride Belle.

He swung his leg up and over Morning Lightning. "No more lies, Kylee, I promise." They took off at a leisurely gait even though Jesse would rather have raced to their destination.

After a few minutes, Kylee tilted her head toward him. "Are you going to tell me what this is all about?"

"Not now, but I'll tell you the whole story as soon as we get to where we're going."

She glanced around at the countryside. "Hastings Landing?"

"Yup, it's the best spot I could think of." His mind reeled with all he wanted to say to her. Everything he'd dreamed about a future with this beautiful girl rode on what he said in the next few minutes as they arrived at the old church.

Jesse dismounted as did Kylee. He tried to reach for her hand, but she pulled away and headed for the bridge. That's where he hoped she'd go. He followed her up to the center then stopped to lean on the top rail.

She folded her arms across her body and leaned back with her elbows on the rail, her head turned toward him.

He clasped his hands in front of him and began his story. "First of all, I'm not engaged, and I've never been engaged. Renee and I dated well over a year ago, but she didn't like the idea of me riding in rodeos, so I broke it off with her. I didn't tell you about her because I never even thought about her. I'm sorry she appeared the way she did. That's the way she was back then—very possessive."

Kylee's face remained impassive. How could he regain her trust?

~~

Her heart said to trust and believe him, but the images in her head from the newspaper said no. "Why did you lie to me about your name?"

"I didn't really lie. My middle name is Jesse and Martin is my mother's maiden name. I planned to tell you last Thursday night at the

364

rodeo, but since I never made it, I didn't have the chance."

"I'm sorry about your mother. I know how hard it can be to see her so ill, but you hid your family, your life from me. You said you loved me, but how can I believe you?" She kept telling herself that Danner women didn't cry, but right now, that's all she wanted to do.

He reached for her hand, and this time she didn't pull back. She missed his touch, and the warmth from it now spread up her arm finding its way to her heart.

"I wanted to be a success on my own merit and not my family name. My father is well known not only for his ranch and marriage to my mother, but also as a politician. Now that Dad is leading the polls to be senator, and Mom is facing surgery, it's going to be that way more than ever. I've stayed off the campaign trail, but I need to show my support for him now."

What he said did make sense. "So, what would that mean for you . . . for us?"

"Kylee, I love you with all of my heart and soul. I meant it when I said I wanted to spend the rest of my life with you. I talked with Dad, and if he wins the election, he's turning the ranch over to me. We have a great foreman who takes care of it now, so I'd still be able to compete in rodeos, and I'd like to do it with you by my side as the best barrel racer in the state."

Doubt still nudged her head, but her heart listened with hope. If that was a proposal, it was the strangest one she'd ever heard, but then she hadn't heard that many.

She scrunched up her nose and peered at him. "So what are you saying, cowboy?"

He sank down on one knee. "I'm saying, or asking, will you make my world brighter and happier by marrying me and being my wife and partner the rest of our lives?"

Her heart kicked the doubt clean out of her mind. "Hmm, that's a long time, but I say yes, Jesse Martin or Connor Morris or whoever you are."

He stood and grabbed her around the waist and lifted her into the air. "Those are the best words I've ever heard."

Then he set her down. "It means you'll have to leave here for the Circle M, and I know how much you love this place."

Kylee looped her arms around his neck. "Yes, I love it here, but I'd also love wherever I am with you. Besides, we won't be that far away." She lifted her head toward his.

He pulled her close and when his lips landed on hers, everything else disappeared. Only the warmth of his embrace and the sweetness of his kiss filled her as she imagined the days ahead.

The kiss ended and he held her close. His heart beat as rapidly as hers, and she inhaled the sweet aroma of horses and the great outdoors that emanated from Jesse. Those would be the scents of their lifetime together.

"I guess we should go back and tell your sisters and brothers. Not sure your brothers trust me just yet. I'd much rather stay here like this with a kiss or two or three in the bargain."

Kylee tilted her head back and grinned. "I'm sure they already know the outcome, so I'll make a deal. Let's stay here for a few more kisses and then we'll go back and tell them."

"Now that's a deal I can live with."

This time his kiss held even more promises for the future, and each one got better and filled her with more love than she could ever have imagined.

When the kiss ended, he grabbed her hand and they walked back toward the horses. She glanced over at the church. "I can't wait to see what Serena and Missy do with flowers decorations for the wedding. If they're half as beautiful as theirs were, it'll be gorgeous."

"Um, about that, I know you want the wedding here, and I'd like that as well, but there may not be enough room."

Kylee frowned and bit her lip. "I hadn't thought of that, but it just has to be here. This is where Mom and I spent so many happy hours, and I feel like she'll really be with me in this church and this place we both loved."

Jesse nodded and hugged her close to his side. "We'll work something out. This place is special in more ways than one."

Kylee snuggled closer and wrapped her arm around his back. No matter how mixed-up the past few days had been, she'd follow this cowboy wherever he led.

Epilogue

Kylee stared at her reflection in the mirror as Brandy Jo fussed with the veil. Spring and her wedding day had finally arrived, and the butterflies in her stomach were having a field day of flitting and flying.

"You look beautiful. Jade did a wonderful job so your hair would fit with the hat. I wasn't sure about a cowgirl hat with a veil, but I like it, and the western style fringe around the scoop neck is different, but beautiful."

"Thank you, the seamstress made it just the way I described, and thank you for finding my size in white boots." She held up her skirt to reveal the footwear trimmed in silver.

"Missy hugged her. "You'd be beautiful no matter what you wore."

"I agree." Serena glanced at her watch. "It's almost time for Bill. Missy, come with me to check on the flower girls. They weren't too happy the last time I saw them. Jade and Chrissy may need help with the all the media camped outside as well."

Kylee hugged Serena. "Thank you so much for all you've done to make this church the way it should be. Mom would have been so proud."

"It was one of my most fun projects." Serena squeezed Kylee's hands. "I'm glad you chose here to get married."

After the two left, Brandy Jo shook her head and giggled. "I heard Jesse's brother-in-law tell his little girls he'd take them to Disneyland if they did this for their uncle Connor."

"That should motivate them. They're adorable in their new dresses."

"Yes, they are and that leads me to tell you a secret. Promise you won't say a word to any of the others." Brandy Jo gripped Kylee's hand.

"Of course, I won't tell anyone."

"We didn't want to horn in on your wedding day, so we're waiting to tell the family tomorrow at dinner, but I wanted you to know before you left for your honeymoon. Dane and I are expecting a baby next fall."

Kylee squealed and hugged Brandy Jo. "I knew it. You've had a glow in your eyes, and it wasn't for me. Besides, I'm not really surprised you're the first since you plan to have a houseful of kids."

"I figured I'd better tell you now because there won't be time after the ceremony. You'll be surrounded by people, especially at the reception."

"That's for sure." Kylee picked up her bouquet. After talking it over with Jesse's parents, they decided to wait until after the election and let his mom recover completely from surgery. Now that his dad had won, their wedding made big news in the state, which accounted for all the media filling the churchyard. The Morris' had agreed to the small wedding with a larger reception to follow at a hotel in town.

Someone knocked, and Brandy Jo hurried to answer. Bill Danner eased around the door. "Is my baby ready for her big day?"

Kylee stepped into his embrace. "Yes, I am, and I guess I'll always be your baby."

"You will, and your mom would be so proud of you. I wish she was here."

"So do I, Pops, but I know her spirit is here. We loved this place and spent so many happy moments together." Now she could add more memories to the precious ones she already held in her heart.

"Then let's do it. Today makes the Danner clan complete. All my children married and out of the nest."

Kylee hugged him and winked at Brandy Jo over his shoulder. This was just the beginning of a bigger and better Danner clan. "I'm ready." She tucked her hand over his arm.

The three of them left the room and joined Missy with the little girls waiting at the back of the church. The music began and her sisters made their way down the aisle followed by the flower girls who displayed their best behavior while sprinkling pink rose petals along the white runner.

The moment she and her father stepped to the aisle, her eyesight fastened on Jesse. He may be Connor to others, but to her he'd always be Jesse, her bronco busting cowboy.

The corners of his eyes crinkled as a wide grin spread across lips. She tugged on her father's arm and stepped up her pace. This may not be a race, but she couldn't wait to cross the finish line and ride into her future with the best-looking cowboy in the state.

Martha Rogers was born in Texas and lived in Dallas the first 18 years of her life. After graduating from Baylor University she moved to Houston and has been there ever since. Martha is a retired teacher at both secondary and college levels. She and her husband Rex enjoy spending time with their grandchildren and attending football, baseball, and basketball games when one of the grandchildren is playing or performing. Her four, soon to be five great-grandchildren are most important right now. Martha loves to cook and experimenting with recipes and enjoys scrapbooking when she has time and isn't on a deadline.

Social Media:
Facebook: Martha L. Rogers
Twitter: @MarthaRogers2
Website: www.marthawrogers.com

Pinterest: www.pinterest.com/grammymartha/

BOOKS BY MARTHA ROGERS

Historical Series
Winds Across the Prairie
Amelia's Journey
Becoming Lucy
Morning for Dove
Finding Becky
Caroline's Choice
Christmas at Holly Hill

Seasons of the Heart
Summer Dream
Autumn Song
Winter Promise
Spring Hope

The Homeward Journey
Love Stays True
Love Finds Faith
Love Never Fails
Christmas at Stoney Creek

Contemporary Series

Love in the Bayou City of Texas
Love on Trial
Forgiving Love
Lessons on Love

Where Love Grows
Garden of Love
Designs for Love
Hearts Open to Love

Mystery
Mulch Ado About Murder
Faces of Her Past

Novella Collections
Not on the Menu in Texas Sweethearts
Key to Her Heart in A River Walk Christmas
Christmas Blessing in Mail Order Christmas Angels
After the Ball in First Love Forever
Best Laid Plans in Bloomfield Series
Icing on the Cupcake in Sweetwater Romances

Novellas
Summer's Surprise
Be True
A House Love Built
Ice Bound Christmas
Love Comes to Bluebonnet Inn
Love Comes Around
The Gardener's Rose
Gamble on Love
Hemmed in Faith
Hidden Heiress
Bride on the Run
Mission of Love
Journey to Freedom
Behind the Mask
Always on My Mind
Meet me At the Fair
Top of the Hill
Mistletoe and Roses

35452342R00222

Made in the USA
Middletown, DE
10 February 2019